THE COUNTRY OF
OTHER SELECTED STORIES

H. G. WELLS, the third son of a small shopkeeper, was born in Bromley in 1866. After two years' apprenticeship in a draper's shop, he became a pupil-teacher at Midhurst Grammar School and won a scholarship to study under T. H. Huxley at the Normal School of Science, South Kensington. He taught biology before becoming a professional writer and journalist. He wrote more than a hundred books, including novels, essays, histories and programmes for world regeneration.

Wells, who rose from obscurity to world fame, had an emotionally and intellectually turbulent life. His prophetic imagination was first displayed in pioneering works of science fiction such as *The Time Machine* (1895), *The Island of Doctor Moreau* (1896), *The Invisible Man* (1897) and *The War of the Worlds* (1898). Later he became an apostle of socialism, science and progress, whose anticipations of a future world state include *The Shape of Things to Come* (1933). His controversial views on sexual equality and women's rights were expressed in the novels *Ann Veronica* (1909) and *The New Machiavelli* (1911). He was, in Bertrand Russell's words, 'an important liberator of thought and action'.

Wells drew on his own early struggles in many of his best novels, including *Love and Mr Lewisham* (1900), *Kipps* (1905), *Tono-Bungay* (1909) and *The History of Mr Polly* (1910). His educational works, some written in collaboration, include *The Outline of History* (1920) and *The Science of Life* (1930). His *Experiment in Autobiography* (2 vols., 1934) reviews his world. He died in London in 1946.

PATRICK PARRINDER took his MA and Ph.D. at Cambridge University, where he held a Fellowship at King's College and published his first two books on Wells, *H. G. Wells* (1970) and *H. G. Wells: The Critical Heritage* (1972). He has been Chairman of the H. G. Wells Society and editor of *The Wellsian*, and has also written on James Joyce, science fiction, literary criticism and the history of the English novel. His book *Nation and Novel* (2006) surveys English fiction from its late Medieval origins to the present day. Since 1986 he has been Professor of English at the University of Reading.

NEIL GAIMAN has won highly respectable awards for writing comics (like *Sandman*) and adult novels (like *American Gods*) and children's books (like *Coraline*). He has written screenplays for films, like the upcoming *Beowulf*. His books have been filmed, like the upcoming *Stardust*. He travels too much and sometimes writes about it at www.neilgaiman.com. He needs a haircut, but has reached the age where he's happy just to have hair.

ANDY SAWYER is the librarian of the Science Fiction Foundation Collection at the University of Liverpool Library, and Course Director of the MA in Science Fiction Studies offered by the School of English. He also teaches a 'speculative fictions' module for undergraduates. He has published widely on science fiction and related literatures, co-edited the collection of essays *Speaking Science Fiction* (2000) and was an Associate Editor of the Greenwood *Encyclopedia of Science Fiction and Fantasy Themes, Works, and Wonders* (2005). He is Reviews Editor of *Foundation: The International Review of Science Fiction*.

H. G. WELLS

The Country of the Blind and Other Selected Stories

Edited by PATRICK PARRINDER
With an Introduction by NEIL GAIMAN
and Notes by ANDY SAWYER

PENGUIN CLASSICS

PENGUIN BOOKS

Published by the Penguin Group
Penguin Books Ltd, 80 Strand, London WC2R ORL, England
Penguin Group (USA) Inc., 375 Hudson Street, New York, New York 10014, USA
Penguin Group (Canada), 90 Eglinton Avenue East, Suite 700, Toronto, Ontario, Canada M4P 2Y3
(a division of Pearson Penguin Canada Inc.)
Penguin Ireland, 25 St Stephen's Green, Dublin 2, Ireland (a division of Penguin Books Ltd)
Penguin Group (Australia), 707 Collins Street, Melbourne, Victoria 3008, Australia
(a division of Pearson Australia Group Pty Ltd)
Penguin Books India Pvt Ltd, 11 Community Centre, Panchsheel Park, New Delhi – 110 017, India
Penguin Group (NZ), 67 Apollo Drive, Rosedale, Auckland 0632, New Zealand
(a division of Pearson New Zealand Ltd)
Penguin Books (South Africa) (Pty) Ltd, Block D, Rosebank Office Park,
181 Jan Smuts Avenue, Parktown North, Gauteng 2193, South Africa

Penguin Books Ltd, Registered Offices: 80 Strand, London WC2R ORL, England

www.penguin.com

This selection first published in Penguin Classics 2007

019

Text copyright © the Literary Executors of the Estate of H. G. Wells
Biographical Note, Further Reading, Note on the Texts
Copyright © Patrick Parrinder, 2005, 2007
Introduction copyright © Neil Gaiman, 2007
'Wells's London and Surrounding Region', Glossary and Notes copyright © Andy Sawyer, 2007
All rights reserved

The moral right of the editors has been asserted

Set in 10.25/12.25 pt PostScript Adbote Sabon
Typeset by Rowland Phototypesetting Ltd, Bury St Edmunds, Suffolk
Printed in England by Clays Ltd, Elcograf S.p.A.

ISBN: 978-0-141-44198-6

www.greenpenguin.co.uk

Contents

Biographical Note

Herbert George Wells was born on 21 September 1866 at Bromley, Kent, a small market town soon to be swallowed up by the suburban growth of outer London. His father, formerly a professional gardener and a county cricketer renowned for his fast bowling, owned a small business in Bromley High Street selling china goods and cricket bats. The house was grandly known as Atlas House, but the centre of family life was a cramped basement kitchen underneath the shop. Soon Joseph Wells's cricketing days were cut short by a broken leg, and the family fortunes looked bleak.

Young 'Bertie' Wells had already shown great academic promise, but when he was thirteen his family broke up and he was forced to earn his own living. His father was bankrupt, and his mother left home to become resident housekeeper at Uppark, the great Sussex country house where she had worked as a lady's maid before her marriage. Wells was taken out of school to follow his two elder brothers into the drapery trade. After serving briefly as a pupil-teacher and a pharmacist's assistant, in 1881 he was apprenticed to a department store in Southsea, working a thirteen-hour day and sleeping in a dormitory with his fellow-apprentices. This was the unhappiest period of his life, though he would later revisit it in comic romances such as *Kipps* (1905) and *The History of Mr Polly* (1910). Kipps and Polly both manage to escape from their servitude as drapers, and in 1883, helped by his long-suffering mother, Wells cancelled his indentures and obtained a post as teaching assistant at Midhurst Grammar School near Uppark. His intellectual development, long held back, now progressed astonishingly.

He passed a series of examinations in science subjects and, in September 1884, entered the Normal School of Science, South Kensington (later to become part of Imperial College of Science and Technology) on a government scholarship.

Wells was a born teacher, as many of his books would show, and at first he was an enthusiastic student. He had the good fortune to be taught biology and zoology by one of the most influential scientific thinkers of the Victorian age, Darwin's friend and supporter T. H. Huxley. Wells never forgot Huxley's teaching, but the other professors were more humdrum, and his interest in their courses rapidly waned. He scraped through second-year physics, but failed his third-year geology exam and left South Kensington in 1887 without taking a degree. He was thrilled by the theoretical framework and imaginative horizons of natural science, but impatient of practical detail and the grinding, routine tasks of laboratory work. He cut his classes and spent his time reading literature and history, satisfying the curiosity he had earlier felt while exploring the long-neglected library at Uppark. He started a college magazine, the *Science Schools Journal*, and argued for socialism in student debates.

In the summer of 1887 Wells became science master at a small private school in North Wales, but a few weeks later he was knocked down and injured by one of his pupils on the football field. Sickly and undernourished as a result of three years of student poverty, he suffered severe kidney and lung damage. After months of convalescence at Uppark he was able to return to science teaching at Henley House School, Kilburn. In 1890 he passed his University of London B.Sc. (Hons.) with a first class in zoology and obtained a post as a biology tutor for the University Correspondence College. In 1891 he married his cousin Isabel Wells, but they had little in common and soon Wells fell in love with one of his students, Amy Catherine Robbins (usually known as 'Jane'). They started living together in 1893, and married two years later when his divorce came through.

During his years as a biology tutor Wells slowly began making his way as a writer and journalist. He wrote for the *Educational Times*, edited the *University Correspondent*, and in 1891 published a philosophical essay, 'The Rediscovery of the Unique', in the prestigious *Fortnightly Review*. His first book was a *Textbook of Biology* (1893). But no sooner was it published than his health again collapsed, forcing him to give up teaching and rely entirely on his literary earnings. His future seemed highly precarious, yet soon he was in regular demand as a writer of short stories and humorous essays for the burgeoning newspapers and magazines of the period. He became a fiction reviewer and, for a short period in 1895, a theatre critic.

Ever since his student days Wells had worked intermittently on a story about time-travelling and the possible future of the human race. An early version was published in the *Science Schools Journal* as 'The Chronic Argonauts', but now, after numerous redrafts and much encouragement from the poet and editor W. E. Henley, it finally took shape as *The Time Machine* (1895). Its success was instantaneous, and while it was running as a magazine serial Wells was already being spoken of as a 'man of genius'. He was celebrated as the inventor of the 'scientific romance', a combination of adventure novel and philosophical tale in which the hero becomes involved in a life-and-death struggle resulting from some unforeseen scientific development. There was now a ready market for his fiction, and *The Island of Doctor Moreau* (1896), *The Invisible Man* (1897), *The War of the Worlds* (1898), *When the Sleeper Wakes* (1899; later revised as *The Sleeper Awakes*, 1910), *The First Men in the Moon* (1901) and several other volumes followed quickly from his pen.

By the turn of the twentieth century Wells was established as a popular author in England and America, and his books were rapidly being translated into French, German, Spanish, Russian and other European languages. Already his fame had begun to eclipse that of his predecessor in scientific romance, the French author Jules Verne, who had dominated the field since the 1860s. But Wells, an increasingly self-conscious artist, had larger ambitions than to go down in history as a boys' adventure novelist like Jules Verne. *Love and Mr Lewisham* (1900) was his first attempt at realistic fiction, comic in spirit and manifestly reflecting his own experiences as a student and teacher. By the end of the Edwardian decade, when he wrote his 'Condition of England' novels *Tono-Bungay* (1909) and *The New Machiavelli* (1911), Wells had become one of the leading novelists of his day, the friend and rival of such literary figures as Arnold Bennett, Joseph Conrad, Ford Madox Ford and Henry James.

But Wells was never a devotee of art for art's sake; he was a prophetic writer with a social and political message. His first major non-fictional work was *Anticipations* (1902), a book of futurological essays setting out the possible effects of scientific and technological progress in the twentieth century. *Anticipations* brought him into contact with the Fabian Society and launched his career as a political journalist and an influential voice of the British left. During his Fabian period Wells wrote *A Modern Utopia* (1905), but failed in his attempt to challenge the bureaucratic, reformist outlook of the Society's leaders such as Bernard Shaw (a lifelong friend and rival) and Beatrice Webb. Wells's Edwardian scientific romances such as *The Food of the Gods* (1904) and *The War in the Air* (1908), though full of humorous touches, are propagandist in intent. In other 'future war' stories of this period he predicted the tank and the atomic bomb.

Success as an author brought about great changes in his personal life. Ill-health had forced him to leave London for the Kent coast in 1898, but in the long run the only legacy of his footballing injury was the diabetes that affected him in old age. He commissioned a house, Spade House, overlooking the English Channel at Sandgate, from the architect C. F. A. Voysey, and here his and Jane's two sons were born – George Philip or 'Gip', who became a zoology professor and collaborated with his father and Julian Huxley on the biology encyclopedia *The Science of Life* (1930), and Frank, who worked in the film industry. Wells gave generous support to his parents and to his eldest brother, who was a fellow-fugitive from the drapery trade. Increasingly, however, he looked for emotional fulfilment outside the family, and his sexual affairs became notorious. He had a daughter in 1909 with Amber Reeves, a leading young Fabian economist, and in 1914 the novelist and critic Rebecca West gave birth to his son Anthony West, whose troubled childhood would later be reflected in his own novel *Heritage* (1955) and in his biography of his father.

As Wells's personal life became the gossip of literary London, his roles as imaginative writer and political journalist or prophet came increasingly into conflict. *Ann Veronica* (1909) was an example of topical, controversial fiction, dramatizing and commenting on such issues as women's rights, sexual equality and contemporary morals. It was the first of Wells's 'discussion novels' in which his personal relationships were often very thinly disguised. His later fiction takes a great variety of forms, but it all belongs to the broad category of the novel of ideas. At one extreme is the realistic reporting of *Mr Britling Sees It Through* (1916) – still valuable and unique as a portrayal of the English 'home front' in the First World War – while at the other extreme are brief fables such as *The Undying Fire* (1919) and *The Croquet Player* (1936), political allegories about world events each cast in the form of a prophetic dialogue.

Wells was by no means an experimental novelist like his younger contemporaries James Joyce and Virginia Woolf, but he was often technically innovative, and in some of his books the boundaries between fiction and non-fiction begin to break down. Sometimes he would take a classic from an earlier, pre-modern epoch as his literary model: *A Modern Utopia* (1905), for example, refers back to Sir Thomas More's *Utopia* and Plato's *Republic*. His bestselling historical works *The Outline of History* (1920) and *A Short History of the World* (1922) break with historical conventions by looking forward to the next stage in history. These works were written in order to draw the lessons of the First World War and to ensure that, if possible, its carnage would never be repeated; Wells saw history as a 'race between education and catastrophe'. The same concerns led to his future-history novel *The Shape of Things to Come* (1933), later rewritten for the cinema as *Things to Come*, an epic science-fiction film produced in 1936 by Alexander Korda. Both novel and film contain dire warnings about the inevitable outbreak and disastrous consequences of the Second World War.

By the 1920s, Wells was not only a famous author but a

public figure whose name was rarely out of the newspapers.
He briefly worked for the Ministry of Propaganda in 1918,
producing a memorandum on war aims which anticipated the
setting-up of the League of Nations. In 1922 and 1923 he stood
for Parliament as a Labour candidate. He sought to influence
world leaders, including two US Presidents, Theodore Roosevelt and Franklin D. Roosevelt. His meeting with Lenin in the
Kremlin in 1920 and his interview in 1934 with Lenin's successor Josef Stalin were publicized all over the world. His high-
pitched, piping voice was often heard on BBC radio. In 1933
he was elected president of International PEN, the writers'
organization campaigning for intellectual freedom. In the same
year his books were publicly burnt by the Nazis in Berlin, and
he was banned from visiting Fascist Italy. His ideas strongly
influenced the Pan-European Union, the pressure group
advocating European unity between the wars.

But Wells became convinced that nothing less than global
unity was needed if humanity was not to destroy itself. In
The Open Conspiracy (1928) and other books he outlined his
theories of world citizenship and world government. As the
Second World War drew nearer he felt that his mission had
been a failure and his warnings had gone unheeded. His last
great campaign, for which he tried to obtain international support, was for human rights. The proposal set out in his Penguin
Special *The Rights of Man* (1940) helped to bring about the
United Nations declaration of 1948. He spent the war years at
his house in Hanover Terrace, Regent's Park, and was awarded
a D.Sc. by London University in 1943. His last book, *Mind at
the End of Its Tether* (1945), was a despairing, pessimistic
work, even bleaker in its prospects for mankind than *The Time
Machine* fifty years earlier. He died at Hanover Terrace on
13 August 1946. He was restless and tireless to the end, a
prophet eternally dissatisfied with himself and with humanity.
'Some day', he had written in a whimsical 'Auto-Obituary'
three years earlier, 'I shall write a book, a *real* book.' He had
published over fifty works of fiction and, in total, some 150
books and pamphlets.

                                                    Patrick Parrinder

Introduction

From the Days of Future Past

H. G. Wells, Bertie to his parents and H.G. to his friends, was, with Jules Verne, the person who gave us the scientific romance – the forerunner of that branch of literature we now know as science fiction. His short stories, and his proto-science fiction novels, have lasted and are still read today, while many of the mainstream novels he considered more important and significant are gone and, for the most part, forgotten, perhaps because they were very much of their time, and swallowed by the change in time, while some of the science fiction and fantasy novels and tales are, for all their late Victorian or Edwardian settings, quite timeless.

Wells's novels set a pattern. The madman on his island making people out of animals, the journey through time or into space, all have been imitated, consciously or unconsciously, ever since, taken as templates for stories by hundreds, perhaps thousands of other authors: the arrival in a small Sussex village of an Invisible Man – his self-imposed confinement to his room, the brilliant but forgettable hero barely introduced until we are past the hundredth page, the revelation and explanation of poor, mad albino Griffin, is not just the story of *The Invisible Man*, but it is the shape, the recipe for a thousand other stories in which there are Some Things Mankind Was Not Meant To Know, in which the borders between science and madness are frayed. Wells's science fiction books were novels of ideas as much as they are novels of people; while arguably they are also all novels of class, either metaphorically (as Dr Moreau creates an underclass of beast-men in *The Island of Doctor Moreau*;

or *The Time Machine's* Traveller encounters in the distant future an effete upper class and a monstrous lower class) or literally – crazy Griffin is a lower-middle-class creature out of his depth.

The short stories, for the most part, tend to be something else. Something unique to Wells.

It has been said that the Golden Age of Science Fiction is when you were twelve years old, and it could certainly be argued that Wells wrote his short stories for twelve year olds, or for the twelve year olds inside adults. His fabulism tends to be asexual, unproblematic, straightforward. (A personal admission: I read most of these stories first as an eleven-year-old boy. I found a thick, red-covered collection of the Science Fiction Short Stories of H. G. Wells on a shelf in a schoolroom and read it several times over the next two years, fascinated and transported. The tales were old, undoubtedly, but they did not feel dusty or anachronistic or even outdated. The flowering of the strange orchid disturbed me and the unsatisfactory nature of the Magic Shop left me wondering.[1] It was good.)

These are tales of obsession and revelation and discovery. Some of them swash, sometimes, buckle and adventure. Mostly, however, they remind us that they are, in some sense, eyewitness reports, with all the limitations and power of such. We are told repeatedly what was seen, and only a little more, and left to draw our own inferences. We are left to wonder. Was a man translated through the fourth dimension, and did he see hungry spirit-creatures there? Was that what he truly saw? Did man-eating cephalopods come ashore on stolid British beaches, to feast on human flesh? What was seen worshipping in the depths of the ocean abyss? How did the crystal egg arrive in the shop, and where is it now? We know only what was seen, and that, in its way, is convincing.

There is an old saw that in a short story one thing happens. Wells's short stories exemplify this. His writing is effective: as good as it needs to be, with little in the way of grace notes. Still, the best of the stories are haunting in their implications.

All too often they are tales of failed revelation. In Wells's world the fruit of the tree of knowledge is not eaten – not because of fear or difficulty, but because of embarrassment – and over and over again, knowledge of something equally as magical (the secret of making diamonds,[2] an egg that shows us life on Mars, the formula for invisibility) is lost to the world. At the end of many of these stories the world is unchanged, and yet it *could* have been changed utterly and irrevocably. If one of the social functions of science fiction is to prepare us for change, Wells's stories began that process. Darwin adumbrated change. Wells was a scientist or at least, when young, a science teacher and science writer, taught by a disciple of Darwin's, and he was not scared by ideas or by the practicalities of science. Wells used his fiction to illuminate change, celebrating it as he warned of what change could mean.

The most successful Wells short stories do not read like stories, not really. They are anecdotes and journalism: carnivorous squid arrive in a tale that feels like an article from a turn-of-the-century scientific paper, while the ants, armed with poison, conclude their tale fifty years away from arriving in Europe (in those slow, comfortable days before container ship and jet plane). It's not a weakness – indeed, it's where these stories derive a significant amount of their power and effect from, and it's one of the places that these stories can be seen as early branches on the science fiction family-tree: part of SF is the literature of ideas, and several of these stories are almost pure idea, uncluttered by plot or narrative. Still, by today's standards (and those of the time Wells was writing) this was not on. They were not proper short stories – a criticism that Wells took to heart in his 1911 introduction to *The Country of the Blind and Other Stories*, when he says that

> we suffered then, as now, from the *à priori* critic. Just as nowadays he goes about declaring that the work of such-and-such a dramatist is all very amusing and delightful, but 'it isn't a Play', so we had a great deal of talk about *the* short story, and found ourselves measured by all kinds of arbitrary standards. There was a tendency to treat the short story as though it was as definable a form as the sonnet, instead of being just exactly what anyone of courage and imagination can get told in twenty

minutes' reading or so. It was either Mr Edward Garnett or Mr
George Moore in a violently anti-Kipling mood who invented
the distinction between the short story and the anecdote. The
short story was Maupassant; the anecdote was damnable. It was
a quite infernal comment in its way, because it permitted no
defence. Fools caught it up and used it freely. Nothing is so
destructive in a field of artistic effort as a stock term of abuse.
Anyone could say of any short story, 'A mere anecdote', just as
anyone can say 'Incoherent!' of any novel or of any sonata that
isn't studiously monotonous. The recession of enthusiasm for
this compact, amusing form is closely associated in my mind
with that discouraging imputation. One felt hopelessly open to a
paralysing and unanswerable charge, and one's ease and happiness in the garden of one's fancies was more and more marred
by the dread of it. It crept into one's mind, a distress as vague
and inexpungible as a sea fog on a spring morning, and presently
one shivered and wanted to go indoors. ... It is the absurd fate
of the imaginative writer that he should be thus sensitive to
atmospheric conditions.[3]

Wells seems painfully aware here that many of his most effective
short stories were not explorations of character and event, and
was uncomfortable with this. He need not have been. The truth
is that they work because they lack, sometimes, plot, often,
character. What they have instead is brevity and conviction.
Arthur Conan Doyle's eleven-thousand-word story 'When the
World Screamed' (1928) in Wells's hands would have been a
journalistic report of half the length, devoid of people. It would
have been only about the event. The world of the finest of
Wells's short stories is one of possibilities, of breakthrough
in science or society or of the Unknown, which reimagine the
world.

The stories, particularly the more fantastic of them, are most
easily read as if they were postcards from an alternate future
that is already long past. Many of these stories are about futures
and changes that have long since been carried away by time
and memory: it is hard to remain on the cutting edge well over
a century after the stories were written.

Wells described the art of the short story as

> the jolly art of making something very bright and moving; it may
> be horrible or pathetic or funny or beautiful or profoundly illumi-
> nating, having only this essential, that it should take from fifteen
> to fifty minutes to read aloud. All the rest is just whatever inven-
> tion and imagination and the mood can give – a vision of buttered
> slides on a busy day or of unprecedented worlds. In that spirit of
> miscellaneous expectation these stories should be received.

And that suggestion holds as true now as when he wrote it.

*(The reader is advised that some plot details are given away in
this section.)*

'The Lord of the Dynamos' – Here we meet the New Theology,
in a tale of 'a blackleg, and Azuma-zi, who was a mere black'.
Azuma-zi, who has come to England from the East, sees the
Dynamo as 'greater and calmer even than the Buddhas he had
seen at Rangoon'. A reminder of attitudes and language we
would no longer view as reasonable, and a story that presaged
one of the themes of science fiction: that our machines, if we
permit them, can become our gods.

'The Remarkable Case of Davidson's Eyes' – An example of
Wells's technique of presenting the reader with an impossibility
and then buttressing it with just enough detail to convince.

'The Moth' – Science fiction in that it is a fiction about scientists,
but it takes on the mantle of a ghost story and then, in its view
of the descent into madness, shades gently into the weird tale.
As our scientist accepts that only he can see the moth he
embraces his madness, and that is true horror.

'A Catastrophe' – A heartbreakingly biographical story, but
one that gives a happy ending to a world that in Wells's own
life ended in disaster. A what-if story. In reality Wells's father

lost his shop, his mother went into service. Here is fiction as time-travel, a way to fix the unfixable.

'The Cone' – A small, tragic, eternal triangle (a cone is a triangle in three dimensions). Reminiscent of the tales of horror and revenge told in the American E. C. Comics line in the 1950s, in which a metaphor is taken literally and lethally: blood boils in the veins of both the artist and the cuckolded husband, and in the case of one of them it is not merely a figure of speech. With its machinery dominating the landscape, the story reminds us of 'Lord of the Dynamos', and the end can be seen as a similar act of sacrifice.

'The Argonauts of the Air' – A small piece of science fiction, now consigned forever to an alternate past. A fascinating little story in which Wells's every guess and instinct was wrong, save for his understanding that mankind would be travelling by air, and sooner than most people believed. Despite the death at the end of the story, this is not shaped as a tragedy. This could be a space-flight story, a little too early: while Wells was wrong about the early days of heavier-than-air flight – it wasn't a millionaire's game, but a relatively cheap playing-field – he would have been right about space travel, which is a billion-aire's game of the kind where one can imagine the gilding of aluminium.

'Under the Knife' – A death that crosses the universe, in a story that is predicated upon changes in scale, as we gaze upon the handiwork, and the hand (although not the face) of God.

'A Slip under the Microscope' – SF in the sense that it is a fiction with scientists in it; a fiction that reminds us of Wells's own early failure to graduate. Again, in every sense, a tale of class. Again, a tale of rivalry, here played out as a morality play in which success and failure mean two very different things to two very different people.

'The Plattner Story' – Again, an anecdote, in which we find ourselves convinced of its truth by the initial shock of the reversal of right-and-left-handedness of things, as if Plattner has been mapped through another dimension and returned to us in mirror-form (the branch of chemistry known as *chirality*). We see ghosts and a nine days' wonder (there are many nine days' wonders in Wells's tales – *Here*, we are told in one way or another, several times, as the stories begin, *is something remarkable – something that has already been replaced in the imagination of the populace, and now I shall tell you something about it you did not know*).

'The Story of the late Mr Elvesham' – A body swap tale, as poor Eden is subsumed into the mysterious Mr Elvesham. It's proto-SF that shades into pure horror.

'In the Abyss' – Again, a fragmentary, almost anecdotal piece, in which we gain a glimpse of a world deep beneath our own, and lose it once more.

'The Sea Raiders' – A tale I last read when I was twelve or thirteen. I remember the fear I felt then at the incursion of something deeply alien and dangerous in places I knew and was familiar with. Another battle in the War of the Worlds, although the threat comes from below, not from Mars. The style is journalistic, the intent purely to convince. The inconclusive nature of the ending adds to the feeling that this happened, or could have happened, just as Wells describes.

'The Crystal Egg' – The nature of seeing is a theme that echoes through many of Wells's short stories and here (as in 'The Remarkable Case of Davidson's Eyes') we encounter seeing at a distance. Once more a revelation that is only partially revealed, wrapped in a series of mysteries and, eventually, lost due to human fallibility, not malevolence. The glimpse of another world the tale (and the Egg) gives us is otherwordly and haunting, and poor Cave, the small businessman on the edge, sustained by his visions of another world, is a perfectly Wellsian character, giving an odd humanity to what would otherwise be an anecdote about an interplanetary television before its time.

'A Story of the Stone Age' – Now an almost forgotten story, it feels like an aborted novel, one that should have continued. Wells is an early explorer of a genre that others have returned to over the years – that of conceptual breakthrough in Stone Age man, in a time when all ideas are new. The hero becomes the first man to ride a horse, and he creates an early doomsday weapon, a club inset with lion's teeth. While the story he gives us is satisfying, it still reads like something Wells meant to go back to and complete, a book that would have been *The Clan of the Cave Bear*[4] of its day.

'The Star' – Wells enjoys changing scale, the slow pull back from the personal to the cosmic, and employs the technique here to great effect.

'The Man who could work Miracles' – Justly famous, often dramatized – this story has been a film, and adapted many times for television and radio. Like many of Wells's fantasies, it loops back to where it began.

'A Dream of Armageddon' – Wells built a 'future history' – a consistent history of the future, in which he set several stories. This tale of a dream of events that have not yet happened, of future war and political and personal disaster, and of death, fits vividly into that history.

'The New Accelerator' – A remarkably joyful story of super speed and mischief. A playful story – for once in a Wells tale the Accelerator is neither lost nor destroyed, nor does it result in madness and death. Instead we end in possibility.

'The Truth about Pyecraft' – In the main, the narrator is indistinguishable from Wells. This is not true of the narrator of 'Pyecraft', who is a thin man, of Indian descent. Pyecraft himself, who thinks he wants to lose weight but actually wants not to be fat, is a real character, in a Bunterish sort of way, a marvellous and memorable 'great, fat, self-indulgent man'. It's a genuinely funny fantasy story which leaves us – almost – where it began.

'The Country of the Blind' – For me, one of the most interesting of Wells's stories, partly because of his need to rewrite the story decades later, or rather, his need to give it a new ending. It's an unusual story in many ways: in its easy reversal of the common saw that in the Country of the Blind, the one-eyed man is king; in the inability of the protagonist to communicate; in the way that entire concepts become meaningless when the sensory information they carry becomes redundant.

The first iteration of the story (1904, given here) follows the classic Wells short-story pattern of an encounter with the impossible, and an unsatisfactory resolution, the story convincing us by its own awkwardness.

The later version (1939, missing the last 300 words and with an additional 2,000 words) is both more and less satisfactory – the convincing anecdote now becomes a real short story. The pattern is more familiar. Now the sighted man does more than simply escape – his vision gives him the power to return to warn the villagers, Cassandra-like, of their impending doom; the ending contains real love between a man and a woman, and the thrust of the story has changed from reportage to art. Each version of the story is perfectly satisfying, but the immediacy and conviction of the first ending is exchanged for something that demonstrates that, had Wells had the spirit for it, he might in later life have produced some remarkably moving short stories of the fantastic. (It was not that he was not asked, nor that he did not have a market. More that the fecundity of ideas went away, and that his mind and attention went elsewhere. As Wells explained, in apology, 'I find it a little difficult to disentangle the causes that have restricted the flow of these inventions. It has happened, I remark, to others as well as to myself, and in spite of the kindliest encouragement to continue from editors and readers. There was a time when life bubbled with short stories; they were always coming to the surface of my mind, and it is no deliberate change of will that has thus restricted my production.')

'The Empire of the Ants' – A story of eco-disaster. An idea that would be seen now as a bouncing-off point, here is the whole story. Which makes sense, of course: the idea was original, and Wells is a remarkable tale-teller. The story ends with the worrying suggestion by the narrator, Wells, that the second act of this disaster story will occur in Europe in 1950 or 1960.

'The Door in the Wall' – One of my favourite stories, by anyone. Haunting, magical and sad, and none the less satisfying for being so perfectly predictable. Like a silent comedy, the delight is not in what happens, but in how each event in the chain happens at the perfect moment for it to happen.

'The Wild Asses of the Devil' – A little brimstone, a little political commentary. What more could anyone wish for?

There are few enough writers in any field whose short stories will be read a hundred years after they were written. Science fiction in particular has a short sell-by date, one that only the finest writers surpass. Ray Bradbury's Martian short stories transcend our knowledge that there are no canals on Mars and no atmosphere. Too many near-future tales from too many fine authors were overtaken by events or by breakthroughs in scientific knowledge and became, simply, redundant. H. G. Wells's stories are, as this collection demonstrates, still astonishingly readable, and, ultimately, the joy of a volume like this is that the stories can and will be read, not as curiosities from the past, but as living things. Wells himself said of his short stories, 'I make no claims for them and no apology; they will be read as long as people read them. Things written either live or die . . .' And of all the things one can say about these stories, to my mind unquestionably the best is this: long after they were written, they live.

Neil Gaiman

NOTES

1. In 'The Magic Shop' (1903) and 'The Flowering of the Strange Orchid' aka 'The Strange Orchid' (1894) respectively, not included in this volume.
2. 'The Diamond Maker' (1894), not in this volume.
3. All Wells quotations below are from his introduction to *The Country of the Blind and Other Stories* (1911): see Appendix. Edward Garnett (1868–1937), English critic and editor. Son of Richard Garnett, author of *Twilight of the Gods*, father of David Garnett, author of *Lady into Fox* and *Aspects of Love*. George Augustus Moore (1852–1933), Anglo-Irish novelist and short-story writer who set out to introduce the techniques of French literary realism and naturalism into English fiction.
4. *The Clan of the Cave Bear* (1980) by Jean M. Auel.

Further Reading

The most vivid and memorable account of Wells's life and times is his own *Experiment in Autobiography* (2 vols., London: Gollancz and Cresset Press, 1934). It has been reprinted several times. A 'postscript' containing the previously suppressed narrative of his sexual liaisons was published as *H. G. Wells in Love*, edited by his son G. P. Wells (London: Faber & Faber, 1984). His more recent biographers draw on this material, as well as on the large body of letters and personal papers archived at the University of Illinois and elsewhere. The fullest and most scholarly biographies are *The Time Traveller* by Norman and Jeanne Mackenzie (2nd edn, London: Hogarth Press, 1987) and *H. G. Wells: Desperately Mortal* by David C. Smith (New Haven and London: Yale University Press, 1986). Smith has also edited a generous selection of Wells's *Correspondence* (4 vols., London: Pickering & Chatto, 1998). Another highly readable, if controversial and idiosyncratic, biography is *H. G. Wells: Aspects of a Life* (London: Hutchinson, 1984) by Wells's son Anthony West. Michael Foot's *H. G.: The History of Mr Wells* (London and New York: Doubleday, 1995) is enlivened by its author's personal knowledge of Wells and his circle.

Two illuminating general interpretations of Wells and his writings are Michael Draper's *H. G. Wells* (Basingstoke: Macmillan, 1987) and Brian Murray's *H. G. Wells* (New York: Continuum, 1990). Both are introductory in scope, but Draper's approach is critical and philosophical, while Murray packs a remarkable amount of biographical and historical detail into a short space. John Hammond's *An H. G. Wells Companion* (London and Basingstoke: Macmillan, 1979) and *H. G.*

Wells (Harlow and London: Longman, 2001) combine criticism with useful contextual material. *H. G. Wells: The Critical Heritage*, edited by Patrick Parrinder (London: Routledge, 1972), is a collection of reviews and essays of Wells published during his lifetime. A number of specialized critical and scholarly studies of Wells concentrate on his scientific romances. These include Bernard Bergonzi's pioneering study of *The Early H. G. Wells* (Manchester: Manchester University Press, 1961); John Huntington, *The Logic of Fantasy: H. G. Wells and Science Fiction* (New York: Columbia University Press, 1982); and Patrick Parrinder, *Shadows of the Future: H. G. Wells, Science Fiction and Prophecy* (Liverpool: Liverpool University Press, 1995). Peter Kemp's *H. G. Wells and the Culminating Ape* (London and Basingstoke: Macmillan, 1982) offers a lively and, at times, lurid tracing of Wells's 'biological themes and imaginative obsessions', while Roslynn D. Haynes's *H. G. Wells: Discoverer of the Future* (London and Basingstoke: Macmillan, 1980) surveys his use of scientific ideas. W. Warren Wagar, *H. G. Wells and the World State* (New Haven: Yale University Press, 1961) and John S. Partington, *Building Cosmopolis* (Aldershot: Ashgate, 2003) are studies of his political thought and his schemes for world government. John S. Partington has also edited *The Wellsian* (The Netherlands: Equilibris, 2003), a selection of essays from the H. G. Wells Society's annual critical journal of the same name. The American branch of the Wells Society maintains a highly informative website at http://hgwellsusa.50megs.com

P.P.

Note on the Texts

H. G. Wells's earliest short stories were published in 1887–8 in the *Science Schools Journal*, the student magazine that he founded and edited at the Normal School of Science in South Kensington. Professionally, however, he owed his inspiration to Lewis Hind, the editor of the *Pall Mall Budget*, one of the new weekly and monthly magazines which made the 1890s an extraordinarily fertile period for short fiction. The 27-year-old Wells was still an obscure author of scientific journalism and textbooks when he first met Hind in 1894. Asked to contribute a series of 'single sitting' stories drawing on his scientific expertise, he jumped at the opportunity. As he recalled in his 1911 introduction to *The Country of the Blind and Other Stories* (see Appendix), 'There was a time when life bubbled with short stories', although it must also be said that his earliest stories, sold to Hind or a rival editor for five guineas each, are quite uneven in quality. For the present selection I have chosen only three of the fifteen items in his first book collection, *The Stolen Bacillus, and Other Incidents* (London: Methuen, 1895). With one exception the remaining stories are drawn from *The Plattner Story, and Others* (London: Methuen, 1897), *Tales of Space and Time* (London and New York: Harper, 1899), *Twelve Stories and a Dream* (London: Macmillan, 1903) and *The Country of the Blind, and Other Stories* (London: Nelson, 1911), the latter being a collection of 33 stories of which only 5 were new. Wells wrote very few original short stories after 1911, although *The Short Stories of H. G. Wells* (London: Ernest Benn, 1927), later retitled *The Complete Short Stories* and much reprinted, includes some 60 stories as well as his novella *The Time Machine*. John Hammond's new edition of Wells's *Complete Short Stories* (London: Dent, 1998) gathers in a further 23 items, the majority of which had not appeared in book form during Wells's lifetime. Thus there are now 83 short stories known to have been published by Wells, excluding the 14 brief sketches involving a fictional uncle collected as *Select Conversations with an Uncle* (1895; revised edition, London: University of North London Press, 1992).

In his *Country of the Blind* introduction Wells wrote that 'I have tried to set a date to most of these stories, but . . . they are not arranged in strictly chronological order.' For the 1927 *Short Stories*, however, he or his editor reverted to the order in which they had appeared in the original volumes detailed above. The same order was followed in the Penguin *Selected Short Stories*, first published in 1958. For the present volume, I have made a new selection, and have arranged the stories in chronological order of first (magazine) publication, following what may have been Wells's intention as he began to compile the 1911 volume. The copy-text for the stories in this book is the 1927 *Short Stories*, modified as set out below, except in the case of 'The Wild Asses of the Devil'. For the latter I follow the text as first published in *Boon* (1915), and not reprinted during Wells's lifetime. For the Appendix the copy-text is Nelson's 1911 edition.

American readers first encountered Wells as a short-story writer in *Thirty Strange Stories* (New York: Arnold, 1897), a compilation of his first two English volumes together with three extra stories. His subsequent volumes of stories were all published in the United States without significant differences from the English publications. In general, Wells made very few revisions to his short stories once they had appeared in book form. (The exception is 'The Country of the Blind', which he enlarged and rewrote near the end of his life for an edition published by Golden Cockerel Press in 1939. The more familiar earlier version is preferred here.) Variant readings are largely confined to the occasional verbal changes that he introduced to eliminate repetitions and careless phrasing as he revised his stories in the 1920s for a series of uniform editions of his works, beginning with the 28-volume Atlantic Edition (London: T. Fisher Unwin, and New York: Scribner's, 1924–7), and including Benn's Essex Edition as well as their separate volume of *Short Stories*. I have accepted all of these deliberate changes. The most significant variants are listed below. Where Wells changed the title of a story, this is indicated under 'Publication History'.

In the present edition, punctuation and spelling have been modernized; capitalized imposed on Negro and Negroid; and hyphens have been removed from some 70 words, e.g. 'blood-stained', 'step-son', 'tooth-brush', 'flying-machine'. Other compound words have been joined together or separated according to modern British practice, e.g. 'everyone' for 'every one', but 'any rate' for 'anyrate', 'market square' for 'market-square' and 'sewing machine' for 'sewing-machine'. The spelling of 'beho(o)ves', 'Burma(h)', 'fetish' ('fetich'), 'Hindustan' ('Hindostan'), 'hy(a)ena' and 'T(h)ibet' has been modernized. Some changes which are authorized by the earlier British line of texts (e.g. 'eh' for 'eigh', 'leapt' for 'leaped', 'therefore' for 'therefor') are also made for the sake of internal consistency. In less than a dozen instances, commas or semi-colons have been restored or added for ease of reading. Other substantive emendations are listed below.

Housestyling of punctuation and spelling has also been implemented to make the text more accessible to the reader: single quotation marks (for doubles) with doubles inside singles as needed; end punctuation placed outside end quotation marks when appropriate; spaced N-dashes (for the heavier, longer M-dash) and M-dashes (for double-length 2M-dash); 'iz' spellings (e.g. recognize, not recognise), and acknowledgements and judgement (not acknowledgments and judgment); no full stop after personal titles (Dr, Mr, Mrs) or story titles, which may not follow the capitalization of the copy-text.

Publication History

The stories in this volume were published as follows (*SB = The Stolen Bacillus, and Other Incidents, PS = The Plattner Story,*

*and Others, TSS = Thirty Strange Stories, TST = Tales of Space
and Time, TSD = Twelve Stories and a Dream, CB = The
Country of the Blind, and Other Stories, SS = The Short Stories
of H. G. Wells*):

'The Lord of the Dynamos': *Pall Mall Budget* (6 September
1894), *SB, TSS, CB, SS*.
'The Remarkable Case of Davidson's Eyes': *Pall Mall Budget*
(28 March 1895), *SB, TSS* (as 'The Story of Davidson's
Eyes'), *CB, SS*.
'The Moth': *Pall Mall Gazette* (28 March 1895), *SB* (as 'A
Moth – "Genus Novo"'), *TSS* (as 'A Moth (Genus
Unknown)'), *CB, SS*.
'A Catastrophe': *New Budget* (4 April 1895), *PS, TSS, SS*.
'The Cone': *Unicorn* (18 September 1895), *PS, TSS, CB, SS*.
'The Argonauts of the Air': *Phil May's Annual* (December
1895), *PS, TSS, SS*.
'Under the Knife': *New Review* (January 1896), *PS, TSS, CB,
SS*.
'A Slip under the Microscope': *Yellow Book* (January 1896),
PS, TSS, CB, SS.
'The Plattner Story': *New Review* (April 1896), *PS, TSS, CB,
SS*.
'The Story of the late Mr Elvesham': *Idler* (May 1896), *PS,
TSS, CB, SS*.
'In the Abyss': *Pearson's Magazine* (1 August 1896), *PS, TSS,
SS*.
'The Sea Raiders': *Weekly Sun Literary Supplement*
(6 December 1896), *PS, TSS, CB, SS* (as 'The
Sea-Raiders').
'The Crystal Egg': *New Review* (May 1897), *TST, CB, SS*.
'A Story of the Stone Age': *Idler* (May–September 1897),
TST, SS.
'The Star': *Graphic* (December 1897), *TST, CB, SS*.
'The Man who could work Miracles': *Illustrated London
News* (July 1898), *TST, CB, SS*. (Filmed as *Man who
could work Miracles*, with a script by H. G. Wells, London
Films, 1935).

'A Dream of Armageddon': *Black and White Budget* (May–
   June 1901), *TSD, CB, SS.*
'The New Accelerator': *Strand Magazine* (December 1901),
   TSD, CB, SS.
'The Truth about Pyecraft': *Strand Magazine* (April 1903),
   TSD, CB, SS.
'The Country of the Blind': *Strand Magazine* (April 1904),
   CB, SS. (Revised version, London: Golden Cockerel Press,
   1939.)
'The Empire of the Ants': *Strand Magazine* (December 1905),
   CB, SS.
'The Door in the Wall': *Daily Chronicle* (14 July 1906), *CB, SS*
'The Wild Asses of the Devil': *Boon, The Mind of the Race,
   The Wild Asses of the Devil, and The Last Trump . . .,*
   Prepared for Publication by Reginald Bliss, with an
   Ambiguous Introduction by H. G. Wells (London: Fisher
   Unwin, 1915).

Sources of Substantive Emendations

Several of these emendations correct obvious misprints in *SS*
(and, in two cases, in all previous editions as well). *CSS* =
Complete Short Stories, 15th impression (reset) (London:
Ernest Benn, 1948).

Page: line	Reading adopted	Reading rejected
14:21	shop (*SB*)	ship
15:35	rubbed (*SB*)	rubbled
18:26	backwards (*SB*)	backward
50:1	had pulled (*PS*)	pulled
68:2	had (*PS*)	have
72:27	trickling (*PS*)	rickling
117:20	picture (*PS*)	pictures
156:20	tentacles (*PS*)	tenacles
281:37	incidentally (*TSD*)	incidenally
318:16	liked (*CSS*)	like
330.35	taxed (*CSS*)	tax
333:5	that for (*CB*)	for that

Selected Variant Readings

Page: line	Revised reading	Earlier reading(s)
22:23–4	Sir Ray	Professor Ray (*SB*, *TSS*, *CB*)
26:18	without seeing.	without seeing.* *[Footnote] The reader unaccustomed to microscopes may easily understand this by rolling a newspaper in the form of a tube and looking through it at a book, keeping the other eye open. (*SB*, *TSS*)
27:1	New Genus	*Genus novo* (*SB*) *Genus unknown* (*TSS*)
68:3–5	themselves. Now . . . hungry.	themselves. (*PS*, *TSS*, *CB*)
69:36–70:33	myself. At . . . indolent,	myself. The doctors were coming at eleven, and I did not get up. It seemed scarcely worth while to trouble about washing and dressing, (*PS*, *TSS*, *CB*)
70:9–10	I had . . . to eat.	I breakfasted in bed. (*PS*, *TSS*, *CB*)
136:34	questions.	questions. Without further comment I leave this extraordinary matter to the reader's individual judgment. (*PS*, *TSS*, *CB*)

254:25–6	experiments . . . type	experiments, at least until he had reconsidered them (*TST, CB*)
317:26–8	agonized. 'Your . . . him.	agonized. (*TSD, CB*)
317:36–7	great-gran—' . . . cried.	great gran——' (*TSD, CB*)

Among minor variants, it is notable that in revising these stories Wells intervened some fifteen times to delete the overused adjective 'little', as in 'little room', 'a little vague', etc. In 'A Dream of Armageddon', the phrase 'a scimitar of beach' (275:21–2) originally read 'a little beach'.

Wells looked back on his career as a short-story writer in the Introduction to *The Country of the Blind and Other Stories*, and again in his *Experiment in Autobiography*.

The surviving manuscripts of many of the short stories are in the H. G. Wells Collection at the Rare Book and Special Collections Library, University of Illinois at Urbana-Champaign. Among the many selections of Wells's stories that have been published, only Michael Sherborne's 'World's Classics' edition of *The Country of the Blind and Other Stories* (New York: Oxford University Press, 1996) has a critical textual apparatus. In preparing this Penguin Classics selection I have been indebted to this edition and to *Selected Stories of H. G. Wells*, ed. Ursula K. Le Guin (New York: Modern Library, 2004), as well as to John Hammond's definitive collection of the *Complete Short Stories* cited on page xxvii. As ever, I am deeply grateful to my editors, Helen Conford and Lindeth Vasey, for their enthusiasm and expertise, to Andy Sawyer for his notes, and to my colleagues in the H. G. Wells Society for their unstinting support for the Penguin Wells editions.

P.P.

THE COUNTRY OF THE
BLIND AND OTHER
SELECTED STORIES

THE LORD OF THE
DYNAMOS

The chief attendant of the three dynamos that buzzed and rattled at Camberwell[1] and kept the electric railway going, came out of Yorkshire, and his name was James Holroyd. He was a practical electrician but fond of whisky, a heavy, red-haired brute with irregular teeth. He doubted the existence of the Deity but accepted Carnot's cycle,[2] and he had read Shakespeare and found him weak in chemistry. His helper came out of the mysterious East, and his name was Azuma-zi.[3] But Holroyd called him Pooh-bah.[4] Holroyd liked a nigger help because he would stand kicking – a habit with Holroyd – and did not pry into the machinery and try to learn the ways of it. Certain odd possibilities of the Negro mind brought into abrupt contact with the crown of our civilization Holroyd never fully realized, though just at the end he got some inkling of them.

To define Azuma-zi was beyond ethnology. He was, perhaps, more Negroid than anything else, though his hair was curly rather than frizzy, and his nose had a bridge. Moreover, his skin was brown rather than black, and the whites of his eyes were yellow. His broad cheek-bones and narrow chin gave his face something of the viperine V. His head, too, was broad behind, and low and narrow at the forehead, as if his brain had been twisted round in the reverse way to a European's. He was short of stature and still shorter of English. In conversation he made numerous odd noises of no known marketable value, and his infrequent words were carved and wrought into heraldic grotesqueness. Holroyd tried to elucidate his religious beliefs, and – especially after whisky – lectured to him against superstition and missionaries. Azuma-zi, however, shirked the discussion of his gods, even though he was kicked for it.

Azuma-zi had come, clad in white but insufficient raiment, out of the stoke-hole of the *Lord Clive*, from the Straits Settlements[5] and beyond, into London. He had heard even in his youth of the greatness and riches of London, where all the women are white and fair and even the beggars in the streets are white; and he had arrived, with newly-earned gold coins in his pocket, to worship at the shrine of civilization. The day of his landing was a dismal one; the sky was dun, and a wind-worried drizzle filtered down to the greasy streets, but he plunged boldly into the delights of Shadwell, and was presently cast up, shattered in health, civilized in costume, penniless, and, except in matters of the direst necessity, practically a dumb animal, to toil for James Holroyd, and to be bullied by him in the dynamo shed at Camberwell. And to James Holroyd bullying was a labour of love.

There were three dynamos with their engines at Camberwell. The two that have been there since the beginning are small machines; the larger one was new. The smaller machines made a reasonable noise; their straps hummed over the drums, every now and then the brushes buzzed and fizzled, and the air churned steadily, whoo! whoo! whoo! between their poles. One was loose in its foundations and kept the shed vibrating. But the big dynamo drowned these little noises altogether with the sustained drone of its iron core, which somehow set part of the ironwork humming. The place made the visitor's head reel with the throb, throb, throb of the engines, the rotation of the big wheels, the spinning ball-valves, the occasional spittings of the steam, and over all the deep, unceasing, surging note of the big dynamo. This last noise was from an engineering point of view a defect, but Azuma-zi accounted it unto the monster for mightiness and pride.

If it were possible we would have the noises of that shed always about the reader as he reads, we would tell all our story to such an accompaniment. It was a steady stream of din, from which the ear picked out first one thread and then another; there was the intermittent snorting, panting, and seething of the

steam-engines, the suck and thud of their pistons, the dull beat
on the air as the spokes of the great driving-wheels came round,
a note the leather straps made as they ran tighter and looser,
and a fretful tumult from the dynamos; and, over all, sometimes
inaudible, as the ear tired of it, and then creeping back upon the
senses again, was this trombone note of the big machine. The
floor never felt steady and quiet beneath one's feet, but quivered
and jarred. It was a confusing, unsteady place, and enough to
send anyone's thoughts jerking into odd zigzags. And for three
months, while the big strike of the engineers was in progress,
Holroyd who was a blackleg, and Azuma-zi who was a mere
black, were never out of the stir and eddy of it, but slept and
fed in the little wooden shanty between the shed and the gates.

Holroyd delivered a theological lecture on the text of his big
machine soon after Azuma-zi came. He had to shout to be
heard in the din. 'Look at that,' said Holroyd; 'where's your
'eathen idol to match 'im?' And Azuma-zi looked. For a
moment Holroyd was inaudible, and then Azuma-zi heard: 'Kill
a hundred men. Twelve per cent[6] on the ordinary shares,' said
Holroyd, 'and that's something like a Gord.'

Holroyd was proud of his big dynamo, and expatiated upon
its size and power to Azuma-zi until Heaven knows what odd
currents of thought that and the incessant whirling and shindy
set up within the curly black cranium. He would explain in the
most graphic manner the dozen or so ways in which a man
might be killed by it, and once he gave Azuma-zi a shock as a
sample of its quality. After that, in the breathing times of his
labour – it was heavy labour, being not only his own, but most
of Holroyd's – Azuma-zi would sit and watch the big machine.
Now and then the brushes would sparkle and spit blue flashes,
at which Holroyd would swear, but all the rest was as smooth
and rhythmic as breathing. The band ran shouting over the
shaft, and ever behind one as one watched was the complacent
thud of the piston. So it lived all day in this big airy shed, with
him and Holroyd to wait upon it; not prisoned up and slaving
to drive a ship as the other engines he knew – mere captive
devils of the British Solomon[7] – had been, but a machine
enthroned. Those two smaller dynamos Azuma-zi by force of

contrast despised; the large one he privately christened the Lord
of the Dynamos. They were fretful and irregular, but the big
dynamo was steady. How great it was! How serene and easy in
its working! Greater and calmer even than the Buddhas he had
seen at Rangoon, and yet not motionless, but living! The great
black coils spun, spun, spun, the rings ran round under the
brushes, and the deep note of its coil steadied the whole. It
affected Azuma-zi queerly.

Azuma-zi was not fond of labour. He would sit about and
watch the Lord of the Dynamos while Holroyd went away to
persuade the yard porter to get whisky, although his proper
place was not in the dynamo shed but behind the engines, and,
moreover, if Holroyd caught him skulking he got hit for it with
a rod of stout copper wire. He would go and stand close to the
colossus, and look up at the great leather band running overhead. There was a black patch on the band that came round,
and it pleased him somehow among all the clatter to watch this
return again and again. Odd thoughts spun with the whirl of
it. Scientific people tell us that savages give souls to rocks and
trees – and a machine is a thousand times more alive than a
rock or a tree. And Azuma-zi was practically a savage still; the
veneer of civilization lay no deeper than his slop suit, his bruises,
and the coal grime on his face and hands. His father before him
had worshipped a meteoric stone;[8] kindred blood, it may be,
had splashed the broad wheels of Juggernaut.

He took every opportunity Holroyd gave him of touching
and handling the great dynamo that was fascinating him. He
polished and cleaned it until the metal parts were blinding in
the sun. He felt a mysterious sense of service in doing this. He
would go up to it and touch its spinning coils gently. The gods
he had worshipped were all far away. The people in London
hid their gods.

At last his dim feelings grew more distinct and took shape in
thoughts, and at last in acts. When he came into the roaring
shed one morning he salaamed to the Lord of the Dynamos,
and then, when Holroyd was away, he went and whispered to
the thundering machine that he was its servant, and prayed it
to have pity on him and save him from Holroyd. As he did so

a rare gleam of light came in through the open archway of the throbbing machine-shed, and the Lord of the Dynamos, as he whirled and roared, was radiant with pale gold. Then Azuma-zi knew that his service was acceptable to his Lord. After that he did not feel so lonely as he had done, and he had indeed been very much alone in London. Even when his work-time was over, which was rare, he loitered about the shed.

The next time Holroyd maltreated him, Azuma-zi went presently to the Lord of the Dynamos and whispered, 'Thou seest, O my Lord!' and the angry whirr of the machinery seemed to answer him. Thereafter it appeared to him that whenever Holroyd came into the shed a different note mingled with the sounds of the dynamo. 'My Lord bides his time,' said Azuma-zi to himself. 'The iniquity of the fool is not yet ripe.' And he waited and watched for the reckoning. One day there was evidence of short circuiting, and Holroyd, making an unwary examination – it was in the afternoon – got a rather severe shock. Azuma-zi from behind the engine saw him jump off and curse at the peccant coil.

'He is warned,' said Azuma-zi to himself. 'Surely my Lord is very patient.'

Holroyd had at first initiated his 'nigger' into such elementary conceptions of the dynamo's working as would enable him to take temporary charge of the shed in his absence. But when he noticed the manner in which Azuma-zi hung about the monster he became suspicious. He dimly perceived his assistant was 'up to something', and connecting him with the anointing of the coils with oil[9] that had rotted the varnish in one place, he issued an edict, shouted above the confusion of the machinery, 'Don't 'ee go nigh that big dynamo any more, Pooh-bah, or a'll take thy skin off!' Besides, if it pleased Azuma-zi to be near the big machine, it was plain sense and decency to keep him away from it.

Azuma-zi obeyed at the time, but later he was caught bowing before the Lord of the Dynamos. At which Holroyd twisted his arm and kicked him as he turned to go away. As Azuma-zi presently stood behind the engine and glared at the back of the hated Holroyd, the noises of the machinery took a new rhythm and sounded like four words in his native tongue.

It is hard to say exactly what madness is. I fancy Azuma-zi was mad. The incessant din and whirl of the dynamo shed may have churned up his little store of knowledge and big store of superstitious fancy, at last, into something akin to frenzy. At any rate, when the idea of making Holroyd a sacrifice to the Dynamo Fetish was thus suggested to him, it filled him with a strange tumult of exultant emotion.

That night the two men and their black shadows were alone in the shed together. The shed was lit with one big arc-light and winked and flickered purple. The shadows lay black behind the dynamos, the ball governors of the engines whirled from light to darkness, and their pistons beat loud and steadily. The world outside seen through the open end of the shed seemed incredibly dim and remote. It seemed absolutely silent, too, since the riot of the machinery drowned every external sound. Far away was the black fence of the yard with grey shadowy houses behind, and above was the deep blue sky and the pale little stars. Azuma-zi suddenly walked across the centre of the shed above which the leather bands were running, and went into the shadow by the big dynamo. Holroyd heard a click, and the spin of the armature changed.

'What are you dewin' with that switch?' he bawled in surprise. 'Han't I told you—'

Then he saw the set expression of Azuma-zi's eyes as the Asiatic came out of the shadow towards him.

In another moment the two men were grappling fiercely in front of the great dynamo.

'You coffee-headed fool!' gasped Holroyd, with a brown hand at his throat. 'Keep off those contact rings.' In another moment he was tripped and reeling back upon the Lord of the Dynamos. He instinctively loosened his grip upon his antagonist to save himself from the machine.

The messenger, sent in furious haste from the station to find out what had happened in the dynamo shed, met Azuma-zi at the porter's lodge by the gate. Azuma-zi tried to explain something, but the messenger could make nothing of the black's incoherent English, and hurried on to the shed. The machines

were all noisily at work, and nothing seemed to be disarranged.
There was, however, a queer smell of singed hair. Then he saw
an odd-looking crumpled mass clinging to the front of the big
dynamo, and, approaching, recognized the distorted remains
of Holroyd.

The man stared and hesitated a moment. Then he saw the
face, and shut his eyes convulsively. He turned on his heel
before he opened them, so that he should not see Holroyd
again, and went out of the shed to get advice and help.

When Azuma-zi saw Holroyd die in the grip of the Great
Dynamo he had been a little scared about the consequences of
his act. Yet he felt strangely elated, and knew that the favour
of the Lord Dynamo was upon him. His plan was already settled
when he met the man coming from the station, and the scientific
manager who speedily arrived on the scene jumped at the
obvious conclusion of suicide. This expert scarcely noticed
Azuma-zi, except to ask a few questions. Did he see Holroyd
kill himself? Azuma-zi explained he had been out of sight at
the engine furnace until he heard a difference in the noise
from the dynamo. It was not a difficult examination, being
untinctured by suspicion.

The distorted remains of Holroyd, which the electrician
removed from the machine, were hastily covered by the porter
with a coffee-stained tablecloth. Somebody, by a happy inspiration, fetched a medical man. The expert was chiefly anxious
to get the machine at work again, for seven or eight trains had
stopped midway in the stuffy tunnels of the electric railway.
Azuma-zi, answering or misunderstanding the questions of the
people who had by authority or impudence come into the
shed, was presently sent back to the stoke-hole by the scientific
manager. Of course a crowd collected outside the gates of the
yard – a crowd, for no known reason, always hovers for a day
or two near the scene of a sudden death in London – two or
three reporters percolated somehow into the engine shed, and
one even got to Azuma-zi; but the scientific expert cleared them
out again, being himself an amateur journalist.

Presently the body was carried away, and public interest
departed with it. Azuma-zi remained very quietly at his furnace,

seeing over and over again in the coals a figure that wriggled violently and became still. An hour after the murder, to anyone coming into the shed things would have looked exactly as if nothing remarkable had ever happened there. Peeping presently from his engine-room the black saw the Lord Dynamo spin and whirl beside his little brothers, and the driving-wheels were beating round and the steam in the pistons went thud, thud, exactly as it had been earlier in the evening. After all, from the mechanical point of view it had been a most insignificant incident – the mere temporary deflection of a current. But now the slender form and slender shadow of the scientific manager replaced the sturdy outline of Holroyd travelling up and down the lane of light upon the vibrating floor under the straps between the engines and the dynamos.

'Have I not served my Lord?' said Azuma-zi inaudibly from his shadow, and the note of the great dynamo rang out full and clear. As he looked at the big whirling mechanism the strange fascination of it that had been a little in abeyance since Holroyd's death resumed its sway.

Never had Azuma-zi seen a man killed so swiftly and pitilessly. The big humming machine had slain its victim without wavering for a second from its steady beating. It was indeed a mighty god.

The unconscious scientific manager stood with his back to him, scribbling on a piece of paper. His shadow lay at the foot of the monster.

Was the Lord Dynamo still hungry? His servant was ready.

Azuma-zi made a stealthy step forward; then stopped. The scientific manager suddenly ceased his writing, walked down the shed to the endmost of the dynamos, and began to examine the brushes.

Azuma-zi hesitated, and then slipped across noiselessly into the shadow by the switch. There he waited. Presently the manager's footsteps could be heard returning. He stopped in his old position, unconscious of the stoker crouching ten feet away from him. Then the big dynamo suddenly fizzled, and in another moment Azuma-zi had sprung out of the darkness upon him.

The scientific manager was gripped round the body and

swung towards the big dynamo. Kicking with his knee and forcing his antagonist's head down with his hands, he loosened the grip on his waist and swung round away from the machine. Then the black grasped him again, putting a curly head against his chest, and they swayed and panted as it seemed for an age or so. Then the scientific manager was impelled to catch a black ear in his teeth and bite furiously. The black yelled hideously.

They rolled over on the floor, and the black, who had apparently slipped from the vice of the teeth or parted with some ear – the scientific manager wondered which at the time – tried to throttle him. The scientific manager was making some ineffectual efforts to claw something with his hands and to kick, when the welcome sound of quick footsteps sounded on the floor. The next moment Azuma-zi had left him and darted towards the big dynamo. There was a splutter amid the roar.

The officer of the company who had entered stood staring as Azuma-zi caught the naked terminals in his hands, gave one horrible convulsion, and then hung motionless from the machine, his face violently distorted.

'I'm jolly glad you came in when you did,' said the scientific manager, still sitting on the floor.

He looked at the still quivering figure. 'It is not a nice death to die, apparently – but it is quick.'

The official was still staring at the body. He was a man of slow apprehension.

There was a pause.

The scientific manager got up on his feet rather awkwardly. He ran his fingers along his collar thoughtfully, and moved his head to and fro several times.

'Poor Holroyd! I see now.' Then almost mechanically he went towards the switch in the shadow and turned the current into the railway circuit again. As he did so the singed body loosened its grip upon the machine and fell forward on its face. The core of the dynamo roared out loud and clear, and the armature beat the air.

So ended prematurely the worship of the Dynamo Deity, perhaps the most short-lived of all religions. Yet withal it could at least boast a Martyrdom and a Human Sacrifice.

THE REMARKABLE CASE OF DAVIDSON'S EYES

The transitory mental aberration of Sidney Davidson, remarkable enough in itself, is still more remarkable if Wade's[1] explanation is to be credited. It sets one dreaming of the oddest possibilities of intercommunication in the future, of spending an intercalary five minutes on the other side of the world, or being watched in our most secret operations by unsuspected eyes. It happened that I was the immediate witness of Davidson's seizure, and so it falls naturally to me to put the story upon paper.

When I say that I was the immediate witness of his seizure, I mean that I was the first on the scene. The thing happened at the Harlow Technical College, just beyond the Highgate Archway.[2] He was alone in the larger laboratory when the thing happened. I was in a smaller room, where the balances are, writing up some notes. The thunderstorm had completely upset my work, of course. It was just after one of the louder peals that I thought I heard some glass smash in the other room. I stopped writing, and turned round to listen. For a moment I heard nothing; the hail was playing the devil's tattoo on the corrugated zinc of the roof. Then came another sound, a smash – no doubt of it this time. Something heavy had been knocked off the bench. I jumped up at once and went and opened the door leading into the big laboratory.

I was surprised to hear a queer sort of laugh, and saw Davidson standing unsteadily in the middle of the room, with a dazzled look on his face. My first impression was that he was drunk. He did not notice me. He was clawing out at something invisible a yard in front of his face. He put out his hand slowly, rather hesitatingly, and then clutched nothing. 'What's come to it?' he said. He held up his hands to his face, fingers spread out. 'Great Scott!' he said. The thing happened three or four years ago, when everyone swore by that personage.[3] Then he began raising his feet clumsily, as though he had expected to find them glued to the floor.

'Davidson!' cried I. 'What's the matter with you?' He turned round in my direction and looked about for me. He looked over me and at me and on either side of me, without the slightest sign of seeing me. 'Waves,' he said; 'and a remarkably neat schooner. I'd swear that was Bellows's voice. *Hullo!*' He shouted suddenly at the top of his voice.

I thought he was up to some foolery. Then I saw littered about his feet the shattered remains of the best of our electrometers. 'What's up, man?' said I, 'You've smashed the electrometer!'

'Bellows again!' said he. 'Friends left, if my hands are gone. Something about electrometers. Which way *are* you, Bellows?' He suddenly came staggering towards me. 'The damned stuff cuts like butter,' he said. He walked straight into the bench and recoiled. 'None so buttery that!' he said, and stood swaying.

I felt scared. 'Davidson,' said I, 'what on earth's come over you?'

He looked round him in every direction. 'I could swear that was Bellows. Why don't you show yourself like a man, Bellows?'

It occurred to me that he must be suddenly struck blind. I walked round the table and laid my hand upon his arm. I never saw a man more startled in my life. He jumped away from me, and came round into an attitude of self-defence, his face fairly distorted with terror. 'Good God!' he cried. 'What was that?'

'It's I – Bellows. Confound it, Davidson!'

He jumped when I answered him and stared – how can I express it? – right through me. He began talking, not to me, but to himself. 'Here in broad daylight on a clear beach. Not a place to hide in.' He looked about him wildly. 'Here! I'm *off.*' He suddenly turned and ran headlong into the big electro-magnet – so violently that, as we found afterwards, he bruised his shoulder and jawbone cruelly. At that he stepped back a pace, and cried out with almost a whimper: 'What, in Heaven's name, has come over me?' He stood, blanched with terror and trembling violently, with his right arm clutching his left, where that had collided with the magnet.

By that time I was excited and fairly scared. 'Davidson,' said I, 'don't be afraid.'

He was startled at my voice, but not so excessively as before. I repeated my words in as clear and as firm a tone as I could assume. 'Bellows,' he said, 'is that you?'

'Can't you see it's me?'

He laughed. 'I can't even see it's myself. Where the devil are we?'

'Here,' said I, 'in the laboratory.'

'The laboratory!' he answered in a puzzled tone, and put his hand to his forehead. 'I *was* in the laboratory – till that flash came, but I'm hanged if I'm there now. What ship is that?'

'There's no ship,' said I. 'Do be sensible, old chap.'

'No ship!' he repeated, and seemed to forget my denial forthwith. 'I suppose,' said he slowly, 'we're both dead. But the rummy part is I feel just as though I still had a body. Don't get used to it all at once, I suppose. The old shop was struck by lightning, I suppose. Jolly quick thing, Bellows – eh?'

'Don't talk nonsense. You're very much alive. You are in the laboratory, blundering about. You've just smashed a new electrometer. I don't envy you when Boyce arrives.'

He stared away from me towards the diagrams of cryohydrates. 'I must be deaf,' said he. 'They've fired a gun, for there goes the puff of smoke, and I never heard a sound.'

I put my hand on his arm again, and this time he was less alarmed. 'We seem to have a sort of invisible bodies,' said he. 'By Jove! there's a boat coming round the headland. It's very much like the old life after all – in a different climate.'

I shook his arm. 'Davidson,' I cried, 'wake up!'

It was just then that Boyce came in. So soon as he spoke Davidson exclaimed: 'Old Boyce! Dead too! What a lark!' I hastened to explain that Davidson was in a kind of somnambulistic trance. Boyce was interested at once. We both did all we could to rouse the fellow out of his extraordinary state. He answered our questions, and asked us some of his own, but his attention seemed distracted by his hallucination about a beach and a ship. He kept interpolating observations concerning some boat and the davits, and sails filling with the wind. It made one feel queer, in the dusky laboratory, to hear him saying such things.

He was blind and helpless. We had to walk him down the passage, one at each elbow, to Boyce's private room, and while Boyce talked to him there, and humoured him about this ship idea, I went along the corridor and asked old Wade to come and look at him. The voice of our Dean sobered him a little, but not very much. He asked where his hands were, and why he had to walk about up to his waist in the ground. Wade thought over him a long time – you know how he knits his brows – and then made him feel the couch, guiding his hands to it. 'That's a couch,' said Wade. 'The couch in the private room of Prof. Boyce. Horsehair stuffing.'

Davidson felt about, and puzzled over it, and answered presently that he could feel it all right, but he couldn't see it.

'What *do* you see?' asked Wade. Davidson said he could see nothing but a lot of sand and broken-up shells. Wade gave him some other things to feel, telling him what they were, and watching him keenly.

'The ship is almost hull down,'[4] said Davidson presently, apropos of nothing.

'Never mind the ship,' said Wade. 'Listen to me, Davidson. Do you know what hallucination means?'

'Rather,' said Davidson.

'Well, everything you see is hallucinatory.'

'Bishop Berkeley,'[5] said Davidson.

'Don't mistake me,' said Wade. 'You are alive and in this room of Boyce's. But something has happened to your eyes. You cannot see; you can feel and hear, but not see. Do you follow me?'

'It seems to me that I see too much.' Davidson rubbed his knuckles into his eyes. 'Well?' he said.

'That's all. Don't let it perplex you. Bellows here and I will take you home in a cab.'

'Wait a bit.' Davidson thought. 'Help me to sit down,' said he presently; 'and now – I'm sorry to trouble you – but will you tell me all that over again?'

Wade repeated it very patiently. Davidson shut his eyes, and pressed his hands upon his forehead. 'Yes,' said he. 'It's quite right. Now my eyes are shut I know you're right. That's you, Bellows, sitting by me on the couch. I'm in England again. And we're in the dark.'

Then he opened his eyes. 'And there,' said he, 'is the sun just rising, and the yards of the ship, and a tumbled sea, and a couple of birds flying. I never saw anything so real. And I'm sitting up to my neck in a bank of sand.'

He bent forward and covered his face with his hands. Then he opened his eyes again. 'Dark sea and sunrise! And yet I'm sitting on a sofa in old Boyce's room! . . . God help me!'

That was the beginning. For three weeks this strange affection of Davidson's eyes continued unabated. It was far worse than being blind. He was absolutely helpless, and had to be fed like a newly hatched bird, and led about and undressed. If he attempted to move, he fell over things or struck himself against walls or doors. After a day or so he got used to hearing our voices without seeing us, and willingly admitted he was at home, and that Wade was right in what he told him. My sister, to whom he was engaged, insisted on coming to see him, and would sit for hours every day while he talked about this beach of his. Holding her hand seemed to comfort him immensely. He explained that when we left the College and drove home – he lived in Hampstead village – it appeared to him as if we drove right through a sandhill – it was perfectly black until he emerged again – and through rocks and trees and solid obstacles, and when he was taken to his own room it made him giddy and almost frantic with the fear of falling, because going upstairs seemed to lift him thirty or forty feet above the rocks of his imaginary island. He kept saying he should smash all the eggs. The end was that he had to be taken down into his father's consulting-room and laid upon a couch that stood there.

He described the island as being a bleak kind of place on the whole, with very little vegetation, except some peaty stuff, and

a lot of bare rock. There were multitudes of penguins,[6] and
they made the rocks white and disagreeable to see. The sea was
often rough, and once there was a thunderstorm, and he lay
and shouted at the silent flashes. Once or twice seals pulled up
on the beach, but only on the first two or three days. He said it
was very funny the way in which the penguins used to waddle
right through him, and how he seemed to lie among them
without disturbing them.

I remember one odd thing, and that was when he wanted
very badly to smoke. We put a pipe in his hands – he almost
poked his eye out with it – and lit it. But he couldn't taste
anything. I've since found it's the same with me – I don't know
if it's the usual case – that I cannot enjoy tobacco at all unless
I can see the smoke.

But the queerest part of his vision came when Wade sent him
out in a bath-chair to get fresh air. The Davidsons hired a chair,
and got that deaf and obstinate dependant of theirs, Widgery,
to attend to it. Widgery's ideas of healthy expeditions were
peculiar. My sister, who had been to the Dogs' Home, met
them in Camden Town, towards King's Cross,[7] Widgery trot-
ting along complacently, and Davidson, evidently most distressed, trying in his feeble, blind way to attract Widgery's
attention.

He positively wept when my sister spoke to him. 'Oh, get me
out of this horrible darkness!' he said, feeling for her hand. 'I
must get out of it, or I shall die.' He was quite incapable of
explaining what was the matter, but my sister decided he must
go home, and presently, as they went uphill towards Hampstead, the horror seemed to drop from him. He said it was good
to see the stars again, though it was then about noon and a
blazing day.

'It seemed,' he told me afterwards, 'as if I was being carried
irresistibly towards the water. I was not very much alarmed at
first. Of course it was night there – a lovely night.'

'Of course?' I asked, for that struck me as odd.

'Of course?' said he. 'It's always night there when it is day
here. ... Well, we went right into the water, which was calm
and shining under the moonlight – just a broad swell that

seemed to grow broader and flatter as I came down into it. The surface glistened just like a skin – it might have been empty space underneath for all I could tell to the contrary. Very slowly, for I rode slanting into it, the water crept up to my eyes. Then I went under and the skin seemed to break and heal again about my eyes. The moon gave a jump up in the sky and grew green and dim, and fish, faintly glowing, came darting round me – and things that seemed made of luminous glass; and I passed through a tangle of seaweeds that shone with an oily lustre. And so I drove down into the sea, and the stars went out one by one, and the moon grew greener and darker, and the seaweed became a luminous purple-red. It was all very faint and mysterious, and everything seemed to quiver. And all the while I could hear the wheels of the bath-chair creaking, and the footsteps of people going by, and a man in the distance selling the special *Pall Mall*.[8]

'I kept sinking down deeper and deeper into the water. It became inky black about me, not a ray from above came down into that darkness, and the phosphorescent things grew brighter and brighter. The snaky branches of the deeper weeds flickered like the flames of spirit-lamps; but, after a time, there were no more weeds. The fishes came staring and gaping towards me, and into me and through me. I never imagined such fishes before. They had lines of fire along the sides of them as though they had been outlined with a luminous pencil. And there was a ghastly thing swimming backwards with a lot of twining arms. And then I saw, coming very slowly towards me through the gloom, a hazy mass of light that resolved itself as it drew nearer into multitudes of fishes, struggling and darting round something that drifted. I drove on straight towards it, and presently I saw in the midst of the tumult, and by the light of the fish, a bit of splintered spar looming over me, and a dark hull tilting over, and some glowing phosphorescent forms that were shaken and writhed as the fish bit at them. Then it was I began to try to attract Widgery's attention. A horror came upon me. Ugh! I should have driven right into those half-eaten — things. If your sister had not come! They had great holes in them, Bellows, and . . . Never mind. But it was ghastly!'

For three weeks Davidson remained in this singular state, seeing what at the time we imagined was an altogether phantasmal world, and stone blind to the world around him. Then, one Tuesday, when I called I met old Davidson in the passage. 'He can see his thumb!' the old gentleman said, in a perfect transport. He was struggling into his overcoat. 'He can see his thumb, Bellows!' he said, with the tears in his eyes. 'The lad will be all right yet.'

I rushed in to Davidson. He was holding up a little book before his face, and looking at it and laughing in a weak kind of way.

'It's amazing,' said he. 'There's a kind of patch come there.' He pointed with his finger. 'I'm on the rocks as usual, and the penguins are staggering and flapping about as usual, and there's been a whale showing every now and then, but it's got too dark now to make him out. But put something *there*, and I see it – I do see it. It's very dim and broken in places, but I see it all the same, like a faint spectre of itself. I found it out this morning while they were dressing me. It's like a hole in this infernal phantom world. Just put your hand by mine. No – not there. Ah! Yes! I see it. The base of your thumb and a bit of cuff! It looks like the ghost of a bit of your hand sticking out of the darkling sky. Just by it there's a group of stars like a cross[9] coming out.'

From that time Davidson began to mend. His account of the change, like his account of the vision, was oddly convincing. Over patches of his field of vision, the phantom world grew fainter, grew transparent, as it were, and through these translucent gaps he began to see dimly the real world about him. The patches grew in size and number, ran together and spread until only here and there were blind spots left upon his eyes. He was able to get up and steer himself about, feed himself once more, read, smoke, and behave like an ordinary citizen again. At first it was very confusing to him to have these two pictures overlapping each other like the changing views of a lantern,[10] but in a little while he began to distinguish the real from the illusory.

At first he was unfeignedly glad, and seemed only too anxious to complete his cure by taking exercise and tonics. But as that odd island of his began to fade away from him, he became queerly interested in it. He wanted particularly to go down into the deep sea again, and would spend half his time wandering about the low-lying parts of London, trying to find the water-logged wreck he had seen drifting. The glare of real daylight very soon impressed him so vividly as to blot out everything of his shadowy world, but of a night-time, in a darkened room, he could still see the white-splashed rocks of the island, and the clumsy penguins staggering to and fro. But even these grew fainter and fainter, and, at last, soon after he married my sister, he saw them for the last time.

And now to tell of the queerest thing of all. About two years after his cure I dined with the Davidsons, and after dinner a man named Atkins called in. He is a lieutenant in the Royal Navy, and a pleasant, talkative man. He was on friendly terms with my brother-in-law, and was soon on friendly terms with me. It came out that he was engaged to Davidson's cousin, and incidentally he took out a kind of pocket photograph case to show us a new rendering of his fiancée. 'And, by the bye,' said he, 'here's the old *Fulmar*.'[11]

Davidson looked at it casually. Then suddenly his face lit up. 'Good heavens!' said he. 'I could almost swear—'

'What?' said Atkins.

'That I had seen that ship before.'

'Don't see how you can have. She hasn't been out of the South Seas for six years, and before then—'

'But,' began Davidson, and then: 'Yes – that's the ship I dreamt of; I'm sure that's the ship I dreamt of. She was standing off an island that swarmed with penguins, and she fired a gun.'

'Good Lord!' said Atkins, who had now heard the particulars of the seizure. 'How the deuce could you dream that?'

And then, bit by bit, it came out that on the very day Davidson was seized, H.M.S. *Fulmar* had actually been off a little rock to the south of Antipodes Island. A boat had landed overnight to get penguins' eggs, had been delayed, and a thunderstorm drifting up, the boat's crew had waited until the morning before rejoining the ship. Atkins had been one of them, and he corroborated, word for word, the descriptions Davidson had given of the island and the boat. There is not the slightest doubt in any of our minds that Davidson has really seen the place. In some unaccountable way, while he moved hither and thither in London, his sight moved hither and thither in a manner that corresponded, about this distant island. *How* is absolutely a mystery.

That completes the remarkable story of Davidson's eyes. It's perhaps the best authenticated case in existence of real vision at a distance. Explanation there is none forthcoming, except what Prof. Wade has thrown out. But his explanation involves the Fourth Dimension,[12] and a dissertation on theoretical kinds of space. To talk of there being 'a kink in space' seems mere nonsense to me; it may be because I am no mathematician. When I said that nothing would alter the fact that the place is eight thousand miles away, he answered that two points might be a yard away on a sheet of paper, and yet be brought together by bending the paper round. The reader may grasp his argument, but I certainly do not. His idea seems to be that Davidson, stooping between the poles of the big electromagnet, had some extraordinary twist given to his retinal elements through the sudden change in the field of force due to the lightning.

He thinks, as a consequence of this, that it may be possible to live visually in one part of the world, while one lives bodily in another. He has even made some experiments in support of his views; but, so far, he has simply succeeded in blinding a few dogs. I believe that is the net result of his work, though I have not seen him for some weeks. Latterly I have been so busy with my work in connection with the Saint Pancras installation[13] that I have had little opportunity of calling to see him. But the whole of his theory seems fantastic to me. The facts concerning Davidson stand on an altogether different footing, and I can testify personally to the accuracy of every detail I have given.

THE MOTH

Probably you have heard of Hapley – not W. T. Hapley, the son, but the celebrated Hapley, the Hapley of *Periplaneta Hapliia*,[1] Hapley the entomologist.

If so you know at least of the great feud between Hapley and Professor Pawkins, though certain of its consequences may be new to you. For those who have not, a word or two of explanation is necessary, which the idle reader may go over with a glancing eye if his indolence so incline him.

It is amazing how very widely diffused is the ignorance of such really important matters as this Hapley–Pawkins feud. Those epoch-making controversies, again, that have convulsed the Geological Society[2] are, I verily believe, almost entirely unknown outside the fellowship of that body. I have heard men of fair general education even refer to the great scenes at these meetings as vestry-meeting squabbles. Yet the great hate of the English and Scotch geologists has lasted now half a century, and has 'left deep and abundant marks upon the body of the science'. And this Hapley–Pawkins business, though perhaps a more personal affair, stirred passions as profound, if not profounder. Your common man has no conception of the zeal that animates a scientific investigator, the fury of contradiction you can arouse in him. It is the *odium theologicum* in a new form. There are men, for instance, who would gladly burn Sir Ray Lankester at Smithfield[3] for his treatment of the Mollusca in the Encyclopaedia. That fantastic extension of the Cephalopods to cover the Pteropods. . . . But I wander from Hapley and Pawkins.

It began years and years ago with a revision of the Microlepidoptera (whatever these may be) by Pawkins, in which he extinguished a new species created by Hapley. Hapley, who was always quarrelsome, replied by a stinging impeachment of the entire classification of Pawkins.* Pawkins in his 'Rejoinder'† suggested that Hapley's microscope was as defective as his power of observation, and called him an 'irresponsible meddler' – Hapley was not a professor at that time. Hapley in his retort,‡ spoke of 'blundering collectors', and described, as if inadvertently, Pawkins's revision as a 'miracle of ineptitude'. It was war to the knife. However, it would scarcely interest the reader to detail how these two great men quarrelled, and how the split between them widened until from the Microlepidoptera they were at war upon every open question in entomology. There were memorable occasions. At times the Royal Entomological Society[4] meetings resembled nothing so much as the Chamber of Deputies.[5] On the whole, I fancy Pawkins was nearer the truth than Hapley. But Hapley was skilful with his rhetoric, had a turn for ridicule rare in a scientific man, was endowed with vast energy, and had a fine sense of injury in the matter of the extinguished species; while Pawkins was a man of dull presence, prosy of speech, in shape not unlike a water-barrel, over-conscientious with testimonials, and suspected of jobbing museum appointments. So the young men gathered round Hapley and applauded him. It was a long struggle, vicious from the beginning and growing at last to pitiless antagonism. The successive turns of fortune, now an advantage to one side and now to another – now Hapley tormented by some success of Pawkins, and now Pawkins outshone by Hapley, belong rather to the history of entomology than to this story.

But in 1891 Pawkins, whose health had been bad for some time, published some work upon the 'mesoblast' of the Death's-Head Moth. What the mesoblast of the Death's-Head Moth may be does not matter a rap in this story. But the work was far below his usual standard, and gave Hapley an opening

* 'Remarks on a Recent Revision of Microlepidoptera', *Quart. Journ. Entomological Soc.*,[6] 1863.
† 'Rejoinder to Certain Remarks', etc. *Ibid.* 1864.
‡ 'Further Remarks', etc. *Ibid.*

he had coveted for years. He must have worked night and day to make the most of his advantage.

In an elaborate critique he rent Pawkins to tatters – one can fancy the man's disordered black hair, and his queer dark eyes flashing as he went for his antagonist – and Pawkins made a reply, halting, ineffectual, with painful gaps of silence, and yet malignant. There was no mistaking his will to wound Hapley, nor his incapacity to do it. But few of those who heard him – I was absent from that meeting – realized how ill the man was.

Hapley got his opponent down, and meant to finish him. He followed with a brutal attack upon Pawkins, in the form of a paper upon the development of moths in general, a paper showing evidence of an extraordinary amount of labour, couched in a violently controversial tone. Violent as it was, an editorial note witnesses that it was modified. It must have covered Pawkins with shame and confusion of face. It left no loophole; it was murderous in argument, and utterly contemptuous in tone; an awful thing for the declining years of a man's career.

The world of entomologists waited breathlessly for the rejoinder from Pawkins. He would try one, for Pawkins had always been game. But when it came it surprised them. For the rejoinder of Pawkins was to catch influenza, proceed to pneumonia, and die.

It was perhaps as effectual a reply as he could make under the circumstances, and largely turned the current of feeling against Hapley. The very people who had most gleefully cheered on those gladiators became serious at the consequence. There could be no reasonable doubt the fret of the defeat had contributed to the death of Pawkins. There was a limit even to scientific controversy, said serious people. Another crushing attack was already in the press and appeared on the day before the funeral. I don't think Hapley exerted himself to stop it. People remembered how Hapley had hounded down his rival and forgot that rival's defects. Scathing satire reads ill over fresh mould. The thing provoked comment in the daily papers. It was that made me think you had probably heard of Hapley and this controversy. But, as I have already remarked, scientific workers live very much in a world of their own; half the people, I dare say, who go along Piccadilly to the Academy every year could not tell you where the learned societies abide.[7] Many even think that research is a kind of happy-family cage in which all kinds of men lie down together in peace.

In his private thoughts Hapley could not forgive Pawkins for dying. In the first place, it was a mean dodge to escape the absolute pulverization Hapley had in hand for him, and in the second, it left Hapley's mind with a queer gap in it. For twenty years he had worked hard, sometimes far into the night, and seven days a week, with microscope, scalpel, collecting-net, and pen, and almost entirely with reference to Pawkins. The European reputation he had won had come as an incident in that great antipathy. He had gradually worked up to a climax in this last controversy. It had killed Pawkins, but it had also thrown Hapley out of gear, so to speak, and his doctor advised him to give up work for a time, and rest. So Hapley went down into a quiet village in Kent, and thought day and night of Pawkins and good things it was now impossible to say about him.

At last Hapley began to realize in what direction the preoccupation tended. He determined to make a fight for it, and started by trying to read novels. But he could not get his mind off Pawkins, white in the face and making his last speech – every sentence a beautiful opening for Hapley. He turned to fiction – and found it had no grip on him. He read the 'Island Nights' Entertainments'[8] until his 'sense of causation' was shocked beyond endurance by the Bottle Imp. Then he went to Kipling,[9] and found he 'proved nothing' besides being irreverent and vulgar. These scientific people have their limitations. Then unhappily he tried Besant's 'Inner House',[10] and the opening chapter set his mind upon learned societies and Pawkins at once.

So Hapley turned to chess, and found it a little more soothing. He soon mastered the moves and the chief gambits and commoner closing positions, and began to beat the Vicar. But then the cylindrical contours of the opposite king began to resemble Pawkins standing up and gasping ineffectually against checkmate, and Hapley decided to give up chess.

Perhaps the study of some new branch of science would after

all be better diversion. The best rest is change of occupation. Hapley determined to plunge at diatoms, and had one of his smaller microscopes and Halibut's monograph[11] sent down from London. He thought that perhaps if he could get up a vigorous quarrel with Halibut, he might be able to begin life afresh and forget Pawkins. And very soon he was hard at work in his habitual strenuous fashion at these microscopic denizens of the wayside pool.

It was on the third day of the diatoms that Hapley became aware of a novel addition to the local fauna. He was working late at the microscope, and the only light in the room was the brilliant little lamp with the special form of green shade. Like all experienced microscopists, he kept both eyes open. It is the only way to avoid excessive fatigue. One eye was over the instrument, and bright and distinct before that was the circular field of the microscope, across which a brown diatom was slowly moving. With the other eye Hapley saw, as it were, without seeing. He was only dimly conscious of the brass side of the instrument, the illuminated part of the tablecloth, a sheet of notepaper, the foot of the lamp, and the darkened room beyond.

Suddenly his attention drifted from one eye to the other. The tablecloth was of the material called tapestry by shopmen, and rather brightly coloured. The pattern was in gold, with a small amount of crimson and pale blue upon a greyish ground. At one point the pattern seemed displaced, and there was a vibrating movement of the colours at this point.

Hapley suddenly moved his head back and looked with both eyes. His mouth fell open with astonishment.

It was a large moth or butterfly; its wings spread in butterfly fashion!

It was strange it should be in the room at all, for the windows were closed. Strange that it should not have attracted his attention when fluttering to its present position. Strange that it should match the tablecloth. Stranger far that to him, Hapley, the great entomologist, it was altogether unknown. There was no delusion. It was crawling slowly towards the foot of the lamp.

'New Genus, by heavens! And in England!' said Hapley, staring.

Then he suddenly thought of Pawkins. Nothing would have maddened Pawkins more. . . . And Pawkins was dead!

Something about the head and body of the insect became singularly suggestive of Pawkins, just as the chess king had been.

'Confound Pawkins!' said Hapley. 'But I must catch this.' And looking round him for some means of capturing the moth, he rose slowly out of his chair. Suddenly the insect rose, struck the edge of the lampshade – Hapley heard the 'ping' – and vanished into the shadow.

In a moment Hapley had whipped off the shade, so that the whole room was illuminated. The thing had disappeared, but soon his practised eye detected it upon the wallpaper near the door. He went towards it poising the lampshade for capture. Before he was within striking distance, however, it had risen and was fluttering round the room. After the fashion of its kind, it flew with sudden starts and turns, seeming to vanish here and reappear there. Once Hapley struck, and missed; then again.

The third time he hit his microscope. The instrument swayed, struck and overturned the lamp, and fell noisily upon the floor. The lamp turned over on the table and, very luckily, went out. Hapley was left in the dark. With a start he felt the strange moth blunder into his face.

It was maddening. He had no lights. If he opened the door of the room the thing would get away. In the darkness he saw Pawkins quite distinctly laughing at him. Pawkins had ever an oily laugh. He swore furiously and stamped his foot on the floor.

There was a timid rapping at the door.

Then it opened, perhaps a foot, and very slowly. The alarmed face of the landlady appeared behind a pink candle flame; she wore a nightcap over her grey hair and had some purple garment over her shoulders. 'What *was* that fearful smash?' she said. 'Has anything—' The strange moth appeared fluttering about the chink of the door. 'Shut that door!' said Hapley, and suddenly rushed at her.

The door slammed hastily. Hapley was left alone in the dark. Then in the pause he heard his landlady scuttle upstairs, lock her door, and drag something heavy across the room and put against it.

It became evident to Hapley that his conduct and appearance had been strange and alarming. Confound the moth! and Pawkins! However, it was a pity to lose the moth now. He felt his way into the hall and found the matches, after sending his hat down upon the floor with a noise like a drum. With the lighted candle he returned to the sitting-room. No moth was to be seen. Yet once for a moment it seemed that the thing was fluttering round his head. Hapley very suddenly decided to give up the moth and go to bed. But he was excited. All night long his sleep was broken by dreams of the moth, Pawkins, and his landlady. Twice in the night he turned out and soused his head in cold water.

One thing was very clear to him. His landlady could not possibly understand about the strange moth, especially as he had failed to catch it. No one but an entomologist would understand quite how he felt. She was probably frightened at his behaviour, and yet he failed to see how he could explain it. He decided to say nothing further about the events of last night. After breakfast he saw her in her garden, and decided to go out and talk to reassure her. He talked to her about beans and potatoes, bees, caterpillars, and the price of fruit. She replied in her usual manner, but she looked at him a little suspiciously, and kept walking as he walked, so that there was always a bed of flowers, or a row of beans, or something of the sort, between them. After a while he began to feel singularly irritated at this, and, to conceal his vexation, went indoors and presently went out for a walk.

The moth, or butterfly, trailing an odd flavour of Pawkins with it, kept coming into that walk though he did his best to keep his mind off it. Once he saw it quite distinctly, with its wings flattened out, upon the old stone wall that runs along the west edge of the park, but going up to it he found it was only two lumps of grey and yellow lichen. 'This,' said Hapley, 'is the reverse of mimicry. Instead of a butterfly looking like a

stone, here is a stone looking like a butterfly!' Once something
hovered and fluttered round his head, but by an effort of will
he drove that impression out of his mind again.

In the afternoon Hapley called upon the Vicar, and argued
with him upon theological questions. They sat in the little
arbour covered with brier, and smoked as they wrangled. 'Look
at that moth!' said Hapley, suddenly, pointing to the edge of
the wooden table.

'Where?' said the Vicar.

'You don't see a moth on the edge of the table there?' said
Hapley.

'Certainly not,' said the Vicar.

Hapley was thunderstruck. He gasped. The Vicar was staring
at him. Clearly the man saw nothing. 'The eye of faith is no
better than the eye of science,' said Hapley awkwardly.

'I don't see your point,' said the Vicar, thinking it was part
of the argument.

That night Hapley found the moth crawling over his counter-
pane. He sat on the edge of the bed in his shirt-sleeves and
reasoned with himself. Was it pure hallucination? He knew he
was slipping, and he battled for his sanity with the same silent
energy he had formerly displayed against Pawkins. So persistent
is mental habit that he felt as if it were still a struggle with
Pawkins. He was well versed in psychology. He knew that such
visual illusions do come as a result of mental strain. But the
point was, he did not only *see* the moth, he had heard it when
it touched the edge of the lampshade and afterwards when
it hit against the wall, and he had felt it strike his face in the dark.

He looked at it. It was not at all dream-like but perfectly
clear and solid-looking in the candlelight. He saw the hairy
body and the short feathery antennae, the jointed legs, even a
place where the down was rubbed from the wing. He suddenly
felt angry with himself for being afraid of a little insect.

His landlady had got the servant to sleep with her that night,
because she was afraid to be alone. In addition she had locked
the door and put the chest of drawers against it. They listened
and talked in whispers after they had gone to bed, but nothing
occurred to alarm them. About eleven they had ventured to put

the candle out and had both dozed off to sleep. They woke with a start, and sat up in bed, listening in the darkness.

Then they heard slippered feet going to and fro in Hapley's room. A chair was overturned and there was a violent dab at the wall. Then a china mantel ornament smashed upon the fender. Suddenly the door of the room opened, and they heard him upon the landing. They clung to one another, listening. He seemed to be dancing upon the staircase. Now he would go down three or four steps quickly, then up again, then hurry down into the hall. They heard the umbrella-stand go over, and the fanlight break. Then the bolt shot and the chain rattled. He was opening the door.

They hurried to the window. It was a dim grey night; an almost unbroken sheet of watery cloud was sweeping across the moon, and the hedge and trees in front of the house were black against the pale roadway. They saw Hapley, looking like a ghost in his shirt and white trousers, running to and fro in the road and beating the air. Now he would stop, now he would dart very rapidly at something invisible, now he would move upon it with stealthy strides. At last he went out of sight up the road towards the down. Then while they argued who should go down and lock the door, he returned. He was walking very fast, and he came straight into the house, closed the door carefully, and went quietly up to his bedroom. Then everything was silent.

'Mrs Colville,' said Hapley, calling down the staircase next morning, 'I hope I did not alarm you last night.'

'You may well ask that!' said Mrs Colville.

'The fact is, I am a sleep-walker, and the last two nights I have been without my sleeping mixture. There is nothing to be alarmed about, really. I am sorry I made such an ass of myself. I will go over the down to Shoreham, and get some stuff to make me sleep soundly. I ought to have done that yesterday.'

But halfway over the down, by the chalk pits, the moth came upon Hapley again. He went on, trying to keep his mind upon chess problems, but it was no good. The thing fluttered into his face, and he struck at it with his hat in self-defence. Then rage, the old rage – the rage he had so often felt against Pawkins –

came upon him again. He went on, leaping and striking at the
eddying insect. Suddenly he trod on nothing, and fell headlong.

There was a gap in his sensations, and Hapley found himself
sitting on the heap of flints in front of the opening of the chalk
pits, with a leg twisted back under him. The strange moth was
still fluttering round his head. He struck at it with his hand,
and turning his head saw two men approaching him. One was
the village doctor. It occurred to Hapley that this was lucky.
Then it came into his mind with extraordinary vividness, that
no one would ever be able to see the strange moth except
himself, and that it behoved him to keep silent about it.

Late that night, however, after his broken leg was set, he was
feverish and forgot his self-restraint. He was lying flat on his
bed, and he began to run his eyes round the room to see if the
moth was still about. He tried not to do this, but it was no
good. He soon caught sight of the thing resting close to his
hand, by the night-light, on the green tablecloth. The wings
quivered. With a sudden wave of anger he smote at it with his
fist, and the nurse woke up with a shriek. He had missed it.

'That moth!' he said; and then: 'It was fancy. Nothing!'

All the time he could see quite clearly the insect going round
the cornice and darting across the room, and he could also see
that the nurse saw nothing of it and looked at him strangely.
He must keep himself in hand. He knew he was a lost man if
he did not keep himself in hand. But as the night waned the
fever grew upon him, and the very dread he had of seeing the
moth made him see it. About five, just as the dawn was grey,
he tried to get out of bed and catch it, though his leg was afire
with pain. The nurse had to struggle with him.

On account of this, they tied him down to the bed. At this
the moth grew bolder, and once he felt it settle in his hair. Then,
because he struck out violently with his arms, they tied these
also. At this the moth came and crawled over his face, and
Hapley wept, swore, screamed, prayed for them to take it off
him, unavailingly.

The doctor was a blockhead, a just-qualified general prac-
titioner, and quite ignorant of mental science. He simply said
there was no moth. Had he possessed the wit, he might still

perhaps have saved Hapley from his fate by entering into his delusion, and covering his face with gauze as he prayed might be done. But, as I say, the doctor was a blockhead; and until the leg was healed Hapley was kept tied to his bed, with the imaginary moth crawling over him. It never left him while he was awake and it grew to a monster in his dreams. While he was awake he longed for sleep, and from sleep he awoke screaming.

So now Hapley is spending the remainder of his days in a padded room, worried by a moth that no one else can see. The asylum doctor calls it hallucination; but Hapley, when he is in his easier mood and can talk, says it is the ghost of Pawkins, and consequently a unique specimen and well worth the trouble of catching.

A CATASTROPHE

The little shop was not paying. The realization came insensibly. Winslow was not the man for definite addition and subtraction and sudden discovery. He became aware of the truth in his mind gradually, as though it had always been there. A lot of facts had converged and led him there. There was that line of cretonnes – four half-pieces – untouched, save for half a yard sold to cover a stool. There were those shirtings at 4¾d.[1] – Bandersnatch,[2] in the Broadway, was selling them at 2¾d. – under cost, in fact. (Surely Bandersnatch might let a man live!) Those servants' caps, a selling line, needed replenishing, and that brought back the memory of Winslow's sole wholesale dealers, Helter, Skelter, & Grab. Why! how about their account?

Winslow stood with a big green box open on the counter before him when he thought of it. His pale grey eyes grew a little rounder; his pale, straggling moustache twitched. He had been drifting along, day after day. He went round to the ramshackle cash-desk in the corner – it was Winslow's weakness to sell his goods over the counter, give his customers a duplicate bill, and then dodge into the desk to receive the money, as though he doubted his own honesty. His lank forefinger, with the prominent joints, ran down the bright little calendar ('Clack's Cottons last for All Time'). 'One – two – three; three weeks an' a day!' said Winslow, staring. 'March! Only three weeks and a day. It *can't* be.'

'Tea, dear,' said Mrs Winslow, opening the door with the glass window and the white blind that communicated with the parlour.

'One minute,' said Winslow, and began unlocking the desk.

An irritable old gentleman, very hot and red about the face, and in a heavy fur-lined coat, came in noisily. Mrs Winslow vanished.

'Ugh!' said the old gentleman. 'Pocket-handkerchief.'

'Yes, sir,' said Winslow. 'About what price' –

'Ugh!' said the old gentleman. 'Poggit-handkerchief, quig!'

Winslow began to feel flustered. He produced two boxes.

'These sir' – began Winslow.

'Sheed tin!' said the old gentleman, clutching the stiffness of the linen. 'Wad to blow my nose – not haggit about.'

'A cotton one, p'raps, sir?' said Winslow.

'How much?' said the old gentleman over the handkerchief.

'Sevenpence, sir. There's nothing more I can show you? No ties, braces –?'

'Damn!' said the old gentleman, fumbling in his ticket-pocket, and finally producing half a crown. Winslow looked round for his metallic duplicate-book which he kept in various fixtures, according to circumstances, and then he caught the old gentleman's eye. He went straight to the desk at once and got the change, with an entire disregard of the routine of the shop.

Winslow was always more or less excited by a customer. But the open desk reminded him of his trouble. It did not come back to him all at once. He heard a fingernail softly tapping on the glass, and, looking up, saw Minnie's eyes over the blind. It seemed like retreat opening. He shut and locked the desk, and went into the back room to tea.

But he was preoccupied. Three weeks and a day! He took unusually large bites of his bread and butter, and stared hard at the little pot of jam. He answered Minnie's conversational advances distractedly. The shadow of Helter, Skelter, & Grab lay upon the tea-table. He was struggling with this new idea of failure, the tangible realization that was taking shape and substance, condensing, as it were, out of the misty uneasiness of many days. At present it was simply one concrete fact; there were thirty-nine pounds left in the bank, and that day three weeks Messrs Helter, Skelter, & Grab, those enterprising outfitters of young men, would demand their eighty pounds.

After tea there was a customer or so – small purchases: some muslin and buckram, dress-protectors, tape, and a pair of Lisle hose. Then, knowing that Black Care[3] was lurking in the dusky corners of the shop, he lit the three lamps early and set to, refolding his cotton prints, the most vigorous and least meditative proceeding of which he could think. He could see Minnie's shadow in the other room as she moved about the table. She was busy turning an old dress. He had a walk after supper, looked in at the Y.M.C.A.,[4] but found no one to talk to, and finally went to bed. Minnie was already there. And there, too, waiting for him, nudging him gently, until about midnight he was hopelessly awake, sat Black Care.

He had had one or two nights lately in that company, but this was much worse. First came Messrs Helter, Skelter, & Grab, and their demand for eighty pounds – an enormous sum when your original capital was only a hundred and seventy. They camped, as it were, before him, sat down and beleaguered him. He clutched feebly at the circumambient darkness for expedients. Suppose he had a sale, sold things for almost anything? He tried to imagine a sale miraculously successful in some unexpected manner, and mildly profitable, in spite of reductions below cost. Then Bandersnatch Limited, 101, 102, 103, 105, 106, 107 Broadway, joined the siege, a long caterpillar of frontage, a battery of shop fronts, wherein things were sold at a farthing above cost. How could he fight such an establishment? Besides, what had he to sell? He began to review his resources. What taking line was there to bait the sale? Then straightway came those pieces of cretonne, yellow and black, with a bluish-green flower; those discredited skirtings, prints without buoyancy, skirmishing haberdashery, some despairful four-button gloves by an inferior maker – a hopeless crew. And that was his force against Bandersnatch, Helter, Skelter, & Grab, and the pitiless world behind them. Whatever had made him think a mortal would buy such things? Why had he bought this and neglected that? He suddenly realized the intensity of his hatred for Helter, Skelter, & Grab's salesman. Then he drove towards an agony of self-reproach. He had spent too much on that cash-desk. What real need was there of a desk?

He saw his vanity of that desk in a lurid glow of self-discovery.
And the lamps? Five pounds! Then suddenly, with what was
almost physical pain, he remembered the rent.

He groaned and turned over. And there, dim in the darkness,
was the hummock of Mrs Winslow's shoulder. That set him off
in another direction. He became acutely sensible of Minnie's
want of feeling. Here he was, worried to death about business,
and she sleeping like a little child. He regretted having married,
with that infinite bitterness that only comes to the human heart
in the small hours of the morning. That hummock of white
seemed absolutely without helpfulness, a burden, a responsibility. What fools men were to marry! Minnie's inert repose
irritated him so much that he was almost provoked to wake her
up and tell her that they were 'Ruined'. She would have to go
back to her uncle; her uncle had always been against him: and
as for his own future, Winslow was exceedingly uncertain. A
shop assistant who has once set up for himself finds the utmost
difficulty in getting into a situation again. He began to figure
himself 'crib-hunting' once more, going from this wholesale
house to that, writing innumerable letters. How he hated
writing letters! 'Sir, – Referring to your advertisement in the
Christian World.'[5] He beheld an infinite vista of discomfort and
disappointment, ending – in a gulf.

He dressed, yawning, and went down to open the shop. He
felt tired before the day began. As he carried the shutters in, he
kept asking himself what good he was doing. The end was
inevitable, whether he bothered or not. The clear daylight smote
into the place, and showed how old and rough and splintered
was the floor, how shabby the secondhand counter, how hopeless the whole enterprise. He had been dreaming these past six
months of a bright shop, of a happy couple, of a modest but
comely profit flowing in. He had suddenly awakened from his
dream. The braid that bound his decent black coat – it was a
trifle loose – caught against the catch of the shop door, and was
torn away. This suddenly turned his wretchedness to wrath. He
stood quivering for a moment, then, with a spiteful clutch, tore
the braid looser, and went in to Minnie.

'Here,' he said, with infinite reproach; 'look here! You might look after a chap a bit.'

'I didn't see it was torn,' said Minnie.

'You never do,' said Winslow, with gross injustice, 'until things are too late.'

Minnie looked suddenly at his face. 'I'll sew it now, Sid, if you like.'

'Let's have breakfast first,' said Winslow, 'and do things at their proper time.'

He was preoccupied at breakfast, and Minnie watched him anxiously. His only remark was to declare his egg a bad one. It wasn't; it was flavoury, – being one of those at fifteen a shilling, – but quite nice. He pushed it away from him, and then, having eaten a slice of bread and butter, admitted himself in the wrong by resuming the egg.

'Sid,' said Minnie, as he stood up to go into the shop again, 'you're not well.'

'I'm *well* enough.' He looked at her as though he hated her.

'Then there's something else the matter. You aren't angry with me, Sid, are you, about that braid? *Do* tell me what's the matter. You were just like this at tea yesterday, and at supper-time. It wasn't the braid then.'

'And I'm likely to be.'

She looked interrogation. 'Oh, what *is* the matter?' she said.

It was too good a chance to miss, and he brought the evil news out with dramatic force. 'Matter?' he said. 'I done my best, and here we are. That's the matter! If I can't pay Helter, Skelter, & Grab eighty pounds, this day three weeks' – Pause. 'We shall be sold up! Sold up! That's the matter, Min! SOLD UP!'

'Oh, Sid!' began Minnie.

He slammed the door. For the moment he felt relieved of at least half his misery. He began dusting boxes that did not require dusting, and then reblocked a cretonne already fault-lessly blocked. He was in a state of grim wretchedness; a martyr under the harrow of fate. At any rate, it should not be said he failed for want of industry. And how he had planned and contrived and worked! All to this end! He felt horrible doubts.

Providence and Bandersnatch – surely they were incompatible!
Perhaps he was being 'tried'? That sent him off upon a new tack,
a very comforting one. The martyr pose, the gold-in-the-furnace
attitude, lasted all the morning.

At dinner – 'potato pie' – he looked up suddenly, and saw
Minnie's face regarding him. Pale she looked, and a little red
about the eyes. Something caught him suddenly with a queer
effect upon his throat. All his thoughts seemed to wheel round
into quite a new direction.

He pushed back his plate and stared at her blankly. Then he
got up, went round the table to her – she staring at him. He
dropped on his knees beside her without a word. 'Oh, Minnie!'
he said, and suddenly she knew it was peace, and put her arms
about him, as he began to sob and weep.

He cried like a little boy, slobbering on her shoulder that he
was a knave to have married her and brought her to this, that
he hadn't the wits to be trusted with a penny, that it was all his
fault, that he 'had hoped so' – ending in a howl. And she, crying
gently herself, patting his shoulders, said 'Ssh!' softly to his
noisy weeping, and so soothed the outbreak. Then suddenly
the crazy bell upon the shop door began, and Winslow had to
jump to his feet, and be a man again.

After that scene they 'talked it over' at tea, at supper, in
bed, at every possible interval in between, solemnly – quite
inconclusively – with set faces and eyes for the most part staring
in front of them – and yet with a certain mutual comfort. 'What
to do I don't know,' was Winslow's main proposition. Minnie
tried to take a cheerful view of service – with a probable baby.
But she found she needed all her courage. And her uncle would
help her again, perhaps, just at the critical time. It didn't do for
folks to be too proud. Besides, 'something might happen', a
favourite formula with her.

One hopeful line was to anticipate a sudden afflux of customers. 'Perhaps,' said Minnie, 'you might get together fifty.
They know you well enough to trust you a bit.' They debated
that point. Once the possibility of Helter, Skelter, & Grab
giving credit was admitted, it was pleasant to begin sweating
the acceptable minimum. For some half-hour over tea the

second day after Winslow's discoveries they were quite cheerful
again, laughing even at their terrific fears. Even twenty pounds
to go on with might be considered enough. Then in some
mysterious way the pleasant prospect of Messrs Helter, Skelter,
& Grab tempering the wind to the shorn retailer[6] vanished –
vanished absolutely, and Winslow found himself again in the
pit of despair.

He began looking about at the furniture, and wondering idly
what it would fetch. The chiffonier was good, anyhow, and
there were Minnie's old plates that her mother used to have.
Then he began to think of desperate expedients for putting off
the evil day. He had heard somewhere of Bills of Sale – there
was to his ears something comfortingly substantial in the
phrase. Then, why not 'Go to the Money-Lenders'?

One cheering thing happened on Thursday afternoon; a little
girl came in with a pattern of 'print', and he was able to match
it. He had not been able to match anything out of his meagre
stock before. He went in and told Minnie. The incident is
mentioned lest the reader should imagine it was uniform despair
with him.

The next morning, and the next, after the discovery, Winslow
opened shop late. When one has been awake most of the night,
and has no hope, what *is* the good of getting up punctually?
But as he went into the dark shop on Friday he saw something
lying on the floor, something lit by the bright light that came
under the ill-fitting door – a black oblong. He stooped and
picked up an envelope with a deep mourning edge. It was
addressed to his wife. Clearly a death in her family – perhaps
her uncle. He knew the man too well to have expectations. And
they would have to get mourning and go to the funeral. The
brutal cruelty of people dying! He saw it all in a flash – he
always visualized his thoughts. Black trousers to get, black
crape, black gloves – none in stock – the railway fares, the shop
closed for the day.

'I'm afraid there's bad news, Minnie,' he said.

She was kneeling before the fireplace, blowing the fire. She
had her housemaid's gloves on and the old country sun-bonnet
she wore of a morning, to keep the dust out of her hair. She

turned, saw the envelope, gave a gasp, and pressed two bloodless lips together.

'I'm afraid it's uncle,' she said, holding the letter and staring
with eyes wide open into Winslow's face. '*It's a strange hand!*'

'The postmark's Hull,' said Winslow.

'The postmark's Hull.'

Minnie opened the letter slowly, drew it out, hesitated, turned
it over, saw the signature. 'It's Mr Speight!'

'What does he say?' said Winslow.

Minnie began to read. '*Oh!*' she screamed. She dropped the
letter, collapsed into a crouching heap, her hands covering her
eyes. Winslow snatched at it. 'A most terrible accident has
occurred,' he read; 'Melchior's chimney fell down yesterday
evening right on the top of your uncle's house, and every living
soul was killed – your uncle, your cousin Mary, Will and Ned,
and the girl – every one of them, and smashed – you would
hardly know them. I'm writing to you to break the news before
you see it in the papers' – The letter fluttered from Winslow's
fingers. He put out his hand against the mantel to steady
himself.

All of them dead! Then he saw, as in a vision, a row of seven
cottages, each let at seven shillings a week, a timber yard,
two villas, and the ruins – still marketable – of the avuncular
residence. He tried to feel a sense of loss and could not. They
were sure to have been left to Minnie's aunt. All dead! $7 \times 7 \times
52 \div 20$ began insensibly to work itself out in his mind, but
discipline was ever weak in his mental arithmetic; figures kept
moving from one line to another, like children playing at
Widdy, Widdy Way. Was it two hundred pounds about – or
one hundred pounds? Presently he picked up the letter again,
and finishing reading it. 'You being the next of kin,' said
Mr Speight.

'How *awful*!' said Minnie in a horror-struck whisper, and
looking up at last. Winslow stared back at her, shaking his
head solemnly. There were a thousand things running through
his mind, but none that, even to his dull sense, seemed appropriate as a remark. 'It was the Lord's will,' he said at last.

'It seems so very, very terrible,' said Minnie; 'auntie, dear auntie – Ted – poor, dear uncle' –

'It was the Lord's will, Minnie,' said Winslow, with infinite feeling. A long silence.

'Yes,' said Minnie, very slowly, staring thoughtfully at the crackling black paper in the grate. The fire had gone out. 'Yes, perhaps it was the Lord's will.'

They looked gravely at one another. Each would have been terribly shocked at any mention of the property by the other. She turned to the dark fireplace and began tearing up an old newspaper slowly. Whatever our losses may be, the world's work still waits for us. Winslow gave a deep sigh and walked in a hushed manner towards the front door. As he opened it, a flood of sunlight came streaming into the dark shadows of the closed shop. Bandersnatch, Helter, Skelter, & Grab, had vanished out of his mind like the mists before the rising sun.

Presently he was carrying in the shutters, and in the briskest way, the fire in the kitchen was crackling exhilaratingly, with a little saucepan walloping above it, for Minnie was boiling two eggs, – one for herself this morning, as well as one for him, – and Minnie herself was audible, laying breakfast with the greatest *éclat*. The blow was a sudden and terrible one – but it behoves us to face such things bravely in this sad, unaccountable world. It was quite midday before either of them mentioned the cottages.

THE CONE

The night was hot and overcast, the sky red-rimmed with the lingering sunset of midsummer. They sat at the open window, trying to fancy the air was fresher there. The trees and shrubs of the garden stood stiff and dark; beyond in the roadway a gas lamp burnt, bright orange against the hazy blue of the evening. Farther were the three lights of the railway signal against the lowering sky. The man and woman spoke to one another in low tones.

'He does not suspect?' said the man, a little nervously.

'Not he,' she said peevishly, as though that too irritated her. 'He thinks of nothing but the works and the prices of fuel. He has no imagination, no poetry.'

'None of these men of iron have,' he said sententiously. 'They have no hearts.'

'*He* has not,' she said. She turned her discontented face towards the window. The distant sound of a roaring and rushing drew nearer and grew in volume; the house quivered; one heard the metallic rattle of the tender. As the train passed, there was a glare of light above the cutting and a driving tumult of smoke; one, two, three, four, five, six, seven, eight black oblongs – eight trucks – passed across the dim grey of the embankment, and were suddenly extinguished one by one in the throat of the tunnel, which, with the last, seemed to swallow down train, smoke, and sound in one abrupt gulp.

'This country was all fresh and beautiful once,' he said; 'and now – it is Gehenna.[1] Down that way – nothing but pot-banks and chimneys belching fire and dust into the face of heaven. ... But what does it matter? An end comes, an end to all this cruelty. . . . *Tomorrow.*' He spoke the last word in a whisper.

'*Tomorrow,*' she said, speaking in a whisper too, and still staring out of the window.

'Dear!' he said, putting his hand on hers.

She turned with a start, and their eyes searched one another's. Hers softened to his gaze. 'My dear one!' she said, and then: 'It seems so strange – that you should have come into my life like this – to open' – She paused.

'To open?' he said.

'All this wonderful world' – she hesitated, and spoke still more softly – 'this world of *love* to me.'

Then suddenly the door clicked and closed. They turned their heads, and he started violently back. In the shadow of the room stood a great shadowy figure – silent. They saw the face dimly in the half-light, with unexpressive dark patches under the penthouse brows.[2] Every muscle in Raut's body suddenly became tense. When could the door have opened? What had he heard? Had he heard all? What had he seen? A tumult of questions.

The newcomer's voice came at last, after a pause that seemed interminable. 'Well?' he said.

'I was afraid I had missed you, Horrocks,' said the man at the window, gripping the window-ledge with his hand. His voice was unsteady.

The clumsy figure of Horrocks came forward out of the shadow. He made no answer to Raut's remark. For a moment he stood above them.

The woman's heart was cold within her. 'I told Mr Raut it was just possible you might come back,' she said, in a voice that never quivered.

Horrocks, still silent, sat down abruptly in the chair by her little work-table. His big hands were clenched; one saw now the fire of his eyes under the shadow of his brows. He was trying to get his breath. His eyes went from the woman he had trusted to the friend he had trusted, and then back to the woman.

By this time and for the moment all three half understood one another. Yet none dared say a word to ease the pent-up things that choked them.

It was the husband's voice that broke the silence at last.

'You wanted to see me?' he said to Raut.

Raut started as he spoke. 'I came to see you,' he said, resolved to lie to the last.

'Yes,' said Horrocks.

'You promised,' said Raut, 'to show me some fine effects of moonlight and smoke.'

'I promised to show you some fine effects of moonlight and smoke,' repeated Horrocks in a colourless voice.

'And I thought I might catch you tonight before you went down to the works,' proceeded Raut, 'and come with you.'

There was another pause. Did the man mean to take the thing coolly? Did he after all know? How long had he been in the room? Yet even at the moment when they heard the door, their attitudes ... Horrocks glanced at the profile of the woman, shadowy pallid in the half-light. Then he glanced at Raut, and seemed to recover himself suddenly. 'Of course,' he said, 'I promised to show you the works under their proper dramatic conditions. It's odd how I could have forgotten.'

'If I am troubling you' – began Raut.

Horrocks started again. A new light had suddenly come into the sultry gloom of his eyes. 'Not in the least,' he said.

'Have you been telling Mr Raut of all these contrasts of flame and shadow you think so splendid?' said the woman, turning now to her husband for the first time, her confidence creeping back again, her voice just one half-note too high. 'That dreadful theory of yours that machinery is beautiful, and everything else in the world ugly. I thought he would not spare you, Mr Raut. It's his great theory, his one discovery in art.'

'I am slow to make discoveries,' said Horrocks grimly, damping her suddenly. 'But what I discover . . .' He stopped.

'Well?' she said.

'Nothing;' and suddenly he rose to his feet.

'I promised to show you the works,' he said to Raut, and put his big, clumsy hand on his friend's shoulder. 'And you are ready to go?'

'Quite,' said Raut, and stood up also.

There was another pause. Each of them peered through the

indistinctness of the dusk at the other two. Horrocks's hand still rested on Raut's shoulder. Raut half fancied still that the incident was trivial after all. But Mrs Horrocks knew her husband better, knew that grim quiet in his voice, and the confusion in her mind took a vague shape of physical evil. 'Very well,' said Horrocks, and, dropping his hand, turned towards the door.

'My hat?' Raut looked round in the half-light.

'That's my work-basket,' said Mrs Horrocks with a gust of hysterical laughter. Their hands came together on the back of the chair. 'Here it is!' he said. She had an impulse to warn him in an undertone, but she could not frame a word. 'Don't go!' and 'Beware of him!' struggled in her mind, and the swift moment passed.

'Got it?' said Horrocks, standing with the door half open.

Raut stepped towards him. 'Better say goodbye to Mrs Horrocks,' said the ironmaster, even more grimly quiet in his tone than before.

Raut started and turned. 'Good evening, Mrs Horrocks,' he said, and their hands touched.

Horrocks held the door open with a ceremonial politeness unusual in him towards men. Raut went out, and then, after a wordless look at her, her husband followed. She stood motionless while Raut's light footfall and her husband's heavy tread, like bass and treble, passed down the passage together. The front door slammed heavily. She went to the window, moving slowly, and stood watching – leaning forward. The two men appeared for a moment at the gateway in the road, passed under the street lamp, and were hidden by the black masses of the shrubbery. The lamplight fell for a moment on their faces, showing only unmeaning pale patches, telling nothing of what she still feared, and doubted, and craved vainly to know. Then she sank down into a crouching attitude in the big arm-chair, her eyes wide open and staring out at the red lights from the furnaces that flickered in the sky. An hour after she was still there, her attitude scarcely changed.

The oppressive stillness of the evening weighed heavily upon Raut. They went side by side down the road in silence, and in

silence turned into the cinder-made byway that presently
opened out the prospect of the valley.

A blue haze, half dust, half mist, touched the long valley with
mystery. Beyond were Hanley and Etruria,[3] grey and black
masses, outlined thinly by the rare golden dots of the street
lamps, and here and there a gaslit window, or the yellow glare
of some late-working factory or crowded public-house. Out of
the masses, clear and slender against the evening sky, rose a
multitude of tall chimneys, many of them reeking, a few smoke-
less during a season of 'play'.[4] Here and there a pallid patch
and ghostly stunted beehive shapes showed the position of a
pot-bank, or a wheel, black and sharp against the hot lower
sky, marked some colliery where they raise the iridescent coal
of the place. Nearer at hand was the broad stretch of railway,
and half invisible trains shunted – a steady puffing and rumbling, with every now and then a ringing concussion and a
series of impacts, and a passage of intermittent puffs of white
steam across the further view. And to the left, between the
railway and the dark mass of the low hill beyond, dominating
the whole view, colossal, inky-black, and crowned with smoke
and fitful flames, stood the great cylinders of the Jeddah[5] Company Blast Furnaces, the central edifices of the big ironworks
of which Horrocks was the manager. They stood heavy and
threatening, full of an incessant turmoil of flames and seething
molten iron, and about the feet of them rattled the rolling-mills,
and the steam-hammer beat heavily and splashed the white iron
sparks hither and thither. Even as they looked, a truckful of
fuel was shot into one of the giants, and the red flames gleamed
out, and a confusion of smoke and black dust came boiling
upwards towards the sky.

'Certainly you get some fine effects of colour with your
furnaces,' said Raut, breaking a silence that had become
apprehensive.

Horrocks grunted. He stood with his hands in his pockets,
frowning down at the dim steaming railway and the busy ironworks beyond, frowning as if he were thinking out some knotty
problem.

Raut glanced at him and away again. 'At present your moonlight effect is hardly ripe,' he continued, looking upward; 'the moon is still smothered by the vestiges of daylight.'

Horrocks stared at him with the expression of a man who has suddenly awakened. 'Vestiges of daylight? ... Of course, of course.' He too looked up at the moon, pale still in the midsummer sky. 'Come along,' he said suddenly, and, gripping Raut's arm in his hand, made a move towards the path that dropped from them to the railway.

Raut hung back. Their eyes met and saw a thousand things in a moment that their lips came near to say. Horrocks's hand tightened and then relaxed. He let go, and before Raut was aware of it, they were arm in arm, and walking, one unwillingly enough, down the path.

'You see the fine effect of the railway signals towards Burslem,' said Horrocks, suddenly breaking into loquacity, striding fast and tightening the grip of his elbow the while. 'Little green lights and red and white lights, all against the haze. You have an eye for effect, Raut. It's a fine effect. And look at those furnaces of mine, how they rise upon us as we come down the hill. That to the right is my pet – seventy feet of him. I packed him myself, and he's boiled away cheerfully with iron in his guts for five long years. I've a particular fancy for *him*. That line of red there – a lovely bit of warm orange you'd call it, Raut – that's the puddlers' furnaces, and there, in the hot light, three black figures – did you see the white splash of the steam-hammer then? – that's the rolling-mills. Come along! Clang, clatter, how it goes rattling across the floor! Sheet tin, Raut, – amazing stuff. Glass mirrors are not in it when that stuff comes from the mill. And, squelch! – there goes the hammer again. Come along!'

He had to stop talking to catch at his breath. His arm twisted into Raut's with benumbing tightness. He had come striding down the black path towards the railway as though he was possessed. Raut had not spoken a word, had simply hung back against Horrocks's pull with all his strength.

'I say,' he said now, laughing nervously, but with an undernote of snarl in his voice, 'why on earth are you nipping my arm off, Horrocks, and dragging me along like this?'

At length Horrocks released him. His manner changed again. 'Nipping your arm off?' he said. 'Sorry. But it's you taught me the trick of walking in that friendly way.'

'You haven't learnt the refinements of it yet then,' said Raut, laughing artificially again. 'By Jove! I'm black and blue.' Horrocks offered no apology. They stood now near the bottom of the hill, close to the fence that bordered the railway. The ironworks had grown larger and spread out with their approach. They looked up to the blast furnaces now instead of down; the further view of Etruria and Hanley had dropped out of sight with their descent. Before them, by the stile, rose a noticeboard, bearing, still dimly visible, the words, 'BEWARE OF THE TRAINS', half hidden by splashes of coaly mud.

'Fine effects,' said Horrocks, waving his arm. 'Here comes a train. The puffs of smoke, the orange glare, the round eye of light in front of it, the melodious rattle. Fine effects! But these furnaces of mine used to be finer, before we shoved cones in their throats, and saved the gas.'

'How?' said Raut. 'Cones?'

'Cones, my man, cones. I'll show you one nearer. The flames used to flare out of the open throats, great – what is it? – pillars of cloud by day,[6] red and black smoke, and pillars of fire by night. Now we run it off in pipes, and burn it to heat the blast, and the top is shut by a cone. You'll be interested in that cone.'

'But every now and then,' said Raut, 'you get a burst of fire and smoke up there.'

'The cone's not fixed, it's hung by a chain from a lever, and balanced by an equipoise. You shall see it nearer. Else, of course, there'd be no way of getting fuel into the thing. Every now and then the cone dips, and out comes the flare.'

'I see,' said Raut. He looked over his shoulder. 'The moon gets brighter,' he said.

'Come along,' said Horrocks abruptly, gripping his shoulder again, and moving him suddenly towards the railway crossing. And then came one of those swift incidents, vivid, but so rapid that they leave one doubtful and reeling. Halfway across, Horrocks's hand suddenly clenched upon him like a vice, and swung him backward and through a half-turn, so that he looked up the line. And there a chain of lamp-lit carriage windows telescoped swiftly as it came towards them, and the red and yellow lights of an engine grew larger and larger, rushing down upon them. As he grasped what this meant, he turned his face to Horrocks, and pushed with all his strength against the arm that held him back between the rails. The struggle did not last a moment. Just as certain as it was that Horrocks held him there, so certain was it that he had been violently lugged out of danger.

'Out of the way,' said Horrocks, with a gasp, as the train came rattling by, and they stood panting by the gate into the ironworks.

'I did not see it coming,' said Raut, still, even in spite of his own apprehensions, trying to keep up an appearance of ordinary intercourse.

Horrocks answered with a grunt. 'The cone,' he said, and then, as one who recovers himself, 'I thought you did not hear.'

'I didn't,' said Raut.

'I wouldn't have had you run over then for the world,' said Horrocks.

'For a moment I lost my nerve,' said Raut.

Horrocks stood for half a minute, then turned abruptly towards the ironworks again. 'See how fine these great mounds of mine, these clinker-heaps, look in the night! That truck yonder, up above there! Up it goes, and out-tilts the slag. See the palpitating red stuff go sliding down the slope. As we get nearer, the heap rises up and cuts the blast furnaces. See the quiver up above the big one. Not that way! This way, between the heaps. That goes to the puddling furnaces, but I want to show you the canal first.' He came and took Raut by the elbow, and so they went along side by side. Raut answered Horrocks vaguely. What, he asked himself, had really happened on the line? Was he deluding himself with his own fancies, or had Horrocks actually held him back in the way of the train? Had he just been within an ace of being murdered?

Suppose this slouching, scowling monster *did* know any-thing? For a minute or two then Raut was really afraid for his life, but the mood passed as he reasoned with himself. After all,

Horrocks might have heard nothing. At any rate, he had pulled him out of the way in time. His odd manner might be due to the mere vague jealousy he had shown once before. He was talking now of the ash-heaps and the canal. 'Eh?' said Horrocks.

'What?' said Raut. 'Rather! The haze in the moonlight. Fine!'

'Our canal,' said Horrocks, stopping suddenly. 'Our canal by moonlight and firelight is an immense effect. You've never seen it? Fancy that! You've spent too many of your evenings philandering up in Newcastle[7] there. I tell you, for real florid effects – But you shall see. Boiling water . . .'

As they came out of the labyrinth of clinker-heaps and mounds of coal and ore, the noises of the rolling-mill sprang upon them suddenly, loud, near, and distinct. Three shadowy workmen went by and touched their caps to Horrocks. Their faces were vague in the darkness. Raut felt a futile impulse to address them, and before he could frame his words, they passed into the shadows. Horrocks pointed to the canal close before them now: a weird-looking place it seemed, in the blood-red reflections of the furnaces. The hot water that cooled the tuyères came into it, some fifty yards up – a tumultuous, almost boiling affluent, and the steam rose up from the water in silent white wisps and streaks, wrapping damply about them, an incessant succession of ghosts coming up from the black and red eddies, a white uprising that made the head swim. The shining black tower of the larger blast furnace rose overhead out of the mist, and its tumultuous riot filled their ears. Raut kept away from the edge of the water, and watched Horrocks.

'Here it is red,' said Horrocks, 'blood-red vapour as red and hot as sin; but yonder there, where the moonlight falls on it, and it drives across the clinker-heaps, it is as white as death.'

Raut turned his head for a moment, and then came back hastily to his watch on Horrocks. 'Come along to the rolling-mills,' said Horrocks. The threatening hold was not so evident that time, and Raut felt a little reassured. But all the same, what on earth did Horrocks mean about 'white as death' and 'red as sin'? Coincidence, perhaps?

They went and stood behind the puddlers for a little while, and then through the rolling-mills, where amidst an incessant

din the deliberate steam-hammer beat the juice out of the succulent iron, and black, half-naked Titans rushed the plastic bars,
like hot sealing-wax, between the wheels. 'Come on,' said
Horrocks in Raut's ear, and they went and peeped through the
little glass hole behind the tuyères, and saw the tumbled fire
writhing in the pit of the blast furnace. It left one eye blinded
for a while. Then, with green and blue patches dancing across
the dark, they went to the lift by which the trucks of ore and
fuel and lime were raised to the top of the big cylinder.

And out upon the narrow rail that overhung the furnace,
Raut's doubts came upon him again. Was it wise to be here? If
Horrocks did know – everything! Do what he would, he could
not resist a violent trembling. Right under foot was a sheer
depth of seventy feet. It was a dangerous place. They pushed
by a truck of fuel to get to the railing that crowned the place.
The reek of the furnace, a sulphurous vapour streaked with
pungent bitterness, seemed to make the distant hillside of
Hanley quiver. The moon was riding out now from among a
drift of clouds, halfway up the sky above the undulating
wooded outlines of Newcastle. The steaming canal ran away
from below them under an indistinct bridge, and vanished into
the dim haze of the flat fields towards Burslem.

'That's the cone I've been telling you of,' shouted Horrocks;
'and, below that, sixty feet of fire and molten metal, with the
air of the blast frothing through it like gas in soda-water.'

Raut gripped the hand-rail tightly, and stared down at the
cone. The heat was intense. The boiling of the iron and the
tumult of the blast made a thunderous accompaniment to
Horrocks's voice. But the thing had to be gone through now.
Perhaps, after all . . .

'In the middle,' bawled Horrocks, 'temperature near a
thousand degrees. If *you* were dropped into it . . . flash into
flame like a pinch of gunpowder in a candle. Put your hand out
and feel the heat of his breath. Why, even up here I've seen the
rainwater boiling off the trucks. And that cone there. It's a
damned sight too hot for roasting cakes. The top side of it's
three hundred degrees.'

'Three hundred degrees!' said Raut.

'Three hundred centigrade, mind!' said Horrocks. 'It will boil the blood out of you in no time.'

'Eh?' said Raut, and turned.

'Boil the blood out of you in . . . No, you don't!'

'Let me go!' screamed Raut. 'Let go my arm!' With one hand he clutched at the hand-rail, then with both. For a moment the two men stood swaying. Then suddenly, with a violent jerk, Horrocks had twisted him from his hold. He clutched at Horrocks and missed, his foot went back into empty air; in mid-air he twisted himself, and then cheek and shoulder and knee struck the hot cone together.

He clutched the chain by which the cone hung, and the thing sank an infinitesimal amount as he struck it. A circle of glowing red appeared about him, and a tongue of flame, released from the chaos within, flickered up towards him. An intense pain assailed him at the knees, and he could smell the singeing of his hands. He raised himself to his feet, and tried to climb up the chain, and then something struck his head. Black and shining with the moonlight, the throat of the furnace rose about him.

Horrocks, he saw, stood above him by one of the trucks of fuel on the rail. The gesticulating figure was bright and white in the moonlight, and shouting, 'Fizzle, you fool! Fizzle, you hunter of women! You hot-blooded hound! Boil! boil! boil!'

Suddenly he caught up a handful of coal out of the truck, and flung it deliberately, lump after lump, at Raut.

'Horrocks!' cried Raut. 'Horrocks!'

He clung crying to the chain, pulling himself up from the burning of the cone. Each missile Horrocks flung hit him. His clothes charred and glowed, and as he struggled the cone dropped, and a rush of hot suffocating gas whooped out and burned round him in a swift breath of flame.

His human likeness departed from him. When the momentary red had passed, Horrocks saw a charred, blackened figure, its head streaked with blood, still clutching and fumbling with the chain, and writhing in agony – a cindery animal, an inhuman, monstrous creature that began a sobbing intermittent shriek.

Abruptly, at the sight, the ironmaster's anger passed. A

deadly sickness came upon him. The heavy odour of burning flesh came drifting up to his nostrils. His sanity returned to him.

'God have mercy upon me!' he cried. 'O God! what have I done?'

He knew the thing below him, save that it still moved and felt, was already a dead man – that the blood of the poor wretch must be boiling in his veins. An intense realization of that agony came to his mind, and overcame every other feeling. For a moment he stood irresolute, and then, turning to the truck, he hastily tilted its contents upon the struggling thing that had once been a man. The mass fell with a thud, and went radiating over the cone. With the thud the shriek ended, and a boiling confusion of smoke, dust, and flame came rushing up towards him. As it passed, he saw the cone clear again.

Then he staggered back, and stood trembling, clinging to the rail with both hands. His lips moved, but no words came to them.

Down below was the sound of voices and running steps. The clangour of rolling in the shed ceased abruptly.

THE ARGONAUTS OF
THE AIR

One saw Monson's flying machine from the windows of the
trains passing either along the South-Western main line[1] or
along the line between Wimbledon and Worcester Park, – to
be more exact, one saw the huge scaffoldings which limited the
flight of the apparatus. They rose over the tree-tops, a massive
alley of interlacing iron and timber, and an enormous web of
ropes and tackle, extending the best part of two miles. From
the Leatherhead branch this alley was foreshortened and in part
hidden by a hill with villas; but from the main line one had it
in profile, a complex tangle of girders and curving bars, very
impressive to the excursionists from Portsmouth and Southampton and the West. Monson had taken up the work where
Maxim[2] had left it, had gone on at first with an utter contempt
for the journalistic wit and ignorance that had irritated and
hampered his predecessor, and had spent (it was said) rather
more than half his immense fortune upon his experiments.
The results, to an impatient generation, seemed inconsiderable. When some five years had passed after the growth of the
colossal iron groves at Worcester Park, and Monson still failed
to put in a fluttering appearance over Trafalgar Square,[3] even
the Isle of Wight trippers[4] felt their liberty to smile. And such
intelligent people as did not consider Monson a fool stricken
with the mania for invention, denounced him as being (for no
particular reason) a self-advertising quack.

Yet now and again a morning trainload of season-ticket
holders would see a white monster rush headlong through the
airy tracery of guides and bars, and hear the further stays,
nettings, and buffers snap, creak, and groan with the impact of

the blow. Then there would be an efflorescence of black-set white-rimmed faces along the sides of the train, and the morning papers would be neglected for a vigorous discussion of the possibility of flying (in which nothing new was ever said by any chance), until the train reached Waterloo, and its cargo of season-ticket holders dispersed themselves over London. Or the fathers and mothers in some multitudinous train of weary excursionists returning exhausted from a day of rest by the sea, would find the dark fabric, standing out against the evening sky, useful in diverting some bilious child from its introspection, and be suddenly startled by the swift transit of a huge black flapping shape that strained upward against the guides. It was a great and forcible thing beyond dispute, and excellent for conversation; yet, all the same, it was but flying in leading-strings, and most of those who witnessed it scarcely counted its flight as flying. More of a switchback it seemed to the run of the folk.

Monson, I say, did not trouble himself very keenly about the opinions of the press at first. But possibly he, even, had formed but a poor idea of the time it would take before the tactics of flying were mastered, the swift assured adjustment of the big soaring shape to every gust and chance movement of the air; nor had he clearly reckoned the money this prolonged struggle against gravitation would cost him. And he was not so pachydermatous as he seemed. Secretly he had his periodical bundles of cuttings sent him by Romeike,[5] he had his periodical reminders from his banker; and if he did not mind the initial ridicule and scepticism, he felt the growing neglect as the months went by and the money dribbled away. Time was when Monson had sent the enterprising journalist, keen after readable matter, empty from his gates. But when the enterprising journalist ceased from troubling,[6] Monson was anything but satisfied in his heart of hearts. Still day by day the work went on, and the multitudinous subtle difficulties of the steering diminished in number. Day by day, too, the money trickled away, until his balance was no longer a matter of hundreds of thousands, but of tens. And at last came an anniversary.

Monson, sitting in the little drawing-shed, suddenly noticed the date on Woodhouse's calendar.

'It was five years ago today that we began,' he said to Wood-house suddenly.

'Is it?' said Woodhouse.

'It's the alterations play the devil with us,' said Monson, biting a paper-fastener.

The drawings for the new vans to the hinder screw lay on the table before him as he spoke. He pitched the mutilated brass paper-fastener into the waste-paper basket and drummed with his fingers. 'These alterations! Will the mathematicians ever be clever enough to save us all this patching and experimenting? Five years – learning by rule of thumb, when one might think that it was possible to calculate the whole thing out beforehand. The cost of it! I might have hired three senior wranglers for life. But they'd only have developed some beautifully useless theorems in pneumatics. What a time it has been, Woodhouse!'

'These mouldings will take three weeks,' said Woodhouse. 'At special prices.'

'Three weeks!' said Monson, and sat drumming.

'Three weeks certain,' said Woodhouse, an excellent engineer, but no good as a comforter. He drew the sheets towards him and began shading a bar.

Monson stopped drumming, and began to bite his fingernails, staring the while at Woodhouse's head.

'How long have they been calling this Monson's Folly?'[7] he said suddenly.

'*Oh!* Year or so,' said Woodhouse carelessly, without looking up.

Monson sucked the air in between his teeth, and went to the window. The stout iron columns carrying the elevated rails upon which the start of the machine was made rose up close by, and the machine was hidden by the upper edge of the window. Through the grove of iron pillars, red painted and ornate with rows of bolts, one had a glimpse of the pretty scenery towards Esher.[8] A train went gliding noiselessly across the middle distance, its rattle drowned by the hammering of the workmen overhead. Monson could imagine the grinning faces at the windows of the carriages. He swore savagely under his breath, and dabbed viciously at a blowfly that suddenly became noisy on the window-pane.

'What's up?' said Woodhouse, staring in surprise at his employer.

'I'm about sick of this.'

Woodhouse scratched his cheek. 'Oh!' he said, after an assimilating pause. He pushed the drawing away from him.

'Here these fools . . . I'm trying to conquer a new element – trying to do a thing that will revolutionize life. And instead of taking an intelligent interest, they grin and make their stupid jokes, and call me and my appliances names.'

'Asses!' said Woodhouse, letting his eye fall again on the drawing.

The epithet, curiously enough, made Monson wince. 'I'm about sick of it, Woodhouse, anyhow,' he said, after a pause.

Woodhouse shrugged his shoulders.

'There's nothing for it but patience, I suppose,' said Monson, sticking his hands in his pockets. 'I've started. I've made my bed, and I've got to lie on it. I can't go back. I'll see it through, and spend every penny I have and every penny I can borrow. But I tell you, Woodhouse, I'm infernally sick of it, all the same. If I'd paid a tenth part of the money towards some political greaser's expenses – I'd have been a baronet before this.'

Monson paused. Woodhouse stared in front of him with a blank expression he always employed to indicate sympathy, and tapped his pencil-case on the table. Monson stared at him for a minute.

'Oh, *damn*!' said Monson suddenly, and abruptly rushed out of the room.

Woodhouse continued his sympathetic rigour for perhaps half a minute. Then he sighed and resumed the shading of the drawings. Something had evidently upset Monson. Nice chap, and generous, but difficult to get on with. It was the way with every amateur who had anything to do with engineering – wanted everything finished at once. But Monson had usually the patience of the expert. Odd he was so irritable. Nice and round that aluminium rod[9] did look now! Woodhouse threw

back his head, and put it, first this side and then that, to
appreciate his bit of shading better.

'Mr Woodhouse,' said Hooper, the foreman of the labourers,
putting his head in at the door.

'Hullo!' said Woodhouse, without turning round.

'Nothing happened, sir?' said Hooper.

'Happened?' said Woodhouse.

'The governor just been up the rails swearing like a tornader.'

'*Oh!*' said Woodhouse.

'It ain't like him, sir.'

'No?'

'And I was thinking perhaps' –

'Don't think,' said Woodhouse, still admiring the drawings.

Hooper knew Woodhouse, and he shut the door suddenly
with a vicious slam. Woodhouse stared stonily before him for
some further minutes, and then made an ineffectual effort to
pick his teeth with his pencil. Abruptly he desisted, pitched
that old, tried, and stumpy servitor across the room, got up,
stretched himself, and followed Hooper.

He looked ruffled – it was visible to every workman he
met. When a millionaire who has been spending thousands on
experiments that employ quite a little army of people suddenly
indicates that he is sick of the undertaking, there is almost
invariably a certain amount of mental friction in the ranks of
the little army he employs. And even before he indicates his
intentions there are speculations and murmurs, a watching of
faces and a study of straws. Hundreds of people knew before
the day was out that Monson was ruffled, Woodhouse ruffled,
Hooper ruffled. A workman's wife, for instance (whom Monson
had never seen), decided to keep her money in the savings-bank
instead of buying a velveteen dress. So far-reaching are even
the casual curses of a millionaire.

Monson found a certain satisfaction in going on the works
and behaving disagreeably to as many people as possible. After
a time even that palled upon him, and he rode off the grounds,
to everyone's relief there, and through the lanes south-eastward,
to the infinite tribulation of his house steward at Cheam.

And the immediate cause of it all, the little grain of annoyance that had suddenly precipitated all this discontent with his life-work was – these trivial things that direct all our great decisions! – half a dozen ill-considered remarks made by a pretty girl, prettily dressed, with a beautiful voice and something more than prettiness in her soft grey eyes. And of these half-dozen remarks, two words especially – 'Monson's Folly'. She had felt she was behaving charmingly to Monson; she reflected the next day how exceptionally effective she had been, and no one would have been more amazed than she, had she learned the effect she had left on Monson's mind. I hope, considering everything, that she never knew.

'How are you getting on with your flying machine?' she asked. ('I wonder if I shall ever meet anyone with the sense not to ask that,' thought Monson.) 'It will be very dangerous at first, will it not?' ('Thinks I'm afraid.') 'Jorgon is going to play presently; have you heard him before?' ('My mania being attended to, we turn to rational conversation.') Gush about Jorgon; gradual decline of conversation, ending with – 'You must let me know when your flying machine is finished, Mr Monson, and then I will consider the advisability of taking a ticket.' ('One would think I was still playing inventions in the nursery.') But the bitterest thing she said was not meant for Monson's ears. To Phlox, the novelist, she was always conscientiously brilliant. 'I have been talking to Mr Monson, and he can think of nothing, positively nothing, but that flying machine of his. Do you know, all his workmen call that place of his "Monson's Folly"? He is quite impossible. It is really very, very sad. I always regard him myself in the light of sunken treasure – the Lost Millionaire, you know.'

She was pretty and well educated, – indeed, she had written an epigrammatic novelette; but the bitterness was that she was typical. She summarized what the world thought of the man who was working sanely, steadily, and surely towards a more tremendous revolution in the appliances of civilization, a more far-reaching alteration in the ways of humanity than has ever been effected since history began. They did not even take him seriously. In a little while he would be proverbial. 'I *must* fly now,' he said on his way home, smarting with a sense of absolute social failure. 'I must fly soon. If it doesn't come off soon, by God! I shall run amuck.'

He said that before he had gone through his passbook and his litter of papers. Inadequate as the cause seems, it was that girl's voice and the expression of her eyes that precipitated his discontent. But certainly the discovery that he had no longer even one hundred thousand pounds' worth of realizable property behind him was the poison that made the wound deadly.

It was the next day after this that he exploded upon Woodhouse and his workmen, and thereafter his bearing was consistently grim for three weeks, and anxiety dwelt in Cheam and Ewell, Malden, Morden, and Worcester Park, places that had thriven mightily on his experiments.

Four weeks after that first swearing of his, he stood with Woodhouse by the reconstructed machine as it lay across the elevated railway, by means of which it gained its initial impetus. The new propeller glittered a brighter white than the rest of the machine, and a gilder, obedient to a whim of Monson's, was picking out the aluminium bars with gold. And looking down the long avenue between the ropes (gilded now with the sunset), one saw red signals, and two miles away an ant-hill of workmen busy altering the last falls of the run into a rising slope.

'I'll *come*,' said Woodhouse. 'I'll come right enough. But I tell you it's infernally foolhardy. If only you would give another year' –

'I tell you I won't. I tell you the thing works. I've given years enough' –

'It's not that,' said Woodhouse. 'We're all right with the machine. But it's the steering' –

'Haven't I been rushing, night and morning, backwards and forwards, through this squirrel's cage? If the thing steers true here, it will steer true all across England. It's just funk, I tell you, Woodhouse. We could have gone a year ago. And besides' –

'Well?' said Woodhouse.

'The money!' snapped Monson over his shoulder.

'Hang it! I never thought of the money,' said Woodhouse, and then, speaking now in a very different tone to that with which he had said the words before, he repeated, 'I'll come. Trust me.'

Monson turned suddenly, and saw all that Woodhouse had not the dexterity to say, shining on his sunset-lit face. He looked for a moment, then impulsively extended his hand. 'Thanks,' he said.

'All right,' said Woodhouse, gripping the hand, and with a queer softening of his features. 'Trust me.'

Then both men turned to the big apparatus that lay with its flat wings extended upon the carrier, and stared at it meditatively. Monson, guided perhaps by a photographic study of the flight of birds, and by Lilienthal's methods,[10] had gradually drifted from Maxim's shapes towards the bird form again. The thing, however, was driven by a huge screw behind in the place of the tail; and so hovering, which needs an almost vertical adjustment of a flat tail, was rendered impossible. The body of the machine was small, almost cylindrical, and pointed. Forward and aft on the pointed ends were two small petroleum[11] engines for the screw, and the navigators sat deep in a canoe-like recess, the foremost one steering, and being protected by a low screen, with two plate-glass windows, from the blinding rush of air. On either side a monstrous flat framework with a curved front border could be adjusted so as either to lie horizontally, or to be tilted upward or down. These wings worked rigidly together, or, by releasing a pin, one could be tilted through a small angle independently of its fellow. The front edge of either wing could also be shifted back so as to diminish the wing-area about one-sixth. The machine was not only not designed to hover, but it was also incapable of fluttering. Monson's idea was to get into the air with the initial rush of the apparatus, and then to skim, much as a playing-card may be skimmed, keeping up the rush by means of the screw at the stern. Rooks and gulls fly enormous distances in that way with scarcely a perceptible movement of the wings. The bird really drives along on an aerial switchback. It glides slanting downward for a space, until it has gained considerable momentum, and then altering the inclination of its wings, glides up again almost to its original altitude. Even a Londoner who has watched the birds in the aviary in Regent's Park knows that.

But the bird is practising this art from the moment it leaves its nest. It has not only the perfect apparatus, but the perfect instinct to use it. A man off his feet has the poorest skill in balancing. Even the simple trick of the bicycle costs him some hours of labour. The instantaneous adjustments of the wings, the quick response to a passing breeze, the swift recovery of equilibrium, the giddy, eddying movements that require such absolute precision – all that he must learn, learn with infinite labour and infinite danger, if ever he is to conquer flying. The flying machine that will start off some fine day, driven by neat 'little levers', with a nice open deck like a liner, and all loaded up with bombshells and guns, is the easy dreaming of a literary man. In lives and in treasure the cost of the conquest of the empire of the air may even exceed all that has been spent in man's great conquest of the sea. Certainly it will be costlier than the greatest war that has ever devastated the world.

No one knew these things better than these two practical men. And they knew they were in the front rank of the coming army. Yet there is hope even in a forlorn hope. Men are killed outright in the reserves sometimes, while others who have been left for dead in the thickest corner crawl out and survive.

'If we miss these meadows' – said Woodhouse presently in his slow way.

'My dear chap,' said Monson, whose spirits had been rising fitfully during the last few days, 'we mustn't miss these meadows. There's a quarter of a square mile for us to hit, fences removed, ditches levelled. We shall come down all right – rest assured. And if we don't' –

'Ah!' said Woodhouse. 'If we don't!'

Before the day of the start, the newspaper people got wind of the alterations at the northward end of the framework, and Monson was cheered by a decided change in the comments Romeike forwarded him. 'He will be off some day,' said the papers. 'He will be off some day,' said the South-Western season-ticket holders one to another; the seaside excursionists, the Saturday-to-Monday trippers from Sussex and Hampshire and Dorset and Devon, the eminent literary people from Haslemere,[12] all remarked eagerly one to another, 'He will be off some day,' as the familiar scaffolding came in sight. And actually, one bright morning, in full view of the ten-past-ten train from Basingstoke, Monson's flying machine started on its journey.

They saw the carrier running swiftly along its rail, and the white and gold screw spinning in the air. They heard the rapid rumble of wheels, and a thud as the carrier reached the buffers at the end of its run. Then a whirr as the flying machine was shot forward into the networks. All that the majority of them had seen and heard before. The thing went with a drooping flight through the framework and rose again, and then every beholder shouted, or screamed, or yelled, or shrieked after his kind. For instead of the customary concussion and stoppage, the flying machine flew out of its five years' cage like a bolt from a crossbow, and drove slantingly upward into the air, curved round a little, so as to cross the line, and soared in the direction of Wimbledon Common.

It seemed to hang momentarily in the air and grow smaller, then it ducked and vanished over the clustering blue tree-tops to the east of Coombe Hill, and no one stopped staring and gasping until long after it had disappeared.

That was what the people in the train from Basingstoke saw. If you had drawn a line down the middle of that train, from engine to guard's van, you would not have found a living soul on the opposite side to the flying machine. It was a mad rush from window to window as the thing crossed the line. And the engine-driver and stoker never took their eyes off the low hills about Wimbledon, and never noticed that they had run clean through Coombe and Malden and Raynes Park, until, with returning animation, they found themselves pelting, at the most indecent pace, into Wimbledon station.

From the moment when Monson had started the carrier with a 'Now!' neither he nor Woodhouse said a word. Both men sat with clenched teeth. Monson had crossed the line with a curve that was too sharp, and Woodhouse had opened and shut his white lips; but neither spoke. Woodhouse simply gripped his seat, and breathed sharply through his teeth, watching the blue country to the west rushing past, and down, and away from him. Monson knelt at his post forward, and his hands trembled on the spoked wheel that moved the wings. He could see nothing before him but a mass of white clouds in the sky.

The machine went slanting upward, travelling with an enormous speed still, but losing momentum every moment. The land ran away underneath with diminishing speed.

'Now!' said Woodhouse at last, and with a violent effort Monson wrenched over the wheel and altered the angle of the wings. The machine seemed to hang for half a minute motionless in mid-air, and then he saw the hazy blue house-covered hills of Kilburn and Hampstead jump up before his eyes and rise steadily, until the little sunlit dome of the Albert Hall[13] appeared through his windows. For a moment he scarcely understood the meaning of this upward rush of the horizon, but as the nearer and nearer houses came into view, he realized what he had done. He had turned the wings over too far, and they were swooping steeply downward towards the Thames.

The thought, the question, the realization were all the business of a second of time. 'Too much!' gasped Woodhouse. Monson brought the wheel halfway back with a jerk, and forthwith the Kilburn and Hampstead ridge dropped again to the lower edge of his windows. They had been a thousand feet above Coombe and Malden station; fifty seconds after they whizzed, at a frightful pace, not eighty feet above the East Putney station, on the Metropolitan District line, to the screaming astonishment of a platformful of people. Monson flung up the vans against the air, and over Fulham they rushed up their atmospheric switchback again, steeply – too steeply. The buses went floundering across the Fulham Road, the people yelled.

Then down again, too steeply still, and the distant trees and houses about Primrose Hill leapt up across Monson's window, and then suddenly he saw straight before him the greenery of Kensington Gardens and the towers of the Imperial Institute.[14] They were driving straight down upon South Kensington. The pinnacles of the Natural History Museum rushed up into view. There came one fatal second of swift thought, a moment of hesitation. Should he try and clear the towers, or swerve eastward?

He made a hesitating attempt to release the right wing, left the catch half released, and gave a frantic clutch at the wheel.

The nose of the machine seemed to leap up before him. The wheel pressed his hand with irresistible force, and jerked itself out of his control.

Woodhouse, sitting crouched together, gave a hoarse cry, and sprang up towards Monson. 'Too far!' he cried, and then he was clinging to the gunwale for dear life, and Monson had been jerked clean overhead, and was falling backwards upon him.

So swiftly had the thing happened that barely a quarter of the people going to and fro in Hyde Park, and Brompton Road, and the Exhibition Road saw anything of the aerial catastrophe. A distant winged shape had appeared above the clustering houses to the south, had fallen and risen, growing larger as it did so; had swooped swiftly down towards the Imperial Institute, a broad spread of flying wings, had swept round in a quarter circle, dashed eastward, and then suddenly sprang vertically into the air. A black object shot out of it, and came spinning downward. A man! Two men clutching each other! They came whirling down, separated as they struck the roof of the Students' Club, and bounded off into the green bushes on its southward side.

For perhaps half a minute, the pointed stem of the big machine still pierced vertically upward, the screw spinning desperately. For one brief instant, that yet seemed an age to all who watched, it had hung motionless in mid-air. Then a spout of yellow flame licked up its length from the stern engine, and swift, swifter, swifter, and flaring like a rocket, it rushed down upon the solid mass of masonry which was formerly the Royal College of Science.[15] The big screw of white and gold touched the parapet, and crumpled up like wet linen. Then the blazing spindle-shaped body smashed and splintered, smashing and splintering in its fall, upon the north-westward angle of the building.

But the crash, the flame of blazing paraffin that shot heavenward from the shattered engines of the machine, the crushed horrors that were found in the garden beyond the Students' Club, the masses of yellow parapet and red brick that fell headlong into the roadway, the running to and fro of people like ants in a broken ant-hill, the galloping of fire-engines, the gathering of crowds – all these things do not belong to this story, which was written only to tell how the first of all success-ful flying machines was launched and flew. Though he failed, and failed disastrously, the record of Monson's work remains – a sufficient monument – to guide the next of that band of gallant experimentalists who will sooner or later master this great problem of flying. And between Worcester Park and Malden there still stands that portentous avenue of ironwork, rusting now, and dangerous here and there, to witness to the first desperate struggle for man's right of way through the air.

UNDER THE KNIFE

'What if I die under it?' The thought recurred again and again as I walked home from Haddon's. It was a purely personal question. I was spared the deep anxieties of a married man, and I knew there were few of my intimate friends but would find my death troublesome chiefly on account of their duty of regret. I was surprised indeed and perhaps a little humiliated, as I turned the matter over, to think how few could possibly exceed the conventional requirement. Things came before me stripped of glamour, in a clear dry light, during that walk from Haddon's house over Primrose Hill. There were the friends of my youth; I perceived now that our affection was a tradition which we foregathered rather laboriously to maintain. There were the rivals and helpers of my later career: I suppose I had been cold-blooded or undemonstrative – one perhaps implies the other. It may be that even the capacity for friendship is a question of physique. There had been a time in my own life when I had grieved bitterly enough at the loss of a friend; but as I walked home that afternoon the emotional side of my imagination was dormant. I could not pity myself, nor feel sorry for my friends, nor conceive of them as grieving for me.

I was interested in this deadness of my emotional nature – no doubt a concomitant of my stagnating physiology; and my thoughts wandered off along the line it suggested. Once before, in my hot youth, I had suffered a sudden loss of blood and had been within an ace of death. I remembered now that my affections as well as my passions had drained out of me, leaving scarcely anything but a tranquil resignation, a dreg of self-pity.

It had been weeks before the old ambitions, and tendernesses, and all the complex moral interplay of a man, had reasserted themselves. Now again I was bloodless; I had been feeding down for a week or more. I was not even hungry. It occurred to me that the real meaning of this numbness might be a gradual slipping away from the pleasure-pain guidance of the animal man. It has been proven, I take it, as thoroughly as anything can be proven in this world, that the higher emotions, the moral feelings, even the subtle tendernesses of love, are evolved from the elemental desires and fears of the simple animal: they are the harness in which man's mental freedom goes. And it may be that, as death overshadows us, as our possibility of acting diminishes, this complex growth of balanced impulse, propensity, and aversion whose interplay inspires our acts, goes with it. Leaving what?

I was suddenly brought back to reality by an imminent collision with a butcher-boy's tray. I found that I was crossing the bridge over the Regent's Park Canal[1] which runs parallel with that in the Zoological Gardens. The boy in blue had been looking over his shoulder at a black barge advancing slowly, towed by a gaunt white horse.[2] In the Gardens a nurse was leading three happy little children over the bridge. The trees were bright green; the spring hopefulness was still unstained by the dusts of summer; the sky in the water was bright and clear, but broken by long waves, by quivering bands of black, as the barge drove through. The breeze was stirring; but it did not stir me as the spring breeze used to do.

Was this dullness of feeling in itself an anticipation? It was curious that I could reason and follow out a network of suggestion as clearly as ever: so, at least, it seemed to me. It was calmness rather than dullness that was coming upon me. Was there any ground for the belief in the presentiment of death? Did a man near to death begin instinctively to withdraw himself from the meshes of matter and sense, even before the cold hand was laid upon his? I felt strangely isolated – isolated without regret – from the life and existence about me. The children playing in the sun and gathering strength and experience for the business of life, the park-keeper gossiping with a nursemaid, the nursing mother, the young couple intent upon each other as they passed me, the trees by the wayside spreading new pleading leaves to the sunlight, the stir in their branches – I had been part of it all, but I had nearly done with it now.

Some way down the Broad Walk I perceived that I was tired, and that my feet were heavy. It was hot that afternoon, and I turned aside and sat down on one of the green chairs that line the way. In a minute I had dozed into a dream, and the tide of my thoughts washed up a vision of the resurrection. I was still sitting in the chair, but I thought myself actually dead, withered, tattered, dried, one eye (I saw) pecked out by birds. 'Awake!' cried a voice; and incontinently the dust of the path and the mould under the grass became insurgent. I had never before thought of Regent's Park as a cemetery, but now through the trees, stretching as far as eye could see, I beheld a flat plain of writhing graves and heeling tombstones. There seemed to be some trouble: the rising dead appeared to stifle as they struggled upward, they bled in their struggles, the red flesh was tattered away from the white bones. 'Awake!' cried a voice: but I determined I would not rise to such horrors. 'Awake!' They would not let me alone. 'Wike up!' said an angry voice. A cockney angel! The man who sells the tickets was shaking me, demanding my penny.

I paid my penny, pocketed my ticket, yawned, stretched my legs, and, feeling now rather less torpid, got up and walked on towards Langham Place. I speedily lost myself again in a shifting maze of thoughts about death. Going across Marylebone Road into that crescent at the end of Langham Place, I had the narrowest escape from the shaft of a cab, and went on my way with a palpitating heart and a bruised shoulder. It struck me that it would have been curious if my meditations on my death on the morrow had led to my death that day.

But I will not weary you with more of my experiences that day and the next. I knew more and more certainly that I should die under the operation; at times I think I was inclined to pose to myself. At home I found everything prepared; my room cleared of needless objects and hung with white sheets; a nurse installed and already at loggerheads with my housekeeper.

They wanted me to go to bed early, and after a little resistance I obeyed.

In the morning I was very indolent, and though I read my newspapers and the letters that came by the first post, I did not find them very interesting. There was a friendly note from Addison, my old school friend, calling my attention to two discrepancies and a printer's error in my new book, with one from Langridge venting some vexation over Minton. The rest were business communications. I had a cup of tea but nothing to eat. The glow of pain at my side seemed more massive. I knew it was pain, and yet, if you can understand, I did not find it very painful. I had been awake and hot and thirsty in the night, but in the morning bed felt comfortable. In the night-time I had lain thinking of things that were past; in the morning I dozed over the question of immortality. Haddon came, punctual to the minute, with a neat black bag; and Mowbray soon followed. Their arrival stirred me up a little. I began to take a more personal interest in the proceedings. Haddon moved the little octagonal table close to the bedside, and, with his broad black back to me, began taking things out of his bag. I heard the light click of steel upon steel. My imagination, I found, was not altogether stagnant. 'Will you hurt me much?' I said in an offhand tone.

'Not a bit,' Haddon answered over his shoulder. 'We shall chloroform you. Your heart's as sound as a bell.' And as he spoke, I had a whiff of the pungent sweetness of the anaesthetic.

They stretched me out, with a convenient exposure of my side, and, almost before I realized what was happening, the chloroform was being administered. It stings the nostrils, and there is a suffocating sensation, at first. I knew I should die – that this was the end of consciousness for me. And suddenly I felt that I was not prepared for death: I had a vague sense of a duty overlooked – I knew not what. What was it I had not done? I could think of nothing more to do, nothing desirable left in life; and yet I had the strangest disinclination for death. And the physical sensation was painfully oppressive. Of course the doctors did not know they were going to kill me. Possibly I struggled. Then I fell motionless, and a great silence, a monstrous silence, and an impenetrable blackness came upon me.

There must have been an interval of absolute unconsciousness, seconds or minutes. Then, with a chilly, unemotional clearness, I perceived that I was not yet dead. I was still in my body; but all the multitudinous sensations that come sweeping from it to make up the background of consciousness had gone, leaving me free of it all. No, not free of it all; for as yet something still held me to the poor stark flesh upon the bed – held me, yet not so closely that I did not feel myself external to it, independent of it, straining away from it. I do not think I saw, I do not think I heard; but I perceived all that was going on, and it was as if I both heard and saw. Haddon was bending over me, Mowbray behind me; the scalpel – it was a large scalpel – was cutting my flesh at the side under the flying ribs. It was interesting to see myself cut like cheese, without a pang, without even a qualm. The interest was much of a quality with that one might feel in a game of chess between strangers. Haddon's face was firm and his hand steady; but I was surprised to perceive (*how* I know not) that he was feeling the gravest doubt as to his own wisdom in the conduct of the operation.

Mowbray's thoughts, too, I could see. He was thinking that Haddon's manner showed too much of the specialist. New suggestions came up like bubbles through a stream of frothing meditation, and burst one after another in the little bright spot of his consciousness. He could not help noticing and admiring Haddon's swift dexterity, in spite of his envious quality and his disposition to detract. I saw my liver exposed. I was puzzled at my own condition. I did not feel that I was dead, but I was different in some way from my living self. The grey depression that had weighed on me for a year or more and coloured all my thoughts, was gone. I perceived and thought without any emotional tint at all. I wondered if everyone perceived things in this way under chloroform, and forgot it again when he came out of it. It would be inconvenient to look into some heads, and not forget.

Although I did not think that I was dead, I still perceived quite clearly that I was soon to die. This brought me back to the consideration of Haddon's proceedings. I looked into his mind, and saw that he was afraid of cutting a branch of the portal vein. My attention was distracted from details by the curious changes going on in his mind. His consciousness was like the quivering little spot of light which is thrown by the mirror of a galvanometer. His thoughts ran under it like a stream, some through the focus bright and distinct, some shadowy in the half-light of the edge. Just now the little glow was steady; but the least movement on Mowbray's part, the slightest sound from outside, even a faint difference in the slow movement of the living flesh he was cutting, set the light-spot shivering and spinning. A new sense-impression came rushing up through the flow of thoughts, and lo! the light-spot jerked away towards it, swifter than a frightened fish. It was wonderful to think that upon that unstable, fitful thing depended all the complex motions of the man; that for the next five minutes, therefore, my life hung upon its movements. And he was growing more and more nervous in his work. It was as if a little picture of a cut vein grew brighter, and struggled to oust from his brain another picture of a cut falling short of the mark. He was afraid: his dread of cutting too little was battling with his dread of cutting too far.

Then, suddenly, like an escape of water from under a lock-gate, a great uprush of horrible realization set all his thoughts swirling, and simultaneously I perceived that the vein was cut. He started back with a hoarse exclamation, and I saw the brown-purple blood gather in a swift bead, and run trickling. He was horrified. He pitched the red-stained scalpel on to the octagonal table; and instantly both doctors flung themselves upon me, making hasty and ill-conceived efforts to remedy the disaster. 'Ice!' said Mowbray, gasping. But I knew that I was killed, though my body still clung to me.

I will not describe their belated endeavours to save me, though I perceived every detail. My perceptions were sharper and swifter than they had ever been in life; my thoughts rushed through my mind with incredible swiftness, but with perfect definition. I can only compare their crowded clarity to the effects of a reasonable dose of opium. In a moment it would all be over, and I should be free. I knew I was immortal, but what would happen I did not know. Should I drift off presently, like a puff of smoke from a gun, in some kind of half-material body, an attenuated version of my material self? Should I find myself suddenly among the innumerable hosts of the dead, and know the world about me for the phantasmagoria it had always seemed? Should I drift to some spiritualistic *séance*, and there make foolish, incomprehensible attempts to affect a purblind medium? It was a state of unemotional curiosity, of colourless expectation. And then I realized a growing stress upon me, a feeling as though some huge human magnet was drawing me upward out of my body. The stress grew and grew. I seemed an atom for which monstrous forces were fighting. For one brief, terrible moment sensation came back to me. That feeling of falling headlong which comes in nightmares, that feeling a thousand times intensified, that and a black horror swept across my thoughts in a torrent. Then the two doctors, the naked body with its cut side, the little room, swept away from under me and vanished as a speck of foam vanishes down an eddy.

I was in mid-air. Far below was the West End of London, receding rapidly, – for I seemed to be flying swiftly upward, – and, as it receded, passing westward, like a panorama. I could see, through the faint haze of smoke, the innumerable roofs chimney-set, the narrow roadways stippled with people and conveyances, the little specks of squares, and the church steeples like thorns sticking out of the fabric. But it spun away as the earth rotated on its axis, and in a few seconds (as it seemed) I was over the scattered clumps of town about Ealing, the little Thames a thread of blue to the south, and the Chiltern Hills and the North Downs coming up like the rim of a basin, far away and faint with haze. Up I rushed. And at first I had not the faintest conception what this headlong rush upward could mean.

Every moment the circle of scenery beneath me grew wider and wider, and the details of town and field, of hill and valley, got more and more hazy and pale and indistinct, a luminous grey was mingled more and more with the blue of the hills and the green of the open meadows; and a little patch of cloud, low and far to the west, shone ever more dazzlingly white. Above, as the veil of atmosphere between myself and outer space grew thinner, the sky, which had been a fair springtime blue at first, grew deeper and richer in colour, passing steadily through the intervening shades until presently it was as dark as the blue sky of midnight, and presently as black as the blackness of a frosty starlight, and at last as black as no blackness I had ever beheld. And first one star and then many, and at last an innumerable host broke out upon the sky: more stars than anyone has ever seen from the face of the earth. For the blueness of the sky is the light of the sun and stars sifted and spread abroad blindingly: there is diffused light even in the darkest skies of winter, and we do not see the stars by day only because of the dazzling irradiation of the sun. But now I saw things – I know not how; assuredly with no mortal eyes – and that defect of bedazzlement blinded me no longer. The sun was incredibly strange and wonderful. The body of it was a disc of blinding white light: not yellowish as it seems to those who live upon the earth, but livid white, all streaked with scarlet streaks and rimmed about with a fringe of writhing tongues of red fire. And, shooting halfway across the heavens from either side of it, and brighter than the Milky Way, were two pinions of silver-white, making it look more like those winged globes[3] I have seen in Egyptian sculpture, than anything else I can remember upon earth. These I knew for the solar corona, though I had never seen anything of it but a picture during the days of my earthly life.

When my attention came back to the earth again, I saw that it had fallen very far away from me. Field and town were long since indistinguishable, and all the varied hues of the country were merging into a uniform bright grey, broken only by the brilliant white of the clouds that lay scattered in flocculent masses over Ireland and the west of England. For now I could see the outlines of the north of France and Ireland, and all this island of Britain save where Scotland passed over the horizon to the north, or where the coast was blurred or obliterated by cloud. The sea was a dull grey, and darker than the land; and the whole panorama was rotating slowly towards the east.

All this had happened so swiftly that, until I was some thousand miles or so from the earth, I had no thought for myself. But now I perceived I had neither hands nor feet, neither parts nor organs, and that I felt neither alarm nor pain. All about me I perceived that the vacancy (for I had already left the air behind) was cold beyond the imagination of man; but it troubled me not. The sun's rays shot through the void, powerless to light or heat until they should strike on matter in their course. I saw things with a serene self-forgetfulness, even as if I were God. And down below there, rushing away from me, – countless miles in a second, – where a little dark spot on the grey marked the position of London, two doctors were struggling to restore life to the poor hacked and outworn shell I had abandoned. I felt then such release, such serenity as I can compare to no mortal delight I have ever known.

It was only after I had perceived all these things that the meaning of that headlong rush of the earth grew into comprehension. Yet it was so simple, so obvious, that I was amazed at my never anticipating the thing that was happening to me. I had suddenly been cut adrift from matter: all that was material of me was there upon earth, whirling away through space, held to the earth by gravitation, partaking of the earth's inertia, moving in its wreath of epicycles round the sun, and with the sun and the planets on their vast march through space. But the immaterial has no inertia, feels nothing of the pull of matter for matter: where it parts from its garment of flesh, there it remains (so far as space concerns it any longer) immovable in space. *I* was not leaving the earth: the earth was leaving *me*, and not only the earth, but the whole solar system was streaming past. And about me in space, invisible to me, scattered in the wake of the earth upon its journey, there must be an innumerable multitude of souls, stripped like myself of the material, stripped like myself of the passions of the individual and the generous emotions of the gregarious brute, naked intelligences, things of newborn wonder and thought, marvelling at the strange release that had suddenly come on them!

As I receded faster and faster from the strange white sun in the black heavens, and from the broad and shining earth upon which my being had begun, I seemed to grow, in some incredible

manner, vast: vast as regards this world I had left, vast as
regards the moments and periods of a human life. Very soon I
saw the full circle of the earth, slightly gibbous, like the moon
when she nears her full, but very large; and the silvery shape of
America was now in the noonday blaze wherein (as it seemed)
little England had been basking but a few minutes ago. At first
the earth was large and shone in the heavens, filling a great part
of them; but every moment she grew smaller and more distant.
As she shrunk, the broad moon in its third quarter crept into
view over the rim of her disc. I looked for the constellations.
Only that part of Aries directly behind the sun, and the Lion,
which the earth covered, were hidden. I recognized the tortuous,
tattered band of the Milky Way, with Vega very bright between
sun and earth; and Sirius and Orion shone splendid against the
unfathomable blackness in the opposite quarter of the heavens.
The Pole Star was overhead, and the Great Bear hung over the
circle of the earth. And away beneath and beyond the shining
corona of the sun were strange groupings of stars I had never
seen in my life – notably, a dagger-shaped group that I knew
for the Southern Cross. All these were no larger than when they
had shone on earth; but the little stars that one scarcely sees
shone now against the setting of black vacancy as brightly as
the first-magnitudes had done, while the larger worlds were
points of indescribable glory and colour. Aldebaran was a spot
of blood-red fire, and Sirius condensed to one point the light of
a world of sapphires. And they shone steadily: they did not
scintillate, they were calmly glorious. My impressions had an
adamantine hardness and brightness: there was no blurring
softness, no atmosphere, nothing but infinite darkness set with
the myriads of these acute and brilliant points and specks of
light. Presently, when I looked again, the little earth seemed no
bigger than the sun, and it dwindled and turned as I looked
until, in a second's space (as it seemed to me), it was halved;
and so it went on swiftly dwindling. Far away in the opposite
direction, a little pinkish pin's head of light, shining steadily,
was the planet Mars. I swam motionless in vacancy, and, without a trace of terror or astonishment, watched the speck of
cosmic dust we call the world fall away from me.

Presently it dawned upon me that my sense of duration had changed: that my mind was moving not faster but infinitely slowlier, that between each separate impression there was a period of many days. The moon spun once round the earth as I noted this; and I perceived clearly the motion of Mars in his orbit. Moreover, it appeared as if the time between thought and thought grew steadily greater, until at last a thousand years was but a moment[4] in my perception.

At first the constellations had shone motionless against the black background of infinite space; but presently it seemed as though the group of stars about Hercules and the Scorpion was contracting, while Orion and Aldebaran and their neighbours were scattering apart. Flashing suddenly out of the darkness there came a flying multitude of particles of rock, glittering like dust-specks in a sunbeam, and encompassed in a faintly luminous haze. They swirled all about me, and vanished again in a twinkling far behind. And then I saw that a bright spot of light, that shone a little to one side of my path, was growing very rapidly larger, and perceived that it was the planet Saturn rushing towards me. Larger and larger it grew, swallowing up the heavens behind it, and hiding every moment a fresh multitude of stars. I perceived its flattened, whirling body, its disc-like belt, and seven of its little satellites. It grew and grew, till it towered enormous; and then I plunged amid a streaming multitude of clashing stones and dancing dust-particles and gas-eddies, and saw for a moment the mighty triple belt like three concentric arches of moonlight above me, its shadow black on the boiling tumult below. These things happened in one-tenth of the time it takes to tell of them. The planet went by like a flash of lightning; for a few seconds it blotted out the sun, and there and then became a mere black, dwindling, winged patch against the light. The earth, the mother mote of my being, I could no longer see.

So with a stately swiftness, in the profoundest silence, the solar system fell from me, as it had been a garment, until the sun was a mere star amid the multitude of stars, with its eddy of planet-specks, lost in the confused glittering of the remoter light. I was no longer a denizen of the solar system: I had come to the Outer Universe, I seemed to grasp and comprehend the whole world of matter. Ever more swiftly the stars closed in about the spot where Antares and Vega had vanished in a luminous haze, until that part of the sky had the semblance of a whirling mass of nebulae, and ever before me yawned vaster gaps of vacant blackness and the stars shone fewer and fewer. It seemed as if I moved towards a point between Orion's belt and sword; and the void about that region opened vaster and vaster every second, an incredible gulf of nothingness, into which I was falling. Faster and ever faster the universe rushed by, a hurry of whirling motes at last, speeding silently into the void. Stars glowing brighter and brighter, with their circling planets catching the light in a ghostly fashion as I neared them, shone out and vanished again into inexistence; faint comets, clusters of meteorites, winking specks of matter, eddying light-points, whizzed past, some perhaps a hundred millions of miles or so from me at most, few nearer, travelling with unimaginable rapidity, shooting constellations, momentary darts of fire, through that black, enormous night. More than anything else it was like a dusty draught, sunbeam-lit. Broader, and wider, and deeper grew the starless space, the vacant Beyond, into which I was being drawn. At last a quarter of the heavens was black and blank, and the whole headlong rush of stellar universe closed in behind me like a veil of light that is gathered together. It drove away from me like a monstrous jack-o'-lantern driven by the wind. I had come out into the wilderness of space. Ever the vacant blackness grew broader, until the hosts of the stars seemed only like a swarm of fiery specks hurrying away from me, inconceivably remote, and the darkness, the nothingness and emptiness, was about me on every side. Soon the little universe of matter, the cage of points in which I had begun to be, was dwindling, now to a whirling disc of luminous glittering, and now to one minute disc of hazy light. In a little while it would shrink to a point, and at last would vanish altogether.

Suddenly feeling came back to me – feeling in the shape of overwhelming terror: such a dread of those dark vastitudes as no words can describe, a passionate resurgence of sympathy and social desire. Were there other souls, invisible to me as I to them, about me in the blackness? or was I indeed, even as I felt, alone? Had I passed out of being into something that was neither being nor not-being? The covering of the body, the covering of matter, had been torn from me, and the hallucinations of companionship and security. Everything was black and silent. I had ceased to be. I was nothing. There was nothing, save only that infinitesimal dot of light that dwindled in the gulf. I strained myself to hear and see, and for a while there was naught but infinite silence, intolerable darkness, horror, and despair.

Then I saw that about the spot of light into which the whole world of matter had shrunk there was a faint glow. And in a band on either side of that the darkness was not absolute. I watched it for ages, as it seemed to me, and through the long waiting the haze grew imperceptibly more distinct. And then about the band appeared an irregular cloud of the faintest, palest brown. I felt a passionate impatience; but the things grew brighter so slowly that they scarcely seemed to change. What was unfolding itself? What was this strange reddish dawn in the interminable night of space?

The cloud's shape was grotesque. It seemed to be looped along its lower side into four projecting masses, and, above, it ended in a straight line. What phantom was it? I felt assured I had seen that figure before; but I could not think what, nor where, nor when it was. Then the realization rushed upon me. *It was a clenched Hand.* I was alone in space, alone with this huge, shadowy Hand, upon which the whole Universe of Matter lay like an unconsidered speck of dust. It seemed as though I watched it through vast periods of time. On the forefinger glittered a ring; and the universe from which I had come was but a spot of light upon the ring's curvature. And the thing that the hand gripped had the likeness of a black rod. Through a long eternity I watched this Hand, with the ring and the rod, marvelling and fearing and waiting helplessly on what might follow. It seemed as though nothing could follow: that I should watch for ever, seeing only the Hand and the thing it held, and understanding nothing of its import. Was the whole universe but a refracting speck upon some greater Being? Were our

worlds but the atoms of another universe, and those again of
another, and so on through an endless progression? And what
was I? Was I indeed immaterial? A vague persuasion of a body
gathering about me came into my suspense. The abysmal darkness about the Hand filled with impalpable suggestions, with
uncertain, fluctuating shapes.

Came a sound, like the sound of a tolling bell; faint, as if
infinitely far, muffled as though heard through thick swathings
of darkness: a deep, vibrating resonance, with vast gulfs of
silence between each stroke. And the Hand appeared to tighten
on the rod. And I saw far above the Hand, towards the apex of
the darkness, a circle of dim phosphorescence, a ghostly sphere
whence these sounds came throbbing; and at the last stroke the
Hand vanished, for the hour had come, and I heard a noise of
many waters. But the black rod remained as a great band across
the sky. And then a voice, which seemed to run to the uttermost
parts of space, spoke, saying, 'There will be no more pain.'[5]

At that an almost intolerable gladness and radiance rushed
upon me, and I saw the circle shining white and bright, and the
rod black and shining, and many things else distinct and clear.
And the circle was the face of the clock, and the rod the rail of
my bed. Haddon was standing at the foot, against the rail, with
a small pair of scissors on his fingers; and the hands of my clock
on the mantel over his shoulder were clasped together over the
hour of twelve. Mowbray was washing something in a basin at
the octagonal table, and at my side I felt a subdued feeling that
could scarce be spoken of as pain.

The operation had not killed me. And I perceived, suddenly,
that the dull melancholy of half a year was lifted from my mind.

A SLIP UNDER THE MICROSCOPE

Outside the laboratory windows was a watery-grey fog, and within a close warmth and the yellow light of the green-shaded gas lamps that stood two to each table down its narrow length. On each table stood a couple of glass jars containing the mangled vestiges of the crayfish, mussels, frogs, and guineapigs upon which the students had been working, and down the side of the room, facing the windows, were shelves bearing bleached dissections in spirits, surmounted by a row of beautifully executed anatomical drawings in whitewood frames and over-hanging a row of cubical lockers. All the doors of the laboratory were panelled with blackboard, and on these were the half-erased diagrams of the previous day's work. The laboratory was empty, save for the demonstrator, who sat near the preparation-room door, and silent, save for a low, continuous murmur, and the clicking of the rocker microtome at which he was working. But scattered about the room were traces of numerous students: handbags, polished boxes of instruments, in one place a large drawing covered by newspaper, and in another a prettily bound copy of *News from Nowhere*,[1] a book oddly at variance with its surroundings. These things had been put down hastily as the students had arrived and hurried at once to secure their seats in the adjacent lecture theatre. Deadened by the closed door, the measured accents of the professor sounded as a featureless muttering.

Presently, faint through the closed windows came the sound of the Oratory clock[2] striking the hour of eleven. The clicking of the microtome ceased, and the demonstrator looked at his watch, rose, thrust his hands into his pockets, and walked slowly down the laboratory towards the lecture theatre door. He stood listening for a moment, and then his eye fell on the little volume by William Morris. He picked it up, glanced at the title, smiled, opened it, looked at the name on the fly-leaf, ran the leaves through with his hand, and put it down. Almost immediately the even murmur of the lecturer ceased, there was a sudden burst of pencils rattling on the desks in the lecture theatre, a stirring, a scraping of feet, and a number of voices speaking together. Then a firm footfall approached the door, which began to open, and stood ajar as some indistinctly heard question arrested the newcomer.

The demonstrator turned, walked slowly back past the microtome, and left the laboratory by the preparation-room door. As he did so, first one, and then several students carrying notebooks entered the laboratory from the lecture theatre, and distributed themselves among the little tables, or stood in a group about the doorway. They were an exceptionally heterogeneous assembly, for while Oxford and Cambridge still recoil from the blushing prospect of mixed classes,[3] the College of Science[4] anticipated America in the matter years ago – mixed socially too, for the prestige of the College is high, and its scholarships, free of any age limit, dredge deeper even than do those of the Scotch universities. The class numbered one-and-twenty, but some remained in the theatre questioning the professor, copying the blackboard diagrams before they were washed off, or examining the special specimens he had produced to illustrate the day's teaching. Of the nine who had come into the laboratory three were girls, one of whom, a little fair woman wearing spectacles and dressed in greyish-green, was peering out of the window at the fog, while the other two, both wholesome-looking, plain-faced schoolgirls, unrolled and put on the brown holland aprons they wore while dissecting. Of the men, two went down the laboratory to their places, one a pallid, dark-bearded man, who had once been a tailor; the other a pleasant-featured, ruddy young man of twenty, dressed in a well-fitting brown suit; young Wedderburn, the son of Wedderburn the eye specialist. The others formed a little knot near the theatre door. One of these, a dwarfed, spectacled figure with a hunchback, sat on a bent wood stool; two others, one a short, dark youngster and the other a flaxen-haired, reddish-complexioned young man, stood leaning side by side against the slate sink, while the fourth stood facing them, and maintained the larger share of the conversation.

This last person was named Hill. He was a sturdily built young fellow, of the same age as Wedderburn; he had a white face, dark grey eyes, hair of an indeterminate colour, and prominent, irregular features. He talked rather louder than was needful, and thrust his hands deeply into his pockets. His collar was frayed and blue with the starch of a careless laundress, his clothes were evidently ready-made, and there was a patch on the side of his boot near the toe. And as he talked or listened to the others, he glanced now and again towards the lecture theatre door. They were discussing the depressing peroration of the lecture they had just heard, the last lecture it was in the introductory course in zoology. 'From ovum to ovum is the goal of the higher vertebrata,' the lecturer had said in his melancholy tones, and so had neatly rounded off the sketch of comparative anatomy he had been developing. The spectacled hunchback had repeated it with noisy appreciation, had tossed it towards the fair-haired student with an evident provocation, and had started one of those vague, rambling discussions on generalities so unaccountably dear to the student mind all the world over.

'That is our goal, perhaps – I admit it, as far as science goes,' said the fair-haired student, rising to the challenge. 'But there are things above science.'

'Science,' said Hill confidently, 'is systematic knowledge. Ideas that don't come into the system – must anyhow – be loose ideas.' He was not quite sure whether that was a clever saying or a fatuity until his hearers took it seriously.

'The thing I cannot understand,' said the hunchback, at large, 'is whether Hill is a materialist or not.'

'There is one thing above matter,' said Hill promptly, feeling he made a better point this time, aware, too, of someone in the doorway behind him, and raising his voice a trifle for her benefit, 'and that is, the delusion that there is something above matter.'

'So we have your gospel at last,' said the fair student. 'It's all a delusion, is it? All our aspirations to lead something more than dogs' lives, all our work for anything beyond ourselves. But see how inconsistent you are. Your socialism, for instance. Why do you trouble about the interests of the race? Why do you concern yourself about the beggar in the gutter? Why are you bothering yourself to lend that book' – he indicated William Morris by a movement of the head – 'to everyone in the lab?'

'Girl,' said the hunchback indistinctly, and glanced guiltily over his shoulder.

The girl in brown, with the brown eyes, had come into the laboratory, and stood on the other side of the table behind him, with her rolled-up apron in one hand, looking over her shoulder, listening to the discussion. She did not notice the hunchback, because she was glancing from Hill to his interlocutor. Hill's consciousness of her presence betrayed itself to her only in his studious ignoring of the fact; but she understood that, and it pleased her. 'I see no reason,' said he, 'why a man should live like a brute because he knows of nothing beyond matter, and does not expect to exist a hundred years hence.'

'Why shouldn't he?' said the fair-haired student.

'Why *should* he?' said Hill.

'What inducement has he?'

'That's the way with all you religious people. It's all a business of inducements. Cannot a man seek after righteousness for righteousness' sake?'

There was a pause. The fair man answered, with a kind of vocal padding, 'But – you see – inducement – when I said inducement,' to gain time. And then the hunchback came to his rescue and inserted a question. He was a terrible person in the debating society with his questions, and they invariably took one form – a demand for a definition. 'What's your definition of righteousness?' said the hunchback at this stage.

Hill experienced a sudden loss of complacency at this question, but even as it was asked, relief came in the person of Brooks, the laboratory attendant, who entered by the preparation-room door, carrying a number of freshly killed guineapigs by their hind legs. 'This is the last batch of material this session,' said the youngster who had not previously spoken. Brooks advanced up the laboratory, smacking down a couple of guineapigs at each table. The rest of the class, scenting the prey from afar, came crowding in by the lecture theatre door, and the discussion perished abruptly as the students who were not already in their places hurried to them to secure the choice of a specimen. There was a noise of keys rattling on split rings as lockers were opened and dissecting instruments taken out. Hill was already standing by his table, and his box of scalpels was sticking out of his pocket. The girl in brown came a step towards him, and leaning over his table said softly, 'Did you see that I returned your book, Mr Hill?'

During the whole scene she and the book had been vividly present in his consciousness; but he made a clumsy pretence of looking at the book and seeing it for the first time. 'Oh yes,' he said, taking it up. 'I see. Did you like it?'

'I want to ask you some questions about it – sometime.'

'Certainly,' said Hill. 'I shall be glad.' He stopped awkwardly. 'You liked it?' he said.

'It's a wonderful book. Only some things I don't understand.'

Then suddenly the laboratory was hushed by a curious braying noise. It was the demonstrator. He was at the blackboard ready to begin the day's instruction, and it was his custom to demand silence by a sound midway between the 'Er' of common intercourse and the blast of a trumpet. The girl in brown slipped back to her place: it was immediately in front of Hill's, and Hill, forgetting her forthwith, took a notebook out of the drawer of his table, turned over its leaves hastily, drew a stumpy pencil from his pocket, and prepared to make a copious note of the coming demonstration. For demonstrations and lectures are the sacred text of the College students. Books, saving only the Professor's own, you may – it is even expedient to – ignore.

Hill was the son of a Landport cobbler, and had been hooked by a chance blue paper[5] the authorities had thrown out to the Landport Technical College. He kept himself in London on his allowance of a guinea a week,[6] and found that, with proper care, this also covered his clothing allowance, an occasional waterproof collar, that is; and ink and needles and cotton and

such-like necessaries for a man about town. This was his first
year and his first session, but the brown old man in Landport
had already got himself detested in many public-houses by
boasting of his son, 'the Professor'. Hill was a vigorous youngster, with a serene contempt for the clergy of all denominations,
and a fine ambition to reconstruct the world. He regarded his
scholarship as a brilliant opportunity. He had begun to read at
seven, and had read steadily whatever came in his way, good
or bad, since then. His worldly experience had been limited to
the island of Portsea, and acquired chiefly in the wholesale
boot factory in which he had worked by day, after passing the
seventh standard of the Board school.[7] He had a considerable
gift of speech, as the College Debating Society, which met
amidst the crushing machines and mine models in the metallur-
gical theatre downstairs, already recognized – recognized by a
violent battering of desks whenever he rose. And he was just at
that fine emotional age when life opens at the end of a narrow
pass like a broad valley at one's feet, full of the promise of
wonderful discoveries and tremendous achievements. And his
own limitations, save that he knew that he knew neither Latin
nor French, were all unknown to him.

At first his interest had been divided pretty equally between
his biological work at the College and social and theological
theorizing, an employment which he took in deadly earnest. Of
a night, when the big museum library was not open, he would
sit on the bed of his room in Chelsea with his coat and a muffler
on, and write out the lecture notes and revise his dissection
memoranda until Thorpe called him out by a whistle – the
landlady objected to open the door to attic visitors – and then
the two would go prowling about the shadowy, shiny, gaslit
streets, talking, very much in the fashion of the sample just
given, of the God Idea and Righteousness and Carlyle[8] and the
Reorganization of Society. And in the midst of it all, Hill,
arguing not only for Thorpe but for the casual passer-by, would
lose the thread of his argument glancing at some pretty painted
face that looked meaningly at him as he passed. Science and
Righteousness! But once or twice lately there had been signs
that a third interest was creeping into his life, and he had found

his attention wandering from the fate of the mesoblastic somites or the probable meaning of the blastopore, to the thought of the girl with the brown eyes who sat at the table before him.

She was a paying student;[9] she descended inconceivable social altitudes to speak to him. At the thought of the education she must have had, and the accomplishments she must possess, the soul of Hill became abject within him. She had spoken to him first over a difficulty about the alisphenoid of a rabbit's skull, and he had found that, in biology at least, he had no reason for self-abasement. And from that, after the manner of young people starting from any starting-point, they got to generalities, and while Hill attacked her upon the question of socialism, – some instinct told him to spare her a direct assault upon her religion – she was gathering resolution to undertake what she told herself was his aesthetic education. She was a year or two older than he, though the thought never occurred to him. The loan of *News from Nowhere* was the beginning of a series of cross loans. Upon some absurd first principle of his, Hill had never 'wasted time' upon poetry, and it seemed an appalling deficiency to her. One day in the lunch hour, when she chanced upon him alone in the little museum where the skeletons were arranged, shamefully eating the bun that constituted his midday meal, she retreated, and returned to lend him, with a slightly furtive air, a volume of Browning.[10] He stood sideways towards her and took the book rather clumsily, because he was holding the bun in the other hand. And in the retrospect his voice lacked the cheerful clearness he could have wished.

That occurred after the examination in comparative anatomy, on the day before the College turned out its students and was carefully locked up by the officials for the Christmas holidays. The excitement of cramming for the first trial of strength had for a little while dominated Hill to the exclusion of his other interests. In the forecasts of the result in which everyone indulged he was surprised to find that no one regarded him as a possible competitor for the Harvey Commemoration Medal,[11] of which this and the two subsequent examinations disposed. It was about this time that Wedderburn, who so far had lived inconspicuously on the uttermost margin of Hill's perceptions, began to take on the appearance of an obstacle. By a mutual agreement, the nocturnal prowlings with Thorpe ceased for the three weeks before the examination, and his landlady pointed out that she really could not supply so much lamp oil at the price. He walked to and fro from the College with little slips of mnemonics in his hand, lists of crayfish appendages, rabbits' skull-bones, and vertebrate nerves, for example, and became a positive nuisance to foot passengers in the opposite direction.

But, by a natural reaction, Poetry and the girl with the brown eyes ruled the Christmas holiday. The pending results of the examination became such a secondary consideration that Hill marvelled at his father's excitement. Even had he wished it, there was no comparative anatomy to read in Landport, and he was too poor to buy books, but the stock of poets in the library was extensive, and Hill's attack was magnificently sustained. He saturated himself with the fluent numbers of Longfellow and Tennyson, and fortified himself with Shakespeare; found a kindred soul in Pope and a master in Shelley, and heard and fled the siren voices of Eliza Cook and Mrs Hemans.[12] But he read no more Browning, because he hoped for the loan of other volumes from Miss Haysman when he returned to London.

He walked from his lodgings to the College with that volume of Browning in his shiny black bag, and his mind teeming with the finest general propositions about poetry. Indeed, he framed first this little speech and then that with which to grace the return. The morning was an exceptionally pleasant one for London; there was a clear hard frost and undeniable blue in the sky, a thin haze softened every outline, and warm shafts of sunlight struck between the house blocks and turned the sunny side of the street to amber and gold. In the hall of the College he pulled off his glove and signed his name with fingers so stiff with cold that the characteristic dash under the signature he cultivated became a quivering line. He imagined Miss Haysman about him everywhere. He turned at the staircase, and there, below, he saw a crowd struggling at the foot of the noticeboard. This, possibly, was the biology list. He forgot Browning and Miss Haysman for the moment, and joined the scrimmage. And at last, with his cheek flattened against the sleeve of the man on the step above him, he read the list –

CLASS I
H. J. Somers Wedderburn
William Hill

and thereafter followed a second class that is outside our present sympathies. It was characteristic that he did not trouble to look for Thorpe on the physics list, but backed out of the struggle at once, and in a curious emotional state between pride over common second-class humanity and acute disappointment at Wedderburn's success, went on his way upstairs. At the top, as he was hanging up his coat in the passage, the zoological demonstrator, a young man from Oxford who secretly regarded him as a blatant 'mugger'[13] of the very worst type, offered his heartiest congratulations.

At the laboratory door Hill stopped for a second to get his breath, and then entered. He looked straight up the laboratory and saw all five girl students grouped in their places, and Wedderburn, the once retiring Wedderburn, leaning rather gracefully against the window, playing with the blind tassel and talking apparently to the five of them. Now, Hill could talk bravely enough and even overbearingly to one girl, and he could have made a speech to a roomful of girls, but this business of standing at ease and appreciating, fencing, and returning quick remarks round a group was, he knew, altogether beyond him. Coming up the staircase his feelings for Wedderburn had been generous, a certain admiration perhaps, a willingness to shake his hand conspicuously and heartily as one who had fought but the first round. But before Christmas Wedderburn had never gone up to that end of the room to talk. In a flash Hill's mist of vague excitement condensed abruptly to a vivid dislike of Wedderburn. Possibly his expression changed. As he came up to his place, Wedderburn nodded carelessly to him, and the others glanced round. Miss Haysman looked at him and away again, the faintest touch of her eyes. 'I can't agree with you, Mr Wedderburn,' she said.

'I must congratulate you on your first class, Mr Hill,' said the spectacled girl in green, turning round and beaming at him.

'It's nothing,' said Hill, staring at Wedderburn and Miss Haysman talking together, and eager to hear what they talked about.

'We poor folks in the second class don't think so,' said the girl in spectacles.

What was it Wedderburn was saying? Something about William Morris! Hill did not answer the girl in spectacles, and the smile died out of his face. He could not hear, and failed to see how he could 'cut in'. Confound Wedderburn! He sat down, opened his bag, hesitated whether to return the volume of Browning forthwith, in the sight of all, and instead drew out his new notebooks for the short course in elementary botany that was now beginning, and which would terminate in February. As he did so, a fat heavy man with a white face and pale grey eyes – Bindon, the professor of botany, who came up from Kew for January and February – came in by the lecture theatre door, and passed, rubbing his hands together and smiling, in silent affability down the laboratory.

In the subsequent six weeks Hill experienced some very rapid and curiously complex emotional developments. For the most part he had Wedderburn in focus – a fact that Miss Haysman never suspected. She told Hill (for in the comparative privacy of the museum she talked a good deal to him of socialism and Browning and general propositions) that she had met Wedderburn at the house of some people she knew, and 'he's inherited his cleverness; for his father, you know, is the great eye specialist'.

'My father is a cobbler,' said Hill, quite irrelevantly, and perceived the want of dignity even as he said it. But the gleam of jealousy did not offend her. She conceived herself the fundamental source of it. He suffered bitterly from a sense of Wedderburn's unfairness, and a realization of his own handicap. Here was this Wedderburn had picked up a prominent man for a father, and instead of his losing so many marks on the score of that advantage, it was counted to him for righteousness![14]

And while Hill had to introduce himself and talk to Miss Haysman clumsily over mangled guineapigs in the laboratory, this Wedderburn, in some backstairs way, had access to her social altitudes, and could converse in a polished argot that Hill understood perhaps, but felt incapable of speaking. Not, of course, that he wanted to. Then it seemed to Hill that for Wedderburn to come there day after day with cuffs unfrayed, neatly tailored, precisely barbered, quietly perfect, was in itself an ill-bred, sneering sort of proceeding. Moreover, it was a stealthy thing for Wedderburn to behave insignificantly for a space, to mock modesty, to lead Hill to fancy that he himself was beyond dispute the man of the year, and then suddenly to dart in front of him, and incontinently to swell up in this fashion. In addition to these things, Wedderburn displayed an increasing disposition to join in any conversational grouping that included Miss Haysman; and would venture, and indeed seek occasion, to pass opinions derogatory to socialism and atheism. He goaded Hill to incivilities by neat, shallow, and exceedingly effective personalities about the socialist leaders, until Hill hated Bernard Shaw's graceful egotisms, William Morris's limited editions and luxurious wallpapers, and Walter Crane's[15] charmingly absurd ideal working men, about as much as he hated Wedderburn. The dissertations in the laboratory, that had been his glory in the previous term, became a danger, degenerated into inglorious tussles with Wedderburn, and Hill kept to them only out of an obscure perception that his honour was involved. In the debating society Hill knew quite clearly that, to a thunderous accompaniment of banged desks, he could have pulverized Wedderburn. Only Wedderburn never attended the debating society to be pulverized, because – nauseous affectation! – he 'dined late'.[16]

You must not imagine that these things presented themselves in quite such a crude form to Hill's perception. Hill was a born generalizer. Wedderburn to him was not so much an individual obstacle as a type, the salient angle of a class. The economic theories that, after infinite ferment, had shaped themselves in Hill's mind, became abruptly concrete at the contact. The world became full of easy-mannered, graceful, gracefully-dressed, conversationally dexterous, finally shallow Wedderburns, Bishops Wedderburn, Wedderburn M.P.s, Professors Wedderburn, Wedderburn landlords, all with finger-bowl shibboleths[17] and epigrammatic cities of refuge from a sturdy debater. And everyone ill-clothed or ill-dressed, from the cobbler to the cab-runner, was, to Hill's imagination, a man and a brother, a fellow-sufferer. So that he became, as it were, a champion of the fallen and oppressed, albeit to outward seeming only a self-assertive, ill-mannered young man, and an unsuccessful champion at that. Again and again a skirmish over the afternoon tea that the girl students had inaugurated left Hill with flushed cheeks and a tattered temper, and the debating society noticed a new quality of sarcastic bitterness in his speeches.

You will understand now how it was necessary, if only in the interests of humanity, that Hill should demolish Wedderburn in the forthcoming examination and outshine him in the eyes of Miss Haysman; and you will perceive, too, how Miss Haysman fell into some common feminine misconceptions. The Hill–Wedderburn quarrel, for in his unostentatious way Wedderburn reciprocated Hill's ill-veiled rivalry, became a tribute to her indefinable charm: she was the Queen of Beauty in a tournament of scalpels and stumpy pencils. To her confidential friend's secret annoyance, it even troubled her conscience, for she was a good girl, and painfully aware, through Ruskin[18] and contemporary fiction, how entirely men's activities are determined by women's attitudes. And if Hill never by any chance mentioned the topic of love to her, she only credited him with the finer modesty for that omission.

So the time came on for the second examination, and Hill's increasing pallor confirmed the general rumour that he was working hard. In the aerated bread shop[19] near South Kensington Station you would see him, breaking his bun and sipping his milk with his eyes intent upon a paper of closely written notes. In his bedroom there were propositions about buds and stems round his looking-glass, a diagram to catch his eye, if soap should chance to spare it, above his washing basin. He missed several meetings of the debating society, but he found the chance encounters with Miss Haysman in the spacious ways of the adjacent art museum, or in the little museum at the top of the College, or in the College corridors, more frequent and very restful. In particular, they used to meet in a little gallery full of wrought-iron chests and gates near the art library, and there Hill used to talk, under the gentle stimulus of her flattering attention, of Browning and his personal ambitions. A characteristic she found remarkable in him was his freedom from avarice. He contemplated quite calmly the prospect of living all his life on an income below a hundred pounds a year. But he was determined to be famous, to make, recognizably in his own proper person, the world a better place to live in. He took Bradlaugh and John Burns[20] for his leaders and models, poor, even impecunious, great men. But Miss Haysman thought that such lives were deficient on the aesthetic side, by which, though she did not know it, she meant good wallpaper and upholstery, pretty books, tasteful clothes, concerts, and meals nicely cooked and respectfully served.

At last came the day of the second examination, and the professor of botany, a fussy, conscientious man, rearranged all the tables in a long narrow laboratory to prevent copying, and put his demonstrator on a chair on a table (where he felt, he said, like a Hindu god),[21] to see all the cheating, and stuck a notice outside the door, 'Door closed', for no earthly reason that any human being could discover. And all the morning from ten till one the quill of Wedderburn shrieked defiance at Hill's, and the quills of the others chased their leaders in a tireless pack, and so also it was in the afternoon. Wedderburn was a little quieter than usual, and Hill's face was hot all day, and his overcoat bulged with textbooks and notebooks against the last moment's revision. And the next day, in the morning and in the afternoon, was the practical examination, when sections had to be cut and slides identified. In the morning Hill was depressed because he knew he had cut a thick section, and in the afternoon came the mysterious slip.

It was just the kind of thing that the botanical professor was always doing. Like the income tax, it offered a premium to the cheat. It was a preparation under the microscope, a little glass slip, held in its place on the stage of the instrument by light steel clips, and the inscription set forth that the slip was not to be moved. Each student was to go in turn to it, sketch it, write in his book of answers what he considered it to be, and return to his place. Now, to move such a slip is a thing one can do by a chance movement of the finger, and in a fraction of a second. The professor's reason for decreeing that the slip should not be moved depended on the fact that the object he wanted identified was characteristic of a certain tree-stem. In the position in which it was placed it was a difficult thing to recognize, but once the slip was moved so as to bring other parts of the preparation into view, its nature was obvious enough.

Hill came to this, flushed from a contest with staining reagents, sat down on the little stool before the microscope, turned the mirror to get the best light, and then, out of sheer habit, shifted the slip. At once he remembered the prohibition, and, with an almost continuous motion of his hands, moved it back, and sat paralysed with astonishment at his action.

Then, slowly, he turned his head. The professor was out of the room; the demonstrator sat aloft on his impromptu rostrum, reading the *Q. Jour. Mi. Sci.*;[22] the rest of the examinees were busy, and with their backs to him. Should he own up to the accident now? He knew quite clearly what the thing was. It was a lenticel, a characteristic preparation from the elder-tree. His eyes roved over his intent fellow-students and Wedderburn suddenly glanced over his shoulder at him with a queer expression in his eyes. The mental excitement that had kept Hill at an abnormal pitch of vigour these two days gave way to a curious nervous tension. His book of answers was beside him. He did not write down what the thing was, but with one eye at the microscope he began making a hasty sketch of it. His mind was full of this grotesque puzzle in ethics that had suddenly been sprung upon him. Should he identify it? or should he leave this question unanswered? In that case Wedderburn would probably come out first in the second result. How could he tell now whether he might not have identified the thing without shifting it? It was possible that Wedderburn had failed to recognize it, of course. Suppose Wedderburn too had shifted the slide? He looked up at the clock. There were fifteen minutes in which to make up his mind. He gathered up his book of answers and the coloured pencils he used in illustrating his replies and walked back to his seat.

He read through his manuscript, and then sat thinking and gnawing his knuckle. It would look queer now if he owned up. He *must* beat Wedderburn. He forgot the examples of those starry gentlemen, John Burns and Bradlaugh. Besides, he reflected, the glimpse of the rest of the slip he had had was after all quite accidental, forced upon him by chance, a kind of providential revelation rather than an unfair advantage. It was not nearly so dishonest to avail himself of that as it was of Broome, who believed in the efficacy of prayer, to pray daily for a first-class. 'Five minutes more,' said the demonstrator, folding up his paper and becoming observant. Hill watched the clock hands until two minutes remained; then he opened the book of answers, and, with hot ears and an affectation of ease, gave his drawing of the lenticel its name.

When the second pass list appeared, the previous positions of Wedderburn and Hill were reversed, and the spectacled girl in green, who knew the demonstrator in private life (where he was practically human), said that in the result of the two examinations taken together Hill had the advantage of a mark – 167 to 166 out of a possible 200. Everyone admired Hill in a way, though the suspicion of 'mugging' clung to him. But Hill was to find congratulations and Miss Haysman's enhanced opinion of him, and even the decided decline in the crest of Wedderburn, tainted by an unhappy memory. He felt a remarkable access of energy at first, and the note of a democracy marching to triumph returned to his debating society speeches; he worked at his comparative anatomy with tremendous zeal and effect, and he went on with his aesthetic education. But through it all, a vivid little picture was continually coming before his mind's eye – of a sneakish person manipulating a slide.

No human being had witnessed the act, and he was cocksure that no higher power existed to see it; but for all that it worried him. Memories are not dead things, but alive; they dwindle in disuse, but they harden and develop in all sorts of queer ways

if they are being continually fretted. Curiously enough, though
at the time he perceived clearly that the shifting was accidental,
as the days wore on his memory became confused about it, until
at last he was not sure – although he assured himself that he *was*
sure – whether the movement had been absolutely involuntary.
Then it is possible that Hill's dietary was conducive to morbid
conscientiousness; a breakfast frequently eaten in a hurry, a
midday bun, and, at such hours after five as chanced to be
convenient, such meat as his means determined, usually in a
chop-house in a back street off the Brompton Road. Occasionally he treated himself to threepenny or ninepenny classics,[23]
and they usually represented a suppression of potatoes or chops.
It is indisputable that outbreaks of self-abasement and emotional revival have a distinct relation to periods of scarcity. But
apart from this influence on the feelings, there was in Hill a
distinct aversion to falsity that the blasphemous Landport
cobbler had inculcated by strap and tongue from his earliest
years. Of one fact about professed atheists I am convinced; they
may be – they usually are – fools, void of subtlety, revilers of
holy institutions, brutal speakers, and mischievous knaves, but
they lie with difficulty. If it were not so, if they had the faintest
grasp of the idea of compromise, they would simply be liberal
churchmen. And, moreover, this memory poisoned his regard
for Miss Haysman. For she now so evidently preferred him
to Wedderburn that he felt sure he cared for her, and began
reciprocating her attentions by timid marks of personal regard;
at one time he even bought a bunch of violets, carried it about
in his pocket, and produced it with a stumbling explanation,
withered and dead, in the gallery of old iron. It poisoned, too,
the denunciation of capitalist dishonesty that had been one
of his life's pleasures. And, lastly, it poisoned his triumph in
Wedderburn. Previously he had been Wedderburn's superior in
his own eyes, and had raged simply at a want of recognition.
Now he began to fret at the darker suspicion of positive inferiority. He fancied he found justifications for his position in
Browning, but they vanished on analysis. At last – moved,
curiously enough, by exactly the same motive forces that had
resulted in his dishonesty – he went to Professor Bindon, and

made a clean breast of the whole affair. As Hill was a paid student, Professor Bindon did not ask him to sit down, and he stood before the professor's desk as he made his confession.

'It's a curious story,' said Professor Bindon, slowly realizing how the thing reflected on himself, and then letting his anger rise, – 'A most remarkable story. I can't understand your doing it, and I can't understand this avowal. You're a type of student – Cambridge men would never dream – I suppose I ought to have thought – Why *did* you cheat?'

'I didn't cheat,' said Hill.

'But you have just been telling me you did.'

'I thought I explained –'

'Either you cheated or you did not cheat.' –

'I said my motion was involuntary.'

'I am not a metaphysician, I am a servant of science – of fact. You were told not to move the slip. You did move the slip. If that is not cheating –'

'If I was a cheat,' said Hill, with the note of hysterics in his voice, 'should I come here and tell you?'

'Your repentance, of course, does you credit,' said Professor Bindon, 'but it does not alter the original facts.'

'No, sir,' said Hill, giving in in utter self-abasement.

'Even now you cause an enormous amount of trouble. The examination list will have to be revised.'

'I suppose so, sir.'

'Suppose so? Of course it must be revised. And I don't see how I can conscientiously pass you.'

'Not pass me?' said Hill. 'Fail me?'

'It's the rule in all examinations. Or where should we be? What else did you expect? You don't want to shirk the consequences of your own acts?'

'I thought, perhaps' – said Hill. And then, 'Fail me? I thought, as I told you, you would simply deduct the marks given for that slip.'

'Impossible!' said Bindon. 'Besides, it would still leave you above Wedderburn. Deduct only the marks – Preposterous! The Departmental Regulations distinctly say –'

'But it's my own admission, sir.'

'The Regulations say nothing whatever of the manner in which the matter comes to light. They simply provide –'

'It will ruin me. If I fail this examination, they won't renew my scholarship.'

'You should have thought of that before.'

'But, sir, consider all my circumstances –'

'I cannot consider anything. Professors in this College are machines. The Regulations will not even let us recommend our students for appointments. I am a machine, and you have worked me. I have to do –'

'It's very hard, sir.'

'Possibly it is.'

'If I am to be failed this examination, I might as well go home at once.'

'That is as you think proper.' Bindon's voice softened a little; he perceived he had been unjust, and, provided he did not contradict himself, he was disposed to amelioration. 'As a private person,' he said, 'I think this confession of yours goes far to mitigate your offence. But you have set the machinery in motion, and now it must take its course. I – I am really sorry you gave way.'

A wave of emotion prevented Hill from answering. Suddenly, very vividly, he saw the heavily-lined face of the old Landport cobbler, his father. 'Good God! What a fool I have been!' he said hotly and abruptly.

'I hope,' said Bindon, 'that it will be a lesson to you.'

But, curiously enough, they were not thinking of quite the same indiscretion.

There was a pause.

'I would like a day to think, sir, and then I will let you know – about going home, I mean,' said Hill, moving towards the door.

The next day Hill's place was vacant. The spectacled girl in green was, as usual, first with the news. Wedderburn and Miss Haysman were talking of a performance of *The Meistersingers*[24] when she came up to them.

'Have you heard?' she said.

'Heard what?'

'There was cheating in the examination.'

'Cheating!' said Wedderburn, with his face suddenly hot. 'How?'

'That slide' –

'Moved? Never!'

'It was. That slide that we weren't to move' –

'Nonsense!' said Wedderburn. 'Why! How could they find out? Who do they say – ?'

'It was Mr Hill.'

'*Hill!*'

'Mr Hill!'

'Not – surely not the immaculate Hill?' said Wedderburn, recovering.

'I don't believe it,' said Miss Haysman. 'How do you know?'

'I *didn't*,' said the girl in spectacles. 'But I know it now for a fact. Mr Hill went and confessed to Professor Bindon himself.'

'By Jove!' said Wedderburn. 'Hill of all people. But I am always inclined to distrust these philanthropists-on-principle' –

'Are you quite sure?' said Miss Haysman, with a catch in her breath.

'Quite. It's dreadful, isn't it? But, you know, what can you expect? His father is a cobbler.'

Then Miss Haysman astonished the girl in spectacles.

'I don't care. I will not believe it,' she said, flushing darkly under her warm-tinted skin. 'I will not believe it until he has told me so himself – face to face. I would scarcely believe it then,' and abruptly she turned her back on the girl in spectacles, and walked to her own place.

'It's true, all the same,' said the girl in spectacles, peering and smiling at Wedderburn.

But Wedderburn did not answer her. She was indeed one of those people who seem destined to make unanswered remarks.

THE PLATTNER STORY

Whether the story of Gottfried Plattner is to be credited or not, is a pretty question in the value of evidence. On the one hand, we have seven witnesses – to be perfectly exact, we have six and a half pairs of eyes, and one undeniable fact; and on the other we have – what is it? – prejudice, common sense, the inertia of opinion. Never were there seven more honest-seeming witnesses; never was there a more undeniable fact than the inversion of Gottfried Plattner's anatomical structure, and – never was there a more preposterous story than the one they have to tell! The most preposterous part of the story is the worthy Gottfried's contribution (for I count him as one of the seven). Heaven forbid that I should be led into giving countenance to superstition by a passion for impartiality, and so come to share the fate of Eusapia's[1] patrons! Frankly, I believe there is something crooked about this business of Gottfried Plattner; but what that crooked factor is, I will admit as frankly, I do not know. I have been surprised at the credit accorded to the story in the most unexpected and authoritative quarters. The fairest way to the reader, however, will be for me to tell it without further comment.

Gottfried Plattner is, in spite of his name, a free-born Englishman. His father was an Alsatian[2] who came to England in the Sixties, married a respectable English girl of unexceptionable antecedents, and died, after a wholesome and uneventful life (devoted, I understand, chiefly to the laying of parquet flooring), in 1887. Gottfried's age is seven-and-twenty. He is, by virtue of his heritage of three languages, Modern Languages Master in a small private school in the South of England. To the casual observer he is singularly like any other Modern Languages Master in any other small private school. His costume is neither very costly nor very fashionable, but, on the other hand, it is not markedly cheap or shabby; his complexion, like his height and his bearing, is inconspicuous. You would notice perhaps that, like the majority of people, his face was not absolutely symmetrical, his right eye a little larger than the left, and his jaw a trifle heavier on the right side. If you, as an ordinary careless person, were to bare his chest and feel his heart beating, you would probably find it quite like the heart of anyone else. But here you and the trained observer would part company. If you found his heart quite ordinary, the trained observer would find it quite otherwise. And once the thing was pointed out to you, you too would perceive the peculiarity easily enough. It is that Gottfried's heart beats on the right side of his body.

Now that is not the only singularity of Gottfried's structure, although it is the only one that would appeal to the untrained mind. Careful sounding of Gottfried's internal arrangements, by a well-known surgeon, seems to point to the fact that all the other unsymmetrical parts of his body are similarly misplaced. The right lobe of his liver is on the left side, the left on his right; while his lungs, too, are similarly contraposed. What is still more singular, unless Gottfried is a consummate actor we must believe that his right hand has recently become his left. Since the occurrences we are about to consider (as impartially as possible), he has found the utmost difficulty in writing except from right to left across the paper with his left hand. He cannot throw with his right hand, he is perplexed at meal times between knife and fork, and his ideas of the rule of the road – he is a cyclist[3] – are still a dangerous confusion. And there is not a scrap of evidence to show that before these occurrences Gottfried was at all left-handed.

There is yet another wonderful fact in this preposterous business. Gottfried produces three photographs of himself. You have him at the age of five or six, thrusting fat legs at you from under a plaid frock, and scowling. In that photograph his left eye is a little larger than his right, and his jaw is a trifle heavier on the left side. This is the reverse of his present living conditions. The photograph of Gottfried at fourteen seems to contradict these facts, but that is because it is one of those cheap 'Gem' photographs[4] that were then in vogue, taken direct upon metal, and therefore reversing things just as a looking-glass would. The third photograph represents him at one-and-twenty, and confirms the record of the others. There seems here evidence of the strongest confirmatory character that Gottfried has exchanged his left side for his right. Yet how a human being can be so changed, short of a fantastic and pointless miracle, it is exceedingly hard to suggest.

In one way, of course, these facts might be explicable on the supposition that Plattner has undertaken an elaborate mystification on the strength of his heart's displacement. Photographs may be fudged, and left-handedness imitated. But the character of the man does not lend itself to any such theory. He is quiet, practical, unobtrusive, and thoroughly sane from the Nordau[5] standpoint. He likes beer and smokes moderately, takes walking exercise daily, and has a healthily high estimate of the value of his teaching. He has a good but untrained tenor voice, and takes a pleasure in singing airs of a popular and cheerful character. He is fond, but not morbidly fond, of reading – chiefly fiction pervaded with a vaguely pious optimism, – sleeps well, and rarely dreams. He is, in fact, the very last person to evolve a fantastic fable. Indeed, so far from forcing this story upon the world, he has been singularly reticent on the matter. He meets inquirers with a certain engaging – bashfulness is almost the word, that disarms the most suspicious. He seems genuinely ashamed that anything so unusual has occurred to him.

It is to be regretted that Plattner's aversion to the idea of post-mortem dissection may postpone, perhaps for ever, the positive proof that his entire body has had its left and right sides transposed. Upon that fact mainly the credibility of his story hangs. There is no way of taking a man and moving him about *in space*, as ordinary people understand space, that will result in our changing his sides. Whatever you do, his right is still his right, his left his left. You can do that with a perfectly thin and flat thing, of course. If you were to cut a figure out of paper, any figure with a right and left side, you could change its sides simply by lifting it up and turning it over. But with a solid it is different. Mathematical theorists tell us that the only way in which the right and left sides of a solid body can be changed is by taking that body clean out of space as we know it, – taking it out of ordinary existence, that is, and turning it somewhere outside space. This is a little abstruse, no doubt, but anyone with a slight knowledge of mathematical theory will assure the reader of its truth. To put the thing in technical language, the curious inversion of Plattner's right and left sides is proof that he has moved out of our space into what is called the Fourth Dimension,[6] and that he has returned again to our world. Unless we choose to consider ourselves the victims of an elaborate and motiveless fabrication, we are almost bound to believe that this has occurred.

So much for the tangible facts. We come now to the account of the phenomena that attended his temporary disappearance from the world. It appears that in the Sussexville Proprietary School, Plattner not only discharged the duties of Modern Languages Master, but also taught chemistry, commercial geography, book-keeping, shorthand, drawing, and any other additional subject to which the changing fancies of the boys' parents might direct attention. He knew little or nothing of these various subjects, but in secondary as distinguished from Board or elementary schools,[7] knowledge in the teacher is, very properly, by no means so necessary as high moral character and gentlemanly tone. In chemistry he was particularly deficient, knowing, he says, nothing beyond the Three Gases[8] (whatever the three gases may be). As, however, his pupils began by knowing nothing, and derived all their information from him, this caused him (or anyone) but little inconvenience for several terms. Then a little boy named Whibble joined the school, who had been educated, it seems, by some mischievous relative into an inquiring habit of mind. This little boy followed Plattner's lessons with marked and sustained interest, and in order to exhibit his zeal on the subject, brought at various times substances for Plattner to analyse. Plattner, flattered by this evidence of his power to awaken interest and trusting to the boy's ignorance, analysed these and even made general statements as to their composition. Indeed he was so far stimulated by his pupil as to obtain a work upon analytical chemistry, and study it during his supervision of the evening's preparation. He was surprised to find chemistry quite an interesting subject.

So far the story is absolutely commonplace. But now the greenish powder comes upon the scene. The source of that greenish powder seems, unfortunately, lost. Master Whibble tells a tortuous story of finding it done up in a packet in a disused limekiln near the Downs. It would have been an excellent thing for Plattner, and possibly for Master Whibble's family, if a match could have been applied to that powder there and then. The young gentleman certainly did not bring it to school in a packet, but in a common eight-ounce graduated medicine bottle, plugged with masticated newspaper. He gave it to Plattner at the end of the afternoon school. Four boys had been detained after school prayers in order to complete some neglected tasks, and Plattner was supervising these in the small classroom in which the chemical teaching was conducted. The appliances for the practical teaching of chemistry in the Sussexville Proprietary School, as in most private schools in this country, are characterized by a severe simplicity. They are kept in a cupboard standing in a recess and having about the same capacity as a common travelling trunk. Plattner, being bored with his passive superintendence, seems to have welcomed the intervention of Whibble with his green powder as an agreeable diversion, and, unlocking this cupboard, proceeded at once with his analytical experiments. Whibble sat, luckily for himself, at a safe distance, regarding him. The four malefactors, feigning a profound absorption in their work, watched him furtively with the keenest interest. For even within the limits of the Three Gases, Plattner's practical chemistry was, I understand, temerarious.

They are practically unanimous in their account of Plattner's proceedings. He poured a little of the green powder into a test-tube, and tried the substance with water, hydrochloric acid, nitric acid, and sulphuric acid in succession. Getting no result, he emptied out a little heap – nearly half the bottleful, in fact – upon a slate and tried a match. He held the medicine bottle in his left hand. The stuff began to smoke and melt, and then – exploded with deafening violence and a blinding flash.

The five boys, seeing the flash and being prepared for catastrophes, ducked below their desks, and were none of them seriously hurt. The window was blown out into the playground, and the blackboard on its easel was upset. The slate was smashed to atoms. Some plaster fell from the ceiling. No other damage was done to the school edifice or appliances, and the boys at first, seeing nothing of Plattner, fancied he was knocked down and lying out of their sight below the desks. They jumped out of their places to go to his assistance, and were amazed to find the space empty. Being still confused by the sudden violence of the report, they hurried to the open door, under the impression that he must have been hurt, and have rushed out of the room. But Carson, the foremost, nearly collided in the doorway with the principal, Mr Lidgett.

Mr Lidgett is a corpulent, excitable man with one eye. The boys describe him as stumbling into the room mouthing some of those tempered expletives irritable schoolmasters accustom themselves to use – lest worse befall. 'Wretched mumchancer!' he said. 'Where's Mr Plattner?' The boys are agreed on the very words. ('Wobbler', 'snivelling puppy', and 'mumchancer' are, it seems, among the ordinary small change of Mr Lidgett's scholastic commerce.)

Where's Mr Plattner? That was a question that was to be repeated many times in the next few days. It really seemed as though that frantic hyperbole, 'blown to atoms', had for once realized itself. There was not a visible particle of Plattner to be seen; not a drop of blood nor a stitch of clothing to be found. Apparently he had been blown clean out of existence and left not a wrack behind.[9] Not so much as would cover a sixpenny piece, to quote a proverbial expression! The evidence of his absolute disappearance, as a consequence of that explosion, is indubitable.

It is not necessary to enlarge here upon the commotion excited in the Sussexville Proprietary School, and in Sussexville and elsewhere, by this event. It is quite possible, indeed, that some of the readers of these pages may recall the hearing of some remote and dying version of that excitement during the last summer holidays. Lidgett, it would seem, did everything in his power to suppress and minimize the story. He instituted a penalty of twenty-five lines for any mention of Plattner's name among the boys, and stated in the schoolroom that he was clearly aware of his assistant's whereabouts. He was afraid, he explains, that the possibility of an explosion happening, in spite of the elaborate precautions taken to minimize the practical teaching of chemistry, might injure the reputation of the school; and so might any mysterious quality in Plattner's departure. Indeed, he did everything in his power to make the occurrence seem as ordinary as possible. In particular, he cross-examined the five eye-witnesses of the occurrence so searchingly that they began to doubt the plain evidence of their senses. But, in spite of these efforts, the tale, in a magnified and distorted state, made a nine days' wonder in the district, and several parents withdrew their sons on colourable pretexts. Not the least remarkable point in the matter is the fact that a large number of people in the neighbourhood dreamed singularly vivid dreams of Plattner during the period of excitement before his return, and that these dreams had a curious uniformity. In almost all of them Plattner was seen, sometimes singly, sometimes in company, wandering about through a coruscating iridescence. In all cases his face was pale and distressed, and in some he gesticulated towards the dreamer. One or two of the boys, evidently under the influence of nightmare, fancied that Plattner approached them with remarkable swiftness, and seemed to look closely into their very eyes. Others fled with Plattner from the pursuit of vague and extraordinary creatures of a globular shape. But all these fancies were forgotten in inquiries and speculations when, on the Wednesday next but one after the Monday of the explosion, Plattner returned.

The circumstances of his return were as singular as those of his departure. So far as Mr Lidgett's somewhat choleric outline can be filled in from Plattner's hesitating statements, it would appear that on Wednesday evening, towards the hour of sunset, the former gentleman, having dismissed evening preparation, was engaged in his garden, picking and eating strawberries, a fruit of which he is inordinately fond. It is a large old-fashioned garden, secured from observation, fortunately, by a high and ivy-covered red-brick wall. Just as he was stooping over a particularly prolific plant, there was a flash in the air and a heavy thud, and before he could look round, some heavy body struck him violently from behind. He was pitched forward, crushing the strawberries he held in his hand, and with such force that his silk hat – Mr Lidgett adheres to the older ideas of scholastic costume – was driven violently down upon his forehead, and almost over one eye. This heavy missile, which slid over him sideways and collapsed into a sitting posture among the strawberry plants, proved to be our long-lost Mr Gottfried Plattner, in an extremely dishevelled condition. He was collarless and hatless, his linen was dirty, and there was blood upon his hands. Mr Lidgett was so indignant and surprised that he remained on all fours, and with his hat jammed down on his eye, while he expostulated vehemently with Plattner for his disrespectful and unaccountable conduct.

This scarcely idyllic scene completes what I may call the exterior version of the Plattner story – its exoteric aspect. It is quite unnecessary to enter here into all the details of his dismissal by Mr Lidgett. Such details, with the full names and dates and references, will be found in the larger report of these occurrences that was laid before the Society for the Investigation of Abnormal Phenomena.[10] The singular transposition of Plattner's right and left sides was scarcely observed for the first day or so, and then first in connection with his disposition to write from right to left across the blackboard. He concealed rather than ostended this curious confirmatory circumstance, as he considered it would unfavourably affect his prospects in a new situation. The displacement of his heart was discovered some months after, when he was having a tooth extracted under anaesthetics. He then, very unwillingly, allowed a cursory surgical examination to be made of himself, with a view to a brief account in the *Journal of Anatomy*.[11] That exhausts the statement of the material facts; and we may now go on to consider Plattner's account of the matter.

But first let us clearly differentiate between the preceding portion of this story and what is to follow. All I have told thus far is established by such evidence as even a criminal lawyer would approve. Every one of the witnesses is still alive; the reader, if he have the leisure, may hunt the lads out tomorrow, or even brave the terrors of the redoubtable Lidgett, and cross-examine and trap and test to his heart's content; Gottfried Plattner, himself, and his twisted heart and his three photographs are producible. It may be taken as proved that he did disappear for nine days as the consequence of an explosion; that he returned almost as violently, under circumstances in their nature annoying to Mr Lidgett, whatever the details of those circumstances may be; and that he returned inverted, just as a reflection returns from a mirror. From the last fact, as I have already stated, it follows almost inevitably that Plattner, during those nine days, must have been in some state of existence altogether out of space. The evidence to these statements is, indeed, far stronger than that upon which most murderers are hanged. But for his own particular account of where he had been, with its confused explanations and well-nigh self-contradictory details, we have only Mr Gottfried Plattner's word. I do not wish to discredit that, but I must point out – what so many writers upon obscure psychic phenomena fail to do – that we are passing here from the practically undeniable to that kind of matter which any reasonable man is entitled to believe or reject as he thinks proper. The previous statements render it plausible; its discordance with common experience tilts it towards the incredible. I would prefer not to sway the beam of the reader's judgement either way, but simply to tell the story as Plattner told it me.

He gave me his narrative, I may state, at my house at Chislehurst; and so soon as he had left me that evening, I went into my study and wrote down everything as I remembered it. Subsequently he was good enough to read over a typewritten copy, so that its substantial correctness is undeniable.

He states that at the moment of the explosion he distinctly thought he was killed. He felt lifted off his feet and driven forcibly backward. It is a curious fact for psychologists that he thought clearly during his backward flight, and wondered whether he should hit the chemistry cupboard or the black-board easel. His heels struck ground, and he staggered and fell heavily into a sitting position on something soft and firm. For a moment the concussion stunned him. He became aware at once of a vivid scent of singed hair, and he seemed to hear the voice of Lidgett asking for him. You will understand that for a time his mind was greatly confused.

At first he was distinctly under the impression that he was still in the classroom. He perceived quite distinctly the surprise of the boys and the entry of Mr Lidgett. He is quite positive upon that score. He did not hear their remarks, but that he ascribed to the deafening effect of the experiment. Things about him seemed curiously dark and faint, but his mind explained that on the obvious but mistaken idea that the explosion had engendered a huge volume of dark smoke. Through the dimness the figures of Lidgett and the boys moved, as faint and silent as ghosts. Plattner's face still tingled with the stinging heat of the flash. He was, he says, 'all muddled'. His first definite thoughts seem to have been of his personal safety. He thought he was perhaps blinded and deafened. He felt his limbs and face in a gingerly manner. Then his perceptions grew clearer, and he was astonished to miss the old familiar desks and other schoolroom furniture about him. Only dim, uncertain, grey shapes stood in the place of these. Then came a thing that made him shout aloud, and awoke his stunned faculties to instant activity. *Two of the boys, gesticulating, walked one after the other clean through him!* Neither manifested the slightest consciousness of his presence. It is difficult to imagine the sensation he felt. They came against him, he says, with no more force than a wisp of mist.

Plattner's first thought after that was that he was dead. Having been brought up with thoroughly sound views in these matters, however, he was a little surprised to find his body still about him. His second conclusion was that he was not dead, but that the others were: that the explosion had destroyed the Sussexville Proprietary School and every soul in it except himself. But that, too, was scarcely satisfactory. He was thrown back upon astonished observation.

Everything about him was extraordinarily dark: at first it seemed to have an altogether ebony blackness. Overhead was a black firmament. The only touch of light in the scene was a faint greenish glow at the edge of the sky in one direction, which threw into prominence a horizon of undulating black hills. This, I say, was his impression at first. As his eye grew accustomed to the darkness, he began to distinguish a faint quality of differentiating greenish colour in the circumambient night. Against this background the furniture and occupants of the classroom, it seems, stood out like phosphorescent spectres, faint and impalpable. He extended his hand, and thrust it without an effort through the wall of the room by the fireplace.

He describes himself as making a strenuous effort to attract attention. He shouted to Lidgett, and tried to seize the boys as they went to and fro. He only desisted from these attempts when Mrs Lidgett, whom he as an Assistant Master naturally disliked, entered the room. He says the sensation of being in the world, and yet not a part of it, was an extraordinarily disagreeable one. He compared his feelings not inaptly to those of a cat watching a mouse through a window. Whenever he made a motion to communicate with the dim, familiar world about him, he found an invisible, incomprehensible barrier preventing intercourse.

He then turned his attention to his solid environment. He found the medicine bottle still unbroken in his hand, with the remainder of the green powder therein. He put this in his pocket, and began to feel about him. Apparently, he was sitting on a boulder of rock covered with a velvety moss. The dark country about him he was unable to see, the faint, misty picture of the schoolroom blotting it out, but he had a feeling (due perhaps to a cold wind) that he was near the crest of a hill, and that a steep valley fell away beneath his feet. The green glow along the edge of the sky seemed to be growing in extent and intensity. He stood up, rubbing his eyes.

It would seem that he made a few steps, going steeply downhill, and then stumbled, nearly fell, and sat down again upon a jagged mass of rock to watch the dawn. He became aware that the world about him was absolutely silent. It was as still as it was dark, and though there was a cold wind blowing up the hill-face, the rustle of grass, the soughing of the boughs that should have accompanied it, were absent. He could hear, therefore, if he could not see, that the hillside upon which he stood was rocky and desolate. The green grew brighter every moment, and as it did so a faint, transparent blood-red mingled with, but did not mitigate, the blackness of the sky overhead and the rocky desolations about him. Having regard to what follows, I am inclined to think that that redness may have been an optical effect due to contrast. Something black fluttered momentarily against the livid yellow-green of the lower sky, and then the thin and penetrating voice of a bell rose out of the black gulf below him. An oppressive expectation grew with the growing light.

It is probable that an hour or more elapsed while he sat there, the strange green light growing brighter every moment, and spreading slowly, in flamboyant fingers, upward towards the zenith. As it grew, the spectral vision of *our* world became relatively or absolutely fainter. Probably both, for the time must have been about that of our earthly sunset. So far as his vision of our world went, Plattner by his few steps downhill, had passed through the floor of the classroom, and was now, it seemed, sitting in mid-air in the larger schoolroom downstairs. He saw the boarders distinctly, but much more faintly than he had seen Lidgett. They were preparing their evening tasks, and he noticed with interest that several were cheating with their Euclid riders[12] by means of a crib, a compilation whose existence he had hitherto never suspected. As the time passed they faded steadily, as steadily as the light of the green dawn increased.

Looking down into the valley, he saw that the light had crept far down its rocky sides, and that the profound blackness of the abyss was now broken by a minute green glow, like the light of a glow-worm. And almost immediately the limb of a huge heavenly body of blazing green rose over the basaltic undulations of the distant hills, and the monstrous hill-masses about him came out gaunt and desolate, in green light and deep, ruddy black shadows. He became aware of a vast number of ball-shaped objects drifting as thistledown drifts over the high ground. There were none of these nearer to him than the opposite side of the gorge. The bell below twanged quicker and quicker, with something like impatient insistence, and several lights moved hither and thither. The boys at work at their desks were now almost imperceptibly faint.

This extinction of our world, when the green sun of this other universe rose, is a curious point upon which Plattner insists. During the Other-World night it is difficult to move about, on account of the vividness with which the things of this world are visible. It becomes a riddle to explain why, if this is the case, we in this world catch no glimpse of the Other-World. It is due, perhaps, to the comparatively vivid illumination of this world of ours. Plattner describes the midday of the Other-World, at its brightest, as not being nearly so bright as this world at full moon, while its night is profoundly black. Consequently, the amount of light, even in an ordinary dark room, is sufficient to render the things of the Other-World invisible, on the same principle that faint phosphorescence is only visible in the profoundest darkness. I have tried, since he told me his story, to see something of the Other-World by sitting for a long space in a photographer's dark room at night. I have certainly seen indistinctly the form of greenish slopes and rocks, but only, I must admit, very indistinctly indeed. The reader may possibly be more successful. Plattner tells me that since his return he has seen and recognized places in the Other-World in his dreams, but this is probably due to his memory of these scenes. It seems quite possible that people with unusually keen eyesight may occasionally catch a glimpse of this strange Other-World about us.

However, this is a digression. As the green sun rose, a long street of black buildings became perceptible, though only darkly and indistinctly, in the gorge, and, after some hesitation, Plattner began to clamber down the precipitous descent towards them. The descent was long and exceedingly tedious, being so not only by the extraordinary steepness, but also by reason of the looseness of the boulders with which the whole face of the hill was strewn. The noise of his descent – now and then his heels struck fire from the rocks – seemed now the only sound in the universe, for the beating of the bell had ceased. As he drew nearer he perceived that the various edifices had a singular resemblance to tombs and mausoleums and monuments, saving only that they were all uniformly black instead of being white as most sepulchres are. And then he saw, crowding out of the largest building very much as people disperse from church, a number of pallid, rounded, pale-green figures. These scattered in several directions about the broad street of the place, some going through side alleys and reappearing upon the steepness of the hill, others entering some of the small black buildings which lined the way.

At the sight of these things drifting up towards him, Plattner stopped, staring. They were not walking, they were indeed limbless; and they had the appearance of human heads beneath which a tadpole-like body swung.[13] He was too astonished at their strangeness, too full indeed of strangeness, to be seriously alarmed by them. They drove towards him, in front of the chill wind that was blowing uphill, much as soap-bubbles drive before a draught. And as he looked at the nearest of those approaching, he saw it was indeed a human head, albeit with singularly large eyes, and wearing such an expression of distress and anguish as he had never seen before upon mortal countenance. He was surprised to find that it did not turn to regard him, but seemed to be watching and following some unseen moving thing. For a moment he was puzzled, and then it occurred to him that this creature was watching with its enormous eyes something that was happening in the world he had just left. Nearer it came, and nearer, and he was too astonished to cry out. It made a very faint fretting sound as it came close to him. Then it struck his face with a gentle pat – its touch was very cold – and drove past him, and upward towards the crest of the hill.

An extraordinary conviction flashed across Plattner's mind that this head had a strong likeness to Lidgett. Then he turned his attention to the other heads that were now swarming thickly up the hillside. None made the slightest sign of recognition. One or two, indeed, came close to his head and almost followed the example of the first, but he dodged convulsively out of the way. Upon most of them he saw the same expression of unavailing regret he had seen upon the first, and heard the same faint sounds of wretchedness from them. One or two wept, and one rolling swiftly uphill wore an expression of diabolical rage. But others were cold, and several had a look of gratified interest in their eyes. One, at least, was almost in an ecstasy of happiness. Plattner does not remember that he recognized any more likenesses in those he saw at this time.

For several hours, perhaps, Plattner watched these strange things dispersing themselves over the hills, and not till long after they had ceased to issue from the clustering black buildings in the gorge did he resume his downward climb. The darkness about him increased so much that he had a difficulty in stepping true. Overhead the sky was now a bright pale green. He felt neither hunger nor thirst. Later, when he did, he found a chilly stream running down the centre of the gorge, and the rare moss upon the boulders, when he tried it at last in desperation, was good to eat.

He groped about among the tombs that ran down the gorge, seeking vaguely for some clue to these inexplicable things. After a long time he came to the entrance of the big mausoleum-like building from which the heads had issued. In this he found a group of green lights burning upon a kind of basaltic altar, and a bell-rope from a belfry overhead hanging down into the centre of the place. Round the wall ran a lettering of fire in a character unknown to him. While he was still wondering at the purport of these things, he heard the receding tramp of heavy feet echoing far down the street. He ran out into the darkness again, but he could see nothing. He had a mind to pull the bell-rope, and finally decided to follow the footsteps. But although he ran far, he never overtook them; and his shouting was of no avail. The gorge seemed to extend an interminable distance. It was as dark as earthly starlight throughout its length, while the ghastly green day lay along the upper edge of its precipices. There were none of the heads, now, below. They were all, it seemed, busily occupied along the upper slopes. Looking up, he saw them drifting hither and thither, some hovering stationary, some flying swiftly through the air. It reminded him, he said, of 'big snowflakes'; only these were black and pale green.

In pursuing the firm, undeviating footsteps that he never overtook, in groping into new regions of this endless devil's dyke,[14] in clambering up and down the pitiless heights, in wandering about the summits, and in watching the drifting faces, Plattner states that he spent the better part of seven or eight days. He did not keep count, he says. Though once or twice he found eyes watching him, he had word with no living soul. He slept among the rocks on the hillside. In the gorge things earthly were invisible, because, from the earthly standpoint, it was far underground. On the altitudes, so soon as the earthly day began, the world became visible to him. He found himself sometimes stumbling over the dark green rocks, or arresting himself on a precipitous brink, while all about him the green branches of the Sussexville lanes were swaying; or, again, he seemed to be walking through the Sussexville streets, or watching unseen the private business of some household. And then it was he discovered, that to almost every human being in our world there pertained some of these drifting heads; that everyone in the world is watched intermittently by these helpless disembodiments.

What are they – these Watchers of the Living? Plattner never learned. But two that presently found and followed him, were like his childhood's memory of his father and mother. Now and then other faces turned their eyes upon him: eyes like those of dead people who had swayed him, or injured him, or helped him in his youth and manhood. Whenever they looked at him, Plattner was overcome with a strange sense of responsibility. To his mother he ventured to speak; but she made no answer. She looked sadly, steadfastly, and tenderly – a little reproachfully, too, it seemed – into his eyes.

He simply tells this story: he does not endeavour to explain. We are left to surmise who these Watchers of the Living may be, or if they are indeed the Dead, why they should so closely and passionately watch a world they have left for ever. It may be – indeed to my mind it seems just – that, when our life has closed, when evil or good is no longer a choice for us, we may

still have to witness the working out of the train of consequences we have laid. If human souls continue after death, then
surely human interests continue after death. But that is merely
my own guess at the meaning of the things seen. Plattner offers
no interpretation, for none was given him. It is well the reader
should understand this clearly. Day after day, with his head
reeling, he wandered about this green-lit world outside the
world, weary and, towards the end, weak and hungry. By day
– by our earthly day, that is – the ghostly vision of the old
familiar scenery of Sussexville, all about him, irked and worried
him. He could not see where to put his feet, and ever and again
with a chilly touch one of these Watching Souls would come
against his face. And after dark the multitude of these Watchers
about him, and their intent distress, confused his mind beyond
describing. A great longing to return to the earthly life that was
so near and yet so remote consumed him. The unearthliness of
things about him produced a positively painful mental distress.
He was worried beyond describing by his own particular followers. He would shout at them to desist from staring at him,
scold at them, hurry away from them. They were always mute
and intent. Run as he might over the uneven ground, they
followed his destinies.

On the ninth day, towards evening, Plattner heard the invisible footsteps approaching, far away down the gorge. He was
then wandering over the broad crest of the same hill upon
which he had fallen in his entry into this strange Other-World
of his. He turned to hurry down into the gorge, feeling his way
hastily, and was arrested by the sight of the thing that was
happening in a room in a back street near the school. Both of
the people in the room he knew by sight. The windows were
open, the blinds up, and the setting sun shone clearly into it, so
that it came out quite brightly at first, a vivid oblong of room,
lying like a magic-lantern picture upon the black landscape and
the livid green dawn. In addition to the sunlight, a candle had
just been lit in the room.

On the bed lay a lank man, his ghastly white face terrible
upon the tumbled pillow. His clenched hands were raised above
his head. A little table beside the bed carried a few medicine

bottles, some toast and water, and an empty glass. Every now and then the lank man's lips fell apart, to indicate a word he could not articulate. But the woman did not notice that he wanted anything, because she was busy turning out papers from an old-fashioned bureau in the opposite corner of the room. At first the picture was very vivid indeed, but as the green dawn behind it grew brighter and brighter, so it became fainter and more and more transparent.

As the echoing footsteps paced nearer and nearer, those footsteps that sound so loud in that Other-World and come so silently in this, Plattner perceived about him a great multitude of dim faces gathering together out of the darkness and watching the two people in the room. Never before had he seen so many of the Watchers of the Living. A multitude had eyes only for the sufferer in the room, another multitude, in infinite anguish, watched the woman as she hunted with greedy eyes for something she could not find. They crowded about Plattner, they came across his sight and buffeted his face, the noise of their unavailing regrets was all about him. He saw clearly only now and then. At other times the picture quivered dimly, through the veil of green reflections upon their movements. In the room it must have been very still, and Plattner says the candle flame streamed up into a perfectly vertical line of smoke, but in his ears each footfall and its echoes beat like a clap of thunder. And the faces! Two more particularly, near the woman's: one a woman's also, white and clear-featured, a face which might have once been cold and hard but which was now softened by the touch of a wisdom strange to earth. The other might have been the woman's father. Both were evidently absorbed in the contemplation of some act of hateful meanness, so it seemed, which they could no longer guard against and prevent. Behind were others, teachers it may be who had taught ill, friends whose influence had failed. And over the man, too – a multitude, but none that seemed to be parents or teachers! Faces that might once have been coarse, now purged to strength by sorrow! And in the forefront one face, a girlish one, neither angry nor remorseful but merely patient and weary, and, as it seemed to Plattner, waiting for relief. His powers of description fail him at the memory of this multitude of ghastly countenances. They gathered on the stroke of the bell. He saw them all in the space of a second. It would seem that he was so worked upon by his excitement that quite involuntarily his restless fingers took the bottle of green powder out of his pocket and held it before him. But he does not remember that.

Abruptly the footsteps ceased. He waited for the next and there was silence, and then suddenly, cutting through the unexpected stillness like a keen, thin blade, came the first stroke of the bell. At that the multitudinous faces swayed to and fro, and a louder crying began all about him. The woman did not hear; she was burning something now in the candle flame. At the second stroke everything grew dim, and a breath of wind, icy cold, blew through the host of watchers. They swirled about him like an eddy of dead leaves in the spring, and at the third stroke something was extended through them to the bed. You have heard of a beam of light. This was like a beam of darkness, and looking again at it, Plattner saw that it was a shadowy arm and hand.

The green sun was now topping the black desolations of the horizon, and the vision of the room was very faint. Plattner could see that the white of the bed struggled, and was convulsed; and that the woman looked round over her shoulder at it, startled.

The cloud of watchers lifted high like a puff of green dust before the wind, and swept swiftly downward towards the temple in the gorge. Then suddenly Plattner understood the meaning of the shadowy black arm that stretched across his shoulder and clutched its prey. He did not dare turn his head to see the Shadow behind the arm. With a violent effort, and covering his eyes, he set himself to run, made perhaps twenty strides, then slipped on a boulder and fell. He fell forward on his hands; and the bottle smashed and exploded as he touched the ground.

In another moment he found himself, stunned and bleeding, sitting face to face with Lidgett in the old walled garden behind the school.

*

There the story of Plattner's experiences ends. I have resisted, I believe successfully, the natural disposition of a writer of fiction to dress up incidents of this sort. I have told the thing as far as possible in the order in which Plattner told it to me. I have carefully avoided any attempt at style, effect, or construction. It would have been easy, for instance, to have worked the scene of the death-bed into a kind of plot in which Plattner might have been involved. But quite apart from the objectionableness of falsifying a most extraordinary true story, any such trite devices would spoil, to my mind, the peculiar effect of this dark world, with its livid green illumination and its drifting Watchers of the Living, which, unseen and unapproachable to us, is yet lying all about us.

It remains to add, that a death did actually occur in Vincent Terrace, just beyond the school garden, and, so far as can be proved, at the moment of Plattner's return. Deceased was a rate-collector and insurance agent. His widow, who was much younger than himself, married last month a Mr Whymper, a veterinary surgeon of Allbeeding. As the portion of this story given here has in various forms circulated orally in Sussexville, she has consented to my use of her name, on condition that I make it distinctly known that she emphatically contradicts every detail of Plattner's account of her husband's last moments. She burnt no will, she says, although Plattner never accused her of doing so: her husband made but one will, and that just after their marriage. Certainly, from a man who had never seen it, Plattner's account of the furniture of the room was curiously accurate.

One other thing, even at the risk of an irksome repetition, I must insist upon lest I seem to favour the credulous superstitious view. Plattner's absence from the world for nine days is, I think, proved. But that does not prove his story. It is quite conceivable that even outside space hallucinations may be possible. That, at least, the reader must bear distinctly in mind.

THE STORY OF THE LATE MR ELVESHAM

I set this story down, not expecting it will be believed, but, if possible, to prepare a way of escape for the next victim. He perhaps may profit by my misfortune. My own case, I know, is hopeless, and I am now in some measure prepared to meet my fate.

My name is Edward George Eden. I was born at Trentham,[1] in Staffordshire, my father being employed in the gardens there. I lost my mother when I was three years old and my father when I was five, my uncle, George Eden, then adopting me as his own son. He was a single man, self-educated, and well-known in Birmingham as an enterprising journalist; he educated me generously, fired my ambition to succeed in the world, and at his death, which happened four years ago, left me his entire fortune, a matter of about five hundred pounds after all out-going charges were paid. I was then eighteen. He advised me in his will to expend the money in completing my education. I had already chosen the profession of medicine, and through his posthumous generosity, and my good fortune in a scholarship competition, I became a medical student at University College, London.[2] At the time of the beginning of my story I lodged at 11A University Street, in a little upper room, very shabbily furnished, and draughty, overlooking the back of Shoolbred's premises.[3] I used this little room both to live in and sleep in, because I was anxious to eke out my means to the very last shillingsworth.

I was taking a pair of shoes to be mended at a shop in the Tottenham Court Road when I first encountered the little old man with the yellow face, with whom my life has now become so inextricably entangled. He was standing on the kerb, and staring at the number on the door in a doubtful way, as I opened it. His eyes – they were dull grey eyes, and reddish under the rims – fell to my face, and his countenance immediately assumed an expression of corrugated amiability.

'You come,' he said, 'apt to the moment. I had forgotten the number of your house. How do you do, Mr Eden?'

I was a little astonished at his familiar address, for I had never set eyes on the man before. I was annoyed, too, at his catching me with my boots under my arm. He noticed my lack of cordiality.

'Wonder who the deuce I am, eh? A friend, let me assure you. I have seen you before, though you haven't seen me. Is there anywhere where I can talk to you?'

I hesitated. The shabbiness of my room upstairs was not a matter for every stranger. 'Perhaps,' said I, 'we might walk down the street. I'm unfortunately prevented' – My gesture explained the sentence before I had spoken it.

'The very thing,' he said, and faced this way and then that. 'The street? Which way shall we go?' I slipped my boots down in the passage. 'Look here!' he said abruptly; 'this business of mine is a rigmarole. Come and lunch with me, Mr Eden. I'm an old man, a very old man, and not good at explanations, and what with my piping voice and the clatter of the traffic' –

He laid a persuasive skinny hand that trembled a little upon my arm.

I was not so old that an old man might not treat me to a lunch. Yet at the same time I was not altogether pleased by this abrupt invitation. 'I had rather' – I began. 'But *I* had rather,' he said, catching me up, 'and a certain civility is surely due to my grey hairs.' And so I consented, and went away with him.

He took me to Blavitski's; I had to walk slowly to accommodate myself to his paces; and over such a lunch as I had never tasted before, he fended off my leading questions, and I took a better note of his appearance. His clean-shaven face was lean and wrinkled, his shrivelled lips fell over a set of false teeth, and his white hair was thin and rather long; he seemed small to me – though, indeed, most people seemed small to me – and his shoulders were rounded and bent. And, watching him, I could not help but observe that he too was taking note of me, running his eyes, with a curious touch of greed in them, over me from my broad shoulders to my sun-tanned hands and up to my freckled face again. 'And now,' said he, as we lit our cigarettes, 'I must tell you of the business in hand.

'I must tell you, then, that I am an old man, a very old man.' He paused momentarily. 'And it happens that I have money that I must presently be leaving, and never a child have I to leave it to.' I thought of the confidence trick, and resolved I would be on the alert for the vestiges of my five hundred pounds. He proceeded to enlarge on his loneliness, and the trouble he had to find a proper disposition of his money. 'I have weighed this plan and that plan, charities, institutions, and scholarships, and libraries, and I have come to this conclusion at last,' – he fixed his eyes on my face, – 'that I will find some young fellow, ambitious, pure-minded, and poor, healthy in body and healthy in mind, and, in short, make him my heir, give him all that I have.' He repeated, 'Give him all that I have. So that he will suddenly be lifted out of all the trouble and struggle in which his sympathies have been educated, to freedom and influence.'

I tried to seem disinterested. With a transparent hypocrisy, I said, 'And you want my help, my professional services maybe, to find that person.'

He smiled and looked at me over his cigarette, and I laughed at his quiet exposure of my modest pretence.

'What a career such a man might have!' he said. 'It fills me with envy to think how I have accumulated that another man may spend –

'But there are conditions, of course, burdens to be imposed. He must, for instance, take my name. You cannot expect everything without some return. And I must go into all the circumstances of his life before I can accept him. He *must* be sound. I must know his heredity, how his parents and grandparents died, have the strictest inquiries made into his private morals' –

This modified my secret congratulations a little. 'And do I understand,' said I, 'that I – ?'

'Yes,' he said, almost fiercely. 'You. *You.*'

I answered never a word. My imagination was dancing wildly, my innate scepticism was useless to modify its transports. There was not a particle of gratitude in my mind – I did not know what to say nor how to say it. 'But why me in particular?' I said at last.

He had chanced to hear of me from Professor Haslar, he said, as a typically sound and sane young man, and he wished, as far as possible, to leave his money where health and integrity were assured.

That was my first meeting with the little old man. He was mysterious about himself; he would not give his name yet, he said, and after I had answered some questions of his, he left me at the Blavitski portal. I noticed that he drew a handful of gold coins from his pocket when it came to paying for the lunch. His insistence upon bodily health was curious. In accordance with an arrangement we had made I applied that day for a life policy in the Loyal Insurance Company for a large sum, and I was exhaustively overhauled by the medical advisers of that company in the subsequent week. Even that did not satisfy him, and he insisted I must be re-examined by the great Doctor Henderson. It was Friday in Whitsun week before he came to a decision. He called me down quite late in the evening, – nearly nine it was, – from cramming chemical equations for my Preliminary Scientific examination. He was standing in the passage under the feeble gas lamp, and his face was a grotesque interplay of shadows. He seemed more bowed than when I had first seen him, and his cheeks had sunk in a little.

His voice shook with emotion. 'Everything is satisfactory, Mr Eden,' he said. 'Everything is quite, quite satisfactory. And this night of all nights, you must dine with me and celebrate your – accession.' He was interrupted by a cough. 'You won't have long to wait, either,' he said, wiping his handkerchief across his lips, and gripping my hand with his long bony claw that was disengaged. 'Certainly not very long to wait.'

We went into the street and called a cab. I remember every incident of that drive vividly, the swift, easy motion, the contrast of gas and oil and electric light, the crowds of people in the streets, the place in Regent Street to which we went, and the sumptuous dinner we were served with there. I was disconcerted at first by the well-dressed waiter's glances at my rough clothes, bothered by the stones of the olives, but as the champagne warmed my blood, my confidence revived. At first the old man talked of himself. He had already told me his name in the cab; he was Egbert Elvesham, the great philosopher, whose name I had known since I was a lad at school. It seemed incredible to me that this man, whose intelligence had so early dominated mine, this great abstraction, should suddenly realize itself as this decrepit, familiar figure. I dare say every young fellow who has suddenly fallen among celebrities has felt something of my disappointment. He told me now of the future that the feeble streams of his life would presently leave dry for me, houses, copyrights, investments; I had never suspected that philosophers were so rich. He watched me drink and eat with a touch of envy. 'What a capacity for living you have!' he said; and then, with a sigh, a sigh of relief I could have thought it, 'It will not be long.'

'Ay,' said I, my head swimming now with champagne; 'I have a future perhaps – of a fairly agreeable sort, thanks to you. I shall now have the honour of your name. But you have a past. Such a past as is worth all my future.'

He shook his head and smiled, as I thought with half-sad appreciation of my flattering admiration. 'That future,' he said; 'would you in truth change it?' The waiter came with liqueurs. 'You will not perhaps mind taking my name, taking my position, but would you indeed – willingly – take my years?'

'With your achievements,' said I gallantly.

He smiled again. 'Kümmel – both,' he said to the waiter, and turned his attention to a little paper packet he had taken from his pocket. 'This hour,' said he, 'this after-dinner hour is the hour of small things. Here is a scrap of my unpublished wisdom.' He opened the packet with his shaking yellow fingers, and showed a little pinkish powder on the paper. 'This,' said he – 'well, you must guess what it is. But Kümmel – put but a dash of this powder in it – is Himmel.' His large greyish eyes watched mine with an inscrutable expression.

It was a bit of a shock to me to find this great teacher gave his mind to the flavour of liqueurs. However, I feigned a great interest in his weakness, for I was drunk enough for such small sycophancy.

He parted the powder between the little glasses, and rising suddenly with a strange unexpected dignity, held out his hand towards me. I imitated his action, and the glasses rang. 'To a quick succession,' said he, and raised his glass towards his lips.

'Not that,' I said hastily. 'Not that.'

He paused, with the liqueur at the level of his chin, and his eyes blazing into mine.

'To a long life,' said I.

He hesitated. 'To a long life,' said he, with a sudden bark of laughter, and with eyes fixed on one another we tilted the little glasses. His eyes looked straight into mine, and as I drained the stuff off, I felt a curiously intense sensation. The first touch of it set my brain in a furious tumult; I seemed to feel an actual physical stirring in my skull, and a seething humming filled my ears. I did not notice the flavour in my mouth, the aroma that filled my throat; I saw only the grey intensity of his gaze that burnt into mine. The draught, the mental confusion, the noise and stirring in my head, seemed to last an interminable time. Curious vague impressions of half-forgotten things danced and vanished on the edge of my consciousness. At last he broke the spell. With a sudden explosive sigh he put down his glass.

'Well?' he said.

'It's glorious,' said I, though I had not tasted the stuff.

My head was spinning. I sat down. My brain was chaos. Then my perception grew clear and minute as though I saw things in a concave mirror. His manner seemed to have changed into something nervous and hasty. He pulled out his watch and grimaced at it. 'Eleven-seven! And tonight I must – Seven – twenty-five. Waterloo! I must go at once.' He called for the bill, and struggled with his coat. Officious waiters came to our assistance. In another moment I was wishing him goodbye, over the apron of a cab, and still with an absurd feeling of minute distinctness, as though – how can I express it? – I not only saw but *felt* through an inverted opera-glass.

'That stuff,' he said. He put his hand to his forehead. 'I ought not to have given it to you. It will make your head split tomorrow. Wait a minute. Here.' He handed me out a little flat thing like a seidlitz-powder. 'Take that in water as you are going to bed. The other thing was a drug. Not till you're ready to go to bed, mind. It will clear your head. That's all. One more shake – Futurus!'

I gripped his shrivelled claw. 'Goodbye,' he said, and by the droop of his eyelids I judged he too was a little under the influence of that brain-twisting cordial.

He recollected something else with a start, felt in his breast-pocket, and produced another packet, this time a cylinder the size and shape of a shaving-stick. 'Here,' said he. 'I'd almost forgotten. Don't open this until I come tomorrow – but take it now.'

It was so heavy that I well-nigh dropped it. 'All ri'!' said I, and he grinned at me through the cab window as the cabman flicked his horse into wakefulness. It was a white packet he had given me, with red seals at either end and along its edge. 'If this isn't money,' said I, 'it's platinum or lead.'

I stuck it with elaborate care into my pocket, and with a whirling brain walked home through the Regent Street loiterers and the dark back streets beyond Portland Road. I remember the sensations of that walk very vividly, strange as they were. I was still so far myself that I could notice my strange mental state, and wonder whether this stuff I had had was opium – a drug beyond my experience. It is hard now to describe the peculiarity of my mental strangeness – mental doubling vaguely expresses it. As I was walking up Regent Street I found in my mind a queer persuasion that it was Waterloo station, and had an odd impulse to get into the Polytechnic as a man might get into a train. I put a knuckle in my eye, and it was Regent Street. How can I express it? You see a skilful actor looking quietly at you, he pulls a grimace, and lo! – another person. Is it too extravagant if I tell you that it seemed to me as if Regent Street had, for the moment, done that? Then, being persuaded it was Regent Street again, I was oddly muddled about some fantastic reminiscences that cropped up. 'Thirty years ago,' thought I, 'it was here that I quarrelled with my brother.' Then I burst out laughing, to the astonishment and encouragement of a group of night prowlers. Thirty years ago I did not exist, and never in my life had I boasted a brother. The stuff was surely liquid folly, for the poignant regret for that lost brother still clung to me. Along Portland Road the madness took another turn. I began to recall vanished shops, and to compare the street with what it used to be. Confused, troubled thinking was comprehensible enough after the drink I had taken, but what puzzled me were these curiously vivid phantasmal memories that had crept into my mind; and not only the memories that had crept in, but also the memories that had slipped out. I stopped opposite Stevens', the natural history dealer's, and cudgelled my brains to think what he had to do with me. A bus went by, and sounded exactly like the rumbling of a train. I seemed to be dipped into some dark, remote pit for the recollection. 'Of course,' said I, at last, 'he has promised me three frogs tomorrow. Odd I should have forgotten.'

Do they still show children dissolving views?[4] In those I remember one view would begin like a faint ghost, and grow and oust another. In just that way it seemed to me that a ghostly set of new sensations was struggling with those of my ordinary self.

I went on through Euston Road to Tottenham Court Road, puzzled, and a little frightened, and scarcely noticed the unusual way I was taking, for commonly I used to cut through the intervening network of back streets. I turned into University Street, to discover that I had forgotten my number. Only by a strong effort did I recall 11A, and even then it seemed to me that it was a thing some forgotten person had told me. I tried to steady my mind by recalling the incidents of the dinner, and for the life of me I could conjure up no picture of my host's face; I saw him only as a shadowy outline, as one might see oneself reflected in a window through which one was looking. In his place, however, I had a curious exterior vision of myself sitting at a table, flushed, bright-eyed, and talkative.

'I must take this other powder,' said I. 'This is getting impossible.'

I tried the wrong side of the hall for my candle and the matches, and had a doubt of which landing my room might be on. 'I'm drunk,' I said, 'that's certain,' and blundered needlessly on the staircase to sustain the proposition.

At the first glance my room seemed unfamiliar. 'What rot!' I said, and stared about me. I seemed to bring myself back by the effort and the odd phantasmal quality passed into the concrete familiar. There was the old looking-glass, with my notes on the albumens stuck in the corner of the frame, my old everyday suit of clothes pitched about the floor. And yet it was not so real after all. I felt an idiotic persuasion trying to creep into my mind, as it were, that I was in a railway carriage in a train just stopping, that I was peering out of the window at some unknown station. I gripped the bed-rail firmly to reassure myself. 'It's clairvoyance, perhaps,' I said. 'I must write to the Psychical Research Society.'[5]

I put the rouleau on my dressing-table, sat on my bed and began to take off my boots. It was as if the picture of my present sensations was painted over some other picture that was trying to show through. 'Curse it!' said I; 'my wits are going, or am I in two places at once?' Half-undressed, I tossed the powder into a glass and drank it off. It effervesced, and became a fluorescent amber colour. Before I was in bed my mind was already tranquillized. I felt the pillow at my cheek, and thereupon I must have fallen asleep.

I awoke abruptly out of a dream of strange beasts, and found myself lying on my back. Probably everyone knows that dismal emotional dream from which one escapes, awake indeed but strangely cowed. There was a curious taste in my mouth, a tired feeling in my limbs, a sense of cutaneous discomfort. I lay with my head motionless on my pillow, expecting that my feeling of strangeness and terror would probably pass away, and that I should then doze off again to sleep. But instead of that, my uncanny sensations increased. At first I could perceive nothing wrong about me. There was a faint light in the room, so faint that it was the very next thing to darkness, and the furniture stood out in it as vague blots of absolute darkness. I stared with my eyes just over the bedclothes.

It came into my mind that someone had entered the room to rob me of my rouleau of money, but after lying for some moments, breathing regularly to simulate sleep, I realized this was mere fancy. Nevertheless, the uneasy assurance of something wrong kept fast hold of me. With an effort I raised my head from the pillow, and peered about me at the dark. What it was I could not conceive. I looked at the dim shapes around me, the greater and lesser darknesses that indicated curtains, table, fireplace, bookshelves, and so forth. Then I began to perceive something unfamiliar in the forms of the darkness. Had the bed turned round? Yonder should be the bookshelves, and something shrouded and pallid rose there, something that would not answer to the bookshelves, however I looked at it. It was far too big to be my shirt thrown on a chair.

Overcoming a childish terror, I threw back the bedclothes and thrust my leg out of bed. Instead of coming out of my truckle-bed upon the floor, I found my foot scarcely reached the edge of the mattress. I made another step, as it were, and sat up on the edge of the bed. By the side of my bed should be the candle, and the matches upon the broken chair. I put out my hand and touched – nothing. I waved my hand in the darkness, and it came against some heavy hanging, soft and thick in texture, which gave a rustling noise at my touch. I grasped this and pulled it; it appeared to be a curtain suspended over the head of my bed.

I was now thoroughly awake, and beginning to realize that I was in a strange room. I was puzzled. I tried to recall the overnight circumstances, and I found them now, curiously enough, vivid in my memory: the supper, my reception of the little packages, my wonder whether I was intoxicated, my slow undressing, the coolness to my flushed face of my pillow. I felt a sudden distrust. Was that last night, or the night before? At any rate, this room was strange to me, and I could not imagine how I had got into it. The dim, pallid outline was growing paler, and I perceived it was a window, with the dark shape of

an oval toilet-glass against the weak intimation of the dawn
that filtered through the blind. I stood up, and was surprised by
a curious feeling of weakness and unsteadiness. With trembling
hands outstretched, I walked slowly towards the window, getting, nevertheless, a bruise on the knee from a chair by the way.
I fumbled round the glass, which was large, with handsome
brass sconces, to find the blind-cord. I could not find any. By
chance I took hold of the tassel, and with the click of a spring
the blind ran up.

I found myself looking out upon a scene that was altogether
strange to me. The night was overcast, and through the flocculent grey of the heaped clouds there filtered a faint half-light of
dawn. Just at the edge of the sky, the cloud-canopy had a
blood-red rim. Below, everything was dark and indistinct, dim
hills in the distance, a vague mass of buildings running up into
pinnacles, trees like spilt ink, and below the window a tracery
of black bushes and pale grey paths. It was so unfamiliar that
for the moment I thought myself still dreaming. I felt the toilet-
table; it appeared to be made of some polished wood, and was
rather elaborately furnished – there were little cut-glass bottles
and a brush upon it. There was also a queer little object, horse-
shoe-shaped it felt, with smooth, hard projections, lying in a
saucer. I could find no matches nor candlestick.

I turned my eyes to the room again. Now the blind was up,
faint spectres of its furnishing came out of the darkness. There
was a huge curtained bed, and the fireplace at its foot had a
large white mantel with something of the shimmer of marble.

I leant against the toilet-table, shut my eyes and opened them
again, and tried to think. The whole thing was far too real for
dreaming. I was inclined to imagine there was still some hiatus
in my memory as a consequence of my draught of that strange
liqueur; that I had come into my inheritance perhaps, and
suddenly lost my recollection of everything since my good fortune had been announced. Perhaps if I waited a little, things
would be clearer to me again. Yet my dinner with old Elvesham
was now singularly vivid and recent. The champagne, the
observant waiters, the powder, and the liqueurs – I could have
staked my soul it all happened a few hours ago.

And then occurred a thing so trivial and yet so terrible to me that I shiver now to think of that moment. I spoke aloud. I said, 'How the devil did I get here?' ... *And the voice was not my own.*

It was not my own, it was thin, the articulation was slurred, the resonance of my facial bones was different. Then to reassure myself I ran one hand over the other, and felt loose folds of skin, the bony laxity of age. 'Surely,' I said in that horrible voice that had somehow established itself in my throat, 'surely this thing is a dream!' Almost as quickly as if I did it involuntarily, I thrust my fingers into my mouth. My teeth had gone. My fingertips ran on the flaccid surface of an even row of shrivelled gums. I was sick with dismay and disgust.

I felt then a passionate desire to see myself, to realize at once in its full horror the ghastly change that had come upon me. I tottered to the mantel, and felt along it for matches. As I did so, a barking cough sprang up in my throat, and I clutched the thick flannel nightdress I found about me. There were no matches there, and I suddenly realized that my extremities were cold. Sniffing and coughing, whimpering a little perhaps, I fumbled back to bed. 'It is surely a dream,' I whimpered to myself as I clambered back, 'surely a dream.' It was a senile repetition. I pulled the bedclothes over my shoulders, over my ears, I thrust my withered hand under the pillow, and determined to compose myself to sleep. Of course it was a dream. In the morning the dream would be over, and I should wake up strong and vigorous again to my youth and studies. I shut my eyes, breathed regularly, and, finding myself wakeful, began to count slowly through the powers of three.[6]

But the thing I desired would not come. I could not get to sleep. And the persuasion of the inexorable reality of the change that had happened to me grew steadily. Presently I found myself with my eyes wide open, the powers of three forgotten, and my skinny fingers upon my shrivelled gums. I was indeed, suddenly and abruptly, an old man. I had in some unaccountable manner fallen through my life and come to old age, in some way I had been cheated of all the best of my life, of love, of struggle, of strength and hope. I grovelled into the pillow and tried to persuade myself that such hallucination was possible. Imperceptibly, steadily, the dawn grew clearer.

At last, despairing of further sleep, I sat up in bed and looked about me. A chill twilight rendered the whole chamber visible. It was spacious and well-furnished, better furnished than any room I had ever slept in before. A candle and matches became dimly visible upon a little pedestal in a recess. I threw back the bedclothes, and shivering with the rawness of the early morning, albeit it was summer-time, I got out and lit the candle. Then, trembling horribly so that the extinguisher rattled on its spike, I tottered to the glass and saw – *Elvesham's face!* It was none the less horrible because I had already dimly feared as much. He had already seemed physically weak and pitiful to me, but seen now, dressed only in a coarse flannel nightdress that fell apart and showed the stringy neck, seen now as my own body, I cannot describe its desolate decrepitude. The hollow cheeks, the straggling tail of dirty grey hair, the rheumy bleared eyes, the quivering, shrivelled lips, the lower displaying a gleam of the pink interior lining, and those horrible dark gums showing. You who are mind and body together at your natural years, cannot imagine what this fiendish imprisonment meant to me. To be young and full of the desire and energy of youth, and to be caught, and presently to be crushed in this tottering ruin of a body. . . .

But I wander from the course of my story. For some time I must have been stunned at this change that had come upon me. It was daylight when I did so far gather myself together as to think. In some inexplicable way I had been changed, though how, short of magic, the thing had been done, I could not say. And as I thought, the diabolical ingenuity of Elvesham came home to me. It seemed plain to me that as I found myself in his, so he must be in possession of *my* body, of my strength that is, and my future. But how to prove it? Then as I thought, the thing became so incredible even to me, that my mind reeled, and I had to pinch myself, to feel my toothless gums, to see myself in the glass, and touch the things about me before I could steady myself to face the facts again. Was all life hallucination? Was I indeed Elvesham, and he me? Had I been dreaming of Eden overnight? Was there any Eden? But if I was Elvesham, I should remember where I was on the previous morning, the name of the town in which I lived, what happened before the dream began. I struggled with my thoughts. I recalled the queer doubleness of my memories overnight. But now my mind was clear. Not the ghost of any memories but those proper to Eden could I raise.

'This way lies insanity!' I cried in my piping voice. I staggered to my feet, dragged my feeble, heavy limbs to the washhand-stand, and plunged my grey head into a basin of cold water. Then, towelling myself, I tried again. It was no good. I felt beyond all question that I was indeed Eden, not Elvesham. But Eden in Elvesham's body!

Had I been a man of any other age, I might have given myself up to my fate as one enchanted. But in these sceptical days miracles do not pass current. Here was some trick of psychology. What a drug and a steady stare could do, a drug and a steady stare, or some similar treatment, could surely undo. Men have lost their memories before. But to exchange memories as one does umbrellas! I laughed. Alas! not a healthy laugh, but a wheezing, senile titter. I could have fancied old Elvesham laughing at my plight, and a gust of petulant anger, unusual to me, swept across my feelings. I began dressing eagerly in the clothes I found lying about on the floor, and only realized when I was dressed that it was an evening suit I had assumed. I opened the wardrobe and found some ordinary clothes, a pair of plaid trousers, and an old-fashioned dressing-gown. I put a venerable smoking-cap on my venerable head, and, coughing a little from my exertions, tottered out upon the landing.

It was then perhaps a quarter to six, and the blinds were closely drawn and the house quite silent. The landing was a spacious one, a broad, richly-carpeted staircase went down into the darkness of the hall below, and before me a door ajar showed me a writing-desk, a revolving bookcase, the back of a study chair, and a fine array of bound books, shelf upon shelf.

'My study,' I mumbled, and walked across the landing. Then at the sound of my voice a thought struck me, and I went back to the bedroom and put in the set of false teeth. They slipped in with the ease of old habit. 'That's better,' said I, gnashing them, and so returned to the study.

The drawers of the writing-desk were locked. Its revolving top was also locked. I could see no indications of the keys, and there were none in the pockets of my trousers. I shuffled back at once to the bedroom, and went through the dress suit, and afterwards the pockets of all the garments I could find. I was very eager; and one might have imagined that burglars had been at work, to see my room when I had done. Not only were there no keys to be found, but not a coin, nor a scrap of paper – save only the receipted bill of the overnight dinner.

A curious weariness asserted itself. I sat down and stared at the garments flung here and there, their pockets turned inside out. My first frenzy had already flickered out. Every moment I was beginning to realize the immense intelligence of the plans of my enemy, to see more and more clearly the hopelessness of my position. With an effort I rose and hurried into the study again. On the staircase was a housemaid pulling up the blinds. She stared, I think, at the expression of my face. I shut the door of the study behind me, and, seizing a poker, began an attack upon the desk. That is how they found me. The cover of the desk was split, the lock smashed, the letters torn out of the pigeon-holes and tossed about the room. In my senile rage I had flung about the pens and other such light stationery, and overturned the ink. Moreover, a large vase upon the mantel had got broken – I do not know how. I could find no cheque-book, no money, no indications of the slightest use for the recovery of my body. I was battering madly at the drawers, when the butler, backed by two women-servants, intruded upon me.

That simply is the story of my change. No one will believe my frantic assertions. I am treated as one demented, and even at this moment I am under restraint. But I am sane, absolutely sane, and to prove it I have sat down to write this story minutely as the thing happened to me. I appeal to the reader, whether there is any trace of insanity in the style or method of the story he has been reading. I am a young man locked away in an old man's body. But the clear fact is incredible to everyone.

Naturally I appear demented to those who will not believe this, naturally I do not know the names of my secretaries, of the doctors who come to see me, of my servants and neighbours, of this town (wherever it is) where I find myself. Naturally I lose myself in my own house, and suffer inconveniences of every sort. Naturally I ask the oddest questions. Naturally I weep and cry out, and have paroxysms of despair. I have no money and no cheque-book. The bank will not recognize my signature, for I suppose that, allowing for the feeble muscles I now have, my handwriting is still Eden's. These people about me will not let me go to the bank personally. It seems, indeed, that there is no bank in this town, and that I have taken an account in some part of London. It seems that Elvesham kept the name of his solicitor secret from all his household – I can ascertain nothing. Elvesham was, of course, a profound student of mental science, and all my declarations of the facts of the case merely confirm the theory that my insanity is the outcome of overmuch brooding upon psychology. Dreams of the personal identity indeed! Two days ago I was a healthy youngster, with all life before me; now I am a furious old man, unkempt and desperate and miserable, prowling about a great luxurious strange house, watched, feared, and avoided as a lunatic by everyone about me. And in London is Elvesham beginning life again in a vigorous body, and with all the accumulated knowledge and wisdom of threescore and ten. He has stolen my life.

What has happened I do not clearly know. In the study are volumes of manuscript notes referring chiefly to the psychology of memory, and parts of what may be either calculations or ciphers in symbols absolutely strange to me. In some passages there are indications that he was also occupied with the philosophy of mathematics. I take it he has transferred the whole of his memories, the accumulation that makes up his personality, from this old withered brain of his to mine, and, similarly, that he has transferred mine to his discarded tenement. Practically, that is, he has changed bodies. But how such a change may be possible is without the range of my philosophy. I have been a materialist for all my thinking life, but here, suddenly, is a clear case of man's detachability from matter.

One desperate experiment I am about to try. I sit writing here before putting the matter to issue. This morning, with the help of a table-knife that I had secreted at breakfast, I succeeded in breaking open a fairly obvious secret drawer in this wrecked writing-desk. I discovered nothing save a little green glass phial containing a white powder. Round the neck of the phial was a label, and thereon was written this one word, '*Release*'. This may be – is most probably, poison. I can understand Elvesham placing poison in my way, and I should be sure that it was his intention so to get rid of the only living witness against him, were it not for this careful concealment. The man has practically solved the problem of immortality. Save for the spite of chance, he will live in my body until it has aged, and then, again, throwing that aside, he will assume some other victim's youth and strength. When one remembers his heartlessness, it is terrible to think of the ever-growing experience, that ... How long has he been leaping from body to body? ... But I tire of writing. The powder appears to be soluble in water. The taste is not unpleasant.

There the narrative found upon Mr Elvesham's desk ends. His dead body lay between the desk and the chair. The latter had been pushed back, probably by his last convulsions. The story was written in pencil, and in a crazy hand quite unlike his usual minute characters. There remain only two curious facts to record. Indisputably there was some connection between Eden and Elvesham, since the whole of Elvesham's property was bequeathed to the young man. But he never inherited. When Elvesham committed suicide, Eden was, strangely enough, already dead. Twenty-four hours before, he had been knocked down by a cab and killed instantly, at the crowded crossing at the intersection of Gower Street and Euston Road. So that the only human being who could have thrown light upon this fantastic narrative is beyond the reach of questions.

IN THE ABYSS

The lieutenant stood in front of the steel sphere and gnawed a piece of pine splinter. 'What do you think of it, Steevens?' he asked.

'It's an idea,' said Steevens, in the tone of one who keeps an open mind.

'I believe it will smash – flat,' said the lieutenant.

'He seems to have calculated it all out pretty well,' said Steevens, still impartial.

'But think of the pressure,' said the lieutenant. 'At the surface of the water it's fourteen pounds to the inch, thirty feet down it's double that; sixty, treble; ninety, four times; nine hundred, forty times; five thousand, three hundred – that's a mile – it's two hundred and forty times fourteen pounds; that's – let's see – thirty hundredweight – a ton and a half, Steevens; *a ton and a half* to the square inch. And the ocean where he's going is five miles deep. That's seven and a half ' –

'Sounds a lot,' said Steevens, 'but it's jolly thick steel.'

The lieutenant made no answer, but resumed his pine splinter. The object of their conversation was a huge ball of steel, having an exterior diameter of perhaps nine feet. It looked like the shot for some Titanic piece of artillery. It was elaborately nested in a monstrous scaffolding built into the framework of the vessel, and the gigantic spars that were presently to sling it overboard gave the stern of the ship an appearance that had raised the curiosity of every decent sailor who had sighted it, from the Pool of London to the Tropic of Capricorn. In two places, one above the other, the steel gave place to a couple of circular windows of enormously thick glass, and one of these, set in a steel frame of great solidity, was now partially un-screwed. Both the men had seen the interior of this globe for the first time that morning. It was elaborately padded with air cushions, with little studs sunk between bulging pillows to work the simple mechanism of the affair. Everything was elaborately padded, even the Myers apparatus[1] which was to absorb car-bonic acid and replace the oxygen inspired by its tenant, when he had crept in by the glass manhole, and had been screwed in. It was so elaborately padded that a man might have been fired from a gun in it with perfect safety. And it had need to be, for presently a man was to crawl in through that glass manhole, to be screwed up tightly, and to be flung overboard, and to sink down – down – down, for five miles, even as the lieutenant said. It had taken the strongest hold of his imagination; it made him a bore at mess; and he found Steevens, the new arrival aboard, a godsend to talk to about it, over and over again.

'It's my opinion,' said the lieutenant, 'that that glass will simply bend in and bulge and smash, under a pressure of that sort. Daubrée[2] has made rocks run like water under big pressures – and, you mark my words' –

'If the glass did break in,' said Steevens, 'what then?'

'The water would shoot in like a jet of iron. Have you ever felt a straight jet of high pressure water? It would hit as hard as a bullet. It would simply smash him and flatten him. It would tear down his throat, and into his lungs; it would blow in his ears' –

'What a detailed imagination you have!' protested Steevens, who saw things vividly.

'It's a simple statement of the inevitable,' said the lieutenant.

'And the globe?'

'Would just give out a few little bubbles, and it would settle down comfortably against the day of judgement, among the oozes and the bottom clay – with poor Elstead spread over his own smashed cushions like butter over bread.'

He repeated this sentence as though he liked it very much. 'Like butter over bread,' he said.

'Having a look at the jigger?' said a voice, and Elstead stood behind them, spick and span in white, with a cigarette between his teeth, and his eyes smiling out of the shadow of his ample hat-brim. 'What's that about bread and butter, Weybridge? Grumbling as usual about the insufficient pay of naval officers? It won't be more than a day now before I start. We are to get the slings ready today. This clean sky and gentle swell is just the kind of thing for swinging off a dozen tons of lead and iron, isn't it?'

'It won't affect you much,' said Weybridge.

'No. Seventy or eighty feet down, and I shall be there in a dozen seconds, there's not a particle moving, though the wind shriek itself hoarse up above, and the water lifts halfway to the clouds. No. Down there' – He moved to the side of the ship and the other two followed him. All three leant forward on their elbows and stared down into the yellow-green water.

'*Peace*,' said Elstead, finishing his thought aloud.

'Are you dead certain that clockwork will act?' asked Weybridge presently.

'It has worked thirty-five times,' said Elstead. 'It's bound to work.'

'But if it doesn't?'

'Why shouldn't it?'

'I wouldn't go down in that confounded thing,' said Weybridge, 'for twenty thousand pounds.'

'Cheerful chap you are,' said Elstead, and spat sociably at a bubble below.

'I don't understand yet how you mean to work the thing,' said Steevens.

'In the first place, I'm screwed into the sphere,' said Elstead, 'and when I've turned the electric light off and on three times to show I'm cheerful, I'm swung out over the stern by that crane, with all those big lead sinkers slung below me. The top lead weight has a roller carrying a hundred fathoms of strong cord rolled up, and that's all that joins the sinkers to the sphere, except the slings that will be cut when the affair is dropped. We use cord rather than wire-rope because it's easier to cut and more buoyant – necessary points, as you will see.

'Through each of these lead weights you notice there is a hole, and an iron rod will be run through that and will project six feet on the lower side. If that rod is rammed up from below, it knocks up a lever and sets the clockwork in motion at the side of the cylinder on which the cord winds.

'Very well. The whole affair is lowered gently into the water, and the slings are cut. The sphere floats, – with the air in it, it's lighter than water, – but the lead weights go down straight and the cord runs out. When the cord is all paid out, the sphere will go down too, pulled down by the cord.'

'But why the cord?' asked Steevens. 'Why not fasten the weights directly to the sphere?'

'Because of the smash down below. The whole affair will go rushing down, mile after mile, at a headlong pace at last. It would be knocked to pieces on the bottom if it wasn't for that cord. But the weights will hit the bottom, and directly they do, the buoyancy of the sphere will come into play. It will go on sinking slower and slower; come to a stop at last, and then begin to float upward again.

'That's where the clockwork comes in. Directly the weights smash against the sea bottom, the rod will be knocked through and will kick up the clockwork, and the cord will be rewound on the reel. I shall be lugged down to the sea bottom. There I shall stay for half an hour, with the electric light on, looking about me. Then the clockwork will release a spring knife, the cord will be cut, and up I shall rush again, like a soda-water bubble. The cord itself will help the flotation.'

'And if you should chance to hit a ship?' said Weybridge.

'I should come up at such a pace, I should go clean through it,' said Elstead, 'like a cannon ball. You needn't worry about that.'

'And suppose some nimble crustacean should wriggle into your clockwork' –

'It would be a pressing sort of invitation for me to stop,' said Elstead, turning his back on the water and staring at the sphere.

They had swung Elstead overboard by eleven o'clock. The day was serenely bright and calm, with the horizon lost in haze. The electric glare in the little upper compartment beamed cheerfully three times. Then they let him down slowly to the surface of the water, and a sailor in the stern-chains hung ready to cut the tackle that held the lead weights and the sphere together. The globe, which had looked so large on deck, looked the smallest thing conceivable under the stern of the ship. It rolled a little, and its two dark windows, which floated uppermost, seemed like eyes turned up in round wonderment at the people who crowded the rail. A voice wondered how Elstead liked the rolling. 'Are you ready?' sang out the commander. 'Ay, ay, sir!' 'Then let her go!'

The rope of the tackle tightened against the blade and was cut, and an eddy rolled over the globe in a grotesquely helpless fashion. Someone waved a handkerchief, someone else tried an ineffectual cheer, a middy was counting slowly, 'Eight, nine, ten!' Another roll, then with a jerk and a splash the thing righted itself.

It seemed to be stationary for a moment, to grow rapidly smaller, and then the water closed over it, and it became visible, enlarged by refraction and dimmer, below the surface. Before one could count three it had disappeared. There was a flicker of white light far down in the water, that diminished to a speck and vanished. Then there was nothing but a depth of water going down into blackness, through which a shark was swimming.

Then suddenly the screw of the cruiser began to rotate, the water was crickled, the shark disappeared in a wrinkled confusion, and a torrent of foam rushed across the crystalline clearness that had swallowed up Elstead. 'What's the idee?' said one A. B. to another.

'We're going to lay off about a couple of miles, 'fear he should hit us when he comes up,' said his mate.

The ship steamed slowly to her new position. Aboard her almost everyone who was unoccupied remained watching the breathing swell into which the sphere had sunk. For the next half-hour it is doubtful if a word was spoken that did not bear directly or indirectly on Elstead. The December sun was now high in the sky, and the heat very considerable.

'He'll be cold enough down there,' said Weybridge. 'They say that below a certain depth seawater's always just about freezing.'

'Where'll he come up?' asked Steevens. 'I've lost my bearings.'

'That's the spot,' said the commander, who prided himself on his omniscience. He extended a precise finger south-eastward. 'And this, I reckon, is pretty nearly the moment,' he said. 'He's been thirty-five minutes.'

'How long does it take to reach the bottom of the ocean?' asked Steevens.

'For a depth of five miles, and reckoning – as we did – an acceleration of two feet per second, both ways, is just about three-quarters of a minute.'

'Then he's overdue,' said Weybridge.

'Pretty nearly,' said the commander. 'I suppose it takes a few minutes for that cord of his to wind in.'

'I forgot that,' said Weybridge, evidently relieved.

And then began the suspense. A minute slowly dragged itself out, and no sphere shot out of the water. Another followed, and nothing broke the low oily swell. The sailors explained to one another that little point about the winding-in of the cord. The rigging was dotted with expectant faces. 'Come up, Elstead!' called one hairy-chested salt impatiently, and the others caught it up, and shouted as though they were waiting for the curtain of a theatre to rise.

The commander glanced irritably at them.

'Of course, if the acceleration's less than two,' he said, 'he'll be all the longer. We aren't absolutely certain that was the proper figure. I'm no slavish believer in calculations.'

Steevens agreed concisely. No one on the quarterdeck spoke for a couple of minutes. Then Steevens's watchcase clicked.

When, twenty-one minutes after, the sun reached the zenith, they were still waiting for the globe to reappear, and not a man aboard had dared to whisper that hope was dead. It was Weybridge who first gave expression to that realization. He spoke while the sound of eight bells[3] still hung in the air. 'I always distrusted that window,' he said quite suddenly to Steevens.

'Good God!' said Steevens; 'you don't think – ?'

'Well!' said Weybridge, and left the rest to his imagination.

'I'm no great believer in calculations myself,' said the commander dubiously, 'so that I'm not altogether hopeless yet.'

And at midnight the gunboat was steaming slowly in a spiral round the spot where the globe had sunk, and the white beam of the electric light fled and halted and swept discontentedly onward again over the waste of phosphorescent waters under the little stars.

'If his window hasn't burst and smashed him,' said Weybridge, 'then it's a cursed sight worse, for his clockwork has gone wrong, and he's alive now, five miles under our feet, down there in the cold and dark, anchored in that little bubble of his, where never a ray of light has shone or a human being lived, since the waters were gathered together.[4] He's there without food, feeling hungry and thirsty and scared, wondering whether he'll starve or stifle. Which will it be? The Myers apparatus is running out, I suppose. How long do they last?'

'Good Heavens!' he exclaimed; 'what little things we are! What daring little devils! Down there, miles and miles of water – all water, and all this empty water about us and this sky. Gulfs!' He threw his hands out, and as he did so, a little white streak swept noiselessly up the sky, travelled more slowly, stopped, became a motionless dot, as though a new star had fallen up into the sky. Then it went sliding back again and lost itself amidst the reflections of the stars and the white haze of the sea's phosphorescence.

At the sight he stopped, arm extended and mouth open. He shut his mouth, opened it again, and waved his arms with an impatient gesture. Then he turned, shouted 'El-stead ahoy!' to the first watch, and went at a run to Lindley and the searchlight. 'I saw him,' he said. 'Starboard there! His light's on, and he's just shot out of the water. Bring the light round. We ought to see him drifting, when he lifts on the swell.'

But they never picked up the explorer until dawn. Then they almost ran him down. The crane was swung out and a boat's crew hooked the chain to the sphere. When they had shipped the sphere, they unscrewed the manhole and peered into the darkness of the interior (for the electric light chamber was intended to illuminate the water about the sphere, and was shut off entirely from its general cavity).

The air was very hot within the cavity, and the indiarubber

at the lip of the manhole was soft. There was no answer to their eager questions and no sound of movement within. Elstead seemed to be lying motionless, crumpled up in the bottom of the globe. The ship's doctor crawled in and lifted him out to the men outside. For a moment or so they did not know whether Elstead was alive or dead. His face, in the yellow light of the ship's lamps, glistened with perspiration. They carried him down to his own cabin.

He was not dead, they found, but in a state of absolute nervous collapse, and besides cruelly bruised. For some days he had to lie perfectly still. It was a week before he could tell his experiences.

Almost his first words were that he was going down again. The sphere would have to be altered, he said, in order to allow him to throw off the cord if need be, and that was all. He had had the most marvellous experience. 'You thought I should find nothing but ooze,' he said. 'You laughed at my explorations, and I've discovered a new world!' He told his story in disconnected fragments, and chiefly from the wrong end, so that it is impossible to re-tell it in his words. But what follows is the narrative of his experience.

It began atrociously, he said. Before the cord ran out, the thing kept rolling over. He felt like a frog in a football. He could see nothing but the crane and the sky overhead, with an occasional glimpse of the people on the ship's rail. He couldn't tell a bit which way the thing would roll next. Suddenly he would find his feet going up, and try to step, and over he went rolling, head over heels, and just anyhow, on the padding. Any other shape would have been more comfortable, but no other shape was to be relied upon under the huge pressure of the nethermost abyss.

Suddenly the swaying ceased; the globe righted, and when he had picked himself up, he saw the water all about him greeny-blue, with an attenuated light filtering down from above, and a shoal of little floating things went rushing up past him, as it seemed to him, towards the light. And even as he looked, it grew darker and darker, until the water above was as dark as the midnight sky, albeit of a greener shade, and the water below black. And little transparent things in the water developed a faint glint of luminosity, and shot past him in faint greenish streaks.

And the feeling of falling! It was just like the start of a lift, he said, only it kept on. One has to imagine what that means, that keeping on. It was then of all times that Elstead repented of his adventure. He saw the chances against him in an altogether new light. He thought of the big cuttlefish people knew to exist in the middle waters, the kind of things they find half digested in whales at times, or floating dead and rotten and half eaten by fish. Suppose one caught hold and wouldn't let go. And had the clockwork really been sufficiently tested? But whether he wanted to go on or to go back mattered not the slightest now.

In fifty seconds everything was as black as night outside, except where the beam from his light struck through the waters, and picked out every now and then some fish or scrap of sinking matter. They flashed by too fast for him to see what they were. Once he thinks he passed a shark. And then the sphere began to get hot by friction against the water. They had under-estimated this, it seems.

The first thing he noticed was that he was perspiring, and then he heard a hissing growing louder under his feet, and saw a lot of little bubbles – very little bubbles they were – rushing upward like a fan through the water outside. Steam! He felt the window, and it was hot. He turned on the minute glow-lamp that lit his own cavity, looked at the padded watch by the studs, and saw he had been travelling now for two minutes. It came into his head that the window would crack through the conflict of temperatures, for he knew the bottom water is very near freezing.

Then suddenly the floor of the sphere seemed to press against his feet, the rush of bubbles outside grew slower and slower, and the hissing diminished. The sphere rolled a little. The window had not cracked, nothing had given, and he knew that the dangers of sinking, at any rate, were over.

In another minute or so he would be on the floor of the abyss. He thought, he said, of Steevens and Weybridge and the rest of them five miles overhead, higher to him than the very highest clouds that ever floated over land are to us, steaming slowly and staring down and wondering what had happened to him.

He peered out of the window. There were no more bubbles now, and the hissing had stopped. Outside there was a heavy blackness – as black as black velvet – except where the electric light pierced the empty water and showed the colour of it – a yellow-green. Then three things like shapes of fire swam into sight, following each other through the water. Whether they were little and near or big and far off he could not tell.

Each was outlined in a bluish light almost as bright as the lights of a fishing smack, a light which seemed to be smoking greatly, and all along the sides of them were specks of this, like the lighter portholes of a ship. Their phosphorescence seemed to go out as they came into the radiance of his lamp, and he saw then that they were little fish of some strange sort, with huge heads, vast eyes, and dwindling bodies and tails. Their eyes were turned towards him, and he judged they were following him down. He supposed they were attracted by his glare.

Presently others of the same sort joined them. As he went on down, he noticed that the water became of a pallid colour, and that little specks twinkled in his ray like motes in a sunbeam. This was probably due to the clouds of ooze and mud that the impact of his leaden sinkers had disturbed.

By the time he was drawn down to the lead weights he was in a dense fog of white that his electric light failed altogether to pierce for more than a few yards, and many minutes elapsed before the hanging sheets of sediment subsided to any extent. Then, lit by his light and by the transient phosphorescence of a distant shoal of fishes, he was able to see under the huge blackness of the super-incumbent water an undulating expanse of greyish-white ooze, broken here and there by tangled thickets of a growth of sea lilies, waving hungry tentacles in the air.

Farther away were the graceful, translucent outlines of a group of gigantic sponges. About this floor there were scattered a number of bristling flattish tufts of rich purple and black, which he decided must be some sort of sea-urchin, and small, large-eyed or blind things having a curious resemblance, some to woodlice, and others to lobsters, crawled sluggishly across the track of the light and vanished into the obscurity again, leaving furrowed trails behind them.

Then suddenly the hovering swarm of little fishes veered about and came towards him as a flight of starlings might do. They passed over him like a phosphorescent snow, and then he saw behind them some larger creature advancing towards the sphere.

At first he could see it only dimly, a faintly moving figure remotely suggestive of a walking man, and then it came into the spray of light that the lamp shot out. As the glare struck it, it shut its eyes, dazzled. He stared in rigid astonishment.

It was a strange vertebrated animal. Its dark purple head was dimly suggestive of a chameleon, but it had such a high forehead and such a braincase as no reptile ever displayed before; the vertical pitch of its face gave it a most extraordinary resemblance to a human being.

Two large and protruding eyes projected from sockets in chameleon fashion, and it had a broad reptilian mouth with horny lips beneath its little nostrils. In the position of the ears were two huge gill-covers, and out of these floated a branching tree of coralline filaments, almost like the tree-like gills that very young rays and sharks possess.

But the humanity of the face was not the most extraordinary thing about the creature. It was a biped; its almost globular body was poised on a tripod of two frog-like legs and a long thick tail, and its fore limbs, which grotesquely caricatured the human hand, much as a frog's do, carried a long shaft of bone, tipped with copper. The colour of the creature was variegated; its head, hands, and legs were purple; but its skin, which hung loosely upon it, even as clothes might do, was a phosphorescent grey. And it stood there blinded by the light.

At last this unknown creature of the abyss blinked its eyes open, and, shading them with its disengaged hand, opened its mouth and gave vent to a shouting noise, articulate almost as speech might be, that penetrated even the steel case and padded jacket of the sphere. How a shouting may be accomplished without lungs Elstead does not profess to explain. It then moved sideways out of the glare into the mystery of shadow that bordered it on either side, and Elstead felt rather than saw that it was coming towards him. Fancying the light had attracted it, he turned the switch that cut off the current. In another moment something soft dabbed upon the steel, and the globe swayed.

Then the shouting was repeated, and it seemed to him that a distant echo answered it. The dabbing recurred, and the globe swayed and ground against the spindle over which the wire was rolled. He stood in the blackness and peered out into the everlasting night of the abyss. And presently he saw, very faint and remote, other phosphorescent quasi-human forms hurrying towards him.

Hardly knowing what he did, he felt about in his swaying prison for the stud of the exterior electric light, and came by accident against his own small glow-lamp in its padded recess. The sphere twisted, and then threw him down; he heard shouts like shouts of surprise, and when he rose to his feet, he saw two pairs of stalked eyes peering into the lower window and reflecting his light.

In another moment hands were dabbing vigorously at his steel casing, and there was a sound, horrible enough in his position, of the metal protection of the clockwork being vigorously hammered. That, indeed, sent his heart into his mouth, for if these strange creatures succeeded in stopping that, his release would never occur. Scarcely had he thought as much when he felt the sphere sway violently, and the floor of it press hard against his feet. He turned off the small glow-lamp that lit the interior, and sent the ray of the large light in the separate compartment out into the water. The sea-floor and the man-like creatures had disappeared, and a couple of fish chasing each other dropped suddenly by the window.

He thought at once that these strange denizens of the deep sea had broken the rope, and that he had escaped. He drove up faster and faster, and then stopped with a jerk that sent him flying against the padded roof of his prison. For half a minute, perhaps, he was too astonished to think.

Then he felt that the sphere was spinning slowly, and rocking, and it seemed to him that it was also being drawn through the water. By crouching close to the window, he managed to make his weight effective and roll that part of the sphere downward, but he could see nothing save the pale ray of his light striking down ineffectively into the darkness. It occurred to him that he would see more if he turned the lamp off, and allowed his eyes to grow accustomed to the profound obscurity.

In this he was wise. After some minutes the velvety blackness became a translucent blackness, and then, far away, and as faint as the zodiacal light of an English summer evening, he saw shapes moving below. He judged these creatures had detached his cable, and were towing him along the sea bottom.

And then he saw something faint and remote across the undulations of the submarine plain, a broad horizon of pale luminosity that extended this way and that way as far as the range of his little window permitted him to see. To this he was being towed, as a balloon might be towed by men out of the open country into a town. He approached it very slowly, and very slowly the dim irradiation was gathered together into more definite shapes.

It was nearly five o'clock before he came over this luminous area, and by that time he could make out an arrangement suggestive of streets and houses grouped about a vast roofless erection that was grotesquely suggestive of a ruined abbey. It was spread out like a map below him. The houses were all roofless enclosures of walls, and their substance being, as he afterwards saw, of phosphorescent bones, gave the place an appearance as if it were built of drowned moonshine.

Among the inner caves of the place waving trees of crinoid stretched their tentacles, and tall, slender, glassy sponges shot like shining minarets and lilies of filmy light out of the general glow of the city. In the open spaces of the place he could see a stirring movement as of crowds of people, but he was too many fathoms above them to distinguish the individuals in those crowds.

Then slowly they pulled him down, and as they did so, the details of the place crept slowly upon his apprehension. He saw that the courses of the cloudy buildings were marked out with beaded lines of round objects, and then he perceived that at several points below him, in broad open spaces, were forms like the encrusted shapes of ships.

Slowly and surely he was drawn down, and the forms below him became brighter, clearer, more distinct. He was being pulled down, he perceived, towards the large building in the centre of the town, and he could catch a glimpse ever and again of the multitudinous forms that were lugging at his cord. He was astonished to see that the rigging of one of the ships, which formed such a prominent feature of the place, was crowded with a host of gesticulating figures regarding him, and then the walls of the great building rose about him silently, and hid the city from his eyes.

And such walls they were, of water-logged wood, and twisted wire-rope, and iron spars, and copper, and the bones and skulls of dead men. The skulls ran in zigzag lines and spirals and fantastic curves over the building; and in and out of their eye-sockets, and over the whole surface of the place, lurked and played a multitude of silvery little fishes.

Suddenly his ears were filled with a low shouting and a noise like the violent blowing of horns, and this gave place to a fantastic chant. Down the sphere sank, past the huge pointed windows, through which he saw vaguely a great number of these strange, ghostlike people regarding him, and at last he came to rest, as it seemed, on a kind of altar that stood in the centre of the place.

And now he was at such a level that he could see these strange people of the abyss plainly once more. To his astonishment, he perceived that they were prostrating themselves before him, all save one, dressed as it seemed in a robe of placoid scales, and crowned with a luminous diadem, who stood with his reptilian mouth opening and shutting, as though he led the chanting of the worshippers.

A curious impulse made Elstead turn on his small glow-lamp again, so that he became visible to these creatures of the abyss, albeit the glare made them disappear forthwith into night. At this sudden sight of him, the chanting gave place to a tumult of exultant shouts; and Elstead, being anxious to watch them, turned his light off again, and vanished from before their eyes.

But for a time he was too blind to make out what they were doing, and when at last he could distinguish them, they were kneeling again. And thus they continued worshipping him, without rest or intermission, for a space of three hours.

Most circumstantial was Elstead's account of this astounding city and its people, these people of perpetual night, who have never seen sun or moon or stars, green vegetation, nor any living, air-breathing creatures, who know nothing of fire, nor any light but the phosphorescent light of living things.

Startling as is his story, it is yet more startling to find that scientific men, of such eminence as Adams and Jenkins, find nothing incredible in it. They tell me they see no reason why intelligent, water-breathing, vertebrated creatures, inured to a low temperature and enormous pressure, and of such a heavy structure, that neither alive nor dead would they float, might not live upon the bottom of the deep sea, and quite unsuspected by us, descendants like ourselves of the great Theriomorpha of the New Red Sandstone age.

We should be known to them, however, as strange, meteoric creatures, wont to fall catastrophically dead out of the mysterious blackness of their watery sky. And not only we ourselves, but our ships, our metals, our appliances, would come raining down out of the night. Sometimes sinking things would smite down and crush them, as if it were the judgement of some unseen power above, and sometimes would come things of the utmost rarity or utility, or shapes of inspiring suggestion. One can understand, perhaps, something of their behaviour at the descent of a living man, if one thinks what a barbaric people might do, to whom an enhaloed, shining creature came suddenly out of the sky.

At one time or another Elstead probably told the officers of the *Ptarmigan* every detail of his strange twelve hours in the abyss. That he also intended to write them down is certain, but he never did, and so unhappily we have to piece together the discrepant fragments of his story from the reminiscences of Commander Simmons, Weybridge, Steevens, Lindley, and the others.

We see the thing darkly in fragmentary glimpses – the huge

ghostly building, the bowing, chanting people, with their dark chameleon-like heads and faintly luminous clothing, and Elstead, with his light turned on again, vainly trying to convey to their minds that the cord by which the sphere was held was to be severed. Minute after minute slipped away, and Elstead, looking at his watch, was horrified to find that he had oxygen only for four hours more. But the chant in his honour kept on as remorselessly as if it was the marching song of his approaching death.

The manner of his release he does not understand, but to judge by the end of cord that hung from the sphere, it had been cut through by rubbing against the edge of the altar. Abruptly the sphere rolled over, and he swept up, out of their world, as an ethereal creature clothed in a vacuum would sweep through our own atmosphere back to its native ether again. He must have torn out of their sight as a hydrogen bubble hastens upward from our air. A strange ascension it must have seemed to them.

The sphere rushed up with even greater velocity than, when weighted with the lead sinkers, it had rushed down. It became exceedingly hot. It drove up with the windows uppermost, and he remembers the torrent of bubbles frothing against the glass. Every moment he expected this to fly. Then suddenly something like a huge wheel seemed to be released in his head, the padded compartment began spinning about him, and he fainted. His next recollection was of his cabin, and of the doctor's voice.

But that is the substance of the extraordinary story that Elstead related in fragments to the officers of the *Ptarmigan*. He promised to write it all down at a later date. His mind was chiefly occupied with the improvement of his apparatus, which was effected at Rio.

It remains only to tell that on February 2, 1896, he made his second descent into the ocean abyss, with the improvements his first experience suggested. What happened we shall probably never know. He never returned. The *Ptarmigan* beat about over the point of his submersion, seeking him in vain for thirteen days. Then she returned to Rio, and the news was telegraphed to his friends. So the matter remains for the present. But it is hardly probable that no further attempt will be made to verify his strange story of these hitherto unsuspected cities of the deep sea.

THE SEA RAIDERS

Until the extraordinary affair at Sidmouth, the peculiar species
Haploteuthis ferox[1] was known to science only generically, on
the strength of a half-digested tentacle obtained near the Azores,
and a decaying body pecked by birds and nibbled by fish, found
early in 1896 by Mr Jennings, near Land's End.

In no department of zoological science, indeed, are we quite
so much in the dark as with regard to the deep-sea cephalopods. A mere accident, for instance, it was that led to the Prince
of Monaco's discovery[2] of nearly a dozen new forms in the
summer of 1895, a discovery in which the before-mentioned
tentacle was included. It chanced that a cachalot was killed
off Terceira by some sperm whalers, and in its last struggles
charged almost to the Prince's yacht, missed it, rolled under,
and died within twenty yards of his rudder. And in its agony
it threw up a number of large objects, which the Prince,
dimly perceiving they were strange and important, was, by a
happy expedient, able to secure before they sank. He set his
screws in motion, and kept them circling in the vortices thus
created until a boat could be lowered. And these specimens
were whole cephalopods and fragments of cephalopods, some
of gigantic proportions, and almost all of them unknown to
science!

It would seem, indeed, that these large and agile creatures,
living in the middle depths of the sea, must, to a large extent,
for ever remain unknown to us, since under water they are
too nimble for nets, and it is only by such rare unlooked-for
accidents that specimens can be obtained. In the case of

Haploteuthis ferox, for instance, we are still altogether ignorant
of its habitat, as ignorant as we are of the breeding-ground of
the herring or the sea-ways of the salmon. And zoologists are
altogether at a loss to account for its sudden appearance on our
coast. Possibly it was the stress of a hunger migration that drove
it hither out of the deep. But it will be, perhaps, better to avoid
necessarily inconclusive discussion, and to proceed at once with
our narrative.

The first human being to set eyes upon a living *Haploteuthis*
– the first human being to survive, that is, for there can be little
doubt now that the wave of bathing fatalities and boating
accidents that travelled along the coast of Cornwall and Devon
in early May was due to this cause – was a retired tea-dealer of
the name of Fison, who was stopping at a Sidmouth boarding-
house. It was in the afternoon, and he was walking along the
cliff path between Sidmouth and Ladram Bay. The cliffs in this
direction are very high, but down the red face of them in one
place a kind of ladder staircase has been made. He was near
this when his attention was attracted by what at first he thought
to be a cluster of birds struggling over a fragment of food that
caught the sunlight, and glistened pinkish-white. The tide was
right out, and this object was not only far below him, but
remote across a broad waste of rock reefs covered with dark
seaweed and interspersed with silvery shining tidal pools. And
he was, moreover, dazzled by the brightness of the further
water.

In a minute, regarding this again, he perceived that his judgement was in fault, for over this struggle circled a number of
birds, jackdaws and gulls for the most part, the latter gleaming
blindingly when the sunlight smote their wings, and they
seemed minute in comparison with it. And his curiosity was,
perhaps, aroused all the more strongly because of his first
insufficient explanations.

As he had nothing better to do than amuse himself, he decided
to make this object, whatever it was, the goal of his afternoon
walk, instead of Ladram Bay, conceiving it might perhaps be a
great fish of some sort, stranded by some chance, and flapping
about in its distress. And so he hurried down the long steep

ladder, stopping at intervals of thirty feet or so to take breath and scan the mysterious movement.

At the foot of the cliff he was, of course, nearer his object than he had been; but, on the other hand, it now came up against the incandescent sky, beneath the sun, so as to seem dark and indistinct. Whatever was pinkish of it was now hidden by a skerry of weedy boulders. But he perceived that it was made up of seven rounded bodies, distinct or connected, and that the birds kept up a constant croaking and screaming, but seemed afraid to approach it too closely.

Mr Fison, torn by curiosity, began picking his way across the wave-worn rocks, and, finding the wet seaweed that covered them thickly rendered them extremely slippery, he stopped, removed his shoes and socks, and coiled his trousers above his knees. His object was, of course, merely to avoid stumbling into the rocky pools about him, and perhaps he was rather glad, as all men are, of an excuse to resume, even for a moment, the sensations of his boyhood. At any rate, it is to this, no doubt, that he owes his life.

He approached his mark with all the assurance which the absolute security of this country against all forms of animal life gives its inhabitants. The round bodies moved to and fro, but it was only when he surmounted the skerry of boulders I have mentioned that he realized the horrible nature of the discovery. It came upon him with some suddenness.

The rounded bodies fell apart as he came into sight over the ridge, and displayed the pinkish object to be the partially devoured body of a human being, but whether of a man or woman he was unable to say. And the rounded bodies were new and ghastly-looking creatures, in shape somewhat resembling an octopus, and with huge and very long and flexible tentacles, coiled copiously on the ground. The skin had a glistening texture, unpleasant to see, like shiny leather. The downward bend of the tentacle-surrounded mouth, the curious excrescence at the bend, the tentacles, and the large intelligent eyes, gave the creatures a grotesque suggestion of a face.[3] They were the size of a fair-sized swine about the body, and the tentacles seemed to him to be many feet in length. There were, he thinks, seven or eight at least of the creatures. Twenty yards beyond them, amid the surf of the now returning tide, two others were emerging from the sea.

Their bodies lay flatly on the rocks, and their eyes regarded him with evil interest; but it does not appear that Mr Fison was afraid, or that he realized that he was in any danger. Possibly his confidence is to be ascribed to the limpness of their attitudes. But he was horrified, of course, and intensely excited and indignant at such revolting creatures preying upon human flesh. He thought they had chanced upon a drowned body. He shouted to them, with the idea of driving them off, and, finding they did not budge, cast about him, picked up a big rounded lump of rock, and flung it at one.

And then, slowly uncoiling their tentacles, they all began moving towards him – creeping at first deliberately, and making a soft purring sound to each other.

In a moment Mr Fison realized that he was in danger. He shouted again, threw both his boots and started off, with a leap, forthwith. Twenty yards off he stopped and faced about, judging them slow, and behold! the tentacles of their leader were already pouring over the rocky ridge on which he had just been standing!

At that he shouted again, but this time not threatening, but a cry of dismay, and began jumping, striding, slipping, wading across the uneven expanse between him and the beach. The tall red cliffs seemed suddenly at a vast distance, and he saw, as though they were creatures in another world, two minute workmen engaged in the repair of the ladder-way, and little suspecting the race for life that was beginning below them. At one time he could hear the creatures splashing in the pools not a dozen feet behind him, and once he slipped and almost fell.

They chased him to the very foot of the cliffs, and desisted only when he had been joined by the workmen at the foot of the ladder-way up the cliff. All three of the men pelted them with stones for a time, and then hurried to the cliff top and along the path towards Sidmouth, to secure assistance and a boat, and to rescue the desecrated body from the clutches of these abominable creatures.

§ 2

And, as if he had not already been in sufficient peril that day,
Mr Fison went with the boat to point out the exact spot of his
adventure.

As the tide was down, it required a considerable detour to
reach the spot, and when at last they came off the ladder-way,
the mangled body had disappeared. The water was now running
in, submerging first one slab of slimy rock and then another,
and the four men in the boat – the workmen, that is, the
boatman, and Mr Fison – now turned their attention from the
bearings off shore to the water beneath the keel.

At first they could see little below them, save a dark jungle
of laminaria, with an occasional darting fish. Their minds were
set on adventure, and they expressed their disappointment
freely. But presently they saw one of the monsters swimming
through the water seaward, with a curious rolling motion that
suggested to Mr Fison the spinning roll of a captive balloon.
Almost immediately after, the waving streamers of laminaria
were extraordinarily perturbed, parted for a moment, and three
of these beasts became darkly visible, struggling for what was
probably some fragment of the drowned man. In a moment the
copious olive-green ribbons had poured again over this writhing
group.

At that all four men, greatly excited, began beating the water
with oars and shouting, and immediately they saw a tumultuous
movement among the weeds. They desisted to see more clearly,
and as soon as the water was smooth, they saw, as it seemed to
them, the whole sea bottom among the weeds set with eyes.

'Ugly swine!' cried one of the men. 'Why, there's dozens!'

And forthwith the things began to rise through the water
about them. Mr Fison has since described to the writer this
startling eruption out of the waving laminaria meadows. To
him it seemed to occupy a considerable time, but it is probable
that really it was an affair of a few seconds only. For a time
nothing but eyes, and then he speaks of tentacles streaming out
and parting the weed fronds this way and that. Then these
things, growing larger, until at last the bottom was hidden by

their intercoiling forms, and the tips of tentacles rose darkly here and there into the air above the swell of the waters.

One came up boldly to the side of the boat, and, clinging to this with three of its sucker-set tentacles, threw four others over the gunwale, as if with an intention either of oversetting the boat or of clambering into it. Mr Fison at once caught up the boathook, and, jabbing furiously at the soft tentacles, forced it to desist. He was struck in the back and almost pitched overboard by the boatman, who was using his oar to resist a similar attack on the other side of the boat. But the tentacles on either side at once relaxed their hold at this, slid out of sight, and splashed into the water.

'We'd better get out of this,' said Mr Fison, who was trembling violently. He went to the tiller, while the boatman and one of the workmen seated themselves and began rowing. The other workman stood up in the fore part of the boat, with the boathook, ready to strike any more tentacles that might appear. Nothing else seems to have been said. Mr Fison had expressed the common feeling beyond amendment. In a hushed, scared mood, with faces white and drawn, they set about escaping from the position into which they had so recklessly blundered.

But the oars had scarcely dropped into the water before dark, tapering, serpentine ropes had bound them, and were about the rudder; and creeping up the sides of the boat with a looping motion came the suckers again. The men gripped their oars and pulled, but it was like trying to move a boat in a floating raft of weeds. 'Help here!' cried the boatman, and Mr Fison and the second workman rushed to help lug at the oar.

Then the man with the boathook – his name was Ewan, or Ewen – sprang up with a curse, and began striking downward over the side, as far as he could reach, at the bank of tentacles that now clustered along the boat's bottom. And, at the same time, the two rowers stood up to get a better purchase for the recovery of their oars. The boatman handed his to Mr Fison, who lugged desperately, and, meanwhile, the boatman opened a big clasp-knife, and, leaning over the side of the boat, began hacking at the spiring arms upon the oar shaft.

Mr Fison, staggering with the quivering rocking of the boat, his teeth set, his breath coming short, and the veins starting on his hands as he pulled at his oar, suddenly cast his eyes seaward. And there, not fifty yards off, across the long rollers of the incoming tide, was a large boat standing in towards them, with three women and a little child in it. A boatman was rowing, and a little man in a pink-ribboned straw hat and whites[4] stood in the stern, hailing them. For a moment, of course, Mr Fison thought of help, and then he thought of the child. He abandoned his oar forthwith, threw up his arms in a frantic gesture, and screamed to the party in the boat to keep away 'for God's sake!' It says much for the modesty and courage of Mr Fison that he does not seem to be aware that there was any quality of heroism in his action at this juncture. The oar he had abandoned was at once drawn under, and presently reappeared floating about twenty yards away.

At the same moment Mr Fison felt the boat under him lurch violently, and a hoarse scream, a prolonged cry of terror from Hill, the boatman, caused him to forget the party of excursionists altogether. He turned, and saw Hill crouching by the forward rowlock, his face convulsed with terror, and his right arm over the side and drawn tightly down. He gave now a succession of short, sharp cries, 'Oh! oh! oh! – oh!' Mr Fison believes that he must have been hacking at the tentacles below the water-line, and have been grasped by them, but, of course, it is quite impossible to say now certainly what had happened. The boat was heeling over, so that the gunwale was within ten inches of the water, and both Ewan and the other labourer were striking down into the water, with oar and boathook, on either side of Hill's arm. Mr Fison instinctively placed himself to counterpoise them.

Then Hill, who was a burly, powerful man, made a strenuous effort, and rose almost to a standing position. He lifted his arm, indeed, clean out of the water. Hanging to it was a complicated tangle of brown ropes; and the eyes of one of the brutes that had hold of him, glaring straight and resolute, showed momentarily above the surface. The boat heeled more and more, and the green-brown water came pouring in a cascade over the side. Then Hill slipped and fell with his ribs across the side, and his

arm and the mass of tentacles about it splashed back into the
water. He rolled over; his boot kicked Mr Fison's knee as that
gentleman rushed forward to seize him, and in another moment
fresh tentacles had whipped about his waist and neck, and
after a brief, convulsive struggle, in which the boat was nearly
capsized, Hill was lugged overboard. The boat righted with a
violent jerk that all but sent Mr Fison over the other side, and
hid the struggle in the water from his eyes.

He stood staggering to recover his balance for a moment,
and as he did so, he became aware that the struggle and the
inflowing tide had carried them close upon the weedy rocks
again. Not four yards off a table of rock still rose in rhythmic
movements above the inwash of the tide. In a moment Mr Fison
seized the oar from Ewan, gave one vigorous stroke, then,
dropping it, ran to the bows and leapt. He felt his feet slide
over the rock, and, by a frantic effort, leapt again towards a
further mass. He stumbled over this, came to his knees, and
rose again.

'Look out!' cried someone, and a large drab body struck him.
He was knocked flat into a tidal pool by one of the workmen,
and as he went down he heard smothered, choking cries, that
he believed at the time came from Hill. Then he found himself
marvelling at the shrillness and variety of Hill's voice. Someone
jumped over him, and a curving rush of foamy water poured
over him, and passed. He scrambled to his feet dripping, and,
without looking seaward, ran as fast as his terror would let him
shoreward. Before him, over the flat space of scattered rocks,
stumbled the two workmen – one a dozen yards in front of the
other.

He looked over his shoulder at last, and, seeing that he was
not pursued, faced about. He was astonished. From the moment
of the rising of the cephalopods out of the water, he had been
acting too swiftly to fully comprehend his actions. Now it
seemed to him as if he had suddenly jumped out of an evil
dream.

For there were the sky, cloudless and blazing with the afternoon sun, the sea weltering under its pitiless brightness, the soft
creamy foam of the breaking water, and the low, long, dark

ridges of rock. The righted boat floated, rising and falling gently on the swell about a dozen yards from shore. Hill and the monsters, all the stress and tumult of that fierce fight for life, had vanished as though they had never been.

Mr Fison's heart was beating violently; he was throbbing to the fingertips, and his breath came deep.

There was something missing. For some seconds he could not think clearly enough what this might be. Sun, sky, sea, rocks – what was it? Then he remembered the boatload of excursionists. It had vanished. He wondered whether he had imagined it. He turned, and saw the two workmen standing side by side under the projecting masses of the tall pink cliffs. He hesitated whether he should make one last attempt to save the man Hill. His physical excitement seemed to desert him suddenly, and leave him aimless and helpless. He turned shoreward, stumbling and wading towards his two companions.

He looked back again, and there were now two boats floating, and the one farthest out at sea pitched clumsily, bottom upward.

§ 3

So it was *Haploteuthis ferox* made its appearance upon the Devonshire coast. So far, this has been its most serious aggression. Mr Fison's account, taken together with the wave of boating and bathing casualties to which I have already alluded, and the absence of fish from the Cornish coasts that year, points clearly to a shoal of these voracious deep-sea monsters prowling slowly along the sub-tidal coastline. Hunger migration has, I know, been suggested as the force that drove them hither; but, for my own part, I prefer to believe the alternative theory of Hemsley. Hemsley holds that a pack or shoal of these creatures may have become enamoured of human flesh by the accident of a foundered ship sinking among them, and have wandered in search of it out of their accustomed zone; first waylaying and following ships, and so coming to our shores in the wake of the Atlantic traffic. But to discuss Hemsley's cogent and admirably-stated arguments would be out of place here.

It would seem that the appetites of the shoal were satisfied by the catch of eleven people – for so far as can be ascertained, there were ten people in the second boat, and certainly these creatures gave no further signs of their presence off Sidmouth that day. The coast between Seaton and Budleigh Salterton was patrolled all that evening and night by four Preventive Service boats, the men in which were armed with harpoons and cut-lasses, and as the evening advanced, a number of more or less similarly equipped expeditions, organized by private indi-viduals, joined them. Mr Fison took no part in any of these expeditions.

About midnight excited hails were heard from a boat about a couple of miles out at sea to the south-east of Sidmouth, and a lantern was seen waving in a strange manner to and fro and up and down. The nearer boats at once hurried towards the alarm. The venturesome occupants of the boat, a seaman, a curate, and two schoolboys, had actually seen the monsters passing under their boat. The creatures, it seems, like most deep-sea organisms, were phosphorescent, and they had been floating, five fathoms deep or so, like creatures of moonshine through the blackness of the water, their tentacles retracted and as if asleep, rolling over and over, and moving slowly in a wedge-like formation towards the south-east.

These people told their story in gesticulated fragments, as first one boat drew alongside and then another. At last there was a little fleet of eight or nine boats collected together, and from them a tumult, like the chatter of a marketplace, rose into the stillness of the night. There was little or no disposition to pursue the shoal, the people had neither weapons nor experi-ence for such a dubious chase, and presently – even with a certain relief, it may be – the boats turned shoreward.

And now to tell what is perhaps the most astonishing fact in this whole astonishing raid. We have not the slightest know-ledge of the subsequent movements of the shoal, although the whole south-west coast was now alert for it. But it may, per-haps, be significant that a cachalot was stranded off Sark on June 3. Two weeks and three days after this Sidmouth affair, a living *Haploteuthis* came ashore on Calais sands. It was alive, because several witnesses saw its tentacles moving in a convulsive way. But it is probable that it was dying. A gentleman named Pouchet obtained a rifle and shot it.

That was the last appearance of a living *Haploteuthis*. No others were seen on the French coast. On the 15th of June a dead body, almost complete, was washed ashore near Torquay, and a few days later a boat from the Marine Biological station, engaged in dredging off Plymouth, picked up a rotting specimen, slashed deeply with a cutlass wound. How the former specimen had come by its death it is impossible to say. And on the last day of June, Mr Egbert Caine, an artist, bathing near Newlyn, threw up his arms, shrieked, and was drawn under. A friend bathing with him made no attempt to save him, but swam at once for the shore. This is the last fact to tell of this extraordinary raid from the deeper sea. Whether it is really the last of these horrible creatures it is, as yet, premature to say. But it is believed, and certainly it is to be hoped, that they have returned now, and returned for good, to the sunless depths of the middle seas, out of which they have so strangely and so mysteriously arisen.

THE CRYSTAL EGG

There was, until a year ago, a little and very grimy-looking shop near Seven Dials, over which, in weather-worn yellow lettering, the name of 'C. Cave, Naturalist and Dealer in Antiquities', was inscribed. The contents of its window were curiously varied. They comprised some elephant tusks and an imperfect set of chessmen, beads and weapons, a box of eyes, two skulls of tigers and one human, several moth-eaten stuffed monkeys (one holding a lamp), an old-fashioned cabinet, a fly-blown ostrich egg or so, some fishing-tackle, and an extra-ordinarily dirty, empty glass fish-tank. There was also, at the moment the story begins, a mass of crystal, worked into the shape of an egg and brilliantly polished. And at that two people, who stood outside the window, were looking, one of them a tall, thin clergyman, the other a black-bearded young man of dusky complexion and unobtrusive costume. The dusky young man spoke with eager gesticulation, and seemed anxious for his companion to purchase the article.

While they were there, Mr Cave came into his shop, his beard still wagging with the bread and butter of his tea. When he saw these men and the object of their regard, his countenance fell. He glanced guiltily over his shoulder, and softly shut the door. He was a little old man, with pale face and peculiar watery blue eyes; his hair was a dirty grey, and he wore a shabby blue frock-coat, an ancient silk hat, and carpet slippers very much down at heel. He remained watching the two men as they talked. The clergyman went deep into his trouser pocket, examined a handful of money, and showed his teeth in an agreeable smile. Mr Cave seemed still more depressed when they came into the shop.

The clergyman, without any ceremony, asked the price of the crystal egg. Mr Cave glanced nervously towards the door leading into the parlour, and said five pounds. The clergyman protested that the price was high, to his companion as well as to Mr Cave – it was, indeed, very much more than Mr Cave had intended to ask, when he had stocked the article – and an attempt at bargaining ensued. Mr Cave stepped to the shop door, and held it open. 'Five pounds is my price,' he said, as though he wished to save himself the trouble of unprofitable discussion. As he did so, the upper portion of a woman's face appeared above the blind in the glass upper panel of the door leading into the parlour, and stared curiously at the two customers. 'Five pounds is my price,' said Mr Cave, with a quiver in his voice.

The swarthy young man had so far remained a spectator, watching Cave keenly. Now he spoke. 'Give him five pounds,' he said. The clergyman glanced at him to see if he were in earnest, and, when he looked at Mr Cave again, he saw that the latter's face was white. 'It's a lot of money,' said the clergyman, and, diving into his pocket, began counting his resources. He had little more than thirty shillings,[1] and he appealed to his companion, with whom he seemed to be on terms of considerable intimacy. This gave Mr Cave an opportunity of collecting his thoughts, and he began to explain in an agitated manner that the crystal was not, as a matter of fact, entirely free for sale. His two customers were naturally surprised at this, and enquired why he had not thought of that before he began to bargain. Mr Cave became confused, but he stuck to his story, that the crystal was not in the market that afternoon, that a probable purchaser of it had already appeared. The two, treating this as an attempt to raise the price still further, made as if they would leave the shop. But at this point the parlour door opened, and the owner of the dark fringe and the little eyes appeared.

She was a coarse-featured, corpulent woman, younger and

very much larger than Mr Cave; she walked heavily, and her face was flushed. 'That crystal *is* for sale,' she said. 'And five pounds is a good enough price for it. I can't think what you're about, Cave, not to take the gentleman's offer!'

Mr Cave, greatly perturbed by the irruption, looked angrily at her over the rims of his spectacles, and, without excessive assurance, asserted his right to manage his business in his own way. An altercation began. The two customers watched the scene with interest and some amusement, occasionally assisting Mrs Cave with suggestions. Mr Cave, hard driven, persisted in a confused and impossible story of an enquiry for the crystal that morning, and his agitation became painful. But he stuck to his point with extraordinary persistence. It was the young Oriental who ended this curious controversy. He proposed that they should call again in the course of two days – so as to give the alleged enquirer a fair chance. 'And then we must insist,' said the clergyman. 'Five pounds.' Mrs Cave took it on herself to apologize for her husband, explaining that he was sometimes 'a little odd', and as the two customers left, the couple prepared for a free discussion of the incident in all its bearings.

Mrs Cave talked to her husband with singular directness. The poor little man, quivering with emotion, muddled himself between his stories, maintaining on the one hand that he had another customer in view, and on the other asserting that the crystal was honestly worth ten guineas. 'Why did you ask five pounds?' said his wife. '*Do* let me manage my business my own way!' said Mr Cave.

Mr Cave had living with him a stepdaughter and a stepson, and at supper that night the transaction was rediscussed. None of them had a high opinion of Mr Cave's business methods, and this action seemed a culminating folly.

'It's my opinion he's refused that crystal before,' said the stepson, a loose-limbed lout of eighteen.

'But *Five Pounds*!' said the stepdaughter, an argumentative young woman of six-and-twenty.

Mr Cave's answers were wretched; he could only mumble weak assertions that he knew his own business best. They drove him from his half-eaten supper into the shop, to close it for the night, his ears aflame and tears of vexation behind his spectacles. 'Why had he left the crystal in the window so long? The folly of it!' That was the trouble closest in his mind. For a time he could see no way of evading sale.

After supper his stepdaughter and stepson smartened themselves up and went out and his wife retired upstairs to reflect upon the business aspects of the crystal, over a little sugar and lemon and so forth[2] in hot water. Mr Cave went into the shop, and stayed there until late, ostensibly to make ornamental rockeries for goldfish cases but really for a private purpose that will be better explained later. The next day Mrs Cave found that the crystal had been removed from the window, and was lying behind some secondhand books on angling. She replaced it in a conspicuous position. But she did not argue further about it, as a nervous headache disinclined her from debate. Mr Cave was always disinclined. The day passed disagreeably. Mr Cave was, if anything, more absent-minded than usual, and uncommonly irritable withal. In the afternoon, when his wife was taking her customary sleep, he removed the crystal from the window again.

The next day Mr Cave had to deliver a consignment of dogfish at one of the hospital schools, where they were needed for dissection. In his absence Mrs Cave's mind reverted to the topic of the crystal, and the methods of expenditure suitable to a windfall of five pounds. She had already devised some very agreeable expedients, among others a dress of green silk for herself and a trip to Richmond, when a jangling of the front door bell summoned her into the shop. The customer was an examination coach who came to complain of the non-delivery of certain frogs asked for the previous day. Mrs Cave did not approve of this particular branch of Mr Cave's business, and the gentleman, who had called in a somewhat aggressive mood, retired after a brief exchange of words – entirely civil so far as he was concerned. Mrs Cave's eye then naturally turned to the window; for the sight of the crystal was an assurance of the five pounds and of her dreams. What was her surprise to find it gone!

She went to the place behind the locker on the counter, where she had discovered it the day before. It was not there; and she immediately began an eager search about the shop.

When Mr Cave returned from his business with the dogfish, about a quarter to two in the afternoon, he found the shop in some confusion, and his wife, extremely exasperated and on her knees behind the counter, routing among his taxidermic material. Her face came up hot and angry over the counter, as the jangling bell announced his return, and she forthwith accused him of 'hiding it'.

'Hid *what*?' asked Mr Cave.

'The crystal!'

At that Mr Cave, apparently much surprised, rushed to the window. 'Isn't it here?' he said. 'Great Heavens! what has become of it?'

Just then, Mr Cave's stepson re-entered the shop from the inner room – he had come home a minute or so before Mr Cave – and he was blaspheming freely. He was apprenticed to a secondhand furniture dealer down the road, but he had his meals at home, and he was naturally annoyed to find no dinner ready.

But, when he heard of the loss of the crystal, he forgot his meal, and his anger was diverted from his mother to his stepfather. Their first idea, of course, was that he had hidden it. But Mr Cave stoutly denied all knowledge of its fate – freely offering his bedabbled affidavit in the matter – and at last was worked up to the point of accusing, first, his wife and then his stepson of having taken it with a view to a private sale. So began an exceedingly acrimonious and emotional discussion, which ended for Mrs Cave in a peculiar nervous condition midway between hysterics and amuck, and caused the stepson to be half-an-hour late at the furniture establishment in the afternoon. Mr Cave took refuge from his wife's emotions in the shop.

In the evening the matter was resumed, with less passion and in a judicial spirit, under the presidency of the stepdaughter. The supper passed unhappily and culminated in a painful scene. Mr Cave gave way at last to extreme exasperation, and went out banging the front door violently. The rest of the family, having discussed him with the freedom his absence warranted, hunted the house from garret to cellar, hoping to light upon the crystal.

The next day the two customers called again. They were received by Mrs Cave almost in tears. It transpired that no one *could* imagine all that she had stood from Cave at various times in her married pilgrimage. . . . She also gave a garbled account of the disappearance. The clergyman and the Oriental laughed silently at one another, and said it was very extraordinary. As Mrs Cave seemed disposed to give them the complete history of her life they made to leave the shop. Thereupon Mrs Cave, still clinging to hope, asked for the clergyman's address, so that, if she could get anything out of Cave, she might communicate it. The address was duly given, but apparently was afterwards mislaid. Mrs Cave can remember nothing about it.

In the evening of that day, the Caves seem to have exhausted their emotions, and Mr Cave, who had been out in the afternoon, supped in a gloomy isolation that contrasted pleasantly with the impassioned controversy of the previous days. For some time matters were very badly strained in the Cave household, but neither crystal nor customer reappeared.

Now, without mincing the matter, we must admit that Mr Cave was a liar. He knew perfectly well where the crystal was. It was in the rooms of Mr Jacoby Wace, Assistant Demonstrator at St Catherine's Hospital, Westbourne Street. It stood on the sideboard partially covered by a black velvet cloth, and beside a decanter of American whisky. It is from Mr Wace, indeed, that the particulars upon which this narrative is based were derived. Cave had taken off the thing to the hospital hidden in the dogfish sack, and there had pressed the young investigator to keep it for him. Mr Wace was a little dubious at first. His relationship to Cave was peculiar. He had a taste for singular characters, and he had more than once invited the old man to smoke and drink in his rooms, and to unfold his rather amusing views of life in general and of his wife in particular. Mr Wace had encountered Mrs Cave, too, on occasions when Mr Cave was not at home to attend to him. He knew the constant interference to which Cave was subjected, and having weighed the story judicially, he decided to give the crystal a refuge.

Mr Cave promised to explain the reasons for his remarkable affection for the crystal more fully on a later occasion, but he spoke distinctly of seeing visions therein. He called on Mr Wace the same evening.

He told a complicated story. The crystal he said had come into his possession with other oddments at the forced sale of another curiosity dealer's effects, and not knowing what its value might be, he had ticketed it at ten shillings. It had hung upon his hands at that price for some months, and he was thinking of 'reducing the figure', when he made a singular discovery.

At that time his health was very bad – and it must be borne in mind that, throughout all this experience, his physical condition was one of ebb – and he was in considerable distress by reason of the negligence, the positive ill-treatment even, he received from his wife and stepchildren. His wife was vain, extravagant, unfeeling, and had a growing taste for private drinking; his stepdaughter was mean and over-reaching; and his stepson had conceived a violent dislike for him, and lost no chance of showing it. The requirements of his business pressed heavily upon him, and Mr Wace does not think that he was altogether free from occasional intemperance. He had begun life in a comfortable position, he was a man of fair education, and he suffered, for weeks at a stretch, from melancholia and insomnia. Afraid to disturb his family, he would slip quietly from his wife's side, when his thoughts became intolerable, and wander about the house. And about three o'clock one morning, late in August, chance directed him into the shop.

The dirty little place was impenetrably black except in one spot, where he perceived an unusual glow of light. Approaching this, he discovered it to be the crystal egg, which was standing on the corner of the counter towards the window. A thin ray smote through a crack in the shutters, impinged upon the object, and seemed as it were to fill its entire interior.

It occurred to Mr Cave that this was not in accordance with the laws of optics as he had known them in his younger days. He could understand the rays being refracted by the crystal and coming to a focus in its interior, but this diffusion jarred with his physical conceptions. He approached the crystal nearly, peering into it and round it, with a transient revival of the scientific curiosity that in his youth had determined his choice of a calling. He was surprised to find the light not steady, but writhing within the substance of the egg, as though that object was a hollow sphere of some luminous vapour. In moving about to get different points of view, he suddenly found that he had come between it and the ray, and that the crystal none the less remained luminous. Greatly astonished, he lifted it out of the light ray and carried it to the darkest part of the shop. It remained bright for some four or five minutes, when it slowly faded and went out. He placed it in the thin streak of daylight, and its luminousness was almost immediately restored.

So far, at least, Mr Wace was able to verify the remarkable story of Mr Cave. He has himself repeatedly held this crystal in a ray of light (which had to be of a less diameter than one millimetre). And in a perfect darkness, such as could be produced by velvet wrapping, the crystal did undoubtedly appear very faintly phosphorescent. It would seem, however, that the luminousness was of some exceptional sort, and not equally visible to all eyes; for Mr Harbinger – whose name will be familiar to the scientific reader in connection with the Pasteur Institute[3] – was quite unable to see any light whatever. And Mr Wace's own capacity for its appreciation was out of comparison inferior to that of Mr Cave's. Even with Mr Cave the power varied very considerably: his vision was most vivid during states of extreme weakness and fatigue.

Now from the outset this light in the crystal exercised an irresistible fascination upon Mr Cave. And it says more for his loneliness of soul than a volume of pathetic writing could do, that he told no human being of his curious observations. He seems to have been living in such an atmosphere of petty spite that to admit the existence of a pleasure would have been to risk the loss of it. He found that as the dawn advanced, and the amount of diffused light increased, the crystal became to all appearance non-luminous. And for some time he was unable to see anything in it, except at night-time, in dark corners of the shop.

But the use of an old velvet cloth, which he used as a background for a collection of minerals, occurred to him, and by doubling this, and putting it over his head and hands, he was able to get a sight of the luminous movement within the crystal even in the daytime. He was very cautious lest he should be thus discovered by his wife, and he practised this occupation only in the afternoons, while she was asleep upstairs, and then circumspectly in a hollow under the counter. And one day, turning the crystal about in his hands, he saw something. It came and went like a flash, but it gave him the impression that the object had for a moment opened to him the view of a wide and spacious and strange country; and, turning it about, he did, just as the light faded, see the same vision again.

Now, it would be tedious and unnecessary to state all the phases of Mr Cave's discovery from this point. Suffice that the effect was this: the crystal, being peered into at an angle of about 137 degrees from the direction of the illuminating ray, gave a clear and consistent picture of a wide and peculiar countryside. It was not dream-like at all; it produced a definite impression of reality, and the better the light the more real and solid it seemed. It was a moving picture: that is to say, certain objects moved in it, but slowly in an orderly manner like real things, and, according as the direction of the lighting and vision changed, the picture changed also. It must, indeed, have been like looking through an oval glass at a view, and turning the glass about to get at different aspects.

Mr Cave's statements, Mr Wace assures me, were extremely circumstantial, and entirely free from any of that emotional quality that taints hallucinatory impressions. But it must be remembered that all the efforts of Mr Wace to see any similar clarity in the faint opalescence of the crystal were wholly unsuccessful, try as he would. The difference in intensity of the impressions received by the two men was very great, and it is quite conceivable that what was a view to Mr Cave was a mere blurred nebulosity to Mr Wace.

The view, as Mr Cave described it, was invariably of an extensive plain, and he seemed always to be looking at it from a considerable height, as if from a tower or a mast. To the east and to the west the plain was bounded at a remote distance by vast reddish cliffs, which reminded him of those he had seen in some picture; but what the picture was Mr Wace was unable to ascertain. These cliffs passed north and south – he could tell the points of the compass by the stars that were visible of a night – receding in an almost illimitable perspective and fading into the mists of the distance before they met. He was nearer the eastern set of cliffs, on the occasion of his first vision the sun was rising over them, and black against the sunlight and pale against their shadow appeared a multitude of soaring forms that Mr Cave regarded as birds. A vast range of buildings spread below him; he seemed to be looking down upon them; and, as they approached the blurred and refracted edge of the picture, they became indistinct. There were also trees curious in shape, and in colouring, a deep mossy green and an exquisite grey, beside a wide and shining canal.[4] And something great and brilliantly coloured flew across the picture. But the first time Mr Cave saw these pictures he saw only in flashes, his hands shook, his head moved, the vision came and went, and grew foggy and indistinct. And at first he had the greatest difficulty in finding the picture again once the direction of it was lost.

His next clear vision, which came about a week after the first, the interval having yielded nothing but tantalizing glimpses and some useful experience, showed him the view down the length of the valley. The view was different, but he had a curious persuasion, which his subsequent observations abundantly confirmed, that he was regarding this strange world from exactly the same spot, although he was looking in a different direction. The long façade of the great building, whose roof he had looked down upon before, was now receding in perspective. He recognized the roof. In the front of the façade was a terrace of massive proportions and extraordinary length, and down the middle of the terrace, at certain intervals, stood huge but very graceful masts, bearing small shiny objects which reflected the setting sun. The import of these small objects did not occur to Mr Cave until some time after, as he was describing the scene to Mr Wace. The terrace overhung a thicket of the most luxuriant and graceful vegetation, and beyond this was a wide grassy lawn on which certain broad creatures, in form like beetles but enormously larger, reposed. Beyond this again was a richly decorated causeway of pinkish stone; and beyond that, and lined with dense *red* weeds, and passing up the valley exactly parallel with the distant cliffs, was a broad and mirror-like expanse of water. The air seemed full of squadrons of great birds, manoeuvring in stately curves; and across the river was a multitude of splendid buildings, richly coloured and glittering with metallic tracery and facets, among a forest of moss-like and lichenous trees. And suddenly something flapped repeatedly across the vision, like the fluttering of a jewelled fan or the beating of a wing, and a face, or rather the upper part of a face with very large eyes, came as it were close to his own and as if on the other side of the crystal. Mr Cave was so startled and so impressed by the absolute reality of these eyes, that he drew his head back from the crystal to look behind it. He had become so absorbed in watching that he was quite surprised to find himself in the cool darkness of his little shop, with its familiar odour of methyl,[5] mustiness, and decay. And, as he blinked about him, the glowing crystal faded, and went out.

Such were the first general impressions of Mr Cave. The story is curiously direct and circumstantial. From the outset, when the valley first flashed momentarily on his senses, his imagination was strangely affected, and, as he began to appreciate the details of the scene he saw, his wonder rose to the point of a passion. He went about his business listless and distraught, thinking only of the time when he should be able to return to his watching. And then a few weeks after his first sight of the valley came the two customers, the stress and excitement of their offer, and the narrow escape of the crystal from sale, as I have already told.

Now while the thing was Mr Cave's secret, it remained a mere wonder, a thing to creep to covertly and peep at, as a child might peep upon a forbidden garden. But Mr Wace has, for a young scientific investigator, a particularly lucid and consecutive habit of mind. Directly the crystal and its story came to him, and he had satisfied himself, by seeing the phosphorescence with his own eyes, that there really was a certain evidence for Mr Cave's statements, he proceeded to develop the matter systematically. Mr Cave was only too eager to come and feast his eyes on this wonderland he saw, and he came every night from half-past eight until half-past ten, and sometimes, in Mr Wace's absence, during the day. On Sunday afternoons, also, he came. From the outset Mr Wace made copious notes, and it was due to his scientific method that the relation between the direction from which the initiating ray entered the crystal and the orientation of the picture was proved. And, by covering the crystal in a box perforated only with a small aperture to admit the exciting ray, and by substituting black holland for his buff blinds, he greatly improved the conditions of the observations; so that in a little while they were able to survey the valley in any direction they desired.

So having cleared the way, we may give a brief account of this visionary world within the crystal. The things were in all cases seen by Mr Cave, and the method of working was invariably for him to watch the crystal and report what he saw, while Mr Wace (who as a science student had learnt the trick of writing in the dark) wrote a brief note of his report. When the crystal faded, it was put into its box in the proper position and the electric light turned on. Mr Wace asked questions, and suggested observations to clear up difficult points. Nothing, indeed, could have been less visionary and more matter-of-fact.

The attention of Mr Cave had been speedily directed to the bird-like creatures he had seen so abundantly present in each of his earlier visions. His first impression was soon corrected, and he considered for a time that they might represent a diurnal species of bat. Then he thought, grotesquely enough, that they might be cherubs. Their heads were round, and curiously human, and it was the eyes of one of them that had so startled him on his second observation. They had broad, silvery wings, not feathered, but glistening almost as brilliantly as new-killed fish and with the same subtle play of colour, and these wings were not built on the plan of bird-wing or bat, Mr Wace learned, but supported by curved ribs radiating from the body. (A sort of butterfly wing with curved ribs seems best to express their

appearance.) The body was small, but fitted with two bunches
of prehensile organs, like long tentacles, immediately under the
mouth. Incredible as it appeared to Mr Wace, the persuasion
at last became irresistible, that it was these creatures which
owned the great quasi-human buildings and the magnificent
garden that made the broad valley so splendid. And Mr Cave
perceived that the buildings, with other peculiarities, had no
doors, but that the great circular windows, which opened freely,
gave the creatures egress and entrance. They would alight upon
their tentacles, fold their wings to a smallness almost rod-like,
and hop into the interior. But among them was a multitude of
smaller-winged creatures, like great dragonflies and moths and
flying beetles, and across the greensward brilliantly-coloured
gigantic ground-beetles crawled lazily to and fro. Moreover, on
the causeways and terraces, large-headed creatures similar to
the greater winged flies, but wingless, were visible, hopping
busily upon their hand-like tangle of tentacles.

Allusion has already been made to the glittering objects upon
masts that stood upon the terrace of the nearer buildings. It
dawned upon Mr Cave, after regarding one of these masts very
fixedly on one particularly vivid day, that the glittering object
there was a crystal exactly like that into which he peered. And
a still more careful scrutiny convinced him that each one in a
vista of nearly twenty carried a similar object.

Occasionally one of the large flying creatures would flutter
up to one, and, folding its wings and coiling a number of its
tentacles about the mast, would regard the crystal fixedly for a
space, – sometimes for as long as fifteen minutes. And a series
of observations, made at the suggestion of Mr Wace, convinced
both watchers that, so far as this visionary world was concerned, the crystal into which they peered actually stood at the
summit of the endmost mast on the terrace, and that on one
occasion at least one of these inhabitants of this other world
had looked into Mr Cave's face while he was making these
observations.

So much for the essential facts of this very singular story.
Unless we dismiss it all as the ingenious fabrication of Mr Wace,
we have to believe one of two things: either that Mr Cave's

crystal was in two worlds at once, and that, while it was carried about in one, it remained stationary in the other, which seems altogether absurd; or else that it had some peculiar relation of sympathy with another and exactly similar crystal in this other world, so that what was seen in the interior of the one in this world was, under suitable conditions, visible to an observer in the corresponding crystal in the other world; and *vice versa*. At present, indeed, we do not know of any way in which two crystals could so come *en rapport*, but nowadays we know enough to understand that the thing is not altogether imposs- ible. This view of the crystals as *en rapport* was the supposition that occurred to Mr Wace, and to me at least it seems extremely plausible. . .

And where was this other world? On this, also, the alert intelligence of Mr Wace speedily threw light. After sunset, the sky darkened rapidly – there was a very brief twilight interval indeed – and the stars shone out. They were recognizably the same as those we see, arranged in the same constellations. Mr Cave recognized the Bear, the Pleiades, Aldebaran, and Sirius: so that the other world must be somewhere in the solar system, and, at the utmost, only a few hundreds of millions of miles from our own. Following up this clue, Mr Wace learned that the midnight sky was a darker blue even than our midwinter sky, and that the sun seemed a little smaller. *And there were two small moons!* 'like our moon but smaller, and quite differently marked', one of which moved so rapidly that its motion was clearly visible as one regarded it. These moons were never high in the sky, but vanished as they rose: that is, every time they revolved they were eclipsed because they were so near their primary planet. And all this answers quite completely, although Mr Cave did not know it, to what must be the condition of things on Mars.

Indeed, it seems an exceedingly plausible conclusion that peering into this crystal Mr Cave did actually see the planet Mars and its inhabitants. And, if that be the case, then the evening star that shone so brilliantly in the sky of that distant vision, was neither more nor less than our own familiar earth.

For a time the Martians – if they were Martians – do not

seem to have known of Mr Cave's inspection. Once or twice one would come to peer, and go away very shortly to some other mast, as though the vision was unsatisfactory. During this time Mr Cave was able to watch the proceedings of these winged people without being disturbed by their attentions, and, although his report is necessarily vague and fragmentary, it is nevertheless very suggestive. Imagine the impression of humanity a Martian observer would get who, after a difficult process of preparation and with considerable fatigue to the eyes, was able to peer at London from the steeple of St Martin's Church for stretches, at longest, of four minutes at a time. Mr Cave was unable to ascertain if the winged Martians were the same as the Martians who hopped about the causeways and terraces, and if the latter could put on wings at will. He several times saw certain clumsy bipeds,[6] dimly suggestive of apes, white and partially translucent, feeding among certain of the lichenous trees, and once some of these fled before one of the hopping, round-headed Martians. The latter caught one in its tentacles, and then the picture faded suddenly and left Mr Cave most tantalizingly in the dark. On another occasion a vast thing, that Mr Cave thought at first was some gigantic insect, appeared advancing along the causeway beside the canal with extraordinary rapidity. As this drew nearer Mr Cave perceived that it was a mechanism of shining metals and of extraordinary complexity. And then, when he looked again, it had passed out of sight.

After a time Mr Wace aspired to attract the attention of the Martians, and the next time that the strange eyes of one of them appeared close to the crystal Mr Cave cried out and sprang away, and they immediately turned on the light and began to gesticulate in a manner suggestive of signalling. But when at last Mr Cave examined the crystal again the Martian had departed.

Thus far these observations had progressed in early November, and then Mr Cave, feeling that the suspicions of his family about the crystal were allayed, began to take it to and fro with him in order that, as occasion arose in the daytime or night, he might comfort himself with what was fast becoming the most real thing in his existence.

In December Mr Wace's work in connection with a forth-coming examination became heavy, the sittings were reluctantly suspended for a week, and for ten or eleven days – he is not quite sure which – he saw nothing of Cave. He then grew anxious to resume these investigations, and, the stress of his seasonal labours being abated, he went down to Seven Dials. At the corner he noticed a shutter before a bird fancier's window, and then another at a cobbler's. Mr Cave's shop was closed.

He rapped and the door was opened by the stepson in black. He at once called Mrs Cave, who was, Mr Wace could not but observe, in cheap but ample widow's weeds of the most imposing pattern. Without any very great surprise Mr Wace learnt that Cave was dead and already buried. She was in tears, and her voice was a little thick. She had just returned from Highgate. Her mind seemed occupied with her own prospects and the honourable details of the obsequies, but Mr Wace was at last able to learn the particulars of Cave's death. He had been found dead in his shop in the early morning, the day after his last visit to Mr Wace, and the crystal had been clasped in his stone-cold hands. His face was smiling, said Mrs Cave, and the velvet cloth from the minerals lay on the floor at his feet. He must have been dead five or six hours when he was found.

This came as a great shock to Wace, and he began to reproach himself bitterly for having neglected the plain symptoms of the old man's ill-health. But his chief thought was of the crystal. He approached that topic in a gingerly manner, because he knew Mrs Cave's peculiarities. He was dumbfounded to learn that it was sold.

Mrs Cave's first impulse, directly Cave's body had been taken upstairs, had been to write to the mad clergyman who had offered five pounds for the crystal, informing him of its recovery; but after a violent hunt in which her daughter joined her, they were convinced of the loss of his address. As they were without the means required to mourn and bury Cave in the elaborate style the dignity of an old Seven Dials inhabitant demands, they had appealed to a friendly fellow-tradesman in Great Portland Street. He had very kindly taken over a portion of the stock at a valuation. The valuation was his own and the crystal egg was included in one of the lots. Mr Wace, after a few suitable consolatory observations, a little off-handedly proffered perhaps, hurried at once to Great Portland Street. But there he learned that the crystal egg had already been sold to a tall, dark man in grey. And there the material facts in this curious, and to me at least very suggestive, story come abruptly to an end. The Great Portland Street dealer did not know who the tall dark man in grey was, nor had he observed him with sufficient attention to describe him minutely. He did not even know which way this person had gone after leaving the shop. For a time Mr Wace remained in the shop, trying the dealer's patience with hopeless questions, venting his own exasperation. And at last, realizing abruptly that the whole thing had passed out of his hands, had vanished like a vision of the night, he returned to his own rooms, a little astonished to find the notes he had made still tangible and visible upon his untidy table.

His annoyance and disappointment were naturally very great. He made a second call (equally ineffectual) upon the Great Portland Street dealer, and he resorted to advertisements in such periodicals as were likely to come into the hands of a bric-a-brac collector. He also wrote letters to *The Daily Chronicle* and *Nature*,[7] but both those periodicals, suspecting a hoax, asked him to reconsider his action before they printed, and he was advised that such a strange story, unfortunately so bare of supporting evidence, might imperil his reputation as an investigator. Moreover, the calls of his proper work were urgent. So that after a month or so, save for an occasional reminder to certain dealers, he had reluctantly to abandon the quest for the crystal egg, and from that day to this it remains undiscovered. Occasionally however, he tells me, and I can quite believe him, he has bursts of zeal in which he abandons his more urgent occupation and resumes the search.

Whether or not it will remain lost for ever, with the material and origin of it, are things equally speculative at the present time. If the present purchaser is a collector, one would have expected the enquiries of Mr Wace to have reached him through the dealers. He has been able to discover Mr Cave's clergyman and 'Oriental' – no other than the Rev. James Parker and the young Prince of Bosso-Kuni in Java. I am obliged to them for certain particulars. The object of the Prince was simply curiosity – and extravagance. He was so eager to buy, because Cave was so oddly reluctant to sell. It is just as possible that the buyer in the second instance was simply a casual purchaser and not a collector at all, and the crystal egg, for all I know, may at the present moment be within a mile of me, decorating a drawing-room or serving as a paperweight – its remarkable functions all unknown. Indeed, it is partly with the idea of such a possibility that I have thrown this narrative into a form that will give it a chance of being read by the ordinary consumer of fiction.

My own ideas in the matter are practically identical with those of Mr Wace. I believe the crystal on the mast in Mars and the crystal egg of Mr Cave's to be in some physical, but at present quite inexplicable, way *en rapport*, and we both believe further that the terrestrial crystal must have been – possibly at some remote date – sent hither from that planet, in order to give the Martians a near view of our affairs. Possibly the fellows to the crystals in the other masts are also on our globe. No theory of hallucination suffices for the facts.

A STORY OF THE
STONE AGE

I. – Ugh-lomi and Uya

This story is of a time beyond the memory of man, before
the beginning of history, a time when one might have walked
dryshod from France (as we call it now) to England, and when
a broad and sluggish Thames flowed through its marshes to
meet its father Rhine, flowing through a wide and level country
that is under water in these latter days, and which we know by
the name of the North Sea. In that remote age the valley which
runs along the foot of the Downs did not exist, and the south
of Surrey was a range of hills, fir-clad on the middle slopes, and
snow-capped for the better part of the year. The cores of its
summits still remain as Leith Hill, and Pitch Hill, and Hindhead.[1] On the lower slopes of the range, below the grassy spaces
where the wild horses grazed, were forests of yew and sweet
chestnut and elm, and the thickets and dark places hid the
grizzly bear and the hyena, and the grey apes clambered through
the branches. And still lower amidst the woodland and marsh
and open grass along the Wey[2] did this little drama play itself
out to the end that I have to tell. Fifty thousand years ago[3] it
was, fifty thousand years – if the reckoning of geologists is
correct.

And in those days the springtime was as joyful as it is now,
and sent the blood coursing in just the same fashion. The
afternoon sky was blue with piled white clouds sailing through
it, and the south-west wind came like a soft caress. The new-
come swallows drove to and fro. The reaches of the river were
spangled with white ranunculus, the marshy places were starred
with lady's-smock and lit with marshmallow wherever the regi-

ments of the sedges lowered their swords, and the northward moving hippopotami, shiny black monsters, sporting clumsily, came floundering and blundering through it all, rejoicing dimly and possessed with one clear idea, to splash the river muddy.

Up the river and well in sight of the hippopotami, a number of little buff-coloured animals dabbled in the water. There was no fear, no rivalry, and no enmity between them and the hippopotami. As the great bulks came crashing through the reeds and smashed the mirror of the water into silvery splashes, these little creatures shouted and gesticulated with glee. It was the surest sign of high spring. 'Boloo!' they cried. 'Baayah. Boloo!' They were the children of the men folk, the smoke of whose encampment rose from the knoll at the river's bend. Wild-eyed youngsters they were, with matted hair and little broad-nosed impish faces, covered (as some children are covered even nowadays) with a delicate down of hair. They were narrow in the loins and long in the arms. And their ears had no lobes, and had little pointed tips,[4] a thing that still, in rare instances, survives. Stark-naked vivid little gipsies, as active as monkeys and as full of chatter, though a little wanting in words.

Their elders were hidden from the wallowing hippopotami by the crest of the knoll. The human squatting-place was a trampled area among the dead brown fronds of Royal Fern, through which the crosiers of this year's growth were unrolling to the light and warmth. The fire was a smouldering heap of char, light grey and black, replenished by the old women from time to time with brown leaves. Most of the men were asleep – they slept sitting with their foreheads on their knees. They had killed that morning a good quarry, enough for all, a deer that had been wounded by hunting dogs; so that there had been no quarrelling among them, and some of the women were still gnawing the bones that lay scattered about. Others were making a heap of leaves and sticks to feed Brother Fire when the darkness came again, that he might grow strong and tall therewith, and guard them against the beasts. And two were piling flints that they brought, an armful at a time, from the bend of the river where the children were at play.

None of these buff-skinned savages were clothed, but some wore about their hips rude girdles of adder-skin or crackling undressed hide, from which depended little bags, not made, but torn from the paws of beasts, and carrying the rudely-dressed flints that were men's chief weapons and tools. And one woman, the mate of Uya the Cunning Man, wore a wonderful necklace of perforated fossils – that others had worn before her. Beside some of the sleeping men lay the big antlers of the elk, with the tines chipped to sharp edges, and long sticks, hacked at the ends with flints into sharp points. There was little else save these things and the smouldering fire to mark these human beings off from the wild animals that ranged the country. But Uya the Cunning did not sleep, but sat with a bone in his hand and scraped busily thereon with a flint, a thing no animal would do. He was the oldest man in the tribe, beetle-browed, prognathous, lank-armed; he had a beard and his cheeks were hairy, and his chest and arms were black with thick hair. And by virtue both of his strength and cunning he was master of the tribe, and his share was always the most and the best.

Eudena had hidden herself among the alders, because she was afraid of Uya. She was still a girl, and her eyes were bright and her smile pleasant to see. He had given her a piece of the liver, a man's piece, and a wonderful treat for a girl to get; but as she took it the other woman with the necklace had looked at her, an evil glance, and Ugh-lomi had made a noise in his throat. At that, Uya had looked at him long and steadfastly, and Ugh-lomi's face had fallen. And then Uya had looked at her. She was frightened and she had stolen away, while the feeding was still going on, and Uya was busy with the marrow of a bone. Afterwards he had wandered about as if looking for her. And now she crouched among the alders, wondering mightily what Uya might be doing with the flint and the bone. And Ugh-lomi was not to be seen.

Presently a squirrel came leaping through the alders, and she lay so quiet the little man was within six feet of her before he saw her. Whereupon he dashed up a stem in a hurry and began to chatter and scold her. 'What are you doing here,' he asked, 'away from the other men beasts?' 'Peace,' said Eudena, but he only chattered more, and then she began to break off the little black cones to throw at him. He dodged and defied her, and she grew excited and rose up to throw better, and then she saw Uya coming down the knoll. He had seen the movement of her pale arm amidst the thicket – he was very keen-eyed.

At that she forgot the squirrel and set off through the alders and reeds as fast as she could go. She did not care where she went so long as she escaped Uya. She splashed nearly knee-deep through a swampy place, and saw in front of her a slope of ferns – growing more slender and green as they passed up out of the light into the shade of the young chestnuts. She was soon amidst the trees – she was very fleet of foot, and she ran on and on until the forest was old and the vales great, and the vines about their stems where the light came were thick as young trees, and the ropes of ivy stout and tight. On she went, and she doubled and doubled again, and then at last lay down amidst some ferns in a hollow place near a thicket, and listened with her heart beating in her ears.

She heard footsteps presently rustling among the dead leaves, far off, and they died away and everything was still again, except the scandalizing of the midges – for the evening was drawing on – and the incessant whisper of the leaves. She laughed silently to think the cunning Uya should go by her. She was not frightened. Sometimes, playing with the other girls and lads, she had fled into the wood, though never so far as this. It was pleasant to be hidden and alone.

She lay a long time there, glad of her escape, and then she sat up listening.

It was a rapid pattering growing louder and coming towards her, and in a little while she could hear grunting noises and the snapping of twigs. It was a drove of lean grisly wild swine. She turned about her, for a boar is an ill fellow to pass too closely, on account of the sideway slash of his tusks, and she made off slantingly through the trees. But the patter came nearer, they were not feeding as they wandered, but going fast – or else they would not overtake her – and she caught the limb of a tree, swung on to it, and ran up the stem with something of the agility of a monkey.

Down below the sharp bristling backs of the swine were already passing when she looked. And she knew the short, sharp grunts they made meant fear. What were they afraid of? A man? They were in a great hurry for just a man.

And then, so suddenly it made her grip on the branch tighten involuntarily, a fawn started in the brake and rushed after the swine. Something else went by, low and grey, with a long body; she did not know what it was, indeed she saw it only momentarily through the interstices of the young leaves; and then there came a pause.

She remained stiff and expectant, as rigid almost as though she was a part of the tree she clung to, peering down.

Then, far away among the trees, clear for a moment, then hidden, then visible knee-deep in ferns, then gone again, ran a man. She knew it was young Ugh-lomi by the fair colour of his hair, and there was red upon his face. Somehow his frantic flight and that scarlet mark made her feel sick. And then nearer, running heavily and breathing hard, came another man. At first she could not see, and then she saw, foreshortened and clear to her, Uya, running with great strides and his eyes staring. He was not going after Ugh-lomi. His face was white. It was Uya – *afraid!* He passed, and was still loud hearing, when something else, something large and with grizzled fur, swinging along with soft swift strides, came rushing in pursuit of him.

Eudena suddenly became rigid, ceased to breathe, her clutch convulsive, and her eyes starting.

She had never seen the thing before, she did not even see him clearly now, but she knew at once it was the Terror of the Woodshade. His name was a legend, the children would frighten one another, frighten even themselves with his name, and run screaming to the squatting-place. No man had ever killed any of his kind. Even the mighty mammoth feared his anger. It was the grizzly bear, the lord of the world as the world went then.

As he ran he made a continuous growling grumble. 'Men in my very lair! Fighting and blood. At the very mouth of my lair. Men, men, men. Fighting and blood.' For he was the lord of the wood and of the caves.

Long after he had passed she remained, a girl of stone, staring down through the branches. All her power of action had gone from her. She gripped by instinct with hands and knees and feet. It was some time before she could think, and then only one thing was clear in her mind, that the Terror was between her and the tribe – that it would be impossible to descend.

Presently when her fear was a little abated she clambered into a more comfortable position, where a great branch forked. The trees rose about her, so that she could see nothing of Brother Fire, who is black by day. Birds began to stir, and things that had gone into hiding for fear of her movements crept out. . . .

After a time the taller branches flamed out at the touch of the sunset. High overhead the rooks, who were wiser than men, went cawing home to their squatting-places among the elms. Looking down, things were clearer and darker. Eudena thought of going back to the squatting-place; she let herself down some way, and then the fear of the Terror of the Woodshade came again. While she hesitated a rabbit squealed dismally, and she dared not descend farther.

The shadows gathered, and the deeps of the forest began stirring. Eudena went up the tree again to be nearer the light. Down below the shadows came out of their hiding-places and walked abroad. Overhead the blue deepened. A dreadful stillness came, and then the leaves began whispering.

Eudena shivered and thought of Brother Fire.

The shadows now were gathering in the trees, they sat on the branches and watched her. Branches and leaves were turned to ominous, quiet black shapes that would spring on her if she stirred. Then the white owl, flitting silently, came ghostly through the shades. Darker grew the world and darker, until the leaves and twigs against the sky were black, and the ground was hidden.

She remained there all night, an age-long vigil, straining her ears for the things that went on below in the darkness, and keeping motionless lest some stealthy beast should discover her. Man in those days was never alone in the dark, save for such rare accidents as this. Age after age he had learnt the lesson of its terror – a lesson we poor children of his have nowadays painfully to unlearn. Eudena, though in age a woman, was in heart like a little child. She kept as still, poor little animal, as a hare before it is started.

The stars gathered and watched her – her one grain of comfort. In one bright one she fancied there was something like Ugh-lomi. Then she fancied it *was* Ugh-lomi. And near him, red and duller, was Uya, and as the night passed Ugh-lomi fled before him up the sky.

She tried to see Brother Fire, who guarded the squatting-place from beasts, but he was not in sight. And far away she heard the mammoths trumpeting as they went down to the drinking-place, and once some huge bulk with heavy paces hurried along, making a noise like a calf, but what it was she could not see. But she thought from the voice it was Yaaa the rhinoceros, who stabs with his nose, goes always alone, and rages without cause.

At last the little stars began to hide, and then the larger ones. It was like all the animals vanishing before the Terror. The Sun was coming, lord of the sky, as the grizzly was lord of the forest. Eudena wondered what would happen if one star stayed behind. And then the sky paled to the dawn.

When the daylight came the fear of lurking things passed, and she could descend. She was stiff, but not so stiff as you would have been, dear young lady (by virtue of your upbringing), and as she had not been trained to eat at least once in three hours, but instead had often fasted three days, she did not feel uncomfortably hungry. She crept down the tree very cautiously, and went her way stealthily through the wood, and not a squirrel sprang or deer started but the terror of the grizzly bear froze her marrow.

Her desire was now to find her people again. Her dread of Uya the Cunning was consumed by a greater dread of loneliness. But she had lost her direction. She had run heedlessly overnight, and she could not tell whether the squatting-place was sunward or where it lay. Ever and again she stopped and listened, and at last, very far away, she heard a measured chinking. It was so faint even in the morning stillness that she could tell it must be far away. But she knew the sound was that of a man sharpening a flint.

Presently the trees began to thin out, and then came a regiment of nettles barring the way. She turned aside, and then she came to a fallen tree that she knew, with a noise of bees about it. And so presently she was in sight of the knoll, very far off, and the river under it, and the children and the hippopotami just as they had been yesterday, and the thin spire of smoke swaying in the morning breeze. Far away by the river was the cluster of alders where she had hidden. And at the sight of that the fear of Uya returned, and she crept into a thicket of bracken, out of which a rabbit scuttled, and lay awhile to watch the squatting-place.

The men were mostly out of sight, saving Wau, the flint-chopper; and at that she felt safer. They were away hunting food, no doubt. Some of the women, too, were down in the stream, stooping intent, seeking mussels, crayfish, and water-snails, and at the sight of their occupation Eudena felt hungry. She rose, and ran through the fern, designing to join them. As she went she heard a voice among the bracken calling softly. She stopped. Then suddenly she heard a rustle behind her, and turning, saw Ugh-lomi rising out of the fern. There were streaks of brown blood and dirt on his face, and his eyes were fierce, and the white stone of Uya, the white Fire Stone, that none but Uya dared to touch, was in his hand. In a stride he was beside her, and gripped her arm. He swung her about, and thrust her before him towards the woods. 'Uya,' he said, and waved his arms about. She heard a cry, looked back, and saw all the women standing up, and two wading out of the stream. Then came a nearer howling, and the old woman with the beard, who watched the fire on the knoll, was waving her arms and Wau, the man who had been chipping the flint, was getting to his feet. The little children too were hurrying and shouting.

'Come!' said Ugh-lomi, and dragged her by the arm.

She still did not understand.

'Uya has called the death-word,' said Ugh-lomi, and she glanced back at the screaming curve of figures, and understood.

Wau and all the women and children were coming towards them, a scattered array of buff shock-headed figures, howling, leaping, and crying. Over the knoll two youths hurried. Down among the ferns to the right came a man, heading them off from the wood. Ugh-lomi left her arm, and the two began running side by side, leaping the bracken and stepping clear and wide. Eudena, knowing her fleetness and the fleetness of Ugh-lomi, laughed aloud at the unequal chase. They were an exceptionally straight-limbed couple for those days.

They soon cleared the open, and drew near the wood of chestnut-trees again – neither afraid now because neither was alone. They slackened their pace, already not excessive. And suddenly Eudena cried and swerved aside, pointing, and looking up through the tree-stems. Ugh-lomi saw the feet and legs of men running towards him. Eudena was already running off at a tangent. And as he too turned to follow her they heard the voice of Uya coming through the trees, and roaring out his rage at them.

Then terror came in their hearts, not the terror that numbs, but the terror that makes one silent and swift. They were cut off now on two sides. They were in a sort of corner of pursuit. On the right hand, and near by them, came the men swift and heavy, with bearded Uya, antler in hand, leading them; and on the left, scattered as one scatters corn, yellow dashes among the fern and grass, ran Wau and the women; and even the little children from the shallow had joined the chase. The two parties converged upon them. Off they went, with Eudena ahead.

They knew there was no mercy for them. There was no hunting so sweet to these ancient men as the hunting of men. Once the fierce passion of the chase was lit, the feeble beginnings of humanity in them were thrown to the winds. And Uya in the night had marked Ugh-lomi with the death-word. Ugh-lomi was the day's quarry, the appointed feast.

They ran straight – it was their only chance – taking whatever ground came in the way – a spread of stinging nettles, an open glade, a clump of grass out of which a hyena fled snarling. Then woods again, long stretches of shady leaf-mould and moss under the green trunks. Then a stiff slope, tree-clad, and long

vistas of trees, a glade, a succulent green area of black mud, a
wide open space again, and then a clump of lacerating brambles,
with beast tracks through it. Behind them the chase trailed out
and scattered, with Uya ever at their heels. Eudena kept the
first place, running light and with her breath easy, for Ugh-lomi
carried the Fire Stone in his hand.

It told on his pace – not at first, but after a time. His footsteps
behind her suddenly grew remote. Glancing over her shoulder
as they crossed another open space, Eudena saw that Ugh-lomi
was many yards behind her, and Uya close upon him, with
antler already raised in the air to strike him down. Wau and
the others were but just emerging from the shadow of the
woods.

Seeing Ugh-lomi in peril, Eudena ran sideways, looking back,
threw up her arms and cried aloud, just as the antler flew. And
young Ugh-lomi, expecting this and understanding her cry,
ducked his head, so that the missile merely struck his scalp
lightly, making but a trivial wound, and flew over him. He
turned forthwith, the quartzite Fire Stone in both hands, and
hurled it straight at Uya's body as he ran loose from the throw.
Uya shouted, but could not dodge it. It took him under the ribs,
heavy and flat, and he reeled and went down without a cry.
Ugh-lomi caught up the antler – one tine of it was tipped with
his own blood – and came running on again with a red trickle
just coming out of his hair.

Uya rolled over twice, and lay a moment before he got up,
and then he did not run fast. The colour of his face was changed.
Wau overtook him, and then others, and he coughed and
laboured in his breath. But he kept on.

At last the two fugitives gained the bank of the river, where
the stream ran deep and narrow, and they still had fifty yards
in hand of Wau, the foremost pursuer, the man who made the
smiting-stones. He carried one, a large flint, the shape of an
oyster and double the size, chipped to a chisel edge, in either
hand.

They sprang down the steep bank into the stream, rushed
through the water, swam the deep current in two or three
strokes, and came out wading again, dripping and refreshed, to

clamber up the farther bank. It was undermined, and with willows growing thickly therefrom, so that it needed clambering. And while Eudena was still among the silvery branches and Ugh-lomi still in the water – for the antler had encumbered him – Wau came up against the sky on the opposite bank, and the smiting-stone, thrown cunningly, took the side of Eudena's knee. She struggled to the top and fell.

They heard the pursuers shout to one another, and Ugh-lomi climbing to her and moving jerkily to mar Wau's aim, felt the second smiting-stone graze his ear, and heard the water splash below him.

Then it was Ugh-lomi, the stripling, proved himself to have come to man's estate. For running on, he found Eudena fell behind, limping, and at that he turned, and crying savagely and with a face terrible with sudden wrath and trickling blood, ran swiftly past her back to the bank, whirling the antler round his head. And Eudena kept on, running stoutly still, though she must needs limp at every step, and the pain was already sharp.

So that Wau, rising over the edge and clutching the straight willow branches, saw Ugh-lomi towering over him, gigantic against the blue; saw his whole body swing round, and the grip of his hands upon the antler. The edge of the antler came sweeping through the air, and he saw no more. The water under the osiers whirled and eddied and went crimson six feet down the stream. Uya following stopped knee-high across the stream, and the man who was swimming turned about.

The other men who trailed after – they were none of them very mighty men (for Uya was more cunning than strong, brooking no sturdy rivals) – slackened momentarily at the sight of Ugh-lomi standing there above the willows, bloody and terrible, between them and the halting girl, with the huge antler waving in his hand. It seemed as though he had gone into the water a youth, and come out of it a man full grown.

He knew what there was behind him. A broad stretch of grass, and then a thicket, and in that Eudena could hide. That was clear in his mind, though his thinking powers were too feeble to see what should happen thereafter. Uya stood knee-deep, undecided and unarmed. His heavy mouth hung open, showing his canine teeth, and he panted heavily. His side was flushed and bruised under the hair. The other man beside him carried a sharpened stick. The rest of the hunters came up one by one to the top of the bank, hairy, long-armed men clutching flints and sticks. Two ran off along the bank down stream, and then clambered to the water, where Wau had come to the surface struggling weakly. Before they could reach him he went under again. Two others threatened Ugh-lomi from the bank.

He answered back, shouts, vague insults, gestures. Then Uya, who had been hesitating, roared with rage, and whirling his fists plunged into the water. His followers splashed after him.

Ugh-lomi glanced over his shoulder and found Eudena already vanished into the thicket. He would perhaps have waited for Uya, but Uya preferred to spar in the water below him until the others were beside him. Human tactics in those days, in all serious fighting, were the tactics of the pack. Prey that turned at bay they gathered around and rushed. Ugh-lomi felt the rush coming, and hurling the antler at Uya, turned about and fled.

When he halted to look back from the shadow of the thicket, he found only three of his pursuers had followed him across the river, and they were going back again. Uya, with a bleeding mouth, was on the farther side of the stream again, but lower down, and holding his hand to his side. The others were in the river dragging something to shore. For a time at least the chase was intermitted.

Ugh-lomi stood watching for a space, and snarled at the sight of Uya. Then he turned and plunged into the thicket.

In a minute, Eudena came hastening to join him, and they went on hand in hand. He dimly perceived the pain she suffered from the cut and bruised knee, and chose the easier ways. But they went on all that day, mile after mile, through wood and thicket, until at last they came to the chalkland, open grass with rare woods of beech, and the birch growing near water, and they saw the Wealden mountains nearer, and groups of horses grazing together. They went circumspectly, keeping always near thicket and cover, for this was a strange region – even its ways were strange. Steadily the ground rose, until the chestnut forests spread wide and blue below them, and the Thames marshes shone silvery, high and far. They saw no men, for in those days men were still only just come into this part of the world, and were moving but slowly along the river-ways. Towards evening they came on the river again, but now it ran in a gorge, between high cliffs of white chalk that sometimes overhung it. Down the cliffs was a scrub of birches and there were many birds there. And high up the cliff was a little shelf by a tree, whereon they clambered to pass the night.

They had had scarcely any food; it was not the time of year for berries, and they had no time to go aside to snare or waylay. They tramped in a hungry weary silence, gnawing at twigs and leaves. But over the surface of the cliffs were a multitude of snails, and in a bush were the freshly laid eggs of a little bird, and then Ugh-lomi threw at and killed a squirrel in a beech tree, so that at last they fed well. Ugh-lomi watched during the night, his chin on his knees; and he heard young foxes crying hard by, and the noise of mammoths down the gorge, and the hyenas yelling and laughing far away. It was chilly, but they dared not light a fire. Whenever he dozed, his spirit went abroad, and straightway met with the spirit of Uya, and they fought. And always Ugh-lomi was paralysed so that he could not smite nor run, and then he would awake suddenly. Eudena, too, dreamt evil things of Uya, so that they both awoke with the fear of him in their hearts, and by the light of the dawn they saw a woolly rhinoceros go blundering down the valley.

During the day they caressed one another and were glad of the sunshine, and Eudena's leg was so stiff she sat on the ledge all day. Ugh-lomi found great flints sticking out of the cliff face, greater than any he had seen, and he dragged some to the ledge and began chipping, so as to be armed against Uya when he came again. And at one he laughed heartily, and Eudena laughed, and they threw it about in derision. It had a hole in it. They stuck their fingers through it, it was very funny indeed. Then they peeped at one another through it. Afterwards, Ugh-lomi got himself a stick, and thrusting by chance at this foolish flint, the stick went in and stuck there. He had rammed it in too tightly to withdraw it. That was still stranger – scarcely funny, terrible almost, and for a time Ugh-lomi did not greatly care to touch the thing. It was as if the flint had bit and held with its teeth. But then he got familiar with the odd combination. He swung it about, and perceived that the stick with the heavy stone on the end struck a better blow than anything he knew. He went to and fro swinging it, and striking with it; but later he tired of it and threw it aside. In the afternoon he went up over the brow of the white cliff, and lay watching by a rabbit-warren until the rabbits came out to play. There were no men thereabouts, and the rabbits were heedless. He threw a smiting-stone he had made and got a kill.

That night they made a fire from flint sparks and bracken fronds, and talked and caressed by it. And in their sleep Uya's spirit came again, and suddenly, while Ugh-lomi was trying to fight vainly, the foolish flint on the stick came into his hand, and he struck Uya with it, and behold! it killed him. But after-wards came other dreams of Uya – for spirits take a lot of killing, and he had to be killed again. Then after that the stone would not keep on the stick. He awoke tired and rather gloomy, and was sulky all the forenoon, in spite of Eudena's kindliness, and instead of hunting he sat chipping a sharp edge to the singular flint, and looking strangely at her. Then he bound the perforated flint on to the stick with strips of rabbit skin. And afterwards he walked up and down the ledge, striking with it, and muttering to himself, and thinking of Uya. It felt very fine and heavy in the hand.

Several days, more than there was any counting in those days, five days, it may be, or six, did Ugh-lomi and Eudena stay on that shelf in the gorge of the river, and they lost all fear of men, and their fire burnt redly of a night. And they were very merry together; there was food every day, sweet water, and no enemies. Eudena's knee was well in a couple of days, for those ancient savages had quick-healing flesh. Indeed, they were very happy.

On one of those days Ugh-lomi dropped a chunk of flint over the cliff. He saw it fall, and go bounding across the river bank into the river, and after laughing and thinking it over a little he tried another. This smashed a bush of hazel in the most interesting way. They spent all the morning dropping stones from the ledge, and in the afternoon they discovered this new and interesting pastime was also possible from the cliff brow. The next day they had forgotten this delight. Or at least, it seemed they had forgotten.

But Uya came in dreams to spoil the paradise. Three nights he came fighting Ugh-lomi. In the morning after these dreams Ugh-lomi would walk up and down, threatening him and swinging the axe, and at last came the night after Ugh-lomi brained the otter, and they had feasted. Uya went too far. Ugh-lomi awoke, scowling under his heavy brows, and he took his axe, and extending his hand towards Eudena he bade her wait for him upon the ledge. Then he clambered down the white declivity, glanced up once from the foot of it and flourished his axe, and without looking back again went striding along the river bank until the overhanging cliff at the bend hid him.

Two days and nights did Eudena sit alone by the fire on the ledge waiting, and in the night the beasts howled over the cliffs and down the valley, and on the cliff over against her the hunched hyenas prowled black against the sky. But no evil thing came near her save fear. Once, far away, she heard the roaring of a lion, following the horses as they came northward over the grasslands with the spring. All that time she waited – the waiting that is pain.

And the third day Ugh-lomi came back, up the river. The plumes of a raven were in his hair. The first axe was red-stained, and had long dark hairs upon it, and he carried the necklace that had marked the favourite of Uya in his hand. He walked in the soft places, giving no heed to his trail. Save a raw cut below his jaw there was not a wound upon him. 'Uya!' cried Ugh-lomi exultant, and Eudena saw it was well. He put the necklace on Eudena, and they ate and drank together. And after eating he began to rehearse the whole story from the beginning, when Uya had cast his eyes on Eudena, and Uya and Ugh-lomi, fighting in the forest, had been chased by the bear, eking out his scanty words with abundant pantomime, springing to his feet and whirling the stone axe round when it came to the fighting. The last fight was a mighty one, stamping and shouting, and once a blow at the fire that sent a torrent of sparks up into the night. And Eudena sat red in the light of the fire, gloating on him, her face flushed and her eyes shining, and the necklace Uya had made about her neck. It was a splendid time, and the stars that look down on us looked down on her, our ancestor – who has been dead now these fifty thousand years.

II. – The Cave Bear

In the days when Eudena and Ugh-lomi fled from the people of Uya towards the fir-clad mountains of the Weald, across the forests of sweet chestnut and the grass-clad chalkland, and hid themselves at last in the gorge of the river between the chalk cliffs, men were few and their squatting-places far between. The nearest men to them were those of the tribe, a full day's journey down the river, and up the mountains there were none. Man was indeed a newcomer to this part of the world in that ancient time, coming slowly along the rivers, generation after generation, from one squatting-place to another, from the south-westward. And the animals that held the land, the hippopotamus and rhinoceros of the river valleys, the horses of the grass plains, the deer and swine of the woods, the grey apes in the branches, the cattle of the uplands, feared him but little – let alone the mammoths in the mountains and the elephants that came through the land in the summertime out of the south. For why should they fear him, with but the rough, chipped flints that he had not learnt to haft and which he threw but ill, and the poor spear of sharpened wood, as all the weapons he had against hoof and horn, tooth and claw?

Andoo, the huge cave bear, who lived in the cave up the gorge, had never even seen a man in all his wise and respectable life, until midway through one night, as he was prowling down the gorge along the cliff edge, he saw the glare of Eudena's fire upon the ledge, and Eudena red and shining, and Ugh-lomi, with a gigantic shadow mocking him upon the white cliff, going to and fro, shaking his mane of hair, and waving the axe of stone – the first axe of stone – while he chanted of the killing of Uya. The cave bear was far up the gorge, and he saw the thing slanting-ways and far off. He was so surprised he stood quite still upon the edge, sniffing the novel odour of burning bracken, and wondering whether the dawn was coming up in the wrong place.

He was the lord of the rocks and caves, was the cave bear, as his slighter brother, the grizzly, was lord of the thick woods below, and as the dappled lion – the lion of those days was dappled – was lord of the thorn-thickets, reed-beds, and open plains. He was the greatest of all meat-eaters; he knew no fear, none preyed on him, and none gave him battle; only the rhinoceros was beyond his strength. Even the mammoth shunned his country. This invasion perplexed him. He noticed these new beasts were shaped like monkeys, and sparsely hairy like young pigs. 'Monkey and young pig,' said the cave bear. 'It might not be so bad. But that red thing that jumps, and the black thing jumping with it yonder! Never in my life have I seen such things before!'

He came slowly along the brow of the cliff towards them, stopping thrice to sniff and peer, and the reek of the fire grew stronger. A couple of hyenas also were so intent upon the thing below that Andoo, coming soft and easy, was close upon them before they knew of him or he of them. They started guiltily and went lurching off. Coming round in a wheel, a hundred yards off, they began yelling and calling him names to revenge themselves for the start they had had. 'Ya-ha!' they cried. 'Who can't grub his own burrow? Who eats roots like a pig? ... Ya-ha!' for even in those days the hyena's manners were just as offensive as they are now.

'Who answers the hyena?' growled Andoo, peering through the midnight dimness at them, and then going to look at the cliff edge.

There was Ugh-lomi still telling his story, and the fire getting low, and the scent of the burning hot and strong.

Andoo stood on the edge of the chalk cliff for some time, shifting his vast weight from foot to foot, and swaying his head to and fro, with his mouth open, his ears erect and twitching, and the nostrils of his big, black muzzle sniffing. He was very curious, was the cave bear, more curious than any of the bears that live now, and the flickering fire and the incomprehensible movements of the man, let alone the intrusion into his indisputable province, stirred him with a sense of strange new happenings. He had been after red deer fawn that night, for the cave bear was a miscellaneous hunter, but this quite turned him from that enterprise.

'Ya-ha!' yelled the hyenas behind. 'Ya-ha-ha!'

Peering through the starlight, Andoo saw there were now three or four going to and fro against the grey hillside. 'They will hang about me now all the night ... until I kill,' said Andoo. 'Filth of the world!' And mainly to annoy them, he resolved to watch the red flicker in the gorge until the dawn came to drive the hyena scum home. And after a time they vanished, and he heard their voices, like a party of Cockney beanfeasters, away in the beechwoods. Then they came slinking near again. Andoo yawned and went on along the cliff, and they followed. Then he stopped and went back.

It was a splendid night, beset with shining constellations, the same stars, but not the same constellations we know, for since those days all the stars have had time to move into new places. Far away across the open space beyond where the heavy-shouldered, lean-bodied hyenas blundered and howled, was a beechwood, and the mountain slopes rose beyond, a dim mystery, until their snow-capped summits came out white and cold and clear, touched by the first rays of the yet unseen moon. It was a vast silence, save when the yell of the hyenas flung a vanishing discordance across its peace, or when from down the hills the trumpeting of the new-come elephants came faintly on the faint breeze. And below now, the red flicker had dwindled and was steady, and shone a deeper red, and Ugh-lomi had finished his story and was preparing to sleep, and Eudena sat and listened to the strange voices of unknown beasts, and watched the dark eastern sky growing deeply luminous at the advent of the moon. Down below, the river talked to itself, and things unseen went to and fro.

After a time the bear went away, but in an hour he was back again. Then, as if struck by a thought, he turned, and went up the gorge. ...

The night passed, and Ugh-lomi slept on. The waning moon rose and lit the gaunt white cliff overhead with a light that was pale and vague. The gorge remained in a deeper shadow and seemed all the darker. Then by imperceptible degrees, the day came stealing in the wake of the moonlight. Eudena's eyes wandered to the cliff brow overhead once, and then again. Each time the line was sharp and clear against the sky, and yet she had a dim perception of something lurking there. The red of the fire grew deeper and deeper, grey scales spread upon it, its vertical column of smoke became more and more visible, and up and down the gorge things that had been unseen grew clear in a colourless illumination. She may have dozed.

Suddenly she started up from her squatting position, erect and alert, scrutinizing the cliff up and down.

She made the faintest sound, and Ugh-lomi too, light-sleeping like an animal, was instantly awake. He caught up his axe and came noiselessly to her side.

The light was still dim, the world now all in black and dark grey, and one sickly star still lingered overhead. The ledge they were on was a little grassy space, six feet wide, perhaps, and twenty feet long, sloping outwardly, and with a handful of St John's wort growing near the edge. Below it the soft, white rock fell away in a steep slope of nearly fifty feet to the thick bush of hazel that fringed the river. Down the river this slope increased, until some way off a thin grass held its own right up to the crest of the cliff. Overhead, forty or fifty feet of rock bulged into the great masses characteristic of chalk, but at the end of the ledge a gully, a precipitous groove of discoloured rock, slashed the face of the cliff, and gave a footing to a scrubby growth, by which Eudena and Ugh-lomi went up and down.

They stood as noiseless as startled deer, with every sense expectant. For a minute they heard nothing, and then came a faint rattling of dust down the gully, and the creaking of twigs.

Ugh-lomi gripped his axe, and went to the edge of the ledge, for the bulge of the chalk overhead had hidden the upper part of the gully. And forthwith, with a sudden contraction of the heart, he saw the cave bear halfway down from the brow, and making a gingerly backward step with his flat hind-foot. His hind-quarters were towards Ugh-lomi, and he clawed at the rocks and bushes so that he seemed flattened against the cliff. He looked none the less for that. From his shining snout to his stumpy tail he was a lion and a half, the length of two tall men. He looked over his shoulder, and his huge mouth was open with the exertion of holding up his great carcase, and his tongue lay out. . . .

He got his footing, and came down slowly, a yard nearer.

'Bear,' said Ugh-lomi, looking round with his face white.

But Eudena, with terror in her eyes, was pointing down the cliff.

Ugh-lomi's mouth fell open. For down below, with her big forefeet against the rock, stood another big brown-grey bulk – the she-bear. She was not so big as Andoo, but she was big enough for all that.

Then suddenly Ugh-lomi gave a cry, and catching up a handful of the litter of ferns that lay scattered on the ledge, he thrust it into the pallid ash of the fire. 'Brother Fire!' he cried, 'Brother Fire!' And Eudena, starting into activity, did likewise. 'Brother Fire! Help, help! Brother Fire!'

Brother Fire was still red in his heart, but he turned to grey as they scattered him. 'Brother Fire!' they screamed. But he whispered and passed, and there was nothing but ashes. Then Ugh-lomi danced with anger and struck the ashes with his fist. But Eudena began to hammer the firestone against a flint. And the eyes of each were turning ever and again towards the gully by which Andoo was climbing down. Brother Fire!

Suddenly the huge furry hind-quarters of the bear came into view, beneath the bulge of the chalk that had hidden him. He was still clambering gingerly down the nearly vertical surface. His head was yet out of sight, but they could hear him talking to himself. 'Pig and monkey,' said the cave bear. 'It ought to be good.'

Eudena struck a spark and blew at it; it twinkled brighter and then – went out. At that she cast down flint and firestone and stared blankly. Then she sprang to her feet and scrambled a yard or so up the cliff above the ledge. How she hung on even for a moment I do not know, for the chalk was vertical and without grip for a monkey. In a couple of seconds she had slid back to the ledge again with bleeding hands.

Ugh-lomi was making frantic rushes about the ledge – now he would go to the edge, now to the gully. He did not know what to do, he could not think. The she-bear looked smaller than her mate – much. If they rushed down on her together, *one* might live. 'Ugh?' said the cave bear, and Ugh-lomi turned again and saw his little eyes peering under the bulge of the chalk.

Eudena, cowering at the end of the ledge, began to scream like a gripped rabbit.

At that a sort of madness came upon Ugh-lomi. With a mighty cry, he caught up his axe and ran towards Andoo. The monster gave a grunt of surprise. In a moment Ugh-lomi was clinging to a bush right underneath the bear, and in another he was hanging to its back half buried in fur, with one fist clutched in the hair under its jaw. The bear was too astonished at this fantastic attack to do more than cling passive. And then the axe, the first of all axes, rang on its skull.

The bear's head twisted from side to side, and he began a petulant scolding growl. The axe bit within an inch of the left eye, and the hot blood blinded that side. At that the brute roared with surprise and anger, and his teeth gnashed six inches from Ugh-lomi's face. Then the axe, clubbed close, came down heavily on the corner of the jaw.

The next blow blinded the right side and called forth a roar, this time of pain. Eudena saw the huge, flat feet slipping and sliding, and suddenly the bear gave a clumsy leap sideways, as if for the ledge. Then everything vanished, and the hazels smashed, and a roar of pain and a tumult of shouts and growls came up from far below.

Eudena screamed and ran to the edge and peered over. For a moment, man and bears were a heap together, Ugh-lomi uppermost; and then he had sprung clear and was scaling the gully again, with the bears rolling and striking at one another among the hazels. But he had left his axe below, and three knob-ended streaks of carmine were shooting down his thigh. 'Up!' he cried, and in a moment Eudena was leading the way to the top of the cliff.

In half a minute they were at the crest, their hearts pumping noisily, with Andoo and his wife far and safe below them. Andoo was sitting on his haunches, both paws at work, trying with quick exasperated movements to wipe the blindness out of his eyes, and the she-bear stood on all fours a little way off, ruffled in appearance and growling angrily. Ugh-lomi flung himself flat on the grass, and lay panting and bleeding with his face on his arms.

For a second Eudena regarded the bears, then she came and sat beside him, looking at him. . . .

Presently she put forth her hand timidly and touched him, and made the guttural sound that was his name. He turned over and raised himself on his arm. His face was pale, like the face of one who is afraid. He looked at her steadfastly for a moment, and then suddenly he laughed. 'Waugh!' he said exultantly.

'Waugh!' said she – a simple but expressive conversation.

Then Ugh-lomi came and knelt beside her, and on hands and knees peered over the brow and examined the gorge. His breath was steady now, and the blood on his leg had ceased to flow, though the scratches the she-bear had made were open and wide. He squatted up and sat staring at the footmarks of the great bear as they came to the gully – they were as wide as his head and twice as long. Then he jumped up and went along the cliff face until the ledge was visible. Here he sat down for some time thinking, while Eudena watched him. Presently she saw the bears had gone.

At last Ugh-lomi rose, as one whose mind is made up. He returned towards the gully, Eudena keeping close by him, and together they clambered to the ledge. They took the firestone and a flint, and then Ugh-lomi went down to the foot of the cliff very cautiously, and found his axe. They returned to the cliff as quietly as they could, and set off at a brisk walk. The ledge was a home no longer, with such callers in the neighbourhood. Ugh-lomi carried the axe and Eudena the firestone. So simple was a Palaeolithic removal.

They went upstream, although it might lead to the very lair
of the cave bear, because there was no other way to go. Down
the stream was the tribe, and had not Ugh-lomi killed Uya and
Wau? By the stream they had to keep – because of drinking.

So they marched through beech trees, with the gorge
deepening until the river flowed, a frothing rapid, five hundred
feet below them. Of all the changeful things in this world of
change, the courses of rivers in deep valleys change least. It was
the river Wey, the river we know today, and they marched
over the very spots where nowadays stand little Guildford and
Godalming – the first human beings to come into the land.
Once a grey ape chattered and vanished, and all along the cliff
edge, vast and even, ran the spoor of the great cave bear.

And then the spoor of the bear fell away from the cliff,
showing, Ugh-lomi thought, that he came from some place to
the left, and keeping to the cliff's edge, they presently came
to an end. They found themselves looking down on a great
semi-circular space caused by the collapse of the cliff. It had
smashed right across the gorge, banking the upstream water
back in a pool which overflowed in a rapid. The slip had
happened long ago. It was grassed over, but the face of the cliffs
that stood about the semicircle was still almost fresh-looking
and white as on the day when the rock must have broken and
slid down. Starkly exposed and black under the foot of these
cliffs were the mouths of several caves. And as they stood there,
looking at the space, and disinclined to skirt it, because they
thought the bears' lair lay somewhere on the left in the direction
they must needs take, they saw suddenly first one bear and then
two coming up the grass slope to the right and going across the
amphitheatre towards the caves. Andoo was first; he dropped
a little on his forefoot and his mien was despondent, and the
she-bear came shuffling behind.

Eudena and Ugh-lomi stepped back from the cliff until they
could just see the bears over the verge. Then Ugh-lomi stopped.
Eudena pulled his arm, but he turned with a forbidding gesture,
and her hand dropped. Ugh-lomi stood watching the bears,
with his axe in his hand, until they had vanished into the cave.
He growled softly, and shook the axe at the she-bear's receding

quarters. Then to Eudena's terror, instead of creeping off with her, he lay flat down and crawled forward into such a position that he could just see the cave. It was bears – and he did it as calmly as if it had been rabbits he was watching!

He lay still, like a bared log, sun-dappled, in the shadow of the trees. He was thinking. And Eudena had learnt, even when a little girl, that when Ugh-lomi became still like that, jawbone on fist, novel things presently began to happen.

It was an hour before the thinking was over; it was noon when the two little savages had found their way to the cliff brow that overhung the bears' cave. And all the long afternoon they fought desperately with a great boulder of chalk; trundling it, with nothing but their unaided sturdy muscles, from the gully where it had hung like a loose tooth, towards the cliff top. It was full two yards about, it stood as high as Eudena's waist, it was obtuse-angled and toothed with flints. And when the sun set it was poised, three inches from the edge, above the cave of the great cave bear.

In the cave conversation languished during that afternoon. The she-bear snoozed sulkily in her corner – for she was fond of pig and monkey – and Andoo was busy licking the side of his paw and smearing his face to cool the smart and inflammation of his wounds. Afterwards he went and sat just within the mouth of the cave, blinking out at the afternoon sun with his uninjured eye, and thinking.

'I never was so startled in my life,' he said at last. 'They are the most extraordinary beasts. Attacking *me*!'

'I don't like them,' said the she-bear, out of the darkness behind.

'A feebler sort of beast I *never* saw. I can't think what the world is coming to. Scraggy, weedy legs. . . . Wonder how they keep warm in winter?'

'Very likely they don't,' said the she-bear.

'I suppose it's a sort of monkey gone wrong.'

'It's a change,' said the she-bear.

A pause.

'The advantage he had was merely accidental,' said Andoo. 'These things *will* happen at times.'

'*I* can't understand why you let go,' said the she-bear.

That matter had been discussed before, and settled. So Andoo, being a bear of experience, remained silent for a space. Then he resumed upon a different aspect of the matter. 'He has a sort of claw – a long claw that he seemed to have first on one paw and then on the other. Just one claw. They're very odd things. The bright thing, too, they seemed to have – like that glare that comes in the sky in daytime – only it jumps about – it's really worth seeing. It's a thing with a root, too – like grass when it is windy.'

'Does it bite?' asked the she-bear. 'If it bites it can't be a plant.'

'No—I don't know,' said Andoo. 'But it's curious, anyhow.'

'I wonder if they *are* good eating?' said the she-bear.

'They look it,' said Andoo, with appetite – for the cave bear, like the polar bear, was an incurable carnivore – no roots or honey for *him*.

The two bears fell into a meditation for a space. Then Andoo resumed his simple attentions to his eye. The sunlight up the green slope before the cave mouth grew warmer in tone and warmer, until it was a ruddy amber.

'Curious sort of thing – day,' said the cave bear. 'Lot too much of it, I think. Quite unsuitable for hunting. Dazzles me always. I can't smell nearly so well by day.'

The she-bear did not answer, but there came a measured crunching sound out of the darkness. She had turned up a bone. Andoo yawned. 'Well,' he said. He strolled to the cave mouth and stood with his head projecting, surveying the amphitheatre. He found he had to turn his head completely round to see objects on his right-hand side. No doubt that eye would be all right tomorrow.

He yawned again. There was a tap overhead, and a big mass of chalk flew out from the cliff face, dropped a yard in front of his nose, and starred into a dozen unequal fragments. It startled him extremely.

When he had recovered a little from his shock, he went and sniffed curiously at the representative pieces of the fallen projectile. They had a distinctive flavour, oddly reminiscent of the two drab animals of the ledge. He sat up and pawed the larger lump, and walked round it several times, trying to find a man about it somewhere. ....

When night had come he went off down the river gorge to see if he could cut off either of the ledge's occupants. The ledge was empty, there were no signs of the red thing, but as he was rather hungry he did not loiter long that night, but pushed on to pick up a red deer fawn. He forgot about the drab animals. He found a fawn, but the doe was close by and made an ugly fight for her young. Andoo had to leave the fawn, but as her blood was up she stuck to the attack, and at last he got in a blow of his paw on her nose, and so got hold of her. More meat but less delicacy, and the she-bear, following, had her share. The next afternoon, curiously enough, the very fellow of the first white rock fell, and smashed precisely according to precedent.

The aim of the third, that fell the night after, however, was better. It hit Andoo's unspeculative skull with a crack that echoed up the cliff, and the white fragments went dancing to all the points of the compass. The she-bear coming after him and sniffing curiously at him, found him lying in an odd sort of attitude, with his head wet and all out of shape. She was a young she-bear, and inexperienced, and having sniffed about him for some time and licked him a little, and so forth, she decided to leave him until the odd mood had passed, and went on her hunting alone.

She looked up the fawn of the red doe they had killed two nights ago, and found it. But it was lonely hunting without Andoo, and she returned caveward before dawn. The sky was grey and overcast, the trees up the gorge were black and unfamiliar, and into her ursine mind came a dim sense of strange and dreary happenings. She lifted up her voice and called Andoo by name. The sides of the gorge re-echoed her.

As she approached the caves she saw in the half light, and heard a couple of jackals scuttle off, and immediately after a hyena howled and a dozen clumsy bulks went lumbering up the slope, and stopped and yelled derision. 'Lord of the rocks and caves – ya-ha!' came down the wind. The dismal feeling in the she-bear's mind became suddenly acute. She shuffled across the amphitheatre.

'Ya-ha!' said the hyenas, retreating. 'Ya-ha!'

The cave bear was not lying quite in the same attitude, because the hyenas had been busy, and in one place his ribs showed white. Dotted over the turf about him lay the smashed fragments of the three great lumps of chalk. And the air was full of the scent of death.

The she-bear stopped dead. Even now, that the great and wonderful Andoo was killed was beyond her believing. Then she heard far overhead a sound, a queer sound, a little like the shout of a hyena but fuller and lower in pitch. She looked up, her little dawn-blinded eyes seeing little, her nostrils quivering. And there, on the cliff edge, far above her against the bright pink of dawn, were two little shaggy round dark things, the heads of Eudena and Ugh-lomi, as they shouted derision at her. But though she could not see them very distinctly she could hear, and dimly she began to apprehend. A novel feeling as of imminent strange evils came into her heart.

She began to examine the smashed fragments of chalk that lay about Andoo. For a space she stood still, looking about her and making a low continuous sound that was almost a moan. Then she went back incredulously to Andoo to make one last effort to rouse him.

III. – The First Horseman

In the days before Ugh-lomi there was little trouble between the horses and men. They lived apart – the men in the river swamps and thickets, the horses on the wide grassy uplands between the chestnuts and the pines. Sometimes a pony would come straying into the clogging marshes to make a flint-hacked meal, and sometimes the tribe would find one, the kill of a lion, and drive off the jackals, and feast heartily while the sun was high. These horses of the old time were clumsy at the fetlock and dun-coloured, with a rough tail and big head. They came every springtime north-westward into the country, after the swallows and before the hippopotami, as the grass on the wide

downland stretches grew long. They came only in small bodies
thus far, each herd, a stallion and two or three mares and a foal
or so, having its own stretch of country, and they went again
when the chestnut-trees were yellow and the wolves came down
the Wealden mountains.

It was their custom to graze right out in the open, going into
cover only in the heat of the day. They avoided the long
stretches of thorn and beechwood, preferring an isolated group
of trees void of ambuscade, so that it was hard to come upon
them. They were never fighters; their heels and teeth were for
one another, but in the clear country, once they were started,
no living thing came near them, though perhaps the elephant
might have done so had he felt the need. And in those days man
seemed a harmless thing enough. No whisper of prophetic
intelligence told the species of the terrible slavery that was to
come, of the whip and spur and bearing-rein, the clumsy load
and the slippery street, the insufficient food, and the knacker's
yard, that was to replace the wide grassland and the freedom
of the earth.

Down in the Wey marshes Ugh-lomi and Eudena had never
seen the horses closely, but now they saw them every day as
the two of them raided out from their lair on the ledge in the
gorge, raiding together in search of food. They had returned to
the ledge after the killing of Andoo; for of the she-bear they
were not afraid. The she-bear had become afraid of them, and
when she winded them she went aside. The two went together
everywhere; for since they had left the tribe Eudena was not so
much Ugh-lomi's woman as his mate; she learnt to hunt even –
as much, that is, as any woman could. She was indeed a marvellous woman. He would lie for hours watching a beast, or
planning catches in that shock head of his, and she would stay
beside him, with her bright eyes upon him, offering no irritating
suggestions – as still as any man. A wonderful woman!

At the top of the cliff was an open grassy lawn and then
beechwoods, and going through the beechwoods one came to
the edge of the rolling grassy expanse, and in sight of the
horses. Here, on the edge of the wood and bracken, were
the rabbit-burrows, and here among the fronds Eudena and

Ugh-lomi would lie with their throwing-stones ready, until the little people came out to nibble and play in the sunset. And while Eudena would sit, a silent figure of watchfulness, regarding the burrows, Ugh-lomi's eyes were ever away across the greensward at those wonderful grazing strangers.

In a dim way he appreciated their grace and their supple nimbleness. As the sun declined in the evening-time, and the heat of the day passed, they would become active, would start chasing one another, neighing, dodging, shaking their manes, coming round in great curves, sometimes so close that the pounding of the turf sounded like hurried thunder. It looked so fine that Ugh-lomi wanted to join in badly. And sometimes one would roll over on the turf, kicking four hoofs heavenward, which seemed formidable and was certainly much less alluring.

Dim imaginings ran through Ugh-lomi's mind as he watched – by virtue of which two rabbits lived the longer. And sleeping, his brains were clearer and bolder – for that was the way in those days. He came near the horses, he dreamt, and fought, smiting-stone against hoof, but then the horses changed to men, or, at least, to men with horses' heads, and he awoke in a cold sweat of terror.

Yet the next day in the morning, as the horses were grazing, one of the mares whinnied, and they saw Ugh-lomi coming up the wind. They all stopped their eating and watched him. Ugh-lomi was not coming towards them, but strolling obliquely across the open, looking at anything in the world but horses. He had stuck three fern-fronds into the mat of his hair, giving him a remarkable appearance, and he walked very slowly. 'What's up now?' said the Master Horse, who was capable, but inexperienced.

'It looks more like the first half of an animal than anything else in the world,' he said. 'Fore-legs and no hind.'

'It's only one of those pink monkey things,' said the Eldest Mare. 'They're a sort of river monkey. They're quite common on the plains.'

Ugh-lomi continued his oblique advance. The Eldest Mare was struck with the want of motive in his proceedings.

'Fool!' said the Eldest Mare, in a quick conclusive way she

had. She resumed her grazing. The Master Horse and the Second Mare followed suit.

'Look! he's nearer,' said the Foal with a stripe.

One of the younger foals made uneasy movements. Ugh-lomi squatted down, and sat regarding the horses fixedly. In a little while he was satisfied that they meant neither flight nor hostilities. He began to consider his next procedure. He did not feel anxious to kill, but he had his axe with him, and the spirit of sport was upon him. How would one kill one of these creatures? – these great beautiful creatures!

Eudena, watching him with a fearful admiration from the cover of the bracken, saw him presently go on all fours, and so proceed again. But the horses preferred him a biped to a quadruped, and the Master Horse threw up his head and gave the word to move. Ugh-lomi thought they were off for good, but after a minute's gallop they came round in a wide curve, and stood winding him. Then, as a rise in the ground hid him, they tailed out, the Master Horse leading, and approached him spirally.

He was as ignorant of the possibilities of a horse as they were of his. And at this stage it would seem he funked. He knew this kind of stalking would make red deer or buffalo charge, if it were persisted in. At any rate Eudena saw him jump up and come walking towards her with the fern plumes held in his hand.

She stood up, and he grinned to show that the whole thing was an immense lark, and that what he had done was just what he had planned to do from the very beginning. So that incident ended. But he was very thoughtful all that day.

The next day this foolish drab creature with the leonine mane, instead of going about the grazing or hunting he was made for, was prowling round the horses again. The Eldest Mare was all for silent contempt. 'I suppose he wants to learn something from us,' she said, and '*Let* him.' The next day he was at it again. The Master Horse decided he meant absolutely nothing. But as a matter of fact, Ugh-lomi, the first of men to feel that curious spell of the horse that binds us even to this day, meant a great deal. He admired them unreservedly. There was a rudiment of the snob in him, I am afraid, and he wanted to be near these beautifully-curved animals. Then there were vague conceptions of a kill. If only they would let him come near them! But they drew the line, he found, at fifty yards. If he came nearer than that they moved off – with dignity. I suppose it was the way he had blinded Andoo that made him think of leaping on the back of one of them. But though Eudena after a time came out in the open too, and they did some unobtrusive stalking, things stopped there.

Then one memorable day a new idea came to Ugh-lomi. The horse looks down and level, but he does not look up. No animals look up – they have too much common sense. It was only that fantastic creature, man, could waste his wits skyward. Ugh-lomi made no philosophical deductions, but he perceived the thing was so. So he spent a weary day in a beech that stood in the open, while Eudena stalked. Usually the horses went into the shade in the heat of the afternoon, but that day the sky was overcast, and they would not, in spite of Eudena's solicitude.

It was two days after that that Ugh-lomi had his desire. The day was blazing hot, and the multiplying flies asserted themselves. The horses stopped grazing before midday, and came into the shadow below him, and stood in couples nose to tail, flapping.

The Master Horse, by virtue of his heels, came closest to the tree. And suddenly there was a rustle and a creak, a *thud*. .... Then a sharp chipped flint bit him on the cheek. The Master Horse stumbled, came on one knee, rose to his feet, and was off like the wind. The air was full of the whirl of limbs, the prance of hoofs, and snorts of alarm. Ugh-lomi was pitched a foot in the air, came down again, up again, his stomach was hit violently, and then his knees got a grip of something between them. He found himself clutching with knees, feet, and hands, careering violently with extraordinary oscillation through the air – his axe gone heaven knows whither. 'Hold tight,' said Mother Instinct, and he did.

He was aware of a lot of coarse hair in his face, some of it between his teeth, and of green turf streaming past in front of his eyes. He saw the shoulder of the Master Horse, vast and sleek, with the muscles flowing swiftly under the skin. He perceived that his arms were round the neck, and that the violent jerkings he experienced had a sort of rhythm.

Then he was in the midst of a wild rush of tree-stems, and then there were fronds of bracken about, and then more open turf. Then a stream of pebbles rushing past, little pebbles flying sideways athwart the stream from the blow of the swift hoofs. Ugh-lomi began to feel frightfully sick and giddy, but he was not the stuff to leave go simply because he was uncomfortable.

He dared not leave his grip, but he tried to make himself more comfortable. He released his hug on the neck, gripping the mane instead. He slipped his knees forward, and pushing back, came into a sitting position where the quarters broaden. It was nervous work, but he managed it, and at last he was fairly seated astride, breathless indeed, and uncertain, but with that frightful pounding of his body at any rate relieved.

Slowly the fragments of Ugh-lomi's mind got into order again. The pace seemed to him terrific, but a kind of exultation was beginning to oust his first frantic terror. The air rushed by, sweet and wonderful, the rhythm of the hoofs changed and broke up and returned into itself again. They were on turf now, a wide glade – the beech trees a hundred yards away on either side, and a succulent band of green starred with pink blossom and shot with silver water here and there, meandered down the middle. Far off was a glimpse of blue valley – far away. The exultation grew. It was man's first taste of pace.

Then came a wide space dappled with flying fallow deer scattering this way and that, and then a couple of jackals, mistaking Ugh-lomi for a lion, came hurrying after him. And when they saw it was not a lion they still came on out of curiosity. On galloped the horse, with his one idea of escape, and after him the jackals, with pricked ears and quickly-barked remarks. 'Which kills which?' said the first jackal. 'It's the horse being killed,' said the second. They gave the howl of following, and the horse answered to it as a horse answers nowadays to the spur.

On they rushed, a little tornado through the quiet day, putting up startled birds, sending a dozen unexpected things darting to cover, raising a myriad of indignant dung-flies,

smashing little blossoms, flowering complacently, back into
their parental turf. Trees again, and then splash, splash across
a torrent; then a hare shot out of a tuft of grass under the
very hoofs of the Master Horse, and the jackals left them
incontinently. So presently they broke into the open again, a
wide expanse of turfy hillside – the very grassy downs that fall
northward nowadays from the Epsom Stand.[5]

The first hot bolt of the Master Horse was long since over. He
was falling into a measured trot, and Ugh-lomi, albeit bruised
exceedingly and quite uncertain of the future, was in a state of
glorious enjoyment. And now came a new development. The
pace broke again, the Master Horse came round on a short
curve, and stopped dead. . . .

Ugh-lomi became alert. He wished he had a flint, but the
throwing flint he had carried in a thong about his waist was –
like the axe – heaven knows where. The Master Horse turned
his head, and Ugh-lomi became aware of an eye and teeth. He
whipped his leg into a position of security, and hit at the cheek
with his fist. Then the head went down somewhere out of
existence apparently, and the back he was sitting on flew up
into a dome. Ugh-lomi became a thing of instinct again – strictly
prehensile; he held by knees and feet, and his head seemed
sliding towards the turf. His fingers were twisted into the shock
of mane, and the rough hair of the horse saved him. The gradi-
ent he was on lowered again, and then – 'Whup!' said Ugh-lomi
astonished, and the slant was the other way up. But Ugh-lomi
was a thousand generations nearer the primordial than man:
no monkey could have held on better. And the lion had been
training the horse for countless generations against the tactics
of rolling and rearing back. But he kicked like a master, and
buck-jumped rather neatly. In five minutes Ugh-lomi lived a
lifetime. If he came off the horse would kill him, he felt assured.

Then the Master Horse decided to stick to his old tactics
again, and suddenly went off at a gallop. He headed down the
slope, taking the steep places at a rush, swerving neither to the
right nor to the left, and, as they rode down, the wide expanse
of valley sank out of sight behind the approaching skirmishers
of oak and hawthorn. They skirted a sudden hollow with the

pool of a spring, rank weeds and silver bushes. The ground grew softer and the grass taller, and on the right-hand side and the left came scattered bushes of May – still splashed with belated blossom. Presently the bushes thickened until they lashed the passing rider, and little flashes and gouts of blood came out on horse and man. Then the way opened again.

And then came a wonderful adventure. A sudden squeal of unreasonable anger rose amidst the bushes, the squeal of some creature bitterly wronged. And crashing after them appeared a big, grey-blue shape. It was Yaaa, the big-horned rhinoceros, in one of those fits of fury of his, charging full tilt, after the manner of his kind. He had been startled at his feeding, and someone, it did not matter who, was to be ripped and trampled therefore. He was bearing down on them from the left, with his wicked little eye red, his great horn down and his tail like a jury-mast behind him. For a minute Ugh-lomi was minded to slip off and dodge, and then behold! the staccato of the hoofs grew swifter, and the rhinoceros and his stumpy hurrying little legs seemed to slide out at the back corner of Ugh-lomi's eye. In two minutes they were through the bushes of May, and out in the open, going fast. For a space he could hear the ponderous paces in pursuit receding behind him, and then it was just as if Yaaa had not lost his temper, as if Yaaa had never existed.

The pace never faltered, on they rode and on.

Ugh-lomi was now all exultation. To exult in those days was to insult. 'Ya-ha! big nose!' he said, trying to crane back and see some remote speck of a pursuer. 'Why don't you carry your smiting-stone in your fist?' he ended with a frantic whoop.

But that whoop was unfortunate, for coming close to the ear of the horse, and being quite unexpected, it startled the stallion extremely. He shied violently. Ugh-lomi suddenly found himself uncomfortable again. He was hanging on to the horse, he found, by one arm and one knee.

The rest of the ride was honourable but unpleasant. The view was chiefly of blue sky, and that was combined with the most unpleasant physical sensations. Finally, a bush of thorn lashed him and he let go.

He hit the ground with his cheek and shoulder, and then,

after a complicated and extraordinarily rapid movement, hit it again with the end of his backbone. He saw splashes and sparks of light and colour. The ground seemed bouncing about just like the horse had done. Then he found he was sitting on turf, six yards beyond the bush. In front of him was a space of grass, growing greener and greener, and a number of human beings in the distance, and the horse was going round at a smart gallop quite a long way off to the right.

The human beings were on the opposite side of the river, some still in the water, but they were all running away as hard as they could go. The advent of a monster that took to pieces was not the sort of novelty they cared for. For quite a minute Ugh-lomi sat regarding them in a purely spectacular spirit. The bend of the river, the knoll among the reeds and royal ferns, the thin streams of smoke going up to Heaven, were all perfectly familiar to him. It was the squatting-place of the Sons of Uya, of Uya from whom he had fled with Eudena, and whom he had waylaid in the chestnut woods and killed with the First Axe.

He rose to his feet, still dazed from his fall, and as he did so the scattering fugitives turned and regarded him. Some pointed to the receding horse and chattered. He walked slowly towards them, staring. He forgot the horse, he forgot his own bruises, in the growing interest of this encounter. There were fewer of them than there had been – he supposed the others must have hid – the heap of fern for the night fire was not so high. By the flint heaps should have sat Wau – but then he remembered he had killed Wau. Suddenly brought back to this familiar scene, the gorge and the bears and Eudena seemed things remote, things dreamt of.

He stopped at the bank and stood regarding the tribe. His mathematical abilities were of the slightest, but it was certain there were fewer. The men might be away, but there were fewer women and children. He gave the shout of homecoming. His quarrel had been with Uya and Wau – not with the others. 'Children of Uya!' he cried. They answered with his name, a little fearfully because of the strange way he had come.

For a space they spoke together. Then an old woman lifted a shrill voice and answered him. 'Our Lord is a Lion.'

Ugh-lomi did not understand that saying. They answered him again several together, 'Uya comes again. He comes as a Lion. Our Lord is a Lion. He comes at night. He slays whom he will. But none other may slay us, Ugh-lomi, none other may slay us.'

Still Ugh-lomi did not understand.

'Our Lord is a Lion. He speaks no more to men.'

Ugh-lomi stood regarding them. He had had dreams – he knew that though he had killed Uya, Uya still existed. And now they told him Uya was a Lion.

The shrivelled old woman, the mistress of the fire-minders, suddenly turned and spoke softly to those next to her. She was a very old woman indeed, she had been the first of Uya's wives, and he had let her live beyond the age to which it is seemly a woman should be permitted to live. She had been cunning from the first, cunning to please Uya and to get food. And now she was great in counsel. She spoke softly, and Ugh-lomi watched her shrivelled form across the river with a curious distaste. Then she called aloud, 'Come over to us, Ugh-lomi.'

A girl suddenly lifted up her voice. 'Come over to us, Ugh-lomi,' she said. And they all began crying, 'Come over to us, Ugh-lomi.'

It was strange how their manner changed after the old woman called.

He stood quite still watching them all. It was pleasant to be called, and the girl who had called first was a pretty one. But she made him think of Eudena.

'Come over to us, Ugh-lomi,' they cried, and the voice of the shrivelled old woman rose above them all. At the sound of her voice his hesitation returned.

He stood on the river bank, Ugh-lomi – Ugh the Thinker – with his thoughts slowly taking shape. Presently one and then another paused to see what he would do. He was minded to go back, he was minded not to. Suddenly his fear or his caution got the upper hand. Without answering them he turned, and walked back towards the distant thorn-trees, the way he had come. Forthwith the whole tribe started crying to him again very eagerly. He hesitated and turned, then he went on, then he turned again, and then once again, regarding them with troubled eyes as they called. The last time he took two paces back, before his fear stopped him. They saw him stop once more, and suddenly shake his head and vanish among the hawthorn-trees.

Then all the women and children lifted up their voices together, and called to him in one last vain effort.

Far down the river the reeds were stirring in the breeze, where, convenient for his new sort of feeding, the old lion, who had taken to man-eating, had made his lair.

The old woman turned her face that way, and pointed to the hawthorn thickets. 'Uya,' she screamed, 'there goes thine enemy! There goes thine enemy, Uya! Why do you devour us nightly? We have tried to snare him! There goes thine enemy, Uya!'

But the lion who preyed upon the tribe was taking his siesta. The cry went unheard. That day he had dined on one of the plumper girls, and his mood was a comfortable placidity. He really did not understand that he was Uya or that Ugh-lomi was his enemy.

So it was that Ugh-lomi rode the horse, and heard first of Uya the lion, who had taken the place of Uya the Master, and was eating up the tribe. And as he hurried back to the gorge his mind was no longer full of the horse, but of the thought that Uya was still alive, to slay or be slain. Over and over again he saw the shrunken band of women and children crying that Uya was a lion. Uya was a lion!

And presently, fearing the twilight might come upon him, Ugh-lomi began running.

IV. – Uya the Lion

The old lion was in luck. The tribe had a certain pride in their ruler, but that was all the satisfaction they got out of it. He came the very night that Ugh-lomi killed Uya the Cunning, and so it was they named him Uya. It was the old woman, the fire-minder, who first named him Uya. A shower had lowered the fires to a glow, and made the night dark. And as they conversed together, and peered at one another in the darkness, and wondered fearfully what Uya would do to them in their dreams now that he was dead, they heard the mounting reverberations of the lion's roar close at hand. Then everything was still.

They held their breath, so that almost the only sounds were the patter of the rain and the hiss of the raindrops in the ashes. And then, after an interminable time, a crash, and a shriek of fear, and a growling. They sprang to their feet, shouting, screaming, running this way and that, but brands would not burn, and in a minute the victim was being dragged away through the ferns. It was Irk, the brother of Wau.

So the lion came.

The ferns were still wet from the rain the next night, and he came and took Click with the red hair. That sufficed for two nights. And then in the dark between the moons he came three nights, night after night, and that though they had good fires. He was an old lion with stumpy teeth, but very silent and very cool; he knew of fires before; these were not the first of mankind that had ministered to his old age. The third night he came between the outer fire and the inner, and he leapt the flint heap, and pulled down Irm the son of Irk, who had seemed like to be the leader. That was a dreadful night, because they lit great flares of fern and ran screaming, and the lion missed his hold of Irm. By the glare of the fire they saw Irm struggle up, and run a little way towards them, and then the lion in two bounds had him down again. That was the last of Irm.

So fear came, and all the delight of spring passed out of their lives. Already there were five gone out of the tribe, and four nights added three more to the number. Food-seeking became spiritless, none knew who might go next, and all day the women toiled, even the favourite women, gathering litter and sticks for the night fires. And the hunters hunted ill: in the warm springtime hunger came again as though it was still winter. The tribe might have moved, had they had a leader, but they had no leader, and none knew where to go that the lion could not follow them. So the old lion waxed fat and thanked heaven for the kindly race of men. Two of the children and a youth died while the moon was still new, and then it was the shrivelled old fire-minder first bethought herself in a dream of Eudena and Ugh-lomi, and of the way Uya had been slain. She had lived in fear of Uya all her days, and now she lived in fear of the lion. That Ugh-lomi could kill Uya for good – Ugh-lomi whom she had seen born – was impossible. It was Uya still seeking his enemy!

And then came the strange return of Ugh-lomi, a wonderful animal seen galloping far across the river, that suddenly changed into two animals, a horse and a man. Following this portent, the vision of Ugh-lomi on the farther bank of the river. . . . Yes, it was all plain to her. Uya was punishing them, because they had not hunted down Ugh-lomi and Eudena.

The men came straggling back to the chances of the night while the sun was still golden in the sky. They were received with the story of Ugh-lomi. She went across the river with them and showed them his spoor hesitating on the farther bank. Siss the Tracker knew the feet for Ugh-lomi's. 'Uya needs Ugh-lomi,' cried the old woman, standing on the left of the bend, a gesticulating figure of flaring bronze in the sunset. Her cries were strange sounds, flitting to and fro on the borderland of speech, but this was the sense they carried: 'The lion needs Eudena. He comes night after night seeking Eudena and Ugh-lomi. When he cannot find Eudena and Ugh-lomi, he grows angry and he kills. Hunt Eudena and Ugh-lomi, Eudena whom he pursued, and Ugh-lomi for whom he gave the death-word! Hunt Eudena and Ugh-lomi!'

She turned to the distant reed-bed, as sometimes she had turned to Uya in his life. 'Is it not so, my lord?' she cried. And, as if in answer, the tall reeds bowed before a breath of wind.

Far into the twilight the sound of hacking was heard from the squatting-places. It was the men sharpening their ashen spears against the hunting of the morrow. And in the night, early before the moon rose, the lion came and took the girl of Siss the Tracker.

In the morning before the sun had risen, Siss the Tracker, and the lad Wau-hau, who now chipped flints, and One Eye, and Bo, and the Snail-eater, the two red-haired men, and

Cat's-skin and Snake, all the men that were left alive of the Sons of Uya, taking their ash spears and their smiting-stones, and with throwing stones in the beast-paw bags, started forth upon the trail of Ugh-lomi through the hawthorn thickets where Yaaa the Rhinoceros and his brothers were feeding, and up the bare downland towards the beechwoods.

That night the fires burnt high and fierce, as the waxing moon set, and the lion left the crouching women and children in peace.

And the next day, while the sun was still high, the hunters returned – all save One Eye, who lay dead with a smashed skull at the foot of the ledge. (When Ugh-lomi came back that evening from stalking the horses, he found the vultures already busy over him.) And with them the hunters brought Eudena, bruised and wounded, but alive. That had been the strange order of the shrivelled old woman, that she was to be brought alive – 'She is no kill for us. She is for Uya the Lion.' Her hands were tied with thongs, as though she had been a man, and she came weary and drooping – her hair over her eyes and matted with blood. They walked about her, and ever and again the Snail-eater, whose name she had given, would laugh and strike her with his ashen spear. And after he had struck her with his spear, he would look over his shoulder like one who had done an over-bold deed. The others, too, looked over their shoulders ever and again, and all were in a hurry save Eudena. When the old woman saw them coming, she cried aloud with joy.

They made Eudena cross the river with her hands tied, although the current was strong and when she slipped the old woman screamed, first with joy and then for fear she might be drowned. And when they had dragged Eudena to shore, she could not stand for a time, albeit they beat her sore. So they let her sit with her feet touching the water, and her eyes staring before her, and her face set, whatever they might do or say. All the tribe came down to the squatting-place, even curly little Haha, who as yet could scarcely toddle, and stood staring at Eudena and the old woman, as now we should stare at some strange wounded beast and its captor.

The old woman tore off the necklace of Uya that was about

Eudena's neck, and put it on herself – she had been the first to
wear it. Then she tore at Eudena's hair, and took a spear from
Siss and beat her with all her might. And when she had vented
the warmth of her heart on the girl she looked closely into her
face. Eudena's eyes were closed and her features were set, and
she lay so still that for a moment the old woman feared she was
dead. And then her nostrils quivered. At that the old woman
slapped her face and laughed and gave the spear to Siss again,
and went a little way off from her and began to talk and jeer at
her after her manner.

The old woman had more words than any in the tribe. And
her talk was a terrible thing to hear. Sometimes she screamed
and moaned incoherently, and sometimes the shape of her
guttural cries was the mere phantom of thoughts. But she conveyed to Eudena, nevertheless, much of the things that were yet
to come, of the Lion and of the torment he would do her. 'And
Ugh-lomi! Ha, ha! Ugh-lomi is slain?'

And suddenly Eudena's eyes opened and she sat up again,
and her look met the old woman's fair and level. 'No,' she said
slowly, like one trying to remember, 'I did not see my Ugh-lomi
slain. I did not see my Ugh-lomi slain.'

'Tell her,' cried the old woman. 'Tell her – he that killed him.
Tell her how Ugh-lomi was slain.'

She looked, and all the women and children there looked,
from man to man.

None answered her. They stood shamefaced.

'Tell her,' said the old woman. The men looked at one
another.

Eudena's face suddenly lit.

'Tell her,' she said. 'Tell her, mighty men! Tell her the killing
of Ugh-lomi.'

The old woman rose and struck her sharply across her mouth.

'We could not find Ugh-lomi,' said Siss the Tracker, slowly.
'Who hunts two, kills none.'

Then Eudena's heart leapt, but she kept her face hard. It was
as well, for the old woman looked at her sharply, with murder
in her eyes.

Then the old woman turned her tongue upon the men because

they had feared to go on after Ugh-lomi. She dreaded no one now Uya was slain. She scolded them as one scolds children. And they scowled at her, and began to accuse one another. Until suddenly Siss the Tracker raised his voice and bade her hold her peace.

And so when the sun was setting they took Eudena and went – though their hearts sank within them – along the trail the old lion had made in the reeds. All the men went together. At one place was a group of alders, and here they hastily bound Eudena where the lion might find her when he came abroad in the twilight, and having done so they hurried back until they were near the squatting-place. Then they stopped. Siss stopped first and looked back again at the alders. They could see her head even from the squatting-place, a little black shock under the limb of the larger tree. That was as well.

All the women and children stood watching upon the crest of the mound. And the old woman stood and screamed for the lion to take her whom he sought, and counselled him on the torments he might do her.

Eudena was very weary now, stunned by beatings and fatigue and sorrow, and only the fear of the thing that was still to come upheld her. The sun was broad and blood-red between the stems of the distant chestnuts, and the west was all on fire; the evening breeze had died to a warm tranquillity. The air was full of midge swarms, the fish in the river hard by would leap at times, and now and again a cockchafer would drone through the air. Out of the corner of her eye Eudena could see a part of the squatting-knoll, and little figures standing and staring at her. And – a very little sound but very clear – she could hear the beating of the firestone. Dark and near to her and still was the reed-fringed thicket of the lair.

Presently the firestone ceased. She looked for the sun and found he had gone, and overhead and growing brighter was the waxing moon. She looked towards the thicket of the lair, seeking shapes in the reeds, and then suddenly she began to wriggle and wriggle, weeping and calling upon Ugh-lomi.

But Ugh-lomi was far away. When they saw her head moving with her struggles, they shouted together on the knoll, and she

desisted and was still. And then came the bats, and the star that
was like Ugh-lomi crept out of its blue hiding-place in the west.
She called to it, but softly, because she feared the lion. And all
through the coming of the twilight the thicket was still.

So the dark crept upon Eudena, and the moon grew bright,
and the shadows of things that had fled up the hillside and
vanished with the evening came back to them short and black.
And the dark shapes in the thicket of reeds and alders where
the lion lay, gathered, and a faint stir began there. But nothing
came out therefrom all through the gathering of the darkness.

She looked at the squatting-place and saw the fires glowing
smoky-red, and the men and women going to and fro. The
other way, over the river, a white mist was rising. Then far
away came the whimpering of young foxes and the yell of a
hyena.

There were long gaps of aching waiting. After a long time
some animal splashed in the water, and seemed to cross the
river at the ford beyond the lair, but what animal it was she
could not see. From the distant drinking-pools she could hear
the sound of splashing, and the noise of elephants – so still was
the night.

The earth was now a colourless arrangement of white reflections and impenetrable shadows, under the blue sky. The silvery
moon was already spotted with the filigree crests of the chestnut
woods, and over the shadowy eastward hills the stars were
multiplying. The knoll fires were bright red now, and black
figures stood waiting against them. They were waiting for a
scream. . . . Surely it would be soon.

The night suddenly seemed full of movement. She held her
breath. Things were passing – one, two, three – subtly sneaking
shadows. . . . Jackals.

Then a long waiting again.

Then, asserting itself as real at once over all the sounds her
mind had imagined, came a stir in the thicket, then a vigorous
movement. There was a snap. The reeds crashed heavily, once,
twice, thrice, and then everything was still save a measured
swishing. She heard a low tremulous growl, and then everything
was still again. The stillness lengthened – would it never end?

She held her breath; she bit her lips to stop screaming. Then something scuttled through the undergrowth. Her scream was involuntary. She did not hear the answering yell from the mound.

Immediately the thicket woke up to vigorous movement again. She saw the grass stems waving in the light of the setting moon, the alders swaying. She struggled violently – her last struggle. But nothing came towards her. A dozen monsters seemed rushing about in that little place for a couple of minutes, and then again came silence. The moon sank behind the distant chestnuts and the night was dark.

Then an odd sound, a sobbing panting, that grew faster and fainter. Yet another silence, and then dim sounds and the grunting of some animal.

Everything was still again. Far away eastwards an elephant trumpeted, and from the woods came a snarling and yelping that died away.

In the long interval the moon shone out again, between the stems of the trees on the ridge, sending two great bars of light and a bar of darkness across the reedy waste. Then came a steady rustling, a splash, and the reeds swayed wider and wider apart. And at last they broke open, cleft from root to crest. . . . The end had come.

She looked to see the thing that had come out of the reeds. For a moment it seemed certainly the great head and jaw she expected, and then it dwindled and changed. It was a dark low thing, that remained silent, but it was not the lion. It became still – everything became still. She peered. It was like some gigantic frog, two limbs and a slanting body. Its head moved about searching the shadows. . . .

A rustle, and it moved clumsily, with a sort of hopping. And as it moved it gave a low groan.

The blood rushing through her veins was suddenly joy. '*Ugh-lomi!*' she whispered,

The thing stopped. '*Eudena*,' he answered softly with pain in his voice, and peering into the alders.

He moved again, and came out of the shadow beyond the reeds into the moonlight. All his body was covered with dark smears. She saw he was dragging his legs, and that he gripped his axe, the first axe, in one hand. In another moment he had struggled into the position of all fours, and had staggered over to her. 'The lion,' he said in a strange mingling of exultation and anguish. 'Wau! – I have slain a lion. With my own hand. Even as I slew the great bear.' He moved to emphasize his words, and suddenly broke off with a faint cry. For a space he did not move.

'Let me free,' whispered Eudena. . . .

He answered her no words but pulled himself up from his crawling attitude by means of the alder stem, and hacked at her thongs with the sharp edge of his axe. She heard him sob at each blow. He cut away the thongs about her chest and arms, and then his hand dropped. His chest struck against her shoulder and he slipped down beside her and lay still.

But the rest of her release was easy. Very hastily she freed herself. She made one step from the tree, and her head was spinning. Her last conscious movement was towards him. She reeled, and dropped. Her hand fell upon his thigh. It was soft and wet, and gave way under her pressure; he cried out at her touch, and writhed and lay still again.

Presently a dark dog-like shape came very softly through the reeds. Then stopped dead and stood sniffing, hesitated, and at last turned and slunk back into the shadows.

Long was the time they remained there motionless, with the light of the setting moon shining on their limbs. Very slowly, as slowly as the setting of the moon, did the shadow of the reeds towards the mound flow over them. Presently their legs were hidden, and Ugh-lomi was but a bust of silver. The shadow crept to his neck, crept over his face, and so at last the darkness of the night swallowed them up.

The shadow became full of instinctive stirrings. There was a patter of feet, and a faint snarling – the sound of a blow.

There was little sleep that night for the women and children at the squatting-place until they heard Eudena scream. But the men were weary and sat dozing. When Eudena screamed they felt assured of their safety, and hurried to get the nearest places to the fires. The old woman laughed at the scream, and laughed again because Si, the little friend of Eudena, whimpered. Directly the dawn came they were all alert and looking towards the alders. They could see that Eudena had been taken. They could not help feeling glad to think that Uya was appeased. But across the minds of the men the thought of Ugh-lomi fell like a shadow. They could understand revenge, for the world was old in revenge, but they did not think of rescue. Suddenly a hyena fled out of the thicket, and came galloping across the reed space. His muzzle and paws were dark-stained. At that sight all the men shouted and clutched at throwing-stones and ran towards him, for no animal is so pitiful a coward as the hyena by day. All men hated the hyena because he preyed on children, and would come and bite when one was sleeping on the edge of the squatting-place. And Cat's-skin, throwing fair and straight, hit the brute shrewdly on the flank, whereat the whole tribe yelled with delight.

At the noise they made there came a flapping of wings from the lair of the lion, and three white-headed vultures rose slowly and circled and came to rest amidst the branches of an alder, overlooking the lair. 'Our lord is abroad,' said the old woman, pointing. 'The vultures have their share of Eudena.' For a space they remained there, and then first one and then another dropped back into the thicket.

Then over the eastern woods, and touching the whole world of life and colour, poured, with the exaltation of a trumpet blast, the light of the rising sun. At the sight of him the children shouted together, and clapped their hands and began to race off towards the water. Only little Si lagged behind and looked wonderingly at the alders where she had seen the head of Eudena overnight.

But Uya, the old lion, was not abroad, but at home, and he lay very still, and a little on one side. He was not in his lair, but a little way from it in a place of trampled grass. Under one eye was a little wound, the feeble little bite of the first axe. But all the ground beneath his chest was ruddy brown with a vivid streak, and in his chest was a little hole that had been made by Ugh-lomi's stabbing-spear. Along his side and at his neck the vultures had marked their claims. For so Ugh-lomi had slain him, lying stricken under his paw and thrusting haphazard at his chest. He had driven the spear in with all his strength and stabbed the giant to the heart. So it was the reign of the lion, of the second incarnation of Uya the Master, came to an end.

From the knoll the bustle of preparation grew, the hacking of spears and throwing-stones. None spake the name of Ugh-lomi for fear that it might bring him. The men were going to keep together, close together, in the hunting for a day or so. And their hunting was to be Ugh-lomi, lest instead he should come a-hunting them.

But Ugh-lomi was lying very still and silent, outside the lion's lair, and Eudena squatted beside him, with the ash spear, all smeared with lion's blood, gripped in her hand.

V. – The Fight in the Lion's Thicket

Ugh-lomi lay still, his back against an alder, and his thigh was a red mass terrible to see. No civilized man could have lived who had been so sorely wounded, but Eudena got him thorns to close his wounds, and squatted beside him day and night, smiting the flies from him with a fan of reeds by day, and in the night threatening the hyenas with the first axe in her hand; and in a little while he began to heal. It was high summer, and there was no rain. Little food they had during the first two days his wounds were open. In the low place where they hid were no roots nor little beasts, and the stream, with its water-snails and fish, was in the open a hundred yards away. She could not go abroad by day for fear of the tribe, her brothers and sisters, nor by night for fear of the beasts, both on his account and hers. So they shared the lion with the vultures. But there was a trickle of water near by, and Eudena brought him plenty in her hands.

Where Ugh-lomi lay was well hidden from the tribe by a thicket of alders, and all fenced about with bulrushes and tall reeds. The dead lion he had killed lay near his old lair on a place of trampled reeds fifty yards away, in sight through the reed-stems, and the vultures fought each other for the choicest pieces and kept the jackals off him. Very soon a cloud of flies that looked like bees hung over him, and Ugh-lomi could hear their humming. And when Ugh-lomi's flesh was already healing – and it was not many days before that began – only a few bones of the lion remained scattered and shining white.

For the most part Ugh-lomi sat still during the day, looking before him at nothing; sometimes he would mutter of the horses and bears and lions, and sometimes he would beat the ground with the first axe and say the names of the tribe – he seemed to have no fear of bringing the tribe – for hours together. But chiefly he slept, dreaming little because of his loss of blood and the slightness of his food. During the short summer night both kept awake. All the while the darkness lasted things moved about them, things they never saw by day. For some nights the hyenas did not come, and then one moonless night near a dozen came and fought for what was left of the lion. The night was a tumult of growling, and Ugh-lomi and Eudena could hear the bones snap in their teeth. But they knew the hyena dare not attack any creature alive and awake, and so they were not greatly afraid.

Of a daytime Eudena would go along the narrow path the old lion had made in the reeds until she was beyond the bend, and then she would creep into the thicket and watch the tribe. She would lie close by the alders where they had bound her to offer her up to the lion, and thence she could see them on the knoll by the fire, small and clear, as she had seen them that night. But she told Ugh-lomi little of what she saw, because she feared to bring them by their names. For so they believed in those days, that naming called.

She saw the men prepare stabbing-spears and throwing-stones on the morning after Ugh-lomi had slain the lion, and go out to hunt him, leaving the women and children on the knoll. Little they knew how near he was as they tracked off in single file towards the hills, with Siss the Tracker leading them. And she watched the women and children, after the men had gone, gathering fern-fronds and twigs for the night fire, and the boys and girls running and playing together. But the very old woman made her feel afraid. Towards noon, when most of the

others were down at the stream by the bend, she came and
stood on the hither side of the knoll, a gnarled brown figure,
and gesticulated so that Eudena could scarce believe she was
not seen. Eudena lay like a hare in its form, with shining eyes
fixed on the bent witch away there, and presently she dimly
understood it was the lion the old woman was worshipping –
the lion Ugh-lomi had slain.

And the next day the hunters came back weary, carrying a
fawn, and Eudena watched the feast enviously. And then came
a strange thing. She saw – distinctly she heard – the old woman
shrieking and gesticulating and pointing towards her. She was
afraid, and crept like a snake out of sight again. But presently
curiosity overcame her and she was back at her spying-place,
and as she peered her heart stopped, for there were all the men,
with their weapons in their hands, walking together towards
her from the knoll.

She dared not move lest her movement should be seen, but
she pressed herself close to the ground. The sun was low and
the golden light was in the faces of the men. She saw they
carried a piece of rich red meat thrust through by an ashen
stake. Presently they stopped. 'Go on!' screamed the old
woman. Cat's-skin grumbled, and they came on, searching the
thicket with sun-dazzled eyes. 'Here!' said Siss. And they took
the ashen stake with the meat upon it and thrust it into the
ground. 'Uya!' cried Siss, 'behold thy portion. And Ugh-lomi
we have slain. Of a truth we have slain Ugh-lomi. This day we
slew Ugh-lomi, and tomorrow we will bring his body to you.'
And the others repeated the words.

They looked at each other and behind them, and partly
turned and began going back. At first they walked half turned
to the thicket, then, facing the mound, they walked faster,
looking over their shoulders, then faster; soon they ran, it was
a race at last, until they were near the knoll. Then Siss, who
was hindmost, was first to slacken his pace.

The sunset passed and the twilight came, the fires glowed red
against the hazy blue of the distant chestnut-trees, and the
voices over the mound were merry. Eudena lay scarcely stirring,
looking from the mound to the meat and then to the mound.

She was hungry, but she was afraid. At last she crept back to Ugh-lomi.

He looked round at the little rustle of her approach. His face was in shadow. 'Have you got me some food?' he said.

She said she could find nothing, but that she would seek further, and went back along the lion's path until she could see the mound again, but she could not bring herself to take the meat; she had the brute's instinct of a snare. She felt very miserable.

She crept back at last towards Ugh-lomi and heard him stirring and moaning. She turned back to the mound again; then she saw something in the darkness near the stake, and peering distinguished a jackal. In a flash she was brave and angry; she sprang up, cried out, and ran towards the offering. She stumbled and fell, and heard the growling of the jackal going off.

When she arose only the ashen stake lay on the ground, the meat was gone. So she went back, to fast through the night with Ugh-lomi; and Ugh-lomi was angry with her, because she had no food for him; but she told him nothing of the things she had seen.

Two days passed and they were near starving, when the tribe slew a horse. Then came the same ceremony, and a haunch was left on the ashen stake; but this time Eudena did not hesitate.

By acting and words she made Ugh-lomi understand, but he ate most of the food before he understood; and then as her meaning passed to him he grew merry with his food. 'I am Uya,' he said; 'I am the Lion. I am the Great Cave Bear, I who was only Ugh-lomi. I am Wau the Cunning. It is well that they should feed me, for presently I will kill them all.'

Then Eudena's heart was light, and she laughed with him; and afterwards she ate what he had left of the horseflesh with gladness.

After that it was he had a dream, and the next day he made Eudena bring him the lion's teeth and claws – so much of them as she could find – and hack him a club of alder. And he put the teeth and claws very cunningly into the wood so that the points were outward. Very long it took him, and he blunted two of the teeth hammering them in, and was very angry and threw the thing away; but afterwards he dragged himself to where he had thrown it and finished it – a club of a new sort set with teeth. That day there was more meat for them both, an offering to the lion from the tribe.

It was one day – more than a hand's fingers of days, more than anyone had skill to count – after Ugh-lomi had made the club, that Eudena while he was asleep was lying in the thicket watching the squatting-place. There had been no meat for three days. And the old woman came and worshipped after her manner. Now while she worshipped, Eudena's little friend Si and another, the child of the first girl Siss had loved, came over the knoll and stood regarding her skinny figure, and presently they began to mock her. Eudena found this entertaining, but suddenly the old woman turned on them quickly and saw them. For a moment she stood and they stood motionless, and then with a shriek of rage, she rushed towards them, and all three disappeared over the crest of the knoll.

Presently the children reappeared among the ferns beyond the shoulder of the hill. Little Si ran first, for she was an active girl, and the other child ran squealing with the old woman close upon her. And over the knoll came Siss with a bone in his hand, and Bo and Cat's-skin obsequiously behind him, each holding a piece of food, and they laughed aloud and shouted to see the old woman so angry. And with a shriek the child was caught and the old woman set to work slapping and the child scream- ing, and it was very good after-dinner fun for them. Little Si ran on a little way and stopped at last between fear and curiosity.

And suddenly came the mother of the child, with hair stream- ing, panting, and with a stone in her hand, and the old woman turned about like a wild cat. She was the equal of any woman, was the chief of the fire-minders, in spite of her years; but before she could do anything Siss shouted to her and the clamour rose loud. Other shock heads came into sight. It seemed the whole tribe was at home and feasting. But the old woman dared not go on wreaking herself on the child Siss befriended.

Everyone made noises and called names – even little Si. Abruptly the old woman let go of the child she had caught and made a swift run at Si, for Si had no friends; and Si, realizing her danger when it was almost upon her, made off headlong, with a faint cry of terror, not heeding whither she ran, straight to the lair of the lion. She swerved aside into the reeds presently, realizing now whither she went.

But the old woman was a wonderful old woman, as active as she was spiteful, and she caught Si by the streaming hair within thirty yards of Eudena. All the tribe now was running down the knoll and shouting and laughing ready to see the fun.

Then something stirred in Eudena; something that had never stirred in her before; and, thinking all of little Si and nothing of her fear, she sprang up from her ambush and ran swiftly forward. The old woman did not see her, for she was busy beating little Si's face with her hand, beating with all her heart, and suddenly something hard and heavy struck her cheek. She went reeling, and saw Eudena with flaming eyes and cheeks between her and little Si. She shrieked with astonishment and terror, and little Si, not understanding, set off towards the gaping tribe. They were quite close now, for the sight of Eudena had driven their fading fear of the lion out of their heads.

In a moment Eudena had turned from the cowering old woman and overtaken Si. 'Si!' she cried, 'Si!' She caught the child up in her arms as it stopped, pressed the nail-lined face to hers, and turned about to run towards her lair, the lair of the old lion. The old woman stood waist-high in the reeds, and screamed foul things and inarticulate rage, but did not dare to intercept her; and at the bend of the path Eudena looked back and saw all the men of the tribe crying to one another and Siss coming at a trot along the lion's trail.

She ran straight along the narrow way through the reeds to the shady place where Ugh-lomi sat with his healing thigh, just awakened by the shouting and rubbing his eyes. She came to him, a woman, with little Si in her arms. Her heart throbbed in her throat. 'Ugh-lomi!' she cried. 'Ugh-lomi, the tribe comes!'

Ugh-lomi sat staring in stupid astonishment at her and Si.

She pointed with Si in one arm. She sought among her feeble store of words to explain. She could hear the men calling. Apparently they had stopped outside. She put down Si and caught up the new club with the lion's teeth, and put it into Ugh-lomi's hand, and ran three yards and picked up the first axe.

'Ah!' said Ugh-lomi, waving the new club, and suddenly he perceived the occasion and, rolling over, began to struggle to his feet.

He stood but clumsily. He supported himself by one hand against the tree, and just touched the ground gingerly with the toe of his wounded leg. In the other hand he gripped the new club. He looked at his healing thigh; and suddenly the reeds began whispering, and ceased and whispered again, and coming cautiously along the track, bending down and holding his fire-hardened stabbing-stick of ash in his hand, appeared Siss. He stopped dead, and his eyes met Ugh-lomi's.

Ugh-lomi forgot he had a wounded leg. He stood firmly on both feet. Something trickled. He glanced down and saw a little gout of blood had oozed out along the edge of the healing wound. He rubbed his hand there to give him the grip of his club, and fixed his eyes again on Siss.

'Wau!' he cried, and sprang forward, and Siss, still stooping and watchful, drove his stabbing-stick up very quickly in an ugly thrust. It ripped Ugh-lomi's guarding arm and the club came down in a counter that Siss was never to understand. He fell, as an ox falls to the pole-axe, at Ugh-lomi's feet.

To Bo it seemed the strangest thing. He had a comforting sense of tall reeds on either side, and an impregnable rampart, Siss, between him and any danger. Snail-eater was close behind and there was no danger there. He was prepared to shove behind and send Siss to death or victory. That was his place as second man. He saw the butt of the spear Siss carried leap away from him, and suddenly a dull whack and the broad back fell away forward, and he looked Ugh-lomi in the face over his prostrate leader. It felt to Bo as if his heart had fallen down a well. He had a throwing-stone in one hand and an ashen stabbing-stick in the other. He did not live to the end of his momentary hesitation which to use.

Snail-eater was a readier man, and besides Bo did not fall forward as Siss had done, but gave at his knees and hips, crumpling up with the toothed club upon his head. The Snail-eater drove his spear forward swift and straight, and took Ugh-lomi in the muscle of the shoulder, and then he drove him hard with the smiting-stone in his other hand, shouting out as he did so. The new club swished ineffectually through the reeds. Eudena saw Ugh-lomi come staggering back from the narrow path into the open space, tripping over Siss and with a foot of ashen stake sticking out of him over his arm. And then the Snail-eater, whose name she had given, had his final injury from her, as his exultant face came out of the reeds after his spear. For she swung the first axe swift and high, and hit him fair and square on the temple; and down he went on Siss at prostrate Ugh-lomi's feet.

But before Ugh-lomi could get up, the two red-haired men were tumbling out of the reeds, spears and smiting-stones ready, and Snake hard behind them. One she struck on the neck, but not to fell him, and he blundered aside and spoilt his brother's blow at Ugh-lomi's head. In a moment Ugh-lomi dropped his club and had his assailant by the waist, and had pitched him sideways sprawling. He snatched at his club again and recovered it. The man Eudena had hit stabbed at her with his spear as he stumbled from her blow, and involuntarily she gave ground to avoid him. He hesitated between her and Ugh-lomi, half turned, gave a vague cry at finding Ugh-lomi so near, and in a moment Ugh-lomi had him by the throat, and the club had its third victim. As he went down Ugh-lomi shouted – no words, but an exultant cry.

The other red-haired man was six feet from her with his back to her, and a darker red streaking his head. He was struggling to his feet. She had an irrational impulse to stop his rising. She flung the axe at him, missed, saw his face in profile, and he had swerved beyond little Si, and was running through the reeds. She had a transitory vision of Snake standing in the throat of the path, half turned away from her, and then she saw his back. She saw the club whirling through the air, and the shock head of Ugh-lomi, with blood in the hair and blood upon the shoulder, vanishing below the reeds in pursuit. Then she heard Snake scream like a woman.

She ran past Si to where the handle of the axe stuck out of a clump of fern, and turning, found herself panting and alone with three motionless bodies. The air was full of shouts and screams. For a space she was sick and giddy, and then it came into her head that Ugh-lomi was being killed along the reed-path, and with an inarticulate cry she leapt over the body of Bo and hurried after him. Snake's feet lay across the path, and his head was among the reeds. She followed the path until it bent round and opened out by the alders, and thence she saw all that was left of the tribe in the open, scattering like dead leaves before a gale, and going back over the knoll. Ugh-lomi was hard upon Cat's-skin.

But Cat's-skin was fleet of foot and got away, and so did young Wau-Hau when Ugh-lomi turned upon him, and Ugh-lomi pursued Wau-Hau far beyond the knoll before he desisted. He had the rage of battle on him now, and the wood thrust through his shoulder stung him like a spur. When she saw he was in no danger she stopped running and stood panting, watching the distant active figures run up and vanish one by one over the knoll. In a little time she was alone again. Everything had happened very swiftly. The smoke of Brother Fire rose straight and steady from the squatting-place, just as it had done ten minutes ago, when the old woman had stood yonder worshipping the lion.

And after a long time, as it seemed, Ugh-lomi reappeared over the knoll, and came back to Eudena, triumphant and breathing heavily. She stood, her hair about her eyes and hot-faced, with the blood-stained axe in her hand, at the place where the tribe had offered her as a sacrifice to the lion. 'Wau!' cried Ugh-lomi at the sight of her, his face alight with the fellowship of battle, and he waved his new club, red now and hairy; and at the sight of his glowing face her tense pose relaxed somewhat, and she stood sobbing and rejoicing.

Ugh-lomi had a queer unaccountable pang at the sight of her tears; but he only shouted 'Wau!' the louder and shook the axe east and west. He called manfully to her to follow him and turned back, striding, with the club swinging in his hand, towards the squatting-place, as if he had never left the tribe;

and she ceased her weeping and followed quickly as a woman should.

So Ugh-lomi and Eudena came back to the squatting-place from which they had fled many days before from the face of Uya; and by the squatting-place lay a deer half eaten, just as there had been before Ugh-lomi was man or Eudena woman. So Ugh-lomi sat down to eat, and Eudena beside him like a man, and the rest of the tribe watched them from safe hiding-places. And after a time one of the elder girls came back timorously, carrying little Si in her arms, and Eudena called to them by name, and offered them food. But the elder girl was afraid and would not come, though Si struggled to come to Eudena. Afterwards, when Ugh-lomi had eaten, he sat dozing, and at last he slept, and slowly the others came out of the hiding-places and drew near. And when Ugh-lomi woke, save that there were no men to be seen, it seemed as though he had never left the tribe.

Now, there is a thing strange but true: that all through this fight Ugh-lomi forgot that he was lame, and was not lame, and after he had rested behold! he was a lame man; and he remained a lame man to the end of his days.

Cat's-skin and the second red-haired man and Wau-Hau, who chipped flints cunningly, as his father had done before him, fled from the face of Ugh-lomi, and none knew where they hid. But two days after they came and squatted a good way off from the knoll among the bracken under the chestnuts and watched. Ugh-lomi's rage had gone, he moved to go against them and did not, and at sundown they went away. That day, too, they found the old woman among the ferns, where Ugh-lomi had blundered upon her when he had pursued Wau-Hau. She was dead and more ugly than ever, but whole. The jackals and vultures had tried her and left her; – she was ever a wonderful old woman.

The next day the three men came again and squatted nearer, and Wau-Hau had two rabbits to hold up, and the red-haired man a wood-pigeon, and Ugh-lomi stood before the women and mocked them.

The next day they sat again nearer – without stones or sticks,

and with the same offerings, and Cat's-skin had a trout. It was
rare men caught fish in those days, but Cat's-skin would stand
silently in the water for hours and catch them with his hand.
And the fourth day Ugh-lomi suffered these three to come to
the squatting-place in peace, with the food they had with them.
Ugh-lomi ate the trout. Thereafter for many moons Ugh-lomi
was master and had his will in peace. And on the fulness of
time he was killed and eaten even as Uya had been slain.

THE STAR

It was on the first day of the new year that the announcement was made, almost simultaneously from three observatories, that the motion of the planet Neptune,[1] the outermost of all the planets that wheel about the sun, had become very erratic. Ogilvy[2] had already called attention to a suspected retardation in its velocity in December. Such a piece of news was scarcely calculated to interest a world the greater portion of whose inhabitants were unaware of the existence of the planet Neptune, nor outside the astronomical profession did the subsequent discovery of a faint remote speck of light in the region of the perturbed planet cause any very great excitement. Scientific people, however, found the intelligence remarkable enough, even before it became known that the new body was rapidly growing larger and brighter, that its motion was quite different from the orderly progress of the planets, and that the deflection of Neptune and its satellite was becoming now of an unprecedented kind.

Few people without a training in science can realize the huge isolation of the solar system. The sun with its specks of planets, its dust of planetoids, and its impalpable comets, swims in a vacant immensity that almost defeats the imagination. Beyond the orbit of Neptune there is space, vacant so far as human observation has penetrated, without warmth or light or sound, blank emptiness, for twenty million times a million miles. That is the smallest estimate of the distance to be traversed before the very nearest of the stars is attained. And, saving a few comets more unsubstantial than the thinnest flame, no matter had ever to human knowledge crossed this gulf of space, until early in the twentieth century this strange wanderer appeared. A vast mass of matter it was, bulky, heavy, rushing without warning out of the black mystery of the sky into the radiance of the sun. By the second day it was clearly visible to any decent instrument, as a speck with a barely sensible diameter, in the constellation Leo near Regulus. In a little while an opera-glass could attain it.

On the third day of the new year the newspaper readers of two hemispheres were made aware for the first time of the real importance of this unusual apparition in the heavens. 'A Planetary Collision', one London paper headed the news, and proclaimed Duchaine's opinion that this strange new planet would probably collide with Neptune. The leader writers enlarged upon the topic. So that in most of the capitals of the world, on January 3rd, there was an expectation, however vague, of some imminent phenomenon in the sky; and as the night followed the sunset round the globe, thousands of men turned their eyes skyward to see – the old familiar stars just as they had always been.

Until it was dawn in London and Pollux setting and the stars overhead grown pale. The winter's dawn it was, a sickly filtering accumulation of daylight, and the light of gas and candles shone yellow in the windows to show where people were astir. But the yawning policeman saw the thing, the busy crowds in the markets stopped agape, workmen going to their work betimes, milkmen, the drivers of news-carts, dissipation going home jaded and pale, homeless wanderers, sentinels on their beats, and in the country, labourers trudging afield, poachers slinking home, all over the dusky quickening country it could be seen – and out at sea by seamen watching for the day – a great white star, come suddenly into the westward sky!

Brighter it was than any star in our skies; brighter than the evening star at its brightest. It still glowed out white and large, no mere twinkling spot of light, but a small round clear shining disc, an hour after the day had come. And where science has not reached, men stared and feared, telling one another of the wars and pestilences that are foreshadowed by these fiery signs in the Heavens. Sturdy Boers, dusky Hottentots,[3] Gold

Coast Negroes, Frenchmen, Spaniards, Portuguese, stood in the warmth of the sunrise watching the setting of this strange new star.

And in a hundred observatories there had been suppressed excitement, rising almost to shouting pitch, as the two remote bodies had rushed together, and a hurrying to and fro to gather photographic apparatus and spectroscope, and this appliance and that, to record this novel astonishing sight, the destruction of a world. For it was a world, a sister planet of our earth, far greater than our earth indeed, that had so suddenly flashed into flaming death. Neptune it was, had been struck, fairly and squarely, by the strange planet from outer space and the heat of the concussion had incontinently turned two solid globes into one vast mass of incandescence. Round the world that day, two hours before the dawn, went the pallid great white star, fading only as it sank westward and the sun mounted above it. Everywhere men marvelled at it, but of all those who saw it none could have marvelled more than those sailors, habitual watchers of the stars, who far away at sea had heard nothing of its advent and saw it now rise like a pigmy moon and climb zenithward and hang overhead and sink westward with the passing of the night.

And when next it rose over Europe everywhere were crowds of watchers on hilly slopes, on house-roofs, in open spaces, staring eastward for the rising of the great new star. It rose with a white glow in front of it, like the glare of a white fire, and those who had seen it come into existence the night before cried out at the sight of it. 'It is larger,' they cried. 'It is brighter!' And, indeed the moon a quarter full and sinking in the west was in its apparent size beyond comparison, but scarcely in all its breadth had it as much brightness now as the little circle of the strange new star.

'It is brighter!' cried the people clustering in the streets. But in the dim observatories the watchers held their breath and peered at one another. '*It is nearer*,' they said. '*Nearer!*'

And voice after voice repeated, 'It is nearer', and the clicking telegraph took that up, and it trembled along telephone wires,[4] and in a thousand cities grimy compositors fingered the type.

'It is nearer.' Men writing in offices, struck with a strange realization, flung down their pens; men talking in a thousand places suddenly came upon a grotesque possibility in those words, 'It is nearer.' It hurried along awakening streets, it was shouted down the frost-stilled ways of quiet villages, men who had read these things from the throbbing tape[5] stood in yellow-lit doorways shouting the news to the passers-by. 'It is nearer.' Pretty women, flushed and glittering, heard the news told jestingly between the dances, and feigned an intelligent interest they did not feel. 'Nearer! Indeed. How curious! How very, very clever people must be to find out things like that!'

Lonely tramps faring through the wintry night murmured those words to comfort themselves – looking skyward. 'It has need to be nearer, for the night's as cold as charity. Don't seem much warmth from it if it *is* nearer, all the same.'

'What is a new star to me?' cried the weeping woman kneeling beside her dead.

The schoolboy, rising early for his examination work, puzzled it out for himself – with the great white star, shining broad and bright through the frost-flowers of his window. 'Centrifugal, centripetal,'[6] he said, with his chin on his fist. 'Stop a planet in its flight, rob it of its centrifugal force, what then? Centripetal has it, and down it falls into the sun! And this –!'

'Do *we* come in the way? I wonder –'

The light of that day went the way of its brethren, and with the later watches of the frosty darkness rose the strange star again. And it was now so bright that the waxing moon seemed but a pale yellow ghost of itself, hanging huge in the sunset. In a South African city a great man had married, and the streets were alight to welcome his return with his bride. 'Even the skies have illuminated,' said the flatterer. Under Capricorn, two Negro lovers, daring the wild beasts and evil spirits, for love of one another, crouched together in a cane brake where the fireflies hovered. 'That is our star,' they whispered, and felt strangely comforted by the sweet brilliance of its light.

The master mathematician sat in his private room and pushed the papers from him. His calculations were already finished. In a small white phial there still remained a little of the drug that had kept him awake and active for four long nights. Each day, serene, explicit, patient as ever, he had given his lecture to his students, and then had come back at once to this momentous calculation. His face was grave, a little drawn and hectic from his drugged activity. For some time he seemed lost in thought. Then he went to the window, and the blind went up with a click. Halfway up the sky, over the clustering roofs, chimneys and steeples of the city, hung the star.

He looked at it as one might look into the eyes of a brave enemy. 'You may kill me,' he said after a silence. 'But I can hold you – and all the universe for that matter – in the grip of this little brain. I would not change. Even now.'

He looked at the little phial. 'There will be no need of sleep again,' he said. The next day at noon, punctual to the minute, he entered his lecture theatre, put his hat on the end of the table as his habit was, and carefully selected a large piece of chalk. It was a joke among his students that he could not lecture without that piece of chalk to fumble in his fingers, and once he had been stricken to impotence by their hiding his supply. He came and looked under his grey eyebrows at the rising tiers of young fresh faces, and spoke with his accustomed studied common-ness of phrasing. 'Circumstances have arisen – circumstances beyond my control,' he said and paused, 'which will debar me from completing the course I had designed. It would seem, gentlemen, if I may put the thing clearly and briefly, that – Man has lived in vain.'

The students glanced at one another. Had they heard aright? Mad? Raised eyebrows and grinning lips there were, but one or two faces remained intent upon his calm grey-fringed face. 'It will be interesting,' he was saying, 'to devote this morning to an exposition, so far as I can make it clear to you, of the calculations that have led me to this conclusion. Let us assume –'

He turned towards the blackboard, meditating a diagram in the way that was usual to him. 'What was that about "lived in vain"?' whispered one student to another. 'Listen,' said the other, nodding towards the lecturer.

And presently they began to understand.

That night the star rose later, for its proper eastward motion had carried it some way across Leo towards Virgo, and its brightness was so great that the sky became a luminous blue as it rose, and every star was hidden in its turn, save only Jupiter near the zenith, Capella, Aldebaran, Sirius and the pointers of the Bear.[7] It was very white and beautiful. In many parts of the world that night a pallid halo encircled it about. It was perceptibly larger; in the clear refractive sky of the tropics it seemed as if it were nearly a quarter the size of the moon. The frost was still on the ground in England, but the world was as brightly lit as if it were midsummer moonlight. One could see to read quite ordinary print by that cold clear light, and in the cities the lamps burnt yellow and wan.

And everywhere the world was awake that night, and throughout Christendom a sombre murmur hung in the keen air over the countryside like the belling of bees in the heather, and this murmurous tumult grew to a clangour in the cities. It was the tolling of the bells in a million belfry towers and steeples, summoning the people to sleep no more, to sin no more, but to gather in their churches and pray. And overhead, growing larger and brighter as the earth rolled on its way and the night passed, rose the dazzling star.

And the streets and houses were alight in all the cities, the shipyards glared, and whatever roads led to high country were lit and crowded all night long. And in all the seas about the civilized lands, ships with throbbing engines, and ships with bellying sails, crowded with men and living creatures, were standing out to ocean and the north. For already the warning of the master mathematician had been telegraphed all over the world, and translated into a hundred tongues. The new planet and Neptune, locked in a fiery embrace, were whirling head-long, ever faster and faster towards the sun. Already every second this blazing mass flew a hundred miles, and every second its terrific velocity increased. As it flew now, indeed, it must pass a hundred million of miles wide of the earth and scarcely affect it. But near its destined path, as yet only slightly per-turbed, spun the mighty planet Jupiter and his moons sweeping splendid round the sun. Every moment now the attraction between the fiery star and the greatest of the planets grew stronger. And the result of that attraction? Inevitably Jupiter would be deflected from his orbit into an elliptical path, and the burning star, swung by his attraction wide of its sunward rush, would 'describe a curved path' and perhaps collide with, and certainly pass very close to, our earth. 'Earthquakes, volcanic outbreaks, cyclones, sea waves, floods, and a steady rise in temperature to I know not what limit' – so prophesied the master mathematician.

And overhead, to carry out his words, lonely and cold and livid, blazed the star of the coming doom.

To many who stared at it that night until their eyes ached, it seemed that it was visibly approaching. And that night, too, the weather changed, and the frost that had gripped all Central Europe and France and England softened towards a thaw.

But you must not imagine because I have spoken of people praying through the night and people going aboard ships and people fleeing towards mountainous country that the whole world was already in a terror because of the star. As a matter of fact, use and wont still ruled the world, and save for the talk of idle moments and the splendour of the night, nine human beings out of ten were still busy at their common occupations. In all the cities the shops, save one here and there, opened and closed at their proper hours, the doctor and the undertaker plied their trades, the workers gathered in the factories, soldiers drilled, scholars studied, lovers sought one another, thieves lurked and fled, politicians planned their schemes. The presses of the newspapers roared through the nights, and many a priest of this church and that would not open his holy building to further what he considered a foolish panic. The newspapers insisted on the lesson of the year 1000[8] – for then, too, people had anticipated the end. The star was no star – mere gas – a comet; and were it a star it could not possibly strike the earth. There was no precedent for such a thing. Common sense was sturdy everywhere, scornful, jesting, a little inclined to persecute the obdurate fearful. That night, at seven-fifteen by Greenwich time,[9] the star would be at its nearest to Jupiter. Then the world would see the turn things would take. The master mathematician's grim warnings were treated by many as so much mere elaborate self-advertisement. Common sense at last, a little heated by argument, signified its unalterable convictions by going to bed. So, too, barbarism and savagery, already tired of the novelty, went about their mighty business, and save for a howling dog here and there, the beast world left the star unheeded.

And yet, when at last the watchers in the European States saw the star rise, an hour later it is true, but no larger than it had been the night before, there were still plenty awake to laugh at the master mathematician – to take the danger as if it had passed.

But hereafter the laughter ceased. The star grew – it grew with a terrible steadiness hour after hour, a little larger each hour, a little nearer the midnight zenith, and brighter and brighter, until it had turned night into a second day. Had it come straight to the earth instead of in a curved path, had it lost no velocity to Jupiter, it must have leapt the intervening gulf in a day, but as it was it took five days altogether to come by our planet. The next night it had become a third the size of the moon before it set to English eyes, and the thaw was assured. It rose over America near the size of the moon, but blinding white to look at, and *hot*; and a breath of hot wind blew now with its rising and gathering strength, and in Virginia, and Brazil, and down the St Lawrence valley, it shone intermittently through a driving reek of thunder-clouds, flickering violet lightning, and hail unprecedented. In Manitoba was a thaw and devastating floods. And upon all the mountains of the earth the snow and ice began to melt that night, and all the rivers coming out of high country flowed thick and turbid, and soon – in their upper reaches – with swirling trees and the bodies of beasts and men. They rose steadily, steadily in the ghostly brilliance, and came trickling over their banks at last, behind the flying population of their valleys.

And along the coast of Argentina and up the South Atlantic the tides were higher than had ever been in the memory of man, and the storms drove the waters in many cases scores of miles

inland, drowning whole cities. And so great grew the heat
during the night that the rising of the sun was like the coming
of a shadow. The earthquakes began and grew until all down
America from the Arctic Circle to Cape Horn, hillsides were
sliding, fissures were opening, and houses and walls crumbling
to destruction. The whole side of Cotopaxi slipped out in one
vast convulsion, and a tumult of lava poured out so high and
broad and swift and liquid that in one day it reached the sea.

So the star, with the wan moon in its wake, marched across
the Pacific, trailed the thunderstorms like the hem of a robe,
and the growing tidal wave that toiled behind it, frothing and
eager, poured over island and island and swept them clear of
men. Until that wave came at last – in a blinding light and with
the breath of a furnace, swift and terrible it came – a wall of
water, fifty feet high, roaring hungrily, upon the long coasts of
Asia, and swept inland across the plains of China. For a space
the star, hotter now and larger and brighter than the sun in its
strength, showed with pitiless brilliance the wide and populous
country; towns and villages with their pagodas and trees, roads,
wide cultivated fields, millions of sleepless people staring in
helpless terror at the incandescent sky; and then, low and growing, came the murmur of the flood. And thus it was with millions
of men that night – a flight nowhither, with limbs heavy with
heat and breath fierce and scant, and the flood like a wall swift
and white behind. And then death.

China was lit glowing white, but over Japan and Java and all
the islands of Eastern Asia the great star was a ball of dull red
fire because of the steam and smoke and ashes the volcanoes
were spouting forth to salute its coming. Above was the lava,
hot gases and ash, and below the seething floods, and the whole
earth swayed and rumbled with the earthquake shocks. Soon
the immemorial snows of Tibet and the Himalaya were melting
and pouring down by ten million deepening converging channels upon the plains of Burma and Hindustan. The tangled
summits of the Indian jungles were aflame in a thousand places,
and below the hurrying waters around the stems were dark
objects that still struggled feebly and reflected the blood-red
tongues of fire. And in a rudderless confusion a multitude of

men and women fled down the broad river-ways to that one last hope of men – the open sea.

Larger grew the star, and larger, hotter, and brighter with a terrible swiftness now. The tropical ocean had lost its phosphorescence, and the whirling steam rose in ghostly wreaths from the black waves that plunged incessantly, speckled with storm-tossed ships.

And then came a wonder. It seemed to those who in Europe watched for the rising of the star that the world must have ceased its rotation. In a thousand open spaces of down and upland the people who had fled thither from the floods and the falling houses and sliding slopes of hill watched for that rising in vain. Hour followed hour through a terrible suspense, and the star rose not. Once again men set their eyes upon the old constellations they had counted lost to them forever. In England it was hot and clear overhead, though the ground quivered perpetually, but in the tropics, Sirius and Capella and Aldebaran showed through a veil of steam. And when at last the great star rose near ten hours late, the sun rose close upon it, and in the centre of its white heart was a disc of black.

Over Asia it was the star had begun to fall behind the movement of the sky, and then suddenly, as it hung over India, its light had been veiled. All the plain of India from the mouth of the Indus to the mouths of the Ganges[10] was a shallow waste of shining water that night, out of which rose temples and palaces, mounds and hills, black with people. Every minaret was a clustering mass of people, who fell one by one into the turbid waters, as heat and terror overcame them. The whole land seemed a-wailing, and suddenly there swept a shadow across that furnace of despair, and a breath of cold wind, and a gathering of clouds, out of the cooling air. Men looking up, near blinded, at the star, saw that a black disc was creeping across the light. It was the moon, coming between the star and the earth. And even as men cried to God at this respite, out of the East with a strange inexplicable swiftness sprang the sun. And then star, sun, and moon rushed together across the heavens.

So it was that presently, to the European watchers, star and sun rose close upon each other, drove headlong for a space and then slower, and at last came to rest, star and sun merged into one glare of flame at the zenith of the sky. The moon no longer eclipsed the star but was lost to sight in the brilliance of the sky. And though those who were still alive regarded it for the most part with that dull stupidity that hunger, fatigue, heat, and despair engender, there were still men who could perceive the meaning of these signs. Star and earth had been at their nearest, had swung about one another, and the star had passed. Already it was receding, swifter and swifter, in the last stage of its headlong journey downward into the sun.

And then the clouds gathered, blotting out the vision of the sky, the thunder and lightning wove a garment round the world; all over the earth was such a downpour of rain as men had never before seen, and where the volcanoes flared red against the cloud canopy there descended torrents of mud. Everywhere the waters were pouring off the land, leaving mud-silted ruins, and the earth littered like a storm-worn beach with all that had floated, and the dead bodies of the men and brutes, its children. For days the water streamed off the land, sweeping away soil and trees and houses in the way, and piling huge dykes and scooping out Titanic gullies over the countryside. Those were the days of darkness that followed the star and the heat. All through them, and for many weeks and months, the earthquakes continued.

But the star had passed, and men, hunger-driven and gathering courage only slowly, might creep back to their ruined cities, buried granaries, and sodden fields. Such few ships as had escaped the storms of that time came stunned and shattered and sounding their way cautiously through the new marks and shoals of once familiar ports. And as the storms subsided men perceived that everywhere the days were hotter than of yore, and the sun larger, and the moon, shrunk to a third of its former size, took now fourscore days between its new and new.

But of the new brotherhood that grew presently among men, of the saving of laws and books and machines, of the strange change that had come over Iceland and Greenland and the shores of Baffin's Bay, so that the sailors coming there presently found them green and gracious, and could scarce believe their eyes, this story does not tell. Nor of the movement of mankind now that the earth was hotter, northward and southward towards the poles of the earth. It concerns itself only with the coming and the passing of the Star.

The Martian astronomers[11] – for there are astronomers on Mars, although they are very different beings from men – were naturally profoundly interested by these things. They saw them from their own standpoint of course. 'Considering the mass and temperature of the missile that was flung through our solar system into the sun,' one wrote, 'it is astonishing what a little damage the earth, which it missed so narrowly, has sustained. All the familiar continental markings and the masses of the seas remain intact, and indeed the only difference seems to be a shrinkage of the white discoloration (supposed to be frozen water) round either pole.' Which only shows how small the vastest of human catastrophes may seem, at a distance of a few million miles.

THE MAN WHO COULD WORK MIRACLES

A Pantoum in Prose

It is doubtful whether the gift was innate. For my own part, I
think it came to him suddenly. Indeed, until he was thirty he
was a sceptic, and did not believe in miraculous powers. And
here, since it is the most convenient place, I must mention that
he was a little man, and had eyes of a hot brown, very erect red
hair, a moustache with ends that he twisted up, and freckles.
His name was George McWhirter Fotheringay – not the sort of
name by any means to lead to any expectation of miracles –
and he was clerk at Gomshott's. He was greatly addicted to
assertive argument. It was while he was asserting the impossibility of miracles that he had his first intimation of his extraordinary powers. This particular argument was being held in
the bar of the Long Dragon, and Toddy Beamish was con-
ducting the opposition by a monotonous but effective 'So *you*
say', that drove Mr Fotheringay to the very limit of his patience.

There were present, besides these two, a very dusty cyclist,
landlord Cox, and Miss Maybridge, the perfectly respectable
and rather portly barmaid of the Dragon. Miss Maybridge was
standing with her back to Mr Fotheringay, washing glasses; the
others were watching him, more or less amused by the present
ineffectiveness of the assertive method. Goaded by the Torres
Vedras[1] tactics of Mr Beamish, Mr Fotheringay determined to
make an unusual rhetorical effort. 'Looky here, Mr Beamish,'
said Mr Fotheringay. 'Let us clearly understand what a miracle
is. It's something contrariwise to the course of nature done by
power of Will, something what couldn't happen without being
specially willed.'

'So *you* say,' said Mr Beamish, repulsing him.

Mr Fotheringay appealed to the cyclist, who had hitherto been a silent auditor, and received his assent – given with a hesitating cough and a glance at Mr Beamish. The landlord would express no opinion, and Mr Fotheringay, returning to Mr Beamish, received the unexpected concession of a qualified assent to his definition of a miracle.

'For instance,' said Mr Fotheringay, greatly encouraged. 'Here would be a miracle. That lamp, in the natural course of nature, couldn't burn like that upsy-down, could it, Beamish?'

'*You* say it couldn't,' said Beamish.

'And you?' said Fotheringay. 'You don't mean to say – eh?'

'No,' said Beamish reluctantly. 'No, it couldn't.'

'Very well,' said Mr Fotheringay. 'Then here comes someone, as it might be me, along here, and stands as it might be here, and says to that lamp, as I might do, collecting all my will – "Turn upsy-down without breaking, and go on burning steady," and – Hullo!'

It was enough to make anyone say 'Hullo!' The impossible, the incredible, was visible to them all. The lamp hung inverted in the air, burning quietly with its flame pointing down. It was as solid, as indisputable as ever a lamp was, the prosaic common lamp of the Long Dragon bar.

Mr Fotheringay stood with an extended forefinger and the knitted brows of one anticipating a catastrophic smash. The cyclist, who was sitting next the lamp, ducked and jumped across the bar. Everybody jumped, more or less. Miss Maybridge turned and screamed. For nearly three seconds the lamp remained still. A faint cry of mental distress came from Mr Fotheringay. 'I can't keep it up,' he said, 'any longer.' He staggered back, and the inverted lamp suddenly flared, fell against the corner of the bar, bounced aside, smashed upon the floor, and went out.

It was lucky it had a metal receiver, or the whole place would have been in a blaze. Mr Cox was the first to speak, and his remark, shorn of needless excrescences, was to the effect that Fotheringay was a fool. Fotheringay was beyond disputing even so fundamental a proposition as that! He was astonished beyond measure at the thing that had occurred. The subsequent conversation threw absolutely no light on the matter so far as Fotheringay was concerned; the general opinion not only followed Mr Cox very closely but very vehemently. Everyone accused Fotheringay of a silly trick, and presented him to himself as a foolish destroyer of comfort and security. His mind was in a tornado of perplexity, he was himself inclined to agree with them, and he made a remarkably ineffectual opposition to the proposal of his departure.

He went home flushed and heated, coat-collar crumpled, eyes smarting and ears red. He watched each of the ten street lamps nervously as he passed it. It was only when he found himself alone in his little bedroom in Church Row that he was able to grapple seriously with his memories of the occurrence, and ask, 'What on earth happened?'

He had removed his coat and boots, and was sitting on the bed with his hands in his pockets repeating the text of his defence for the seventeenth time, '*I* didn't want the confounded thing to upset', when it occurred to him that at the precise moment he had said the commanding words he had inadvertently willed the thing he said, and that when he had seen the lamp in the air he had felt that it depended on him to maintain it there without being clear how this was to be done. He had not a particularly complex mind, or he might have stuck for a time at that 'inadvertently willed', embracing, as it does, the abstrusest problems of voluntary action; but as it was, the idea came to him with a quite acceptable haziness. And from that, following, as I must admit, no clear logical path, he came to the test of experiment.

He pointed resolutely to his candle and collected his mind, though he felt he did a foolish thing. 'Be raised up,' he said. But in a second that feeling vanished. The candle was raised, hung in the air one giddy moment, and as Mr Fotheringay gasped, fell with a smash on his toilet-table, leaving him in darkness save for the expiring glow of its wick.

For a time Mr Fotheringay sat in the darkness, perfectly still. 'It did happen, after all,' he said. 'And 'ow I'm to explain it I *don't* know.' He sighed heavily, and began feeling in his pockets

for a match. He could find none, and he rose and groped about
the toilet-table. 'I wish I had a match,' he said. He resorted to
his coat, and there were none there, and then it dawned upon
him that miracles were possible even with matches. He extended
a hand and scowled at it in the dark. 'Let there be a match in
that hand,' he said. He felt some light object fall across his
palm, and his fingers closed upon a match.

After several ineffectual attempts to light this, he discovered
it was a safety-match.[2] He threw it down, and then it occurred
to him that he might have willed it lit. He did, and perceived it
burning in the midst of his toilet-table mat. He caught it up
hastily, and it went out. His perception of possibilities enlarged,
and he felt for and replaced the candle in its candlestick. 'Here!
you be lit,' said Mr Fotheringay, and forthwith the candle was
flaring, and he saw a little black hole in the toilet-cover, with a
wisp of smoke rising from it. For a time he stared from this to
the little flame and back, and then looked up and met his
own gaze in the looking-glass. By this help he communed with
himself in silence for a time.

'How about miracles now?' said Mr Fotheringay at last,
addressing his reflection.

The subsequent meditations of Mr Fotheringay were of a
severe but confused description. So far as he could see, it was a
case of pure willing with him. The nature of his first experiences
disinclined him for any further experiments except of the most
cautious type. But he lifted a sheet of paper, and turned a glass
of water pink and then green, and he created a snail, which he
miraculously annihilated, and got himself a miraculous new
toothbrush. Somewhen in the small hours he had reached the
fact that his will-power must be of a particularly rare and
pungent quality, a fact of which he had certainly had inklings
before, but no certain assurance. The scare and perplexity of
his first discovery was now qualified by pride in this evidence of
singularity and by vague intimations of advantage. He became
aware that the church clock was striking one, and as it did not
occur to him that his daily duties at Gomshott's might be
miraculously dispensed with, he resumed undressing, in order
to get to bed without further delay. As he struggled to get his

shirt over his head, he was struck with a brilliant idea. 'Let me be in bed,' he said, and found himself so. 'Undressed,' he stipulated; and, finding the sheets cold, added hastily, 'and in my nightshirt – no, in a nice soft woollen nightshirt. Ah!' he said with immense enjoyment. 'And now let me be comfortably asleep. . . .'

He awoke at his usual hour and was pensive all through breakfast-time, wondering whether his overnight experience might not be a particularly vivid dream. At length his mind turned again to cautious experiments. For instance, he had three eggs for breakfast; two his landlady had supplied, good, but shoppy, and one was a delicious fresh goose-egg, laid, cooked, and served by his extraordinary will. He hurried off to Gomshott's in a state of profound but carefully concealed excitement, and only remembered the shell of the third egg when his landlady spoke of it that night. All day he could do no work because of this astonishingly new self-knowledge, but this caused him no inconvenience, because he made up for it miraculously in his last ten minutes.

As the day wore on his state of mind passed from wonder to elation, albeit the circumstances of his dismissal from the Long Dragon were still disagreeable to recall, and a garbled account of the matter that had reached his colleagues led to some badinage. It was evident he must be careful how he lifted frangible articles, but in other ways his gift promised more and more as he turned it over in his mind. He intended among other things to increase his personal property by unostentatious acts of creation. He called into existence a pair of very splendid diamond studs, and hastily annihilated them again as young Gomshott came across the counting-house to his desk. He was afraid young Gomshott might wonder how he had come by them. He saw quite clearly the gift required caution and watchfulness in its exercise, but so far as he could judge the difficulties attending its mastery would be no greater than those he had already faced in the study of cycling. It was that analogy, perhaps, quite as much as the feeling that he would be unwelcome in the Long Dragon, that drove him out after supper into the lane beyond the gasworks, to rehearse a few miracles in private.

There was possibly a certain want of originality in his attempts, for apart from his will-power Mr Fotheringay was not a very exceptional man. The miracle of Moses' rod came to his mind, but the night was dark and unfavourable to the proper control of large miraculous snakes. Then he recollected the story of Tannhäuser[3] that he had read on the back of the Philharmonic programme. That seemed to him singularly attractive and harmless. He stuck his walking-stick – a very nice Poona-Penang lawyer[4] – into the turf that edged the footpath, and commanded the dry wood to blossom. The air was immediately full of the scent of roses, and by means of a match he saw for himself that this beautiful miracle was indeed accomplished. His satisfaction was ended by advancing footsteps. Afraid of a premature discovery of his powers, he addressed the blossoming stick hastily: 'Go back.' What he meant was 'Change back'; but of course he was confused. The stick receded at a considerable velocity, and incontinently came a cry of anger and a bad word from the approaching person. 'Who are you throwing brambles at, you fool?' cried a voice. 'That got me on the shin.'

'I'm sorry, old chap,' said Mr Fotheringay, and then realizing the awkward nature of the explanation, caught nervously at his moustache. He saw Winch, one of the three Immering[5] constables, advancing.

'What d'yer mean by it?' asked the constable. 'Hullo! It's you, is it? The gent that broke the lamp at the Long Dragon!'

'I don't mean anything by it,' said Mr Fotheringay. 'Nothing at all.'

'What d'yer do it for then?'

'Oh, bother!' said Mr Fotheringay.

'Bother indeed! D'yer know that stick hurt? What d'yer do it for, eh?'

For the moment Mr Fotheringay could not think what he had done it for. His silence seemed to irritate Mr Winch. 'You've been assaulting the police, young man, this time. That's what *you* done.'

'Look here, Mr Winch,' said Mr Fotheringay, annoyed and confused, 'I'm very sorry. The fact is –'

'Well?'

He could think of no way but the truth. 'I was working a miracle.' He tried to speak in an offhand way, but try as he would he couldn't.

'Working a –! 'Ere, don't you talk rot. Working a miracle, indeed! Miracle! Well, that's downright funny! Why, you's the chap that don't believe in miracles. ... Fact is, this is another of your silly conjuring tricks – that's what this is. Now, I tell you –'

But Mr Fotheringay never heard what Mr Winch was going to tell him. He realized he had given himself away, flung his valuable secret to all the winds of heaven. A violent gust of irritation swept him to action. He turned on the constable swiftly and fiercely. 'Here,' he said, 'I've had enough of this, I have! I'll show you a silly conjuring trick, I will! Go to Hades! Go, now!'

He was alone!

Mr Fotheringay performed no more miracles that night, nor did he trouble to see what had become of his flowering stick. He returned to the town, scared and very quiet, and went to his bedroom. 'Lord!' he said, 'it's a powerful gift – an extremely powerful gift. I didn't hardly mean as much as that. Not really. ... I wonder what Hades is like!'

He sat on the bed taking off his boots. Struck by a happy thought he transferred the constable to San Francisco, and without any more interference with normal causation went soberly to bed. In the night he dreamt of the anger of Winch.

The next day Mr Fotheringay heard two interesting items of news. Someone had planted a most beautiful climbing rose against the elder Mr Gomshott's private house in the Lullaborough Road, and the river as far as Rawling's Mill was to be dragged for Constable Winch.

Mr Fotheringay was abstracted and thoughtful all that day, and performed no miracles except certain provisions for Winch, and the miracle of completing his day's work with punctual perfection in spite of all the bee-swarm of thoughts that hummed through his mind. And the extraordinary abstraction and meekness of his manner was remarked by several people, and made a matter for jesting. For the most part he was thinking of Winch.

On Sunday evening he went to chapel, and oddly enough, Mr Maydig, who took a certain interest in occult matters, preached about 'things that are not lawful'. Mr Fotheringay was not a regular chapel goer, but the system of assertive scepticism, to which I have already alluded, was now very much shaken. The tenor of the sermon threw an entirely new light on these novel gifts, and he suddenly decided to consult Mr Maydig immediately after the service. So soon as that was determined, he found himself wondering why he had not done so before.

Mr Maydig, a lean, excitable man with quite remarkably long wrists and neck, was gratified at a request for a private conversation from a young man whose carelessness in religious matters was a subject for general remark in the town. After a few necessary delays, he conducted him to the study of the Manse, which was contiguous to the chapel, seated him comfortably, and, standing in front of a cheerful fire – his legs threw a Rhodian arch of shadow on the opposite wall – requested Mr Fotheringay to state his business.

At first Mr Fotheringay was a little abashed, and found some difficulty in opening the matter. 'You will scarcely believe me, Mr Maydig, I am afraid' – and so forth for some time. He tried a question at last, and asked Mr Maydig his opinion of miracles.

Mr Maydig was still saying 'Well' in an extremely judicial tone, when Mr Fotheringay interrupted again: 'You don't believe, I suppose, that some common sort of person – like myself, for instance – as it might be sitting here now, might have some sort of twist inside him that made him able to do things by his will.'

'It's possible,' said Mr Maydig. 'Something of the sort, perhaps, is possible.'

'If I might make free with something here, I think I might show you by a sort of experiment,' said Mr Fotheringay. 'Now, take that tobacco-jar on the table, for instance. What I want to know is whether what I am going to do with it is a miracle or not. Just half a minute, Mr Maydig, please.'

He knitted his brows, pointed to the tobacco-jar and said: 'Be a bowl of vi'lets.'

The tobacco-jar did as it was ordered.

Mr Maydig started violently at the change, and stood looking from the thaumaturgist to the bowl of flowers. He said nothing. Presently he ventured to lean over the table and smell the violets; they were fresh-picked and very fine ones. Then he stared at Mr Fotheringay again.

'How did you do that?' he asked.

Mr Fotheringay pulled his moustache. 'Just told it – and there you are. Is that a miracle, or is it black art, or what is it? And what do you think's the matter with me? That's what I want to ask.'

'It's a most extraordinary occurrence.'

'And this day last week I knew no more that I could do things like that than you did. It came quite sudden. It's something odd about my will, I suppose, and that's as far as I can see.'

'Is *that* – the only thing. Could you do other things besides that?'

'Lord, yes!' said Mr Fotheringay. 'Just anything.' He thought, and suddenly recalled a conjuring entertainment he had seen. 'Here!' He pointed. 'Change into a bowl of fish – no, not that – change into a glass bowl full of water with goldfish swimming in it. That's better! You see that, Mr Maydig?'

'It's astonishing. It's incredible. You are either a most extraordinary . . . But no –'

'I could change it into anything,' said Mr Fotheringay. 'Just anything. Here! be a pigeon, will you?'

In another moment a blue pigeon was fluttering round the room and making Mr Maydig duck every time it came near him. 'Stop there, will you,' said Mr Fotheringay; and the pigeon hung motionless in the air. 'I could change it back to a bowl of flowers,' he said, and after replacing the pigeon on the table worked that miracle. 'I expect you will want your pipe in a bit,' he said, and restored the tobacco-jar.

Mr Maydig had followed all these later changes in a sort of ejaculatory silence. He stared at Mr Fotheringay and, in a very gingerly manner, picked up the tobacco-jar, examined it, replaced it on the table. '*Well!*' was the only expression of his feelings.

'Now, after that it's easier to explain what I came about,' said Mr Fotheringay; and proceeded to a lengthy and involved narrative of his strange experiences, beginning with the affair of the lamp in the Long Dragon and complicated by persistent allusions to Winch. As he went on, the transient pride Mr Maydig's consternation had caused passed away; he became the very ordinary Mr Fotheringay of everyday intercourse again. Mr Maydig listened intently, the tobacco-jar in his hand, and his bearing changed also with the course of the narrative. Presently, while Mr Fotheringay was dealing with the miracle of the third egg, the minister interrupted with a fluttering extended hand –

'It is possible,' he said. 'It is credible. It is amazing, of course, but it reconciles a number of difficulties. The power to work miracles is a gift – a peculiar quality like genius or second sight – hitherto it has come very rarely and to exceptional people. But in this case . . . I have always wondered at the miracles of Mahomet, and at Yogi's miracles, and the miracles of Madame Blavatsky.[6] But, of course! Yes, it is simply a gift! It carries out so beautifully the arguments of that great thinker' – Mr Maydig's voice sank – 'his Grace the Duke of Argyll.[7] Here we plumb some profounder law – deeper than the ordinary laws of nature. Yes – yes. Go on. Go on!'

Mr Fotheringay proceeded to tell of his misadventure with Winch, and Mr Maydig, no longer overawed or scared, began to jerk his limbs about and interject astonishment. 'It's this what troubled me most,' proceeded Mr Fotheringay; 'it's this I'm most mijitly in want of advice for; of course he's at San Francisco – wherever San Francisco may be – but of course it's awkward for both of us, as you'll see, Mr Maydig. I don't see how he can understand what has happened, and I dare say he's scared and exasperated something tremendous, and trying to get at me. I dare say he keeps on starting off to come here. I send him back, by a miracle, every few hours, when I think of it. And of course, that's a thing he won't be able to understand,

and it's bound to annoy him; and, of course, if he takes a ticket every time it will cost him a lot of money. I done the best I could for him, but of course it's difficult for him to put himself in my place. I thought afterwards that his clothes might have got scorched, you know – if Hades is all it's supposed to be – before I shifted him. In that case I suppose they'd have locked him up in San Francisco. Of course I willed him a new suit of clothes on him directly I thought of it. But, you see, I'm already in a deuce of a tangle –'

Mr Maydig looked serious. 'I see you are in a tangle. Yes, it's a difficult position. How you are to end it . . .' He became diffuse and inconclusive.

'However, we'll leave Winch for a little and discuss the larger question. I don't think this is a case of the black art or anything of the sort. I don't think there is any taint of criminality about it at all. Mr Fotheringay – none whatever, unless you are suppressing material facts. No, it's miracles – pure miracles – miracles, if I may say so, of the very highest class.'

He began to pace the hearthrug and gesticulate, while Mr Fotheringay sat with his arm on the table and his head on his arm, looking worried. 'I don't see how I'm to manage about Winch,' he said.

'A gift of working miracles – apparently a very powerful gift,' said Mr Maydig, 'will find a way about Winch – never fear. My dear Sir, you are a most important man – a man of the most astonishing possibilities. As evidence, for example! And in other ways, the things you may do . . .'

'Yes, I've thought of a thing or two,' said Mr Fotheringay. 'But – some of the things came a bit twisty. You saw that fish at first? Wrong sort of bowl and wrong sort of fish. And I thought I'd ask someone.'

'A proper course,' said Mr Maydig, 'a very proper course – altogether the proper course.' He stopped and looked at Mr Fotheringay. 'It's practically an unlimited gift. Let us test your powers, for instance. If they really are . . . If they really are all they seem to be.'

And so, incredible as it may seem, in the study of the little house behind the Congregational Chapel, on the evening of

Sunday, Nov. 10, 1896,[8] Mr Fotheringay, egged on and inspired by Mr Maydig, began to work miracles. The reader's attention is specially and definitely called to the date. He will object, probably has already objected, that certain points in this story are improbable, that if any things of the sort already described had indeed occurred, they would have been in all the papers a year ago. The details immediately following he will find particularly hard to accept, because among other things they involve the conclusion that he or she, the reader in question, must have been killed in a violent and unprecedented manner more than a year ago. Now a miracle is nothing if not improbable, and as a matter of fact the reader *was* killed in a violent and unprecedented manner a year ago. In the subsequent course of this story that will become perfectly clear and credible, as every right-minded and reasonable reader will admit. But this is not the place for the end of the story, being but little beyond the hither side of the middle. And at first the miracles worked by Mr Fotheringay were timid little miracles – little things with the cups and parlour fitments, as feeble as the miracles of Theosophists, and, feeble as they were, they were received with awe by his collaborator. He would have preferred to settle the Winch business out of hand, but Mr Maydig would not let him. But after they had worked a dozen of these domestic trivialities, their sense of power grew, their imagination began to show signs of stimulation, and their ambition enlarged. Their first larger enterprise was due to hunger and the negligence of Mrs Minchin, Mr Maydig's housekeeper. The meal to which the minister conducted Mr Fotheringay was certainly ill-laid and uninviting as refreshment for two industrious miracle-workers; but they were seated, and Mr Maydig was descanting in sorrow rather than in anger upon his housekeeper's shortcomings, before it occurred to Mr Fotheringay that an opportunity lay before him. 'Don't you think, Mr Maydig,' he said, 'if it isn't a liberty, I –'

'My dear Mr Fotheringay! Of course! No – I didn't think.'

Mr Fotheringay waved his hand. 'What shall we have?' he said, in a large, inclusive spirit, and, at Mr Maydig's order, revised the supper very thoroughly. 'As for me,' he said, eyeing

Mr Maydig's selection, 'I am always particularly fond of a tankard of stout and a nice Welsh rarebit, and I'll order that. I ain't much given to Burgundy,' and forthwith stout and Welsh rarebit promptly appeared at his command. They sat long at their supper, talking like equals, as Mr Fotheringay presently perceived with a glow of surprise and gratification, of all the miracles they would presently do. 'And, by the bye, Mr Maydig,' said Mr Fotheringay, 'I might perhaps be able to help you – in a domestic way.'

'Don't quite follow,' said Mr Maydig, pouring out a glass of miraculous old Burgundy.

Mr Fotheringay helped himself to a second Welsh rarebit out of vacancy, and took a mouthful. 'I was thinking,' he said, 'I might be able (*chum, chum*) to work (*chum, chum*) a miracle with Mrs Minchin (*chum, chum*) – make her a better woman.'

Mr Maydig put down the glass and looked doubtful. 'She's – She strongly objects to interference, you know, Mr Fotheringay. And – as a matter of fact – it's well past eleven and she's probably in bed and asleep. Do you think, on the whole –'

Mr Fotheringay considered these objections. 'I don't see that it shouldn't be done in her sleep.'

For a time Mr Maydig opposed the idea, and then he yielded. Mr Fotheringay issued his orders, and a little less at their ease, perhaps, the two gentlemen proceeded with their repast. Mr Maydig was enlarging on the changes he might expect in his housekeeper next day, with an optimism that seemed even to Mr Fotheringay's supper senses a little forced and hectic, when a series of confused noises from upstairs began. Their eyes exchanged interrogations, and Mr Maydig left the room hastily. Mr Fotheringay heard him calling up to his housekeeper and then his footsteps going softly up to her.

In a minute or so the minister returned, his step light, his face radiant. 'Wonderful!' he said, 'and touching! Most touching!'

He began pacing the hearthrug. 'A repentance – a most touching repentance – through the crack of the door. Poor woman! A most wonderful change! She had got up. She must have got up at once. She had got up out of her sleep to smash a private bottle of brandy in her box. And to confess it too! . . . But this gives us – it opens – a most amazing vista of possibilities. If we can work this miraculous change in *her* . . .'

'The thing's unlimited seemingly,' said Mr Fotheringay. 'And about Mr Winch –'

'Altogether unlimited.' And from the hearthrug Mr Maydig, waving the Winch difficulty aside, unfolded a series of wonderful proposals – proposals he invented as he went along.

Now what those proposals were does not concern the essentials of this story. Suffice it that they were designed in a spirit of infinite benevolence, the sort of benevolence that used to be called post-prandial. Suffice it, too, that the problem of Winch remained unsolved. Nor is it necessary to describe how far that series got to its fulfilment. There were astonishing changes. The small hours found Mr Maydig and Mr Fotheringay careering across the chilly market square under the still moon, in a sort of ecstasy of thaumaturgy, Mr Maydig all flap and gesture, Mr Fotheringay short and bristling, and no longer abashed at his greatness. They had reformed every drunkard in the Parliamentary division, changed all the beer and alcohol to water (Mr Maydig had overruled Mr Fotheringay on this point), they had, further, greatly improved the railway communication of the place, drained Flinder's swamp, improved the soil of One Tree Hill, and cured the Vicar's wart. And they were going to see what could be done with the injured pier at South Bridge. 'The place,' gasped Mr Maydig, 'won't be the same place tomorrow. How surprised and thankful everyone will be!' And just at that moment the church clock struck three.

'I say,' said Mr Fotheringay, 'that's three o'clock! I must be getting back. I've got to be at business by eight. And besides, Mrs Wimms –'

'We're only beginning,' said Mr Maydig, full of the sweetness of unlimited power. 'We're only beginning. Think of all the good we're doing. When people wake –'

'But –,' said Mr Fotheringay.

Mr Maydig gripped his arm suddenly. His eyes were bright and wild. 'My dear chap,' he said, 'there's no hurry. Look' – he pointed to the moon at the zenith – 'Joshua!'[9]

'Joshua?' said Mr Fotheringay.

'Joshua,' said Mr Maydig. 'Why not? Stop it.'

Mr Fotheringay looked at the moon.

'That's a bit tall,' he said after a pause.

'Why not?' said Mr Maydig. 'Of course it doesn't stop. You stop the rotation of the earth, you know. Time stops. It isn't as if we were doing harm.'

'H'm!' said Mr Fotheringay. 'Well.' He sighed. 'I'll try. Here –'

He buttoned up his jacket and addressed himself to the habitable globe, with as good an assumption of confidence as lay in his power. 'Jest stop rotating, will you,' said Mr Fotheringay.

Incontinently he was flying head over heels through the air at the rate of dozens of miles a minute. In spite of the innumerable circles he was describing per second, he thought; for thought is wonderful – sometimes as sluggish as flowing pitch, sometimes as instantaneous as light. He thought in a second, and willed. 'Let me come down safe and sound. Whatever else happens, let me down safe and sound.'

He willed it only just in time, for his clothes, heated by his rapid flight through the air, were already beginning to singe. He came down with a forcible, but by no means injurious bump in what appeared to be a mound of fresh-turned earth. A large mass of metal and masonry, extraordinarily like the clock-tower in the middle of the market square, hit the earth near him, ricochetted over him, and flew into stonework, bricks, and masonry, like a bursting bomb. A hurtling cow hit one of the larger blocks and smashed like an egg. There was a crash that made all the most violent crashes of his past life seem like the sound of falling dust, and this was followed by a descending series of lesser crashes. A vast wind roared throughout earth and heaven, so that he could scarcely lift his head to look. For a while he was too breathless and astonished even to see where he was or what had happened. And his first movement was to feel his head and reassure himself that his streaming hair was still his own.

'Lord!' gasped Mr Fotheringay, scarce able to speak for the gale, 'I've had a squeak! What's gone wrong? Storms and thunder. And only a minute ago a fine night. It's Maydig set me on to this sort of thing. *What* a wind! If I go on fooling in this way I'm bound to have a thundering accident! . . .

'Where's Maydig?

'What a confounded mess everything's in!'

He looked about him so far as his flapping jacket would permit. The appearance of things was really extremely strange. 'The sky's all right anyhow,' said Mr Fotheringay. 'And that's about all that is all right. And even there it looks like a terrific gale coming up. But there's the moon overhead. Just as it was just now. Bright as midday. But as for the rest – Where's the village? Where's – where's anything? And what on earth set this wind a-blowing? *I* didn't order no wind.'

Mr Fotheringay struggled to get to his feet in vain, and after one failure, remained on all fours, holding on. He surveyed the moonlit world to leeward, with the tails of his jacket streaming over his head. 'There's something seriously wrong,' said Mr Fotheringay. 'And what it is – goodness knows.'

Far and wide nothing was visible in the white glare through the haze of dust that drove before a screaming gale but tumbled masses of earth and heaps of inchoate ruins, no trees, no houses, no familiar shapes, only a wilderness of disorder vanishing at last into the darkness beneath the whirling columns and streamers, the lightnings and thunderings of a swiftly rising storm. Near him in the livid glare was something that might once have been an elm tree, a smashed mass of splinters, shivered from boughs to base, and further a twisted mass of iron girders – only too evidently the viaduct – rose out of the piled confusion.

You see, when Mr Fotheringay had arrested the rotation of the solid globe, he had made no stipulation concerning the trifling movables upon its surface. And the earth spins so fast that the surface at its equator is travelling at rather more than a thousand miles an hour,[10] and in these latitudes at more than half that pace. So that the village, and Mr Maydig, and Mr Fotheringay, and everybody and everything had been jerked violently forward at about nine miles per second – that is to say, much more violently than if they had been fired out of a cannon. And every human being, every living creature, every house, and every tree – all the world as we know it – had been so jerked and smashed and utterly destroyed. That was all.

These things Mr Fotheringay did not, of course, fully appreciate. But he perceived that his miracle had miscarried, and with that a great disgust of miracles came upon him. He was in darkness now, for the clouds had swept together and blotted out his momentary glimpse of the moon, and the air was full of fitful struggling tortured wraiths of hail. A great roaring of wind and waters filled earth and sky, and, peering under his hand through the dust and sleet to windward, he saw by the play of the lightnings a vast wall of water pouring towards him.

'Maydig!' screamed Mr Fotheringay's feeble voice amid the elemental uproar. 'Here! – Maydig!'

'Stop!' cried Mr Fotheringay to the advancing water. 'Oh, for goodness' sake, stop!'

'Just a moment,' said Mr Fotheringay to the lightnings and thunder. 'Stop jest a moment while I collect my thoughts. . . . And now what shall I do?' he said. 'What *shall* I do? Lord! I wish Maydig was about.'

'I know,' said Mr Fotheringay. 'And for goodness' sake let's have it right *this* time.'

He remained on all fours, leaning against the wind, very intent to have everything right.

'Ah!' he said. 'Let nothing what I'm going to order happen until I say "Off!" . . . Lord! I wish I'd thought of that before!'

He lifted his little voice against the whirlwind, shouting louder and louder in the vain desire to hear himself speak. 'Now then! – here goes! Mind about that what I said just now. In the first place, when all I've got to say is done, let me lose my miraculous power, let my will become just like anybody else's will, and all these dangerous miracles be stopped. I don't like them. I'd rather I didn't work 'em. Ever so much. That's the first thing. And the second is – let me be back just before the miracles begin; let everything be just as it was before that blessed lamp turned up. It's a big job, but it's the last. Have you got it? No more miracles, everything as it was – me back in the Long Dragon just before I drank my half-pint. That's it! Yes.'

He dug his fingers into the mould, closed his eyes, and said 'Off!'

Everything became perfectly still. He perceived that he was standing erect.

'So *you* say,' said a voice.

He opened his eyes. He was in the bar of the Long Dragon, arguing about miracles with Toddy Beamish. He had a vague sense of some great thing forgotten that instantaneously passed. You see, except for the loss of his miraculous powers, everything was back as it had been, his mind and memory therefore were now just as they had been at the time when this story began. So that he knew absolutely nothing of all that is told here, knows nothing of all that is told here to this day. And among other things, of course, he still did not believe in miracles.

'I tell you that miracles, properly speaking, can't possibly happen,' he said, 'whatever you like to hold. And I'm prepared to prove it up to the hilt.'

'That's what *you* think,' said Toddy Beamish, and 'Prove it if you can.'

'Looky here, Mr Beamish,' said Mr Fotheringay. 'Let us clearly understand what a miracle is. It's something contrariwise to the course of nature done by power of Will. . . .'

A DREAM OF
ARMAGEDDON[1]

The man with the white face entered the carriage at Rugby. He moved slowly in spite of the urgency of his porter, and even while he was still on the platform I noted how ill he seemed. He dropped into the corner over against me with a sigh, made an incomplete attempt to arrange his travelling shawl, and became motionless, with his eyes staring vacantly. Presently he was moved by a sense of my observation, looked up at me, and put out a spiritless hand for his newspaper. Then he glanced again in my direction.

I feigned to read. I feared I had unwittingly embarrassed him, and in a moment I was surprised to find him speaking.

'I beg your pardon?' said I.

'That book,' he repeated, pointing a lean finger, 'is about dreams.'

'Obviously,' I answered, for it was Fortnum-Roscoe's *Dream States*,[2] and the title was on the cover.

He hung silent for a space as if he sought words. 'Yes,' he said at last, 'but they tell you nothing.'

I did not catch his meaning for a second.

'They don't know,' he added.

I looked a little more attentively at his face.

'There are dreams,' he said, 'and dreams.'

That sort of proposition I never dispute.

'I suppose—' he hesitated. 'Do you ever dream? I mean vividly.'

'I dream very little,' I answered. 'I doubt if I have three vivid dreams a year.'

'Ah!' he said, and seemed for a moment to collect his thoughts.

'Your dreams don't mix with your memories?' he asked abruptly. 'You don't find yourself in doubt; did this happen or did it not?'

'Hardly ever. Except just for a momentary hesitation now and then. I suppose few people do.'

'Does *he* say—' he indicated the book.

'Says it happens at times and gives the usual explanation about intensity of impression and the like to account for its not happening as a rule. I suppose you know something of these theories—'

'Very little – except that they are wrong.'

His emaciated hand played with the strap of the window for a time. I prepared to resume reading, and that seemed to precipitate his next remark. He leant forward almost as though he would touch me.

'Isn't there something called consecutive dreaming – that goes on night after night?'

'I believe there is. There are cases given in most books on mental trouble.'

'Mental trouble! Yes. I dare say there are. It's the right place for them. But what I mean—' He looked at his bony knuckles. 'Is that sort of thing always dreaming? *Is* it dreaming? Or is it something else? Mightn't it be something else?'

I should have snubbed his persistent conversation but for the drawn anxiety of his face. I remember now the look of his faded eyes and the lids red stained – perhaps you know that look.

'I'm not just arguing about a matter of opinion,' he said. 'The thing's killing me.'

'Dreams?'

'If you call them dreams. Night after night. Vivid! – so vivid ... this—' (he indicated the landscape that went streaming by the window) 'seems unreal in comparison! I can scarcely remember who I am, what business I am on. ....'

He paused. 'Even now—'

'The dream is always the same – do you mean?' I asked.

'It's over.'

'You mean?'

'I died.'

'Died?'

'Smashed and killed, and now, so much of me as that dream was, is dead. Dead for ever. I dreamt I was another man, you know, living in a different part of the world and in a different time. I dreamt that night after night. Night after night I woke into that other life. Fresh scenes and fresh happenings – until I came upon the last—'

'When you died?'

'When I died.'

'And since then—'

'No,' he said. 'Thank God! That was the end of the dream. . . .'

It was clear I was in for this dream. And after all, I had an hour before me, the light was fading fast, and Fortnum-Roscoe has a dreary way with him. 'Living in a different time,' I said: 'do you mean in some different age?'

'Yes.'

'Past?'

'No – to come – to come.'

'The year three thousand, for example?'

'I don't know what year it was. I did when I was asleep, when I was dreaming, that is, but not now – not now that I am awake. There's a lot of things I have forgotten since I woke out of these dreams, though I knew them at the time when I was – I suppose it was dreaming. They called the year differently from our way of calling the year. . . . What *did* they call it?' He put his hand to his forehead. 'No,' said he, 'I forget.'

He sat smiling weakly. For a moment I feared he did not mean to tell me his dream. As a rule I hate people who tell their dreams, but this struck me differently. I proffered assistance even. 'It began—' I suggested.

'It was vivid from the first. I seemed to wake up in it suddenly. And it's curious that in these dreams I am speaking of I never remembered this life I am living now. It seemed as if the dream life was enough while it lasted. Perhaps— But I will tell you how I find myself when I do my best to recall it all. I don't remember anything clearly until I found myself sitting in a sort of loggia looking out over the sea. I had been dozing, and suddenly I woke up – fresh and vivid – not a bit dream-like – because the girl had stopped fanning me.'

'The girl?'

'Yes, the girl. You must not interrupt or you will put me out.'

He stopped abruptly. 'You won't think I'm mad?' he said.

'No,' I answered; 'you've been dreaming. Tell me your dream.'

'I woke up, I say, because the girl had stopped fanning me. I was not surprised to find myself there or anything of that sort, you understand. I did not feel I had fallen into it suddenly. I simply took it up at that point. Whatever memory I had of *this* life, this nineteenth-century life, faded as I woke, vanished like a dream. I knew all about myself, knew that my name was no longer Cooper but Hedon, and all about my position in the world. I've forgotten a lot since I woke – there's a want of connection – but it was all quite clear and matter of fact then.'

He hesitated again, gripping the window strap, putting his face forward and looking up to me appealingly.

'This seems bosh to you?'

'No, no!' I cried. 'Go on. Tell me what this loggia was like.'

'It was not really a loggia – I don't know what to call it. It faced south. It was small. It was all in shadow except the semicircle above the balcony that showed the sky and sea and the corner where the girl stood. I was on a couch – it was a metal couch with light striped cushions – and the girl was leaning over the balcony with her back to me. The light of the sunrise fell on her ear and cheek. Her pretty white neck and the little curls that nestled there, and her white shoulder were in the sun, and all the grace of her body was in the cool blue shadow. She was dressed – how can I describe it? It was easy and flowing. And altogether there she stood, so that it came to me how beautiful and desirable she was, as though I had never seen her before And when at last I sighed and raised myself upon my arm she turned her face to me—'

He stopped.

'I have lived three-and-fifty years in this world. I have had mother, sisters, friends, wife and daughters – all their faces, the play of their faces, I know. But the face of this girl – it is much more real to me. I can bring it back into memory so that I see it again – I could draw it or paint it. And after all—'

He stopped – but I said nothing.

'The face of a dream – the face of a dream. She was beautiful. Not that beauty which is terrible, cold, and worshipful, like the beauty of a saint; nor that beauty that stirs fierce passions; but a sort of radiation, sweet lips that softened into smiles, and grave grey eyes. And she moved gracefully, she seemed to have part with all pleasant and gracious things—'

He stopped, and his face was downcast and hidden. Then he looked up at me and went on, making no further attempt to disguise his absolute belief in the reality of his story.

'You see, I had thrown up my plans and ambitions, thrown up all I had ever worked for or desired for her sake. I had been a master man away there in the north, with influence and property and a great reputation, but none of it had seemed worth having beside her. I had come to the place, this city of sunny pleasures, with her, and left all those things to wreck and ruin just to save a remnant at least of my life. While I had been in love with her before I knew that she had any care for me, before I had imagined that she would dare – that we should dare, all my life had seemed vain and hollow, dust and ashes. It *was* dust and ashes. Night after night and through the long days I had longed and desired – my soul had beaten against the thing forbidden!

'But it is impossible for one man to tell another just these things. It's emotion, it's a tint, a light that comes and goes. Only while it's there, everything changes, everything. The thing is I came away and left them in their Crisis to do what they could.'

'Left whom?' I asked, puzzled.

'The people up in the north there. You see – in this dream, anyhow – I had been a big man, the sort of man men come to trust in, to group themselves about. Millions of men who had never seen me were ready to do things and risk things because of their confidence in me. I had been playing that game for years, that big laborious game, that vague, monstrous political game amidst intrigues and betrayals, speech and agitation. It was a vast weltering world, and at last I had a sort of leadership against the Gang – you know it was called the Gang – a sort of compromise of scoundrelly projects and base ambitions and vast public emotional stupidities and catch-words – the Gang that kept the world noisy and blind year by year, and all the while that it was drifting, drifting towards infinite disaster. But I can't expect you to understand the shades and complications of the year – the year something or other ahead. I had it all – down to the smallest details – in my dream. I suppose I had been dreaming of it before I awoke, and the fading outline of some queer new development I had imagined still hung about me as I rubbed my eyes. It was some grubby affair that made me thank God for the sunlight. I sat up on the couch and remained looking at the woman and rejoicing – rejoicing that I had come away out of all that tumult and folly and violence before it was too late. After all, I thought, this is life – love and beauty, desire and delight, are they not worth all those dismal struggles for vague, gigantic ends. And I blamed myself for having ever sought to be a leader when I might have given my days to love. But then, thought I, if I had not spent my early days sternly and austerely, I might have wasted myself upon vain and worthless women, and at the thought all my being went out in love and tenderness to my dear mistress, my dear lady, who had come at last and compelled me – compelled me by her invincible charm for me – to lay that life aside.

' "You are worth it," I said, speaking without intending her to hear; "you are worth it, my dearest one; worth pride and praise and all things. Love! to have *you* is worth them all together." And at the murmur of my voice she turned about.

' "Come and see," she cried – I can hear her now – "come and see the sunrise upon Monte Solaro."

'I remember how I sprang to my feet and joined her at the balcony. She put a white hand upon my shoulder and pointed towards great masses of limestone, flushing, as it were, into life. I looked. But first I noted the sunlight on her face caressing the

lines of her cheeks and neck. How can I describe to you the
scene we had before us? We were at Capri—'

'I have been there,' I said. 'I have clambered up Monte Solaro
and drunk *vero Capri* – muddy stuff like cider – at the summit.'

'Ah!' said the man with the white face; 'then perhaps you
can tell me – you will know if this was indeed Capri. For in this
life I have never been there. Let me describe it. We were in a
little room, one of a vast multitude of little rooms, very cool
and sunny, hollowed out of the limestone of a sort of cape, very
high above the sea. The whole island, you know, was one
enormous hotel, complex beyond explaining, and on the other
side there were miles of floating hotels, and huge floating stages
to which the flying machines came. They called it a pleasure
city.[3] Of course, there was none of that in your time – rather,
I should say, *is* none of that *now*. Of course. Now! – yes.

'Well, this room of ours was at the extremity of the cape, so
that one could see east and west. Eastward was a great cliff – a
thousand feet high perhaps – coldly grey except for one bright
edge of gold, and beyond it the Isle of the Sirens, and a falling
coast that faded and passed into the hot sunrise. And when one
turned to the west, distinct and near was a little bay, a scimitar
of beach still in shadow. And out of that shadow rose Solaro
straight and tall, flushed and golden crested, like a beauty
throned, and the white moon was floating behind her in the
sky. And before us from east to west stretched the many-tinted
sea all dotted with sailing boats.

'To the eastward, of course, these little boats were grey and
very minute and clear, but to the westward they were little
boats of gold – shining gold – almost like little flames. And just
below us was a rock with an arch worn through it. The blue
seawater broke to green and foam all round the rock, and a
galley came gliding out of the arch.'

'I know that rock,' I said. 'I was nearly drowned there. It is
called the Faraglioni.'

'*I Faraglioni*? Yes, *she* called it that,' answered the man with
the white face. 'There was some story – but that—'

He put his hand to his forehead again. 'No,' he said, 'I forget
that story.

'Well, that is the first thing I remember, the first dream I had, that shaded room and the beautiful air and sky and that dear lady of mine, with her shining arms and her graceful robe, and how we sat and talked in half whispers to one another. We talked in whispers not because there was anyone to hear, but because there was still such a freshness of mind between us that our thoughts were a little frightened, I think, to find themselves at last in words. And so they went softly.

'Presently we were hungry and we went from our apartment, going by a strange passage with a moving floor, until we came to the great breakfast room – there was a fountain and music. A pleasant and joyful place it was, with its sunlight and splashing, and the murmur of plucked strings. And we sat and ate and smiled at one another, and I would not heed a man who was watching me from a table near by.

'And afterwards we went on to the dancing hall. But I cannot describe that hall. The place was enormous – larger than any building you have ever seen – and in one place there was the old gate of Capri, caught into the wall of a gallery high overhead. Light girders, stems and threads of gold, burst from the pillars like fountains, streamed like an Aurora across the roof and interlaced, like – like conjuring tricks. All about the great circle for the dancers there were beautiful figures, strange dragons, and intricate and wonderful grotesques bearing lights. The place was inundated with artificial light that shamed the newborn day. And as we went through the throng the people turned about and looked at us, for all through the world my name and face were known, and how I had suddenly thrown up pride and struggle to come to this place. And they looked also at the lady beside me, though half the story of how at last she had come to me was unknown or mistold. And few of the men who were there, I know, but judged me a happy man, in spite of all the shame and dishonour that had come upon my name.

'The air was full of music, full of harmonious scents, full of the rhythm of beautiful motions. Thousands of beautiful people swarmed about the hall, crowded the galleries, sat in a myriad recesses; they were dressed in splendid colours and crowned with flowers; thousands danced about the great circle beneath the white images of the ancient gods, and glorious processions of youths and maidens came and went. We two danced, not the dreary monotonies of your days – of this time, I mean – but dances that were beautiful, intoxicating. And even now I can see my lady dancing – dancing joyously. She danced, you know, with a serious face; she danced with a serious dignity, and yet she was smiling at me and caressing me – smiling and caressing with her eyes.

'The music was different,' he murmured. 'It went – I cannot describe it; but it was infinitely richer and more varied than any music that has ever come to me awake.

'And then – it was when we had done dancing – a man came to speak to me. He was a lean, resolute man, very soberly clad for that place, and already I had marked his face watching me in the breakfasting hall, and afterwards as we went along the passage I had avoided his eye. But now, as we sat in an alcove, smiling at the pleasure of all the people who went to and fro across the shining floor, he came and touched me, and spoke to me so that I was forced to listen. And he asked that he might speak to me for a while apart.

'"No," I said. "I have no secrets from this lady. What do you want to tell me?"

'He said it was a trivial matter, or at least a dry matter, for a lady to hear.

'"Perhaps for me to hear," said I.

'He glanced at her, as though almost he would appeal to her. Then he asked me suddenly if I had heard of a great and avenging declaration that Evesham[4] had made. Now, Evesham had always before been the man next to myself in the leadership of that great party in the north. He was a forcible, hard, and tactless man, and only I had been able to control and soften him. It was on his account even more than my own, I think, that the others had been so dismayed at my retreat. So this question about what he had done reawakened my old interest in the life I had put aside just for a moment.

'"I have taken no heed of any news for many days," I said. "What has Evesham been saying?"

'And with that the man began, nothing loth, and I must confess even I was struck by Evesham's reckless folly in the wild and threatening words he had used. And this messenger they had sent to me not only told me of Evesham's speech, but went on to ask counsel and to point out what need they had of me. While he talked, my lady sat a little forward and watched his face and mine.

'My old habits of scheming and organizing reasserted themselves. I could even see myself suddenly returning to the north, and all the dramatic effect of it. All that this man said witnessed to the disorder of the party indeed, but not to its damage. I should go back stronger than I had come. And then I thought of my lady. You see – how can I tell you? There were certain peculiarities of our relationship – as things are I need not tell you about that – which would render her presence with me impossible. I should have had to leave her; indeed, I should have had to renounce her clearly and openly, if I was to do all that I could do in the north. And the man knew *that*, even as he talked to her and me, knew it as well as she did, that my steps to duty were – first, separation, then abandonment. At the touch of that thought my dream of a return was shattered. I turned on the man suddenly, as he was imagining his eloquence was gaining ground with me.

'"What have I to do with these things now?" I said. "I have done with them. Do you think I am coquetting with your people in coming here?"

'"No," he said; "but—"

'"Why cannot you leave me alone. I have done with these things. I have ceased to be anything but a private man."

'"Yes," he answered. "But have you thought? – this talk of war, these reckless challenges, these wild aggressions—"

'I stood up.

'"No," I cried. "I won't hear you. I took count of all those things, I weighed them – and I have come away."

'He seemed to consider the possibility of persistence. He looked from me to where the lady sat regarding us.

'"War," he said, as if he were speaking to himself, and then turned slowly from me and walked away.

'I stood, caught in the whirl of thoughts his appeal had set going.

'I heard my lady's voice.

'"Dear," she said; "but if they have need of you—"

'She did not finish her sentence, she let it rest there. I turned to her sweet face, and the balance of my mood swayed and reeled.

'"They want me only to do the thing they dare not do themselves," I said. "If they distrust Evesham they must settle with him themselves."

'She looked at me doubtfully.

'"But war—" she said.

'I saw a doubt on her face that I had seen before, a doubt of herself and me, the first shadow of the discovery that, seen strongly and completely, must drive us apart for ever.

'Now I was an older mind than hers, and I could sway her to this belief or that.

'"My dear one," I said, "you must not trouble over these things. There will be no war. Certainly there will be no war. The age of wars is past. Trust me to know the justice of this case. They have no right upon me, dearest, and no one has a right upon me. I have been free to choose my life, and I have chosen this."

'"But *war*—," she said.

'I sat down beside her. I put an arm behind her and took her hand in mine. I set myself to drive that doubt away – I set myself to fill her mind with pleasant things again. I lied to her, and in lying to her I lied also to myself. And she was only too ready to believe me, only too ready to forget.

'Very soon the shadow had gone again, and we were hastening to our bathing-place in the Grotta del Bove Marino, where it was our custom to bathe every day. We swam and splashed one another, and in that buoyant water I seemed to become something lighter and stronger than a man. And at last we came out dripping and rejoicing and raced among the rocks. And then I put on a dry bathing-dress, and we sat to bask in the sun, and presently I nodded, resting my head against her knee, and she put her hand upon my hair and stroked it softly

and I dozed. And behold! as it were with the snapping of the
string of a violin, I was awakening, and I was in my own bed
in Liverpool, in the life of today.

'Only for a time I could not believe that all these vivid
moments had been no more than the substance of a dream.

'In truth, I could not believe it a dream for all the sobering
reality of things about me. I bathed and dressed as it were by
habit, and as I shaved I argued why I of all men should leave
the woman I loved to go back to fantastic politics in the hard
and strenuous north. Even if Evesham did force the world back
to war, what was that to me? I was a man with the heart of a
man, and why should I feel the responsibility of a deity for the
way the world might go?

'You know that is not quite the way I think about affairs,
about my real affairs. I am a solicitor, you know, with a point
of view.

'The vision was so real, you must understand, so utterly
unlike a dream that I kept perpetually recalling trivial irrelevant
details; even the ornament of a book-cover that lay on my wife's
sewing machine in the breakfast room recalled with the utmost
vividness the gilt line that ran about the seat in the alcove where
I had talked with the messenger from my deserted party. Have
you ever heard of a dream that had a quality like that?'

'Like—?'

'So that afterwards you remembered details you had forgotten.'

I thought. I had never noticed the point before, but he was
right.

'Never,' I said. 'That is what you never seem to do with
dreams.'

'No,' he answered. 'But that is just what I did. I am a solicitor,
you must understand, in Liverpool, and I could not help
wondering what the clients and business people I found myself
talking to in my office would think if I told them suddenly I
was in love with a girl who would be born a couple of hundred
years or so hence, and worried about the politics of my great-
great-great-grand-children. I was chiefly busy that day negotiat-
ing a ninety-nine-year building lease. It was a private builder in

a hurry, and we wanted to tie him in every possible way. I had an interview with him, and he showed a certain want of temper that sent me to bed still irritated. That night I had no dream. Nor did I dream the next night, at least, to remember.

'Something of that intense reality of conviction vanished. I began to feel sure it *was* a dream. And then it came again.

'When the dream came again, nearly four days later, it was very different. I think it certain that four days had also elapsed in the dream. Many things had happened in the north, and the shadow of them was back again between us, and this time it was not so easily dispelled. I began I know with moody musings. Why, in spite of all, should I go back, go back for all the rest of my days to toil and stress, insults and perpetual dissatisfaction, simply to save hundreds of millions of common people, whom I did not love, whom too often I could do no other than despise, from the stress and anguish of war and infinite misrule? And after all I might fail. *They* all sought their own narrow ends, and why should not I – why should not I also live as a man? And out of such thoughts her voice summoned me, and I lifted my eyes.

'I found myself awake and walking. We had come out above the Pleasure City, we were near the summit of Monte Solaro and looking towards the bay. It was the late afternoon and very clear. Far away to the left Ischia hung in a golden haze between sea and sky, and Naples was coldly white against the hills, and before us was Vesuvius[5] with a tall and slender streamer feathering at last towards the south, and the ruins of Torre Annunziata and Castellamare glittering and near.'

I interrupted suddenly: 'You have been to Capri, of course?'

'Only in this dream,' he said, 'only in this dream. All across the bay beyond Sorrento were the floating palaces of the Pleasure City moored and chained. And northward were the broad floating stages that received the aeroplanes.[6] Aeroplanes fell out of the sky every afternoon, each bringing its thousands of pleasure-seekers from the uttermost parts of the earth to Capri and its delights. All these things, I say, stretched below.

'But we noticed them only incidentally because of an unusual sight that evening had to show. Five war aeroplanes that had long slumbered useless in the distant arsenals of the Rhine-mouth[7] were manoeuvring now in the eastward sky. Evesham had astonished the world by producing them and others, and sending them to circle here and there. It was the threat material in the great game of bluff he was playing, and it had taken even me by surprise. He was one of those incredibly stupid energetic people who seem sent by heaven to create disasters. His energy to the first glance seemed so wonderfully like capacity! But he had no imagination, no invention, only a stupid, vast, driving force of will, and a mad faith in his stupid idiot "luck" to pull him through. I remember how we stood out upon the headland watching the squadron circling far away, and how I weighed the full meaning of the sight, seeing clearly the way things must go. And then even it was not too late. I might have gone back, I think, and saved the world. The people of the north would follow me, I knew, granted only that in one thing I respected their moral standards. The east and south would trust me as they would trust no other northern man. And I knew I had only to put it to her and she would have let me go. . . . Not because she did not love me!

'Only I did not want to go; my will was all the other way about. I had so newly thrown off the incubus of responsibility: I was still so fresh a renegade from duty that the daylight clearness of what I *ought* to do had no power at all to touch my will. My will was to live, to gather pleasures and make my dear lady happy. But though this sense of vast neglected duties had no power to draw me, it could make me silent and preoccupied, it robbed the days I had spent of half their brightness and roused me into dark meditations in the silence of the night. And as I stood and watched Evesham's aeroplanes sweep to and fro – those birds of infinite ill omen – she stood beside me watching me, perceiving the trouble indeed, but not perceiving it clearly – her eyes questioning my face, her expression shaded with perplexity. Her face was grey because the sunset was fading out of the sky. It was no fault of hers that she held me. She had asked me to go from her, and again in the night-time and with tears she had asked me to go.

'At last it was the sense of her that roused me from my mood.

I turned upon her suddenly and challenged her to race down the mountain slopes. "No," she said, as if I jarred with her gravity; but I was resolved to end that gravity, and made her run – no one can be very grey and sad who is out of breath – and when she stumbled I ran with my hand beneath her arm. We ran down past a couple of men, who turned back staring in astonishment at my behaviour – they must have recognized my face. And halfway down the slope came a tumult in the air, clang-clank, clang-clank, and we stopped, and presently over the hill-crest those war things came flying one behind the other.'

The man seemed hesitating on the verge of a description.

'What were they like?' I asked.

'They had never fought,' he said. 'They were just like our ironclads are nowadays; they had never fought. No one knew what they might do, with excited men inside them; few even cared to speculate. They were great driving things shaped like spear-heads without a shaft, with a propeller in the place of the shaft.'

'Steel?'

'Not steel.'

'Aluminium?'

'No, no, nothing of that sort. An alloy that was very common – as common as brass, for example. It was called – let me see—' He squeezed his forehead with the fingers of one hand. 'I am forgetting everything,' he said.

'And they carried guns?'

'Little guns, firing high explosive shells. They fired the guns backwards, out of the base of the leaf, so to speak, and rammed with the beak. That was the theory, you know, but they had never been fought. No one could tell exactly what was going to happen. And meanwhile I suppose it was very fine to go whirling through the air like a flight of young swallows, swift and easy. I guess the captains tried not to think too clearly what the real thing would be like. And these flying war machines, you know, were only one sort of the endless war contrivances that had been invented and had fallen into abeyance during the long peace. There were all sorts of these things that people were routing out and furbishing up; infernal things, silly things;

things that had never been tried; big engines, terrible explosives, great guns. You know the silly way of the ingenious sort of men who make these things; they turn 'em out as beavers build dams, and with no more sense of the rivers they're going to divert and the lands they're going to flood!

'As we went down the winding stepway to our hotel again, in the twilight, I foresaw it all: I saw how clearly and inevitably things were driving for war in Evesham's silly, violent hands, and I had some inkling of what war was bound to be under these new conditions. And even then, though I knew it was drawing near the limit of my opportunity, I could find no will to go back.'

He sighed.

'That was my last chance.

'We didn't go into the city until the sky was full of stars, so we walked out upon the high terrace, to and fro, and – she counselled me to go back.

'"My dearest," she said, and her sweet face looked up to me, "this is Death. This life you lead is Death. Go back to them, go back to your duty—"

'She began to weep, saying, between her sobs, and clinging to my arm as she said it, "Go back – Go back."

'Then suddenly she fell mute, and, glancing down at her face, I read in an instant the thing she had thought to do. It was one of those moments when one *sees*.

'"No!" I said.

'"No?" she asked, in surprise, and I think a little fearful at the answer to her thought.

'"Nothing," I said, "shall send me back. Nothing! I have chosen. Love, I have chosen, and the world must go. Whatever happens I will live this life – I will live for *you*! It – nothing shall turn me aside; nothing, my dear one. Even if you died – even if you died—"

'"Yes?" she murmured, softly.

'"Then – I also would die."

'And before she could speak again I began to talk, talking eloquently – as I *could* do in that life – talking to exalt love, to make the life we were living seem heroic and glorious; and the thing I was deserting something hard and enormously ignoble that it was a fine thing to set aside. I bent all my mind to throw that glamour upon it, seeking not only to convert her but myself to that. We talked, and she clung to me, torn too between all that she deemed noble and all that she knew was sweet. And at last I did make it heroic, made all the thickening disaster of the world only a sort of glorious setting to our unparalleled love, and we two poor foolish souls strutted there at last, clad in that splendid delusion, drunken rather with that glorious delusion, under the still stars.

'And so my moment passed.

'It was my last chance. Even as we went to and fro there, the leaders of the south and east were gathering their resolve, and the hot answer that shattered Evesham's bluffing for ever, took shape and waited. And all over Asia, and the ocean, and the South, the air and the wires were throbbing with their warnings to prepare – prepare.

'No one living, you know, knew what war was; no one could imagine, with all these new inventions, what horror war might bring. I believe most people still believed it would be a matter of bright uniforms and shouting charges and triumphs and flags and bands – in a time when half the world drew its food supply from regions ten thousand miles away—'

The man with the white face paused. I glanced at him, and his face was intent on the floor of the carriage. A little railway station, a string of loaded trucks, a signal-box, and the back of a cottage, shot by the carriage window, and a bridge passed with a clap of noise, echoing the tumult of the train.

'After that,' he said, 'I dreamt often. For three weeks of nights that dream was my life. And the worst of it was there were nights when I could not dream, when I lay tossing on a bed in *this* accursed life; and *there* – somewhere lost to me – things were happening – momentous, terrible things. . . . I lived at nights – my days, my waking days, this life I am living now, became a faded, far-away dream, a drab setting, the cover of the book.'

He thought.

'I could tell you all, tell you every little thing in the dream, but as to what I did in the daytime – no. I could not tell – I do not remember. My memory – my memory has gone. The business of life slips from me—'

He leant forward, and pressed his hands upon his eyes. For a long time he said nothing.

'And then?' said I.

'The war burst like a hurricane.'

He stared before him at unspeakable things.

'And then?' I urged again.

'One touch of unreality,' he said, in the low tone of a man who speaks to himself, 'and they would have been nightmares. But they were not nightmares – they were not nightmares. *No!*'

He was silent for so long that it dawned upon me that there was a danger of losing the rest of the story. But he went on talking again in the same tone of questioning self-communion.

'What was there to do but flight? I had not thought the war would touch Capri – I had seemed to see Capri as being out of it all, as the contrast to it all; but two nights after the whole place was shouting and bawling, every woman almost and every other man wore a badge – Evesham's badge – and there was no music but a jangling war-song over and over again, and everywhere men enlisting, and in the dancing halls they were drilling. The whole island was awhirl with rumours; it was said, again and again, that fighting had begun. I had not expected this. I had seen so little of the life of pleasure that I had failed to reckon with this violence of the amateurs. And as for me, I was out of it. I was like a man who might have prevented the firing of a magazine. The time had gone. I was no one; the vainest stripling with a badge counted for more than I. The crowd jostled us and bawled in our ears; that accursed song deafened us; a woman shrieked at my lady because no badge was on her, and we two went back to our own place again, ruffled and insulted – my lady white and silent, and I aquiver with rage. So furious was I, I could have quarrelled with her if I could have found one shade of accusation in her eyes.

'All my magnificence had gone from me. I walked up and down our rock cell, and outside was the darkling sea and a light to the southward that flared and passed and came again.

' "We must get out of this place," I said over and over. "I have made my choice, and I will have no hand in these troubles. I will have nothing of this war. We have taken our lives out of all these things. This is no refuge for us. Let us go."

'And the next day we were already in flight from the war that covered the world.

'And all the rest was Flight – all the rest was Flight.'

He mused darkly.

'How much was there of it?'

He made no answer.

'How many days?'

His face was white and drawn and his hands were clenched. He took no heed of my curiosity.

I tried to draw him back to his story with questions.

'Where did you go?' I said.

'When?'

'When you left Capri.'

'South-west,'[8] he said, and glanced at me for a second. 'We went in a boat.'

'But I should have thought an aeroplane?'

'They had been seized.'

I questioned him no more. Presently I thought he was beginning again. He broke out in an argumentative monotone:

'But why should it be? If, indeed, this battle, this slaughter and stress *is* life, why have we this craving for pleasure and beauty? If there *is* no refuge, if there is no place of peace, and if all our dreams of quiet places are a folly and a snare, why have we such dreams? Surely it was no ignoble cravings, no base intentions, had brought us to this; it was Love had isolated us. Love had come to me with her eyes and robed in her beauty, more glorious than all else in life, in the very shape and colour of life, and summoned me away. I had silenced all the voices, I had answered all the questions – I had come to her. And suddenly there was nothing but War and Death!'

I had an inspiration. 'After all,' I said, 'it could have been only a dream.'

'A dream!' he cried, flaming upon me, 'a dream – when, even now—'

For the first time he became animated. A faint flush crept into his cheek. He raised his open hand and clenched it, and dropped it to his knee. He spoke, looking away from me, and for all the rest of the time he looked away. 'We are but phantoms,' he said, 'and the phantoms of phantoms, desires like cloud shadows and wills of straw that eddy in the wind; the days pass, use and wont carry us through as a train carries the shadow of its lights – so be it! But one thing is real and certain, one thing is no dreamstuff, but eternal and enduring. It is the centre of my life, and all other things about it are subordinate or altogether vain. I loved her, that woman of a dream. And she and I are dead together!

'A dream! How can it be a dream, when it has drenched a living life with unappeasable sorrow, when it makes all that I have lived for and cared for, worthless and unmeaning?

'Until that very moment when she was killed I believed we had still a chance of getting away,' he said. 'All through the night and morning that we sailed across the sea from Capri to Salerno, we talked of escape. We were full of hope, and it clung about us to the end, hope for the life together we should lead, out of it all, out of the battle and struggle, the wild and empty passions, the empty arbitrary "thou shalt" and "thou shalt not" of the world. We were uplifted, as though our quest was a holy thing, as though love for one another was a mission. . . .

'Even when from our boat we saw the fair face of that great rock Capri – already scarred and gashed by the gun emplacements and hiding-places that were to make it a fastness – we reckoned nothing of the imminent slaughter, though the fury of preparation hung about in puffs and clouds of dust at a hundred points amidst the grey; but, indeed, I made a text of that and talked. There, you know, was the rock, still beautiful for all its scars, with its countless windows and arches and ways, tier upon tier, for a thousand feet, a vast carving of grey, broken by vine-clad terraces and lemon and orange groves and masses of agave and prickly pear, and puffs of almond blossom. And out under the archway that is built over the Marina Piccola[9] other boats were coming; and as we came round the cape and within sight of the mainland, another string of boats came into view, driving before the wind towards the south-west. In a little while a multitude had come out, the remoter just specks of ultramarine in the shadow of the eastward cliff.

' "It is love and reason," I said, "fleeing from all this madness of war."

'And though we presently saw a squadron of aeroplanes flying across the southern sky we did not heed it. There it was – a line of dots in the sky – and then more, dotting the south-eastern horizon, and then still more, until all that quarter of the sky was stippled with blue specks. Now they were all thin little strokes of blue, and now one and now a multitude would heel and catch the sun and become short flashes of light. They came, rising and falling and growing larger like some huge flight of gulls or rooks or such-like birds, moving with a marvellous uniformity, and ever as they drew nearer they spread over a greater width of sky. The southward wing flung itself in an arrow-headed cloud athwart the sun. And then suddenly they swept round to the eastward and streamed eastward, growing smaller and smaller and clearer and clearer again until they vanished from the sky. And after that we noted to the northward and very high Evesham's fighting machines hanging high over Naples like an evening swarm of gnats.

'It seemed to have no more to do with us than a flight of birds.

'Even the mutter of guns far away in the south-east seemed to us to signify nothing. . . .

'Each day, each dream after that, we were still exalted, still seeking that refuge where we might live and love. Fatigue had come upon us, pain and many distresses. For though we were dusty and stained by our toilsome tramping, and half starved and with the horror of the dead men we had seen and the flight of the peasants – for very soon a gust of fighting swept up the peninsula – with these things haunting our minds it still resulted only in a deepening resolution to escape. Oh, but she was brave and patient! She who had never faced hardship and exposure had courage for herself – and me. We went to and fro seeking an outlet, over a country all commandeered and ransacked by the gathering hosts of war. Always we went on foot. At first there were other fugitives, but we did not mingle with them. Some escaped northward, some were caught in the torrent of peasantry that swept along the main roads; many gave themselves into the hands of the soldiery and were sent northward. Many of the men were impressed. But we kept away from these things; we had brought no money to bribe a passage north, and I feared for my lady at the hands of these conscript crowds. We had landed at Salerno, and we had been turned back from Cava, and we had tried to cross towards Taranto by a pass over Monte Alburno, but we had been driven back for want of food, and so we had come down among the marshes by Paestum,[10] where those great temples stand alone. I had some vague idea that by Paestum it might be possible to find a boat or something, and take once more to sea. And there it was the battle overtook us.

'A sort of soul-blindness had me. Plainly I could see that we were being hemmed in; that the great net of that giant Warfare had us in its toils. Many times we had seen the levies that had come down from the north going to and fro, and had come upon them in the distance amidst the mountains making ways for the ammunition and preparing the mounting of the guns. Once we fancied they had fired at us, taking us for spies – at any rate a shot had gone shuddering over us. Several times we had hidden in woods from hovering aeroplanes.

'But all these things do not matter now, these nights of flight and pain. . . . We were in an open place near those great temples at Paestum at last, on a blank stony place dotted with spiky bushes, empty and desolate and so flat that a grove of eucalyptus far away showed to the feet of its stems. How I can see it! My lady was sitting down under a bush resting a little, for she was very weak and weary, and I was standing up watching to see if I could tell the distance of the firing that came and went. They were still, you know, fighting far from each other, with those terrible new weapons that had never before been used: guns that would carry beyond sight, and aeroplanes that would do— What *they* would do no man could foretell.

'I knew that we were between the two armies, and that they drew together. I knew we were in danger, and that we could not stop there and rest!

'Though all these things were in my mind, they were in the background. They seemed to be affairs beyond our concern. Chiefly, I was thinking of my lady. An aching distress filled me. For the first time she had owned herself beaten and had fallen a-weeping. Behind me I could hear her sobbing, but I would not turn round to her because I knew she had need of weeping, and had held herself so far and so long for me. It was well, I thought, that she would weep and rest and then we would toil on again, for I had no inkling of the thing that hung so near. Even now I can see her as she sat there, her lovely hair upon her shoulder, can mark again the deepening hollow of her cheek.

'"If we had parted," she said, "if I had let you go."

'"No," said I. "Even now, I do not repent. I will not repent; I made my choice, and I will hold on to the end."

'And then—

'Overhead in the sky flashed something and burst, and all about us I heard the bullets making a noise like a handful of peas suddenly thrown. They chipped the stones about us, and whirled fragments from the bricks and passed. . . .'

He put his hand to his mouth, and then moistened his lips.

'At the flash I had turned about. . . .

'You know – she stood up—

'She stood up, you know, and moved a step towards me—

'As though she wanted to reach me—

'And she had been shot through the heart.'

He stopped and stared at me. I felt all that foolish incapacity an Englishman feels on such occasions. I met his eyes for a moment, and then stared out of the window. For a long space we kept silence. When at last I looked at him he was sitting back in his corner, his arms folded, and his teeth gnawing at his knuckles.

He bit his nail suddenly, and stared at it.

'I carried her,' he said, 'towards the temples, in my arms – as though it mattered. I don't know why. They seemed a sort of sanctuary, you know; they had lasted so long, I suppose.

'She must have died almost instantly. Only – I talked to her – all the way.'

Silence again.

'I have seen those temples,' I said abruptly, and indeed he had brought those still, sunlit arcades of worn sandstone very vividly before me.

'It was the brown one, the big brown one. I sat down on a fallen pillar and held her in my arms. . . . Silent after the first babble was over. And after a little while the lizards came out and ran about again, as though nothing unusual was going on, as though nothing had changed. . . . It was tremendously still there, the sun high and the shadows still; even the shadows of the weeds upon the entablature were still – in spite of the thudding and banging that went all about the sky.

'I seem to remember that the aeroplanes came up out of the south, and that the battle went away to the west. One aeroplane was struck, and overset and fell. I remember that – though it didn't interest me in the least. It didn't seem to signify. It was like a wounded gull, you know – flapping for a time in the water. I could see it down the aisle of the temple – a black thing in the bright blue water.

'Three or four times shells burst about the beach, and then that ceased. Each time that happened all the lizards scuttled in and hid for a space. That was all the mischief done, except that once a stray bullet gashed the stone hard by – made just a fresh bright surface.

'As the shadows grew longer, the stillness seemed greater.

'The curious thing,' he remarked, with the manner of a man who makes a trivial conversation, 'is that I didn't *think* – I didn't think at all. I sat with her in my arms amidst the stones – in a sort of lethargy – stagnant.

'And I don't remember waking up. I don't remember dressing that day. I know I found myself in my office, with my letters all slit open in front of me, and how I was struck by the absurdity of being there, seeing that in reality I was sitting, stunned, in that Paestum Temple with a dead woman in my arms. I read my letters like a machine. I have forgotten what they were about.'

He stopped, and there was a long silence.

Suddenly I perceived that we were running down the incline from Chalk Farm to Euston. I started at this passing of time.

I turned on him with a brutal question, in the tone of 'Now or never.'

'And did you dream again?'

'Yes.'

He seemed to force himself to finish. His voice was very low.

'Once more, and as it were only for a few instants. I seemed to have suddenly awakened out of a great apathy, to have risen into a sitting position, and the body lay there on the stones beside me. A gaunt body. Not her, you know. So soon – it was not her. . . .

'I may have heard voices. I do not know. Only I knew clearly that men were coming into the solitude and that that was a last outrage.

'I stood up and walked through the temple, and then there came into sight – first one man with a yellow face, dressed in a uniform of dirty white, trimmed with blue, and then several, climbing to the crest of the old wall of the vanished city, and crouching there. They were little bright figures in the sunlight, and there they hung, weapon in hand, peering cautiously before them.

'And further away I saw others and then more at another point in the wall. It was a long lax line of men in open order.

'Presently the man I had first seen stood up and shouted a command, and his men came tumbling down the wall and into the high weeds towards the temple. He scrambled down with them and led them. He came facing towards me, and when he saw me he stopped.

'At first I had watched these men with a mere curiosity, but when I had seen they meant to come to the temple I was moved to forbid them. I shouted to the officer.

' "You must not come here," I cried, "*I* am here. I am here with my dead."

'He stared, and then shouted a question back to me in some unknown tongue.

'I repeated what I had said.

'He shouted again, and I folded my arms and stood still. Presently he spoke to his men and came forward. He carried a drawn sword.

'I signed to him to keep away, but he continued to advance. I told him again very patiently and clearly: "You must not come here. These are old temples and I am here with my dead."

'Presently he was so close I could see his face clearly. It was a narrow face, with dull grey eyes, and a black moustache. He had a scar on his upper lip, and he was dirty and unshaven. He kept shouting unintelligible things, questions, perhaps, at me.

'I know now that he was afraid of me, but at the time that did not occur to me. As I tried to explain to him, he interrupted me in imperious tones, bidding me, I suppose, stand aside.

'He made to go past me, and I caught hold of him.

'I saw his face change at my grip.

'"You fool," I cried. "Don't you know? She is dead!"

'He started back. He looked at me with cruel eyes. I saw a sort of exultant resolve leap into them – delight. Then, suddenly, with a scowl, he swept his sword back – *so* – and thrust.'

He stopped abruptly.

I became aware of a change in the rhythm of the train. The brakes lifted their voices and the carriage jarred and jerked. This present world insisted upon itself, became clamorous. I saw through the steamy window huge electric lights glaring down from tall masts upon a fog, saw rows of stationary empty carriages passing by; and then a signal-box, hoisting its constellation of green and red into the murky London twilight, marched after them. I looked again at his drawn features.

'He ran me through the heart. It was with a sort of astonishment – no fear, no pain – but just amazement, that I felt it pierce me, felt the sword drive home into my body. It didn't hurt, you know. It didn't hurt at all.'

The yellow platform lights came into the field of view, passing first rapidly, then slowly, and at last stopping with a jerk. Dim shapes of men passed to and fro without.

'Euston!' cried a voice.

'Do you mean—?'

'There was no pain, no sting or smart. Amazement and then darkness sweeping over everything. The hot, brutal face before me, the face of the man who had killed me, seemed to recede. It swept out of existence—'

'Euston!' clamoured the voices outside; 'Euston!'

The carriage door opened admitting a flood of sound, and a porter stood regarding us. The sounds of doors slamming, and the hoof-clatter of cab-horses, and behind these things the featureless remote roar of the London cobble-stones, came to my ears. A truckload of lighted lamps blazed along the platform.

'A darkness, a flood of darkness that opened and spread and blotted out all things.'

'Any luggage, sir?' said the porter.

'And that was the end?' I asked.

He seemed to hesitate. Then, almost inaudibly, he answered, '*No.*'

'You mean?'

'I couldn't get to her. She was there on the other side of the temple— And then—'

'Yes,' I insisted. 'Yes?'

'Nightmares,' he cried; 'nightmares indeed! My God! Great birds that fought and tore.'

THE NEW ACCELERATOR

Certainly, if ever a man found a guinea[1] when he was looking for a pin it is my good friend Professor Gibberne. I have heard before of investigators overshooting the mark, but never quite to the extent that he has done. He has really, this time at any rate, without any touch of exaggeration in the phrase, found something to revolutionize human life. And that when he was simply seeking an all-round nervous stimulant to bring languid people up to the stresses of these pushful days. I have tasted the stuff now several times, and I cannot do better than describe the effect the thing had on me. That there are astonishing experiences in store for all in search of new sensations will become apparent enough.

Professor Gibberne, as many people know, is my neighbour in Folkestone. Unless my memory plays me a trick, his portrait at various ages has already appeared in *The Strand Magazine*[2] – I think late in 1899; but I am unable to look it up because I have lent that volume to someone who has never sent it back. The reader may, perhaps, recall the high forehead and the singularly long black eyebrows that give such a Mephistophelian[3] touch to his face. He occupies one of those pleasant detached houses in the mixed style that make the western end of the Upper Sandgate Road[4] so interesting. His is the one with the Flemish gables and the Moorish portico, and it is in the room with the mullioned bay window that he works when he is down here, and in which of an evening we have so often smoked and talked together. He is a mighty jester, but, besides, he likes to talk to me about his work; he is one of those men who find a help and stimulus in talking, and so I have been able to follow the conception of the New Accelerator right up from a very early stage. Of course, the greater portion of his experimental work is not done in Folkestone, but in Gower Street, in the fine new laboratory next to the hospital that he has been the first to use.

As everyone knows, or at least as all intelligent people know, the special department in which Gibberne has gained so great and deserved a reputation among physiologists is the action of drugs upon the nervous system. Upon soporifics, sedatives, and anaesthetics he is, I am told, unequalled. He is also a chemist of considerable eminence, and I suppose in the subtle and complex jungle of riddles that centres about the ganglion cell and the axis fibre there are little cleared places of his making, glades of illumination, that, until he sees fit to publish his results, are inaccessible to every other living man. And in the last few years he has been particularly assiduous upon this question of nervous stimulants, and already, before the discovery of the New Accelerator, very successful with them. Medical science has to thank him for at least three distinct and absolutely safe invigorators of unrivalled value to practising men. In cases of exhaustion the preparation known as Gibberne's B Syrup[5] has, I suppose, saved more lives already than any lifeboat round the coast.

'But none of these things begin to satisfy me yet,' he told me nearly a year ago. 'Either they increase the central energy without affecting the nerves or they simply increase the available energy by lowering the nervous conductivity; and all of them are unequal and local in their operation. One wakes up the heart and viscera and leaves the brain stupefied, one gets at the brain champagne fashion and does nothing good for the solar plexus, and what I want – and what, if it's an earthly possibility, I mean to have – is a stimulant that stimulates all round, that wakes you up for a time from the crown of your head to the tip of your great toe, and makes you go two – or even three to everybody else's one. Eh? That's the thing I'm after.'

'It would tire a man,' I said.

'Not a doubt of it. And you'd eat double or treble – and all that. But just think what the thing would mean. Imagine yourself with a little phial like this' – he held up a bottle of green glass and marked his points with it – 'and in this precious phial is the power to think twice as fast, move twice as quickly, do twice as much work in a given time as you could otherwise do.'

'But is such a thing possible?'

'I believe so. If it isn't, I've wasted my time for a year. These various preparations of the hypophosphites, for example, seem to show that something of the sort. . . . Even if it was only one and a half times as fast it would do.'

'It *would* do,' I said.

'If you were a statesman in a corner, for example, time rushing up against you, something urgent to be done, eh?'

'He could dose his private secretary,' I said.

'And gain – double time. And think if *you*, for example, wanted to finish a book.'

'Usually,' I said, 'I wish I'd never begun 'em.'

'Or a doctor, driven to death, wants to sit down and think out a case. Or a barrister – or a man cramming for an examination.'

'Worth a guinea a drop,' said I, 'and more – to men like that.'

'And in a duel again,' said Gibberne, 'where it all depends on your quickness in pulling the trigger.'

'Or in fencing,' I echoed.

'You see,' said Gibberne, 'if I get it as an all-round thing it will really do you no harm at all – except perhaps to an infinitesimal degree it brings you nearer old age. You will just have lived twice to other people's once—'

'I suppose,' I meditated, 'in a duel – it would be fair?'

'That's a question for the seconds,' said Gibberne.

I harked back further. 'And you really think such a thing *is* possible?' I said.

'As possible,' said Gibberne, and glanced at something that went throbbing by the window, 'as a motor-bus. As a matter of fact—'

He paused and smiled at me deeply, and tapped slowly on the edge of his desk with the green phial. 'I think I know the stuff. . . . Already I've got something coming.' The nervous smile upon his face betrayed the gravity of his revelation. He rarely talked of his actual experimental work unless things were very near the end. 'And it may be, it may be – I shouldn't be surprised – it may even do the thing at a greater rate than twice.'

'It will be rather a big thing,' I hazarded.

'It will be, I think, rather a big thing.'

But I don't think he quite knew what a big thing it was to be, for all that.

I remember we had several subsequent talks about the stuff. 'The New Accelerator' he called it, and his tone about it grew more confident on each occasion. Sometimes he talked nervously of unexpected physiological results its use might have, and then he would get a bit unhappy; at others he was frankly mercenary, and we debated long and anxiously how the preparation might be turned to commercial account. 'It's a good thing,' said Gibberne, 'a tremendous thing. I know I'm giving the world something, and I think it only reasonable we should expect the world to pay. The dignity of science is all very well, but I think somehow I must have the monopoly of the stuff for, say, ten years. I don't see why *all* the fun in life should go to the dealers in ham.'

My own interest in the coming drug certainly did not wane in the time. I have always had a queer twist towards metaphysics in my mind. I have always been given to paradoxes about space and time, and it seemed to me that Gibberne was really preparing no less than the absolute acceleration of life. Suppose a man repeatedly dosed with such a preparation: he would live an active and record life indeed, but he would be an adult at eleven, middle-aged at twenty-five, and by thirty well on the road to senile decay. It seemed to me that so far Gibberne was only going to do for anyone who took his drug exactly what Nature has done for the Jews and Orientals,[6] who are men in their teens and aged by fifty, and quicker in thought and act than we are all the time. The marvel of drugs has always been great to my mind; you can madden a man, calm a man, make him incredibly strong and alert or a helpless log, quicken this passion and allay that, all by means of drugs, and here was a

new miracle to be added to this strange armoury of phials the
doctors use! But Gibberne was far too eager upon his technical
points to enter very keenly into my aspect of the question.

It was the 7th or 8th of August when he told me the distil-
lation that would decide his failure or success for a time was
going forward as we talked, and it was on the 10th that he told
me the thing was done and the New Accelerator a tangible
reality in the world. I met him as I was going up the Sandgate
Hill towards Folkestone – I think I was going to get my hair
cut; and he came hurrying down to meet me – I suppose he was
coming to my house to tell me at once of his success. I remember
that his eyes were unusually bright and his face flushed, and
I noted even then the swift alacrity of his step.

'It's done,' he cried, and gripped my hand, speaking very fast;
'it's more than done. Come up to my house and see.'

'Really?'

'Really!' he shouted. 'Incredibly! Come up and see.'

'And it does – twice?'

'It does more, much more. It scares me. Come up and see the
stuff. Taste it! Try it! It's the most amazing stuff on earth. He
gripped my arm and, walking at such a pace that he forced
me into a trot, went shouting with me up the hill. A whole
charabancful of people turned and stared at us in unison after
the manner of people in charabancs. It was one of those hot,
clear days that Folkestone sees so much of, every colour incredibly bright and every outline hard. There was a breeze,
of course, but not so much breeze as sufficed under these
conditions to keep me cool and dry. I panted for mercy.

'I'm not walking fast, am I?' cried Gibberne, and slackened
his pace to a quick march.

'You've been taking some of this stuff,' I puffed.

'No,' he said. 'At the utmost a drop of water that stood in a
beaker from which I had washed out the last traces of the stuff.
I took some last night, you know. But that is ancient history,
now.'

'And it goes twice?' I said, nearing his doorway in a grateful
perspiration.

'It goes a thousand times, many thousand times!' cried

Gibberne, with a dramatic gesture, flinging open his Early
English carved oak gate.

'Phew!' said I, and followed him to the door.

'I don't know how many times it goes,' he said, with his
latch-key in his hand.

'And you—'

'It throws all sorts of light on nervous physiology, it kicks
the theory of vision into a perfectly new shape! ... Heaven
knows how many thousand times. We'll try all that after— The
thing is to try the stuff now.'

'Try the stuff?' I said, as we went along the passage.

'Rather,' said Gibberne, turning on me in his study. 'There it
is in that little green phial there! Unless you happen to be
afraid?'

I am a careful man by nature, and only theoretically adven-
turous. I *was* afraid. But on the other hand there is pride.

'Well,' I haggled. 'You say you've tried it?'

'I've tried it,' he said, 'and I don't look hurt by it, do I?
I don't even look livery and I *feel*—'

I sat down. 'Give me the potion,' I said. 'If the worst comes
to the worst it will save having my hair cut, and that I think is
one of the most hateful duties of a civilized man. How do you
take the mixture?'

'With water,' said Gibberne, whacking down a carafe.

He stood up in front of his desk and regarded me in his easy
chair; his manner was suddenly affected by a touch of the
Harley Street specialist.[7] 'It's rum stuff, you know,' he said.

I made a gesture with my hand.

'I must warn you in the first place as soon as you've got it
down to shut your eyes, and open them very cautiously in a
minute or so's time. One still sees. The sense of vision is a
question of length of vibration, and not of multitude of impacts;
but there's a kind of shock to the retina, a nasty giddy confusion
just at the time if the eyes are open. Keep 'em shut.'

'Shut,' I said. 'Good!'

'And the next thing is, keep still. Don't begin to whack about.
You may fetch something a nasty rap if you do. Remember you
will be going several thousand times faster than you ever did

before, heart, lungs, muscles, brain – everything – and you will hit hard without knowing it. You won't know it, you know. You'll feel just as you do now. Only everything in the world will seem to be going ever so many thousand times slower than it ever went before. That's what makes it so deuced queer.'

'Lor',' I said. 'And you mean—'

'You'll see,' said he, and took up a measure. He glanced at the material on his desk. 'Glasses,' he said, 'water. All here. Mustn't take too much for the first attempt.'

The little phial glucked out its precious contents. 'Don't forget what I told you,' he said, turning the contents of the measure into a glass in the manner of an Italian waiter measuring whisky. 'Sit with the eyes tightly shut and in absolute stillness for two minutes,' he said. 'Then you will hear me speak.'

He added an inch or so of water to the dose in each glass.

'By the bye,' he said, 'don't put your glass down. Keep it in your hand and rest your hand on your knee. Yes – so. And now—'

He raised his glass.

'The New Accelerator,' I said.

'The New Accelerator,' he answered, and we touched glasses and drank, and instantly I closed my eyes.

You know that blank non-existence into which one drops when one has taken 'gas'.[8] For an indefinite interval it was like that. Then I heard Gibberne telling me to wake up, and I stirred and opened my eyes. There he stood as he had been standing, glass still in hand. It was empty, that was all the difference.

'Well?' said I.

'Nothing out of the way?'

'Nothing. A slight feeling of exhilaration, perhaps. Nothing more.'

'Sounds?'

'Things are still,' I said. 'By Jove! yes! They *are* still. Except the sort of faint pat, patter, like rain falling on different things. What is it?'

'Analysed sounds,'[9] I think he said, but I am not sure. He glanced at the window. 'Have you ever seen a curtain before a window fixed in that way before?'

I followed his eyes, and there was the end of the curtain, frozen, as it were, corner high, in the act of flapping briskly in the breeze.

'No,' said I; 'that's odd.'

'And here,' he said, and opened the hand that held the glass. Naturally I winced, expecting the glass to smash. But so far from smashing it did not even seem to stir; it hung in mid-air – motionless. 'Roughly speaking,' said Gibberne, 'an object in these latitudes falls 16 feet in the first second. This glass is falling 16 feet in a second now. Only, you see, it hasn't been falling yet for the hundredth part of a second. That gives you some idea of the pace of my Accelerator.' And he waved his hand round and round, over and under the slowly sinking glass. Finally he took it by the bottom, pulled it down and placed it very carefully on the table. 'Eh?' he said to me, and laughed.

'That seems all right,' I said, and began very gingerly to raise myself from my chair. I felt perfectly well, very light and comfortable, and quite confident in my mind. I was going fast all over. My heart, for example, was beating a thousand times a second, but that caused me no discomfort at all. I looked out of the window. An immovable cyclist, head down and with a frozen puff of dust behind his driving-wheel, scorched to over-take a galloping charabanc that did not stir. I gaped in amaze-ment at this incredible spectacle. 'Gibberne,' I cried, 'how long will this confounded stuff last?'

'Heaven knows!' he answered. 'Last time I took it I went to bed and slept it off. I tell you, I was frightened. It must have lasted some minutes, I think – it seemed like hours. But after a bit it slows down rather suddenly, I believe.'

I was proud to observe that I did not feel frightened – I suppose because there were two of us. 'Why shouldn't we go out?' I asked.

'Why not?'

'They'll see us.'

'Not they. Goodness, no! Why, we shall be going a thousand times faster than the quickest conjuring trick that was ever done. Come along! Which way shall we go? Window, or door?'

And out by the window we went.

Assuredly of all the strange experiences that I have ever had, or imagined, or read of other people having or imagining, that little raid I made with Gibberne on the Folkestone Leas,[10] under the influence of the New Accelerator, was the strangest and maddest of all. We went out by his gate into the road, and there we made a minute examination of the statuesque passing traffic. The tops of the wheels and some of the legs of the horses of this charabanc, the end of the whiplash and the lower jaw of the conductor – who was just beginning to yawn – were perceptibly in motion, but all the rest of the lumbering conveyance seemed still. And quite noiseless except for a faint rattling that came from one man's throat! And as parts of this frozen edifice there were a driver, you know, and a conductor, and eleven people! The effect as we walked about the thing began by being madly queer and ended by being – disagreeable. There they were, people like ourselves and yet not like ourselves, frozen in careless attitudes, caught in mid-gesture. A girl and a man smiled at one another, a leering smile that threatened to last for evermore; a woman in a floppy capelline rested her arm on the rail and stared at Gibberne's house with the unwinking stare of eternity; a man stroked his moustache like a figure of wax, and another stretched a tiresome stiff hand with extended fingers towards his loosened hat. We stared at them, we laughed at them; we made faces at them, and then a sort of disgust of them came upon us, and we turned away and walked round in front of the cyclist towards the Leas.

'Goodness!' cried Gibberne, suddenly; 'look there!'

He pointed, and there at the tip of his finger and sliding down the air with wings flapping slowly and at the speed of an exceptionally languid snail – was a bee.

And so we came out upon the Leas. There the thing seemed madder than ever. The band was playing in the upper stand, though all the sound it made for us was a low-pitched, wheezy rattle, a sort of prolonged last sigh that passed at times into a sound like the slow, muffled ticking of some monstrous clock. Frozen people stood erect; strange, silent, self-conscious-looking dummies hung unstably in mid-stride, promenading upon the grass. I passed close to a poodle dog suspended in the act of leaping, and watched the slow movement of his legs as he sank to earth. 'Lord, look *here*!' cried Gibberne, and we halted for a moment before a magnificent person in white faint-striped flannels, white shoes, and a Panama hat, who turned back to wink at two gaily dressed ladies he had passed. A wink, studied with such leisurely deliberation as we could afford, is an unattractive thing. It loses any quality of alert gaiety, and one remarks that the winking eye does not completely close, that under its drooping lid appears the lower edge of an eyeball and a line of white. 'Heaven give me memory,' said I, 'and I will never wink again.'

'Or smile,' said Gibberne, with his eye on the lady's answering teeth.

'It's infernally hot, somehow,' said I. 'Let's go slower.'

'Oh, come along!' said Gibberne.

We picked our way among the bath-chairs in the path. Many of the people sitting in the chairs seemed almost natural in their passive poses, but the contorted scarlet of the bandsmen was not a restful thing to see. A purple-faced gentleman was frozen in the midst of a violent struggle to refold his newspaper against the wind; there were many evidences that all these people in their sluggish way were exposed to a considerable breeze, a breeze that had no existence so far as our sensations went. We came out and walked a little way from the crowd, and turned and regarded it. To see all that multitude changed to a picture, smitten rigid, as it were, into the semblance of realistic wax, was impossibly wonderful. It was absurd, of course; but it filled me with an irrational, an exultant sense of superior advantage. Consider the wonder of it! All that I had said and thought and done since the stuff had begun to work in my veins had happened, so far as those people, so far as the world in general went, in the twinkling of an eye. 'The New Accelerator—' I began, but Gibberne interrupted me.

'There's that infernal old woman!' he said.

'What old woman?'

'Lives next door to me,' said Gibberne. 'Has a lapdog that yaps. Gods! The temptation is strong!'

There is something very boyish and impulsive about Gibberne

at times. Before I could expostulate with him he had dashed forward, snatched the unfortunate animal out of visible existence, and was running violently with it towards the cliff of the Leas. It was most extraordinary. The little brute, you know, didn't bark or wriggle or make the slightest sign of vitality. It kept quite stiffly in an attitude of somnolent repose, and Gibberne held it by the neck. It was like running about with a dog of wood. 'Gibberne,' I cried, 'put it down!' Then I said something else. 'If you run like that, Gibberne,' I cried, 'you'll set your clothes on fire. Your linen trousers are going brown as it is!'

He clapped his hand on his thigh and stood hesitating on the verge. 'Gibberne,' I cried, coming up, 'put it down. This heat is too much! It's our running so! Two or three miles a second! Friction of the air!'

'What?' he said, glancing at the dog.

'Friction of the air,' I shouted. 'Friction of the air. Going too fast. Like meteorites and things. Too hot. And, Gibberne! Gibberne! I'm all over pricking and a sort of perspiration. You can see people stirring slightly. I believe the stuff's working off! Put that dog down.'

'Eh?' he said.

'It's working off,' I repeated. 'We're too hot and the stuff's working off! I'm wet through.'

He stared at me. Then at the band, the wheezy rattle of whose performance was certainly going faster. Then with a tremendous sweep of the arm he hurled the dog away from him and it went spinning upward, still inanimate and hung at last over the grouped parasols of a knot of chattering people. Gibberne was gripping my elbow. 'By Jove!' he cried. 'I believe it is! A sort of hot pricking and – yes. That man's moving his pocket-handkerchief! Perceptibly. We must get out of this sharp.'

But we could not get out of it sharply enough. Luckily perhaps! For we might have run, and if we had run we should, I believe, have burst into flames. Almost certainly we should have burst into flames! You know we had neither of us thought of that. ... But before we could even begin to run the action

of the drug had ceased. It was the business of a minute fraction
of a second. The effect of the New Accelerator passed like the
drawing of a curtain, vanished in the movement of a hand. I
heard Gibberne's voice in infinite alarm. 'Sit down,' he said,
and flop, down upon the turf at the edge of the Leas I sat –
scorching as I sat. There is a patch of burnt grass there still
where I sat down. The whole stagnation seemed to wake up as
I did so, the disarticulated vibration of the band rushed together
into a blast of music, the promenaders put their feet down and
walked their ways, the papers and flags began flapping, smiles
passed into words, the winker finished his wink and went on
his way complacently, and all the seated people moved and
spoke.

The whole world had come alive again, was going as fast as
we were, or rather we were going no faster than the rest of the
world. It was like slowing down as one comes into a railway
station. Everything seemed to spin round for a second or two,
I had the most transient feeling of nausea, and that was all. And
the little dog which had seemed to hang for a moment when
the force of Gibberne's arm was expended fell with a swift
acceleration clean through a lady's parasol!

That was the saving of us. Unless it was for one corpulent
old gentleman in a bath-chair, who certainly did start at the
sight of us and afterwards regarded us at intervals with a darkly
suspicious eye, and finally, I believe, said something to his nurse
about us, I doubt if a solitary person remarked our sudden
appearance among them. Plop! We must have appeared
abruptly. We ceased to smoulder almost at once, though the turf
beneath me was uncomfortably hot. The attention of everyone –
including even the Amusements' Association band, which on
this occasion, for the only time in its history, got out of tune –
was arrested by the amazing fact, and the still more amazing
yapping and uproar caused by the fact, that a respectable,
over-fed lapdog sleeping quietly to the east of the bandstand
should suddenly fall through the parasol of a lady on the west
– in a slightly singed condition due to the extreme velocity of
its movements through the air. In these absurd days, too, when
we are all trying to be as psychic and silly and superstitious as

possible! People got up and trod on other people, chairs were overturned, the Leas policeman ran. How the matter settled itself I do not know – we were much too anxious to disentangle ourselves from the affair and get out of range of the eye of the old gentleman in the bath-chair to make minute inquiries. As soon as we were sufficiently cool and sufficiently recovered from our giddiness and nausea and confusion of mind to do so we stood up and, skirting the crowd, directed our steps back along the road below the Metropole towards Gibberne's house. But amidst the din I heard very distinctly the gentleman who had been sitting beside the lady of the ruptured sunshade using quite unjustifiable threats and language to one of those chair-attendants who have 'Inspector' written on their caps. 'If you didn't throw the dog,' he said, 'who *did*?'

The sudden return of movement and familiar noises, and our natural anxiety about ourselves (our clothes were still dreadfully hot, and the fronts of the thighs of Gibberne's white trousers were scorched a drabbish brown), prevented the minute observations I should have liked to make on all these things. Indeed, I really made no observations of any scientific value on that return. The bee, of course, had gone. I looked for that cyclist, but he was already out of sight as we came into the Upper Sandgate Road or hidden from us by traffic; the charabanc, however, with its people now all alive and stirring, was clattering along at a spanking pace almost abreast of the nearer church.

We noted, however, that the window-sill on which we had stepped in getting out of the house was slightly singed, and that the impressions of our feet on the gravel of the path were unusually deep.

So it was I had my first experience of the New Accelerator. Practically we had been running about and saying and doing all sorts of things in the space of a second or so of time. We had lived half an hour while the band had played, perhaps, two bars. But the effect it had upon us was that the whole world had stopped for our convenient inspection. Considering all things, and particularly considering our rashness in venturing out of the house, the experience might certainly have been much more disagreeable than it was. It showed, no doubt, that Gibberne has still much to learn before his preparation is a manageable convenience, but its practicability it certainly demonstrated beyond all cavil.

Since that adventure he has been steadily bringing its use under control, and I have several times, and without the slightest bad result, taken measured doses under his direction; though I must confess I have not yet ventured abroad again while under its influence. I may mention, for example, that this story has been written at one sitting and without interruption, except for the nibbling of some chocolate, by its means. I began at 6.25, and my watch is now very nearly at the minute past the half-hour. The convenience of securing a long, uninterrupted spell of work in the midst of a day full of engagements cannot be exaggerated. Gibberne is now working at the quantitative handling of his preparation, with especial reference to its distinctive effects upon different types of constitution. He then hopes to find a Retarder with which to dilute its present rather excessive potency. The Retarder will, of course, have the reverse effect to the Accelerator; used alone it should enable the patient to spread a few seconds over many hours of ordinary time, and so to maintain an apathetic inaction, a glacierlike absence of alacrity, amidst the most animated or irritating surroundings. The two things together must necessarily work an entire revolution in civilized existence. It is the beginning of our escape from that Time Garment of which Carlyle speaks.[11] While this Accelerator will enable us to concentrate ourselves with tremendous impact upon any moment or occasion that demands our utmost sense and vigour, the Retarder will enable us to pass in passive tranquillity through infinite hardship and tedium. Perhaps I am a little optimistic about the Retarder, which has indeed still to be discovered, but about the Accelerator there is no possible sort of doubt whatever. Its appearance upon the market in a convenient, controllable, and assimilable form is a matter of the next few months. It will be obtainable of all chemists and druggists, in small green bottles, at a high but, considering its extraordinary qualities, by no means excessive price. Gibberne's Nervous Accelerator it will be called, and he hopes to be able to supply it in three strengths: one in 200, one in 900, and one in 2000, distinguished by yellow, pink, and white labels respectively.

No doubt its use renders a great number of very extraordinary things possible; for, of course, the most remarkable and, possibly, even criminal proceedings may be effected with impunity by thus dodging, as it were, into the interstices of time. Like all potent preparations it will be liable to abuse. We have, however, discussed this aspect of the question very thoroughly, and we have decided that this is purely a matter of medical jurisprudence and altogether outside our province. We shall manufacture and sell the Accelerator, and, as for the consequences – we shall see.

THE TRUTH ABOUT
PYECRAFT

He sits not a dozen yards away. If I glance over my shoulder I can see him. And if I catch his eye – and usually I catch his eye – it meets me with an expression—

It is mainly an imploring look – and yet with suspicion in it.

Confound his suspicion! If I wanted to tell on him I should have told long ago. I don't tell and I don't tell, and he ought to feel at his ease. As if anything so gross and fat as he could feel at ease! Who would believe me if I did tell?

Poor old Pyecraft! Great, uneasy jelly of substance! The fattest clubman in London.

He sits at one of the little club tables in the huge bay by the fire, stuffing. What is he stuffing? I glance judiciously and catch him biting at a round of hot buttered teacake, with his eyes on me. Confound him! – with his eyes on me!

That settles it, Pyecraft! Since you *will* be abject, since you *will* behave as though I was not a man of honour, here, right under your embedded eyes, I write the thing down – the plain truth about Pyecraft. The man I helped, the man I shielded, and who has requited me by making my club unendurable, absolutely unendurable, with his liquid appeal, with the perpetual 'don't tell' of his looks.

And, besides, why does he keep on eternally eating?

Well, here goes for the truth, the whole truth, and nothing but the truth!

Pyecraft— I made the acquaintance of Pyecraft in this very smoking-room. I was a young, nervous new member, and he saw it. I was sitting all alone, wishing I knew more of the members, and suddenly he came, a great rolling front of chins and abdomina, towards me, and grunted and sat down in a chair close by me and wheezed for a space, and scraped for a space with a match and lit a cigar, and then addressed me. I forget what he said – something about the matches not lighting properly, and afterwards as he talked he kept stopping the waiters one by one as they went by, and telling them about the matches in that thin, fluty voice he has. But, anyhow, it was in some such way we began our talking.

He talked about various things and came round to games. And thence to my figure and complexion. 'You ought to be a good cricketer,' he said. I suppose I am slender, slender to what some people would call lean, and I suppose I am rather dark, still— I am not ashamed of having a Hindu great-grandmother, but, for all that, I don't want casual strangers to see through me at a glance to *her*. So that I was set against Pyecraft from the beginning.

But he only talked about me in order to get to himself.

'I expect,' he said, 'you take no more exercise than I do, and probably you eat no less.' (Like all excessively obese people he fancied he ate nothing.) 'Yet' – and he smiled an oblique smile – 'we differ.'

And then he began to talk about his fatness and his fatness; all he did for his fatness and all he was going to do for his fatness; what people had advised him to do for his fatness and what he had heard of people doing for fatness similar to his. '*A priori*,' he said, 'one would think a question of nutrition could be answered by dietary and a question of assimilation by drugs.' It was stifling. It was dumpling talk. It made me feel swelled to hear him.

One stands that sort of thing once in a way at a club, but a time came when I fancied I was standing too much. He took to me altogether too conspicuously. I could never go into the smoking-room but he would come wallowing towards me, and sometimes he came and gormandized round and about me while I had my lunch. He seemed at times almost to be clinging to me. He was a bore, but not so fearful a bore as to be limited to me; and from the first there was something in his manner – almost as though he knew, almost as though he penetrated to the fact that I *might* – that there was a remote, exceptional chance in me that no one else presented.

'I'd give anything to get it down,' he would say – 'anything', and peer at me over his vast cheeks and pant.

Poor old Pyecraft! He has just gonged, no doubt to order another buttered teacake!

He came to the actual thing one day. 'Our Pharmacopoeia,' he said, 'our Western Pharmacopoeia, is anything but the last word of medical science. In the East, I've been told—'

He stopped and stared at me. It was like being at an aquarium.

I was quite suddenly angry with him. 'Look here,' I said, 'who told you about my great-grandmother's recipes?'

'Well,' he fenced.

'Every time we've met for a week,' I said – 'and we've met pretty often – you've given me a broad hint or so about that little secret of mine.'

'Well,' he said, 'now the cat's out of the bag, I'll admit, yes, it is so. I had it—'

'From Pattison?'

'Indirectly,' he said, which I believe was lying, 'yes.'

'Pattison,' I said, 'took that stuff at his own risk.'

He pursed his mouth and bowed.

'My great-grandmother's recipes,' I said, 'are queer things to handle. My father was near making me promise—'

'He didn't?'

'No. But he warned me. He himself used one – once.'

'Ah! . . . But do you think—? Suppose – suppose there did happen to be one—'

'The things are curious documents,' I said. 'Even the smell of 'em. . . . No!'

But after going so far Pyecraft was resolved I should go farther. I was always a little afraid if I tried his patience too much he would fall on me suddenly and smother me. I own I was weak. But I was also annoyed with Pyecraft. I had got to that state of feeling for him that disposed me to say, 'Well, *take* the risk!' The little affair of Pattison to which I have alluded was a different matter altogether. What it was doesn't concern us now, but I knew, anyhow, that the particular recipe I used then was safe. The rest I didn't know so much about, and, on the whole, I was inclined to doubt their safety pretty completely.

Yet even if Pyecraft got poisoned—

I must confess the poisoning of Pyecraft struck me as an immense undertaking.

That evening I took that queer, odd-scented sandalwood box out of my safe and turned the rustling skins over. The gentleman who wrote the recipes for my great-grandmother evidently had a weakness for skins of a miscellaneous origin, and his hand-writing was cramped to the last degree. Some of the things are quite unreadable to me – though my family, with its Indian Civil Service associations, has kept up a knowledge of Hin-dustani from generation to generation – and none are absolutely plain sailing. But I found the one that I knew was there soon enough, and sat on the floor by my safe for some time looking at it.

'Look here,' said I to Pyecraft next day, and snatched the slip away from his eager grasp.

'So far as I can make it out, this is a recipe for Loss of Weight. ('Ah!' said Pyecraft.) I'm not absolutely sure, but I think it's that. And if you take my advice you'll leave it alone. Because, you know – I blacken my blood in your interest, Pyecraft – my ancestors on that side were, so far as I can gather, a jolly queer lot. See?'

'Let me try it,' said Pyecraft.

I leant back in my chair. My imagination made one mighty effort and fell flat within me. 'What in Heaven's name, Pye-craft,' I asked, 'do you think you'll look like when you get thin?'

He was impervious to reason. I made him promise never to say a word to me about his disgusting fatness again whatever happened – never, and then I handed him that little piece of skin.

'It's nasty stuff,' I said.

'No matter,' he said, and took it.

He goggled at it. 'But – but—' he said.

He had just discovered that it wasn't English.

'To the best of my ability,' I said, 'I will do you a translation.'
I did my best. After that we didn't speak for a fortnight. Whenever he approached me I frowned and motioned him away, and he respected our compact, but at the end of the fortnight he was as fat as ever. And then he got a word in.

'I must speak,' he said. 'It isn't fair. There's something wrong. It's done me no good. You're not doing your great-grandmother justice.'

'Where's the recipe?'

He produced it gingerly from his pocket-book.

I ran my eye over the items. 'Was the egg addled?' I asked.

'No. Ought it to have been?'

'That,' I said, 'goes without saying in all my poor dear great-grandmother's recipes. When condition or quality is not specified you must get the worst. She was drastic or nothing. . . . And there's one or two possible alternatives to some of these other things. You got *fresh* rattlesnake venom?'

'I got a rattlesnake from Jamrach's.[1] It cost – *it* cost—'

'That's your affair, anyhow. This last item—'

'I know a man who—'

'Yes. H'm. Well, I'll write the alternatives down. So far as I know the language, the spelling of this recipe is particularly atrocious. By the bye, dog here probably means pariah dog.'

For a month after that I saw Pyecraft constantly at the club and as fat and anxious as ever. He kept our treaty, but at times he broke the spirit of it by shaking his head despondently. Then one day in the cloakroom he said, 'Your great-grandmother—'

'Not a word against her,' I said; and he held his peace.

I could have fancied he had desisted, and I saw him one day talking to three new members about his fatness as though he was in search of other recipes. And then, quite unexpectedly his telegram came.

'Mr Formalyn!' bawled a page-boy under my nose and I took the telegram and opened it at once.

'For Heaven's sake come. – Pyecraft.'

'H'm,' said I, and to tell the truth I was so pleased at the rehabilitation of my great-grandmother's reputation this evidently promised that I made a most excellent lunch.

I got Pyecraft's address from the hall porter. Pyecraft inhabited the upper half of a house in Bloomsbury, and I went there so soon as I had done my coffee and Trappistine. I did not wait to finish my cigar.

'Mr Pyecraft?' said I, at the front door.

They believed he was ill; he hadn't been out for two days.

'He expects me,' said I, and they sent me up.

I rang the bell at the lattice-door upon the landing.

'He shouldn't have tried it, anyhow,' I said to myself. 'A man who eats like a pig ought to look like a pig.'

An obviously worthy woman, with an anxious face and a carelessly placed cap, came and surveyed me through the lattice.

I gave my name and she opened his door for me in a dubious fashion.

'Well?' said I, as we stood together inside Pyecraft's piece of the landing.

''E said you was to come in if you came,' she said, and regarded me, making no motion to show me anywhere. And then, confidentially, ''E's locked in, sir.'

'Locked in?'

'Locked himself in yesterday morning and 'asn't let anyone in since, sir. And ever and again *swearing*. Oh, my!'

I stared at the door she indicated by her glances. 'In there?' I said.

'Yes, sir.'

'What's up?'

She shook her head sadly. ''E keeps on calling for vittles, sir. 'Eavy vittles 'e wants. I get 'im what I can. Pork 'e's 'ad, sooit puddin', sossiges, noo bread. Everythink like that. Left outside, if you please, and me go away. 'E's eatin' sir, somethink *awful*.'

There came a piping bawl from inside the door: 'That Formalyn?'

'That you, Pyecraft?' I shouted, and went and banged the door.

'Tell her to go away.'

I did.

Then I could hear a curious pattering upon the door, almost

like someone feeling for the handle in the dark, and Pyecraft's familiar grunts.

'It's all right,' I said, 'she's gone.'

But for a long time the door didn't open.

I heard the key turn. Then Pyecraft's voice said, 'Come in.'

I turned the handle and opened the door. Naturally I expected to see Pyecraft.

Well, you know, he wasn't there!

I never had such a shock in my life. There was his sitting-room in a state of untidy disorder, plates and dishes among the books and writing things, and several chairs overturned, but Pyecraft—

'It's all right, o' man; shut the door,' he said, and then I discovered him.

There he was right up close to the cornice in the corner by the door, as though someone had glued him to the ceiling. His face was anxious and angry. He panted and gesticulated. 'Shut the door,' he said. 'If that woman gets hold of it—'

I shut the door, and went and stood away from him and stared.

'If anything gives way and you tumble down,' I said, 'you'll break your neck, Pyecraft.'

'I wish I could,' he wheezed.

'A man of your age and weight getting up to kiddish gymnastics—'

'Don't,' he said, and looked agonized. 'Your damned great-grandmother—'

'Be careful,' I warned him.

'I'll tell you,' he said, and gesticulated.

'How the deuce,' said I, 'are you holding on up there?'

And then abruptly I realized that he was not holding on at all, that he was floating up there – just as a gas-filled bladder might have floated in the same position. He began a struggle to thrust himself away from the ceiling and to clamber down the wall to me. 'It's that prescription,' he panted, as he did so. 'Your great-gran—'

'No!' I cried.

He took hold of a framed engraving rather carelessly as he spoke and it gave way, and he flew back to the ceiling again, while the picture smashed on to the sofa. Bump he went against the ceiling, and I knew then why he was all over white on the more salient curves and angles of his person. He tried again more carefully, coming down by way of the mantel.

It was really a most extraordinary spectacle, that great, fat, apoplectic-looking man upside down and trying to get from the ceiling to the floor. 'That prescription,' he said. 'Too successful.'

'How?'

'Loss of weight – almost complete.'

And then, of course, I understood.

'By Jove, Pyecraft,' said I, 'what you wanted was a cure for fatness! But you always called it weight. You would call it weight.'

Somehow I was extremely delighted. I quite liked Pyecraft for the time. 'Let me help you!' I said, and took his hand and pulled him down. He kicked about, trying to get foothold somewhere. It was very like holding a flag on a windy day.

'That table,' he said, pointing, 'is solid mahogany and very heavy. If you can put me under that—'

I did, and there he wallowed about like a captive balloon, while I stood on his hearthrug and talked to him.

I lit a cigar. 'Tell me,' I said, 'what happened?'

'I took it,' he said.

'How did it taste?'

'Oh, *beastly*!'

I should fancy they all did. Whether one regards the ingredients or the probable compound or the possible results, almost all my great-grandmother's remedies appear to me at least to be extraordinarily uninviting. For my own part—

'I took a little sip first.'

'Yes?'

'And as I felt lighter and better after an hour, I decided to take the draught.'

'My dear Pyecraft!'

'I held my nose,' he explained. 'And then I kept on getting lighter and lighter – and helpless, you know.'

He gave way suddenly to a burst of passion. 'What the goodness am I to *do*?' he said.

'There's one thing pretty evident,' I said, 'that you mustn't do. If you go out of doors you'll go up and up.' I waved an arm upward. 'They'd have to send Santos-Dumont[2] after you to bring you down again.'

'I suppose it will wear off?'

I shook my head. 'I don't think you can count on that,' I said.

And then there was another burst of passion, and he kicked out at adjacent chairs and banged the floor. He behaved just as I should have expected a great, fat, self-indulgent man to behave under trying circumstances – that is to say, very badly. He spoke of me and of my great-grandmother with an utter want of discretion.

'I never asked you to take the stuff,' I said.

And generously disregarding the insults he was putting upon me, I sat down in his armchair and began to talk to him in a sober, friendly fashion.

I pointed out to him that this was a trouble he had brought upon himself, and that it had almost an air of poetical justice. He had eaten too much. This he disputed, and for a time we argued the point.

He became noisy and violent, so I desisted from this aspect of his lesson. 'And then,' said I, 'you committed the sin of euphuism.[3] You called it, not Fat, which is just and inglorious, but Weight. You—'

He interrupted to say that he recognized all that. What was he to *do*?

I suggested he should adapt himself to his new conditions. So we came to the really sensible part of the business. I suggested that it would not be difficult for him to learn to walk about on the ceiling with his hands—

'I can't sleep,' he said.

But that was no great difficulty. It was quite possible, I pointed out, to make a shake-up under a wire mattress, fasten the under things on with tapes, and have a blanket, sheet, and coverlet to button at the side. He would have to confide in his housekeeper, I said; and after some squabbling he agreed to that. (Afterwards it was quite delightful to see the beautifully matter-of-fact way with which the good lady took all these amazing inversions.) He could have a library ladder in his room, and all his meals could be laid on the top of his bookcase. We also hit on an ingenious device by which he could get to the floor whenever he wanted, which was simply to put the *British Encyclopaedia*[4] (tenth edition) on the top of his open shelves. He just pulled out a couple of volumes and held on, and down he came. And we agreed there must be iron staples along the skirting, so that he could cling to those whenever he wanted to get about the room on the lower level.

As we got on with the thing I found myself almost keenly interested. It was I who called in the housekeeper and broke matters to her, and it was I chiefly who fixed up the inverted bed. In fact, I spent two whole days at his flat. I am a handy, interfering sort of man with a screwdriver, and I made all sorts of ingenious adaptations for him – ran a wire to bring his bells within reach, turned all his electric lights up instead of down, and so on. The whole affair was extremely curious and interesting to me, and it was delightful to think of Pyecraft like some great, fat blowfly, crawling about on his ceiling and clambering round the lintel of his doors from one room to another, and never, never, never coming to the club any more. . . .

Then, you know, my fatal ingenuity got the better of me. I was sitting by his fire drinking his whisky, and he was up in his favourite corner by the cornice, tacking a Turkey carpet to the ceiling, when the idea struck me. 'By Jove, Pyecraft!' I said, 'all this is totally unnecessary.'

And before I could calculate the complete consequences of my notion I blurted it out. 'Lead underclothing,' said I, and the mischief was done.

Pyecraft received the thing almost in tears. 'To be right ways up again—' he said.

I gave him the whole secret before I saw where it would take me. 'Buy sheet lead,' I said, 'stamp it into discs. Sew 'em all over your underclothes until you have enough. Have lead-soled boots, carry a bag of solid lead, and the thing is done! Instead

of being a prisoner here you may go abroad again, Pyecraft;
you may travel—'

A still happier idea came to me. 'You need never fear a
shipwreck. All you need do is just slip off some or all of your
clothes, take the necessary amount of luggage in your hand,
and float up in the air—'

In his emotion he dropped the tack-hammer within an ace of
my head. 'By Jove!' he said, 'I shall be able to come back to the
club again.'

The thing pulled me up short. 'By Jove!' I said, faintly. 'Yes.
Of course – you will.'

He did. He does. There he sits behind me now, stuffing – as
I live! – a third go of buttered teacake. And no one in the whole
world knows – except his housekeeper and me – that he weighs
practically nothing; that he is a mere boring mass of assimila-
tory matter, mere clouds in clothing, *niente, nefas*, the most
inconsiderable of men. There he sits watching until I have done
this writing. Then, if he can, he will waylay me. He will come
billowing up to me. . . .

He will tell me over again all about it, how it feels, how it
doesn't feel, how he sometimes hopes it is passing off a little.
And always somewhere in that fat, abundant discourse he will
say, 'The secret's keeping, eh? If anyone knew of it – I should
be so ashamed. . . . Makes a fellow look such a fool, you know.
Crawling about on a ceiling and all that. . . .'

And now to elude Pyecraft, occupying, as he does, an admirable strategic position between me and the door.

THE COUNTRY OF
THE BLIND

Three hundred miles and more from Chimborazo,[1] one hundred from the snows of Cotopaxi, in the wildest wastes of Ecuador's Andes, there lies that mysterious mountain valley, cut off from the world of men, the Country of the Blind. Long years ago that valley lay so far open to the world that men might come at last through frightful gorges and over an icy pass into its equable meadows; and thither indeed men came, a family or so of Peruvian half-breeds fleeing from the lust and tyranny of an evil Spanish ruler. Then came the stupendous outbreak of Mindobamba,[2] when it was night in Quito for seventeen days, and the water was boiling at Yaguachi and all the fish floating dying even as far as Guayaquil; everywhere along the Pacific slopes there were landslips and swift thawings and sudden floods, and one whole side of the old Arauca crest slipped and came down in thunder, and cut off the Country of the Blind for ever from the exploring feet of men. But one of these early settlers had chanced to be on the hither side of the gorges when the world had so terribly shaken itself, and he perforce had to forget his wife and his child and all the friends and possessions he had left up there, and start life over again in the lower world. He started it again but ill, blindness overtook him, and he died of punishment in the mines; but the story he told begot a legend that lingers along the length of the Cordilleras of the Andes to this day.

He told of his reason for venturing back from that fastness, into which he had first been carried lashed to a llama, beside a vast bale of gear, when he was a child. The valley, he said, had in it all that the heart of man could desire – sweet water, pasture, and even climate, slopes of rich brown soil with tangles of a shrub that bore an excellent fruit, and on one side great hanging forests of pine that held the avalanches high. Far over-head, on three sides, vast cliffs of grey-green rock were capped by cliffs of ice; but the glacier stream came not to them but flowed away by the farther slopes, and only now and then huge ice masses fell on the valley side. In this valley it neither rained nor snowed, but the abundant springs gave a rich green pasture, that irrigation would spread over all the valley space. The settlers did well indeed there. Their beasts did well and multi-plied, and but one thing marred their happiness. Yet it was enough to mar it greatly. A strange disease had come upon them, and had made all the children born to them there – and indeed, several older children also – blind. It was to seek some charm or antidote against this plague of blindness that he had with fatigue and danger and difficulty returned down the gorge. In those days, in such cases, men did not think of germs and infections but of sins; and it seemed to him that the reason of this affliction must lie in the negligence of these priestless immigrants to set up a shrine so soon as they entered the valley. He wanted a shrine – a handsome, cheap, effectual shrine – to be erected in the valley; he wanted relics and such-like potent things of faith, blessed objects and mysterious medals and prayers. In his wallet he had a bar of native silver for which he would not account; he insisted there was none in the valley with something of the insistence of an inexpert liar. They had all clubbed their money and ornaments together, having little need for such treasure up there, he said, to buy them holy help against their ill. I figure this dim-eyed young mountaineer, sunburnt, gaunt, and anxious, hat-brim clutched feverishly, a man all unused to the ways of the lower world, telling this story to some keen-eyed, attentive priest before the great convulsion; I can picture him presently seeking to return with pious and infallible remedies against that trouble, and the infinite dismay with which he must have faced the tumbled vastness where the gorge had once come out. But the rest of his story of mischances is lost to me, save that I know of his evil death after several years. Poor stray from that remoteness! The stream that had once made the gorge now bursts from the mouth of a rocky cave, and the legend his poor, ill-told story set going developed into the legend of a race of blind men somewhere 'over there' one may still hear today.

And amidst the little population of that now isolated and forgotten valley the disease ran its course. The old became groping and purblind, the young saw but dimly, and the children that were born to them saw never at all. But life was very easy in that snow-rimmed basin, lost to all the world, with neither thorns nor briars, with no evil insects nor any beasts save the gentle breed of llamas they had lugged and thrust and followed up the beds of the shrunken rivers in the gorges up which they had come. The seeing had become purblind so gradually that they scarcely noted their loss. They guided the sightless youngsters hither and thither until they knew the whole valley marvellously, and when at last sight died out among them the race lived on. They had even time to adapt themselves to the blind control of fire, which they made carefully in stoves of stone. They were a simple strain of people at the first, unlettered, only slightly touched with the Spanish civilization, but with something of a tradition of the arts of old Peru[3] and of its lost philosophy. Generation followed generation. They forgot many things; they devised many things. Their tradition of the greater world they came from became mythical in colour and uncertain. In all things save sight they were strong and able; and presently the chance of birth and heredity sent one who had an original mind and who could talk and persuade among them, and then afterwards another. These two passed, leaving their effects, and the little community grew in numbers and in understanding, and met and settled social and economic problems that arose. Generation followed generation. Generation followed generation. There came a time when a child was born who was fifteen generations from that ancestor who went out of the valley with a bar of silver to seek God's aid, and who never returned. Thereabouts it chanced that a man came into this community from the outer world. And this is the story of that man.

He was a mountaineer from the country near Quito, a man

who had been down to the sea and had seen the world, a reader
of books in an original way, an acute and enterprising man,
and he was taken on by a party of Englishmen who had come
out to Ecuador to climb mountains, to replace one of their three
Swiss guides who had fallen ill. He climbed here and he climbed
there, and then came the attempt on Parascotopetl, the Matterhorn[4] of the Andes, in which he was lost to the outer world. The
story of the accident has been written a dozen times. Pointer's
narrative is the best. He tells how the party worked their difficult and almost vertical way up to the very foot of the last and
greatest precipice, and how they built a night shelter amidst the
snow upon a little shelf of rock, and, with a touch of real
dramatic power, how presently they found Nunez had gone
from them. They shouted, and there was no reply; shouted and
whistled, and for the rest of that night they slept no more.

As the morning broke they saw the traces of his fall. It seems
impossible he could have uttered a sound. He had slipped
eastward towards the unknown side of the mountain; far below
he had struck a steep slope of snow, and ploughed his way
down it in the midst of a snow avalanche. His track went
straight to the edge of a frightful precipice, and beyond that
everything was hidden. Far, far below, and hazy with distance,
they could see trees rising out of a narrow, shut-in valley – the
lost Country of the Blind. But they did not know it was the lost
Country of the Blind, nor distinguish it in any way from any
other narrow streak of upland valley. Unnerved by this disaster,
they abandoned their attempt in the afternoon, and Pointer was
called away to the war before he could make another attack. To
this day Parascotopetl lifts an unconquered crest, and Pointer's
shelter crumbles unvisited amidst the snows.

And the man who fell survived.

At the end of the slope he fell a thousand feet, and came
down in the midst of a cloud of snow upon a snow slope even
steeper than the one above. Down this he was whirled, stunned
and insensible, but without a bone broken in his body; and
then at last came to gentler slopes, and at last rolled out and
lay still, buried amidst a softening heap of the white masses
that had accompanied and saved him. He came to himself with

a dim fancy that he was ill in bed; then realized his position
with a mountaineer's intelligence, and worked himself loose
and, after a rest or so, out until he saw the stars. He rested flat
upon his chest for a space, wondering where he was and what
had happened to him. He explored his limbs, and discovered
that several of his buttons were gone and his coat turned over
his head. His knife had gone from his pocket and his hat was
lost, though he had tied it under his chin. He recalled that he
had been looking for loose stones to raise his piece of the shelter
wall. His ice-axe had disappeared.

He decided he must have fallen, and looked up to see, exaggerated by the ghastly light of the rising moon, the tremendous
flight he had taken. For a while he lay, gazing blankly at that
vast pale cliff towering above, rising moment by moment out
of a subsiding tide of darkness. Its phantasmal, mysterious
beauty held him for a space, and then he was seized with a
paroxysm of sobbing laughter. . . .

After a great interval of time he became aware that he was
near the lower edge of the snow. Below, down what was now
a moonlit and practicable slope, he saw the dark and broken
appearance of rock-strewn turf. He struggled to his feet, aching
in every joint and limb, got down painfully from the heaped
loose snow about him, went downward until he was on the
turf, and there dropped rather than lay beside a boulder, drank
deep from the flask in his inner pocket, and instantly fell
asleep. . . .

He was awakened by the singing of birds in the trees far
below.

He sat up and perceived he was on a little alp at the foot of
a vast precipice, that was grooved by the gully down which he
and his snow had come. Over against him another wall of rock
reared itself against the sky. The gorge between these precipices
ran east and west and was full of the morning sunlight, which
lit to the westward the mass of fallen mountain that closed the
descending gorge. Below him it seemed there was a precipice
equally steep, but behind the snow in the gully he found a
sort of chimney-cleft dripping with snow-water down which a
desperate man might venture. He found it easier than it seemed,

and came at last to another desolate alp, and then after a rock climb of no particular difficulty to a steep slope of trees. He took his bearings and turned his face up the gorge, for he saw it opened out above upon green meadows, among which he now glimpsed quite distinctly a cluster of stone huts of unfamiliar fashion. At times his progress was like clambering along the face of a wall, and after a time the rising sun ceased to strike along the gorge, the voices of the singing birds died away, and the air grew cold and dark about him. But the distant valley with its houses was all the brighter for that. He came presently to talus, and among the rocks he noted – for he was an observant man – an unfamiliar fern that seemed to clutch out of the crevices with intense green hands. He picked a frond or so and gnawed its stalk and found it helpful.

About midday he came at last out of the throat of the gorge into the plain and the sunlight. He was stiff and weary; he sat down in the shadow of a rock, filled up his flask with water from a spring and drank it down, and remained for a time resting before he went on to the houses.

They were very strange to his eyes, and indeed the whole aspect of that valley became, as he regarded it, queerer and more unfamiliar. The greater part of its surface was lush green meadow, starred with many beautiful flowers, irrigated with extraordinary care, and bearing evidence of systematic cropping piece by piece. High up and ringing the valley about was a wall, and what appeared to be a circumferential water-channel, from which the little trickles of water that fed the meadow plants came, and on the higher slopes above this flocks of llamas cropped the scanty herbage. Sheds, apparently shelters or feeding-places for the llamas, stood against the boundary wall here and there. The irrigation streams ran together into a main channel down the centre of the valley, and this was enclosed on either side by a wall breast high. This gave a singularly urban quality to this secluded place, a quality that was greatly enhanced by the fact that a number of paths paved with black and white stones, and each with a curious little kerb at the side, ran hither and thither in an orderly manner. The houses of the central village were quite unlike the casual and higgledy-piggledy agglomeration of the mountain villages he knew; they stood in a continuous row on either side of a central street of astonishing cleanness; here and there their parti-coloured façade was pierced by a door, and not a solitary window broke their even frontage. They were parti-coloured with extraordinary irregularity; smeared with a sort of plaster that was sometimes grey, sometimes drab, sometimes slate-coloured or dark brown; and it was the sight of this wild plastering first brought the word 'blind' into the thoughts of the explorer. 'The good man who did that,' he thought, 'must have been as blind as a bat.'

He descended a steep place, and so came to the wall and channel that ran about the valley, near where the latter spouted out its surplus contents into the deeps of the gorge in a thin and wavering thread of cascade. He could now see a number of men and women resting on piled heaps of grass, as if taking a siesta, in the remoter part of the meadow, and nearer the village a number of recumbent children, and then nearer at hand three men carrying pails on yokes along a little path that ran from the encircling wall towards the houses. These latter were clad in garments of llama cloth and boots and belts of leather, and they wore caps of cloth with back and ear flaps. They followed one another in single file, walking slowly and yawning as they walked, like men who have been up all night. There was something so reassuringly prosperous and respectable in their bearing that after a moment's hesitation Nunez stood forward as conspicuously as possible upon his rock, and gave vent to a mighty shout that echoed round the valley.

The three men stopped, and moved their heads as though they were looking about them. They turned their faces this way and that, and Nunez gesticulated with freedom. But they did not appear to see him for all his gestures, and after a time, directing themselves towards the mountains far away to the right, they shouted as if in answer. Nunez bawled again, and then once more, and as he gestured ineffectually the word 'blind' came up to the top of his thoughts. 'The fools must be blind,' he said.

When at last, after much shouting and wrath, Nunez crossed

the stream by a little bridge, came through a gate in the wall, and approached them, he was sure that they were blind. He was sure that this was the Country of the Blind of which the legends told. Conviction had sprung upon him, and a sense of great and rather enviable adventure. The three stood side by side, not looking at him, but with their ears directed towards him, judging him by his unfamiliar steps. They stood close together like men a little afraid, and he could see their eyelids closed and sunken, as though the very balls beneath had shrunk away. There was an expression near awe on their faces.

'A man,' one said, in hardly recognizable Spanish – 'a man it is – a man or a spirit – coming down from the rocks.'

But Nunez advanced with the confident steps of a youth who enters upon life. All the old stories of the lost valley and the Country of the Blind had come back to his mind, and through his thoughts ran this old proverb, as if it were a refrain –

'In the Country of the Blind the One-eyed Man is King.'[5]

'In the Country of the Blind the One-eyed Man is King.'

And very civilly he gave them greeting. He talked to them and used his eyes.

'Where does he come from, brother Pedro?' asked one.

'Down out of the rocks.'

'Over the mountains I come,' said Nunez, 'out of the country beyond there – where men can see. From near Bogota, where there are a hundred thousands of people, and where the city passes out of sight.'

'Sight?' muttered Pedro. 'Sight?'

'He comes,' said the second blind man, 'out of the rocks.'

The cloth of their coats Nunez saw was curiously fashioned, each with a different sort of stitching.

They startled him by a simultaneous movement towards him, each with a hand outstretched. He stepped back from the advance of these spread fingers.

'Come hither,' said the third blind man, following his motion and clutching him neatly.

And they held Nunez and felt him over, saying no word further until they had done so.

'Carefully,' he cried, with a finger in his eye, and found they thought that organ, with its fluttering lids, a queer thing in him. They went over it again.

'A strange creature, Correa,' said the one called Pedro. 'Feel the coarseness of his hair. Like a llama's hair.'

'Rough he is as the rocks that begot him,' said Correa, investigating Nunez's unshaven chin with a soft and slightly moist hand. 'Perhaps he will grow finer.' Nunez struggled a little under their examination, but they gripped him firm.

'Carefully,' he said again.

'He speaks,' said the third man. 'Certainly he is a man.'

'Ugh!' said Pedro, at the roughness of his coat.

'And you have come into the world?' asked Pedro.

'*Out* of the world. Over mountains and glaciers; right over above there, halfway to the sun. Out of the great big world that goes down, twelve days' journey to the sea.'

They scarcely seemed to heed him. 'Our fathers have told us men may be made by the forces of Nature,' said Correa. 'It is the warmth of things and moisture, and rottenness – rottenness.'

'Let us lead him to the elders,' said Pedro

'Shout first,' said Correa, 'lest the children be afraid. This is a marvellous occasion.'

So they shouted, and Pedro went first and took Nunez by the hand to lead him to the houses.

He drew his hand away. 'I can see,' he said.

'See?' said Correa.

'Yes, see,' said Nunez, turning towards him, and stumbled against Pedro's pail.

'His senses are still imperfect,' said the third blind man. 'He stumbles, and talks unmeaning words. Lead him by the hand.'

'As you will,' said Nunez, and was led along, laughing.

It seemed they knew nothing of sight.

Well, all in good time he would teach them.

He heard people shouting, and saw a number of figures gathering together in the middle roadway of the village.

He found it taxed his nerve and patience more than he had anticipated, that first encounter with the population of the Country of the Blind. The place seemed larger as he drew near to it, and the smeared plasterings queerer, and a crowd of children and men and women (the women and girls, he was pleased to note, had some of them quite sweet faces, for all that their eyes were shut and sunken) came about him, holding on to him, touching him with soft, sensitive hands, smelling at him, and listening at every word he spoke. Some of the maidens and children, however, kept aloof as if afraid, and indeed his voice seemed coarse and rude beside their softer notes. They mobbed him. His three guides kept close to him with an effect of proprietorship, and said again and again, 'A wild man out of the rocks.'

'Bogota,' he said. 'Bogota. Over the mountain crests.'

'A wild man – using wild words,' said Pedro. 'Did you hear that – Bogota? His mind is hardly formed yet. He has only the beginnings of speech.'

A little boy nipped his hand. 'Bogota!' he said mockingly.

'Ay! A city to your village. I come from the great world – where men have eyes and see.'

'His name's Bogota,' they said.

'He stumbled,' said Correa, 'stumbled twice as we came hither.'

'Bring him to the elders.'

And they thrust him suddenly through a doorway into a room as black as pitch, save at the end there faintly glowed a fire. The crowd closed in behind him and shut out all but the faintest glimmer of day, and before he could arrest himself he had fallen headlong over the feet of a seated man. His arm, outflung, struck the face of someone else as he went down; he felt the soft impact of features and heard a cry of anger, and for a moment he struggled against a number of hands that clutched him. It was a one-sided fight. An inkling of the situation came to him, and he lay quiet.

'I fell down,' he said; 'I couldn't see in this pitchy darkness.'

There was a pause as if the unseen persons about him tried to understand his words. Then the voice of Correa said: 'He is but newly formed. He stumbles as he walks and mingles words that mean nothing with his speech.'

Others also said things about him that he heard or understood imperfectly.

'May I sit up?' he asked, in a pause. 'I will not struggle against you again.'

They consulted and let him rise.

The voice of an older man began to question him, and Nunez found himself trying to explain the great world out of which he had fallen, and the sky and mountains and sight and such-like marvels, to these elders who sat in darkness in the Country of the Blind. And they would believe and understand nothing whatever he told them, a thing quite outside his expectation. They would not even understand many of his words. For fourteen generations these people had been blind and cut off from all the seeing world; the names for all the things of sight had faded and changed; the story of the outer world was faded and changed to a child's story; and they had ceased to concern themselves with anything beyond the rocky slopes above their circling wall. Blind men of genius had arisen among them and questioned the shreds of belief and tradition they had brought with them from their seeing days, and had dismissed all these things as idle fancies, and replaced them with new and saner explanations. Much of their imagination had shrivelled with their eyes, and they had made for themselves new imaginations with their ever more sensitive ears and fingertips. Slowly Nunez realized this; that his expectation of wonder and reverence at his origin and his gifts was not to be borne out; and after his poor attempt to explain sight to them had been set aside as the confused version of a new-made being describing the marvels of his incoherent sensations, he subsided, a little dashed, into listening to their instruction. And the eldest of the blind men explained to him life and philosophy and religion, how that the world (meaning their valley) had been first an empty hollow in the rocks, and then had come, first, inanimate things without the gift of touch, and llamas and a few other creatures that had little sense, and then men, and at last angels, whom one could hear singing and making fluttering sounds, but whom no one could touch at all, which puzzled Nunez greatly until he thought of the birds.

He went on to tell Nunez how this time had been divided into the warm and the cold, which are the blind equivalents of day and night, and how it was good to sleep in the warm and work during the cold, so that now, but for his advent, the whole town of the blind would have been asleep. He said Nunez must have been specially created to learn and serve the wisdom they had acquired, and that for all his mental incoherency and stumbling behaviour he must have courage, and do his best to learn, and at that all the people in the doorway murmured encouragingly. He said the night – for the blind call their day night – was now far gone, and it behoved everyone to go back to sleep. He asked Nunez if he knew how to sleep, and Nunez said he did, but that before sleep he wanted food.

They brought him food – llama's milk in a bowl, and rough salted bread – and led him into a lonely place to eat out of their hearing, and afterwards to slumber until the chill of the mountain evening roused them to begin their day again. But Nunez slumbered not at all.

Instead, he sat up in the place where they had left him, resting his limbs and turning the unanticipated circumstances of his arrival over and over in his mind.

Every now and then he laughed, sometimes with amusement, and sometimes with indignation.

'Unformed mind!' he said. 'Got no senses yet! They little know they've been insulting their heaven-sent king and master. I see I must bring them to reason. Let me think – let me think.'

He was still thinking when the sun set.

Nunez had an eye for all beautiful things, and it seemed to him that the glow upon the snowfields and glaciers that rose about the valley on every side was the most beautiful thing he had ever seen. His eyes went from that inaccessible glory to the village and irrigated fields, fast sinking into the twilight, and suddenly a wave of emotion took him, and he thanked God from the bottom of his heart that the power of sight had been given him.

He heard a voice calling to him from out of the village.

'Ya ho there, Bogota! Come hither!'

At that he stood up smiling. He would show these people once and for all what sight would do for a man. They would seek him, but not find him.

'You move not, Bogota,' said the voice.

He laughed noiselessly, and made two stealthy steps aside from the path.

'Trample not on the grass, Bogota; that is not allowed.'

Nunez had scarcely heard the sound he made himself. He stopped amazed.

The owner of the voice came running up the piebald path towards him.

He stepped back into the pathway. 'Here I am,' he said.

'Why did you not come when I called you?' said the blind man. 'Must you be led like a child? Cannot you hear the path as you walk?'

Nunez laughed. 'I can see it,' he said.

'There is no such word as *see*,' said the blind man, after a pause. 'Cease this folly, and follow the sound of my feet.'

Nunez followed, a little annoyed.

'My time will come,' he said.

'You'll learn,' the blind man answered. 'There is much to learn in the world.'

'Has no one told you, "In the Country of the Blind the One-eyed Man is King"?'

'What is blind?' asked the blind man carelessly over his shoulder.

Four days passed, and the fifth found the King of the Blind still incognito, as a clumsy and useless stranger among his subjects.

It was, he found, much more difficult to proclaim himself than he had supposed, and in the meantime, while he meditated his *coup d'état*, he did what he was told and learned the manners and customs of the Country of the Blind. He found working and going about at night a particularly irksome thing, and he decided that that should be the first thing he would change.

They led a simple, laborious life, these people, with all the elements of virtue and happiness, as these things can be understood by men. They toiled, but not oppressively; they had food and clothing sufficient for their needs; they had days and seasons of rest; they made much of music and singing, and there was love among them, and little children.

It was marvellous with what confidence and precision they

went about their ordered world. Everything, you see, had been made to fit their needs; each of the radiating paths of the valley area had a constant angle to the others, and was distinguished by a special notch upon its kerbing; all obstacles and irregularities of path or meadow had long since been cleared away; all their methods and procedure arose naturally from their special needs. Their senses had become marvellously acute; they could hear and judge the slightest gesture of a man a dozen paces away – could hear the very beating of his heart. Intonation had long replaced expression with them, and touches gesture, and their work with hoe and spade and fork was as free and confident as garden work can be. Their sense of smell was extraordinarily fine; they could distinguish individual differences as readily as a dog can, and they went about the tending of the llamas, who lived among the rocks above and came to the wall for food and shelter, with ease and confidence. It was only when at last Nunez sought to assert himself that he found how easy and confident their movements could be.

He rebelled only after he had tried persuasion.

He tried at first on several occasions to tell them of sight. 'Look you here, you people,' he said. 'There are things you do not understand in me.'

Once or twice one or two of them attended to him; they sat with faces downcast and ears turned intelligently towards him, and he did his best to tell them what it was to see. Among his hearers was a girl, with eyelids less red and sunken than the others, so that one could almost fancy she was hiding eyes, whom especially he hoped to persuade. He spoke of the beauties of sight, of watching the mountains, of the sky and the sunrise, and they heard him with amused incredulity that presently became condemnatory. They told him there were indeed no mountains at all, but that the end of the rocks where the llamas grazed was indeed the end of the world; thence sprang a cavernous roof of the universe, from which the dew and the avalanches fell; and when he maintained stoutly the world had neither end nor roof such as they supposed, they said his thoughts were wicked. So far as he could describe sky and clouds and stars to them it seemed to them a hideous void, a

terrible blankness in the place of the smooth roof to things in
which they believed – it was an article of faith with them that
the cavern roof was exquisitely smooth to the touch. He saw
that in some manner he shocked them, and gave up that aspect
of the matter altogether, and tried to show them the practical
value of sight. One morning he saw Pedro in the path called
Seventeen and coming towards the central houses, but still too
far off for hearing or scent, and he told them as much. 'In a
little while,' he prophesied, 'Pedro will be here.' An old man
remarked that Pedro had no business on Path Seventeen, and
then, as if in confirmation, that individual as he drew near
turned and went transversely into Path Ten, and so back with
nimble paces towards the outer wall. They mocked Nunez when
Pedro did not arrive, and afterwards, when he asked Pedro
questions to clear his character, Pedro denied and outfaced him,
and was afterwards hostile to him.

Then he induced them to let him go a long way up the sloping
meadows towards the wall with one complacent individual,
and to him he promised to describe all that happened among
the houses. He noted certain goings and comings, but the things
that really seemed to signify to these people happened inside of
or behind the windowless houses – the only things they took
note of to test him by – and of these he could see or tell nothing;
and it was after the failure of this attempt, and the ridicule they
could not repress, that he resorted to force. He thought of
seizing a spade and suddenly smiting one or two of them to
earth, and so in fair combat showing the advantage of eyes. He
went so far with that resolution as to seize his spade, and then
he discovered a new thing about himself, and that was that it
was impossible for him to hit a blind man in cold blood.

He hesitated, and found them all aware that he snatched up
the spade. They stood alert, with their heads on one side, and
bent ears towards him for what he would do next.

'Put that spade down,' said one, and he felt a sort of helpless
horror. He came near obedience.

Then he thrust one backwards against a house wall, and fled
past him and out of the village.

He went athwart one of their meadows, leaving a track of

trampled grass behind his feet, and presently sat down by the side of one of their ways. He felt something of the buoyancy that comes to all men in the beginning of a fight, but more perplexity. He began to realize that you cannot even fight happily with creatures who stand upon a different mental basis to yourself. Far away he saw a number of men carrying spades and sticks come out of the street of houses, and advance in a spreading line along the several paths towards him. They advanced slowly, speaking frequently to one another, and ever and again the whole cordon would halt and sniff the air and listen.

The first time they did this Nunez laughed. But afterwards he did not laugh.

One struck his trail in the meadow grass, and came stooping and feeling his way along it.

For five minutes he watched the slow extension of the cordon, and then his vague disposition to do something forthwith became frantic. He stood up, went a pace or so towards the circumferential wall, turned, and went back a little way. There they all stood in a crescent, still and listening.

He also stood still, gripping his spade very tightly in both hands. Should he charge them?

The pulse in his ears ran into the rhythm of 'In the Country of the Blind the One-eyed Man is King!'

Should he charge them?

He looked back at the high and unclimbable wall behind – unclimbable because of its smooth plastering, but withal pierced with many little doors, and at the approaching line of seekers. Behind these, others were now coming out of the street of houses.

Should he charge them?

'Bogota!' called one. 'Bogota! where are you?'

He gripped his spade still tighter, and advanced down the meadows towards the place of habitations, and directly he moved they converged upon him. 'I'll hit them if they touch me,' he swore; 'by Heaven, I will. I'll hit.' He called aloud, 'Look here, I'm going to do what I like in this valley. Do you hear? I'm going to do what I like and go where I like!'

They were moving in upon him quickly, groping, yet moving

rapidly. It was like playing blind man's buff, with everyone blindfolded except one. 'Get hold of him!' cried one. He found himself in the arc of a loose curve of pursuers. He felt suddenly he must be active and resolute.

'You don't understand,' he cried in a voice that was meant to be great and resolute, and which broke. 'You are blind, and I can see. Leave me alone!'

'Bogota! Put down that spade, and come off the grass!'

The last order, grotesque in its urban familiarity, produced a gust of anger.

'I'll hurt you,' he said, sobbing with emotion. 'By Heaven, I'll hurt you. Leave me alone!'

He began to run, not knowing clearly where to run. He ran from the nearest blind man, because it was a horror to hit him. He stopped, and then made a dash to escape from their closing ranks. He made for where a gap was wide, and the men on either side, with a quick perception of the approach of his paces, rushed in on one another. He sprang forward, and then saw he must be caught, and *swish!* the spade had struck. He felt the soft thud of hand and arm, and the man was down with a yell of pain, and he was through.

Through! And then he was close to the street of houses again, and blind men, whirling spades and stakes, were running with a sort of reasoned swiftness hither and thither.

He heard steps behind him just in time, and found a tall man rushing forward and swiping at the sound of him. He lost his nerve, hurled his spade a yard wide at his antagonist, and whirled about and fled, fairly yelling as he dodged another.

He was panic-stricken. He ran furiously to and fro, dodging when there was no need to dodge, and in his anxiety to see on every side of him at once, stumbling. For a moment he was down and they heard his fall. Far away in the circumferential wall a little doorway looked like heaven, and he set off in a wild rush for it. He did not even look round at his pursuers until it was gained, and he had stumbled across the bridge, clambered a little way among the rocks, to the surprise and dismay of a young llama, who went leaping out of sight, and lay down sobbing for breath.

And so his *coup d'état* came to an end.

He stayed outside the wall of the valley of the Blind for two nights and days without food or shelter, and meditated upon the unexpected. During these meditations he repeated very frequently and always with a profounder note of derision the exploded proverb: 'In the Country of the Blind the One-eyed Man is King.' He thought chiefly of ways of fighting and conquering these people, and it grew clear that for him no practicable way was possible. He had no weapons, and now it would be hard to get one.

The canker of civilization had got to him even in Bogota, and he could not find it in himself to go down and assassinate a blind man. Of course, if he did that, he might then dictate terms on the threat of assassinating them all. But – sooner or later he must sleep! . . .

He tried also to find food among the pine trees, to be comfortable under pine boughs while the frost fell at night, and – with less confidence – to catch a llama by artifice in order to try to kill it – perhaps by hammering it with a stone – and so finally, perhaps, to eat some of it. But the llamas had a doubt of him and regarded him with distrustful brown eyes, and spat when he drew near. Fear came on him the second day and fits of shivering. Finally he crawled down to the wall of the Country of the Blind and tried to make terms. He crawled along by the stream, shouting, until two blind men came out to the gate and talked to him.

'I was mad,' he said. 'But I was only newly made.'

They said that was better.

He told them he was wiser now, and repented of all he had done.

Then he wept without intention, for he was very weak and ill now, and they took that as a favourable sign.

They asked him if he still thought he could '*see*'.

'No,' he said. 'That was folly. The word means nothing – less than nothing!'

They asked him what was overhead.

'About ten times ten the height of a man there is a roof above the world – of rock – and very, very smooth.' . . . He burst again into hysterical tears. 'Before you ask me any more, give me some food or I shall die.'

He expected dire punishments, but these blind people were capable of toleration. They regarded his rebellion as but one more proof of his general idiocy and inferiority; and after they had whipped him they appointed him to do the simplest and heaviest work they had for anyone to do, and he, seeing no other way of living, did submissively what he was told.

He was ill for some days, and they nursed him kindly. That refined his submission. But they insisted on his lying in the dark, and that was a great misery. And blind philosophers came and talked to him of the wicked levity of his mind, and reproved him so impressively for his doubts about the lid of rock that covered their cosmic casserole that he almost doubted whether indeed he was not the victim of hallucination in not seeing it overhead.

So Nunez became a citizen of the Country of the Blind, and these people ceased to be a generalized people and became individualities and familiar to him, while the world beyond the mountains became more and more remote and unreal. There was Yacob, his master, a kindly man when not annoyed; there was Pedro, Yacob's nephew; and there was Medina-saroté,[6] who was the youngest daughter of Yacob. She was little esteemed in the world of the blind, because she had a clear-cut face, and lacked that satisfying, glossy smoothness that is the blind man's ideal of feminine beauty; but Nunez thought her beautiful at first, and presently the most beautiful thing in the whole creation. Her closed eyelids were not sunken and red after the common way of the valley, but lay as though they might open again at any moment; and she had long eyelashes, which were considered a grave disfigurement. And her voice was strong, and did not satisfy the acute hearing of the valley swains. So that she had no lover.

There came a time when Nunez thought that, could he win her, he would be resigned to live in the valley for all the rest of his days.

He watched her; he sought opportunities of doing her little services, and presently he found that she observed him. Once at a rest-day gathering they sat side by side in the dim starlight, and the music was sweet. His hand came upon hers and he dared to clasp it. Then very tenderly she returned his pressure. And one day, as they were at their meal in the darkness, he felt her hand very softly seeking him, and as it chanced the fire leapt then and he saw the tenderness of her face.

He sought to speak to her.

He went to her one day when she was sitting in the summer moonlight spinning. The light made her a thing of silver and mystery. He sat down at her feet and told her he loved her, and told her how beautiful she seemed to him. He had a lover's voice, he spoke with a tender reverence that came near to awe, and she had never before been touched by adoration. She made him no definite answer, but it was clear his words pleased her.

After that he talked to her whenever he could take an opportunity. The valley became the world for him, and the world beyond the mountains where men lived in sunlight seemed no more than a fairy tale he would someday pour into her ears. Very tentatively and timidly he spoke to her of sight.

Sight seemed to her the most poetical of fancies, and she listened to his description of the stars and the mountains and her own sweet white-lit beauty as though it was a guilty indulgence. She did not believe, she could only half understand, but she was mysteriously delighted, and it seemed to him that she completely understood.

His love lost its awe and took courage. Presently he was for demanding her of Yacob and the elders in marriage, but she became fearful and delayed. And it was one of her elder sisters who first told Yacob that Medina-saroté and Nunez were in love.

There was from the first very great opposition to the marriage of Nunez and Medina-saroté; not so much because they valued her as because they held him as a being apart, an idiot, incompetent thing below the permissible level of a man. Her sisters opposed it bitterly as bringing discredit on them all; and old Yacob, though he had formed a sort of liking for his clumsy, obedient serf, shook his head and said the thing could not be. The young men were all angry at the idea of corrupting the race, and one went so far as to revile and strike Nunez. He struck back. Then for the first time he found an advantage in seeing, even by twilight, and after that fight was over no one was disposed to raise a hand against him. But they still found his marriage impossible.

Old Yacob had a tenderness for his last little daughter, and was grieved to have her weep upon his shoulder.

'You see, my dear, he's an idiot. He has delusions; he can't do anything right.'

'I know,' wept Medina-saroté. 'But he's better than he was. He's getting better. And he's strong, dear father, and kind – stronger and kinder than any other man in the world. And he loves me – and, father, I love him.'

Old Yacob was greatly distressed to find her inconsolable, and, besides – what made it more distressing – he liked Nunez for many things. So he went and sat in the windowless council-chamber with the other elders and watched the trend of the talk, and said, at the proper time, 'He's better than he was. Very likely, someday, we shall find him as sane as ourselves.'

Then afterwards one of the elders, who thought deeply, had an idea. He was the great doctor among these people, their medicine-man, and he had a very philosophical and inventive mind, and the idea of curing Nunez of his peculiarities appealed to him. One day when Yacob was present he returned to the topic of Nunez.

'I have examined Bogota,' he said, 'and the case is clearer to me. I think very probably he might be cured.'

'That is what I have always hoped,' said old Yacob.

'His brain is affected,' said the blind doctor.

The elders murmured assent.

'Now, *what* affects it?'

'Ah!' said old Yacob.

'*This*,' said the doctor, answering his own question. 'Those queer things that are called the eyes, and which exist to make an agreeable soft depression in the face, are diseased, in the case of Bogota, in such a way as to affect his brain. They are greatly distended, he has eyelashes, and his eyelids move, and consequently his brain is in a state of constant irritation and distraction.'

'Yes?' said old Yacob. 'Yes?'

'And I think I may say with reasonable certainty that, in order to cure him completely, all that we need do is a simple and easy surgical operation – namely, to remove these irritant bodies.'

'And then he will be sane?'

'Then he will be perfectly sane, and a quite admirable citizen.'

'Thank Heaven for science!' said old Yacob, and went forth at once to tell Nunez of his happy hopes.

But Nunez's manner of receiving the good news struck him as being cold and disappointing.

'One might think,' he said, 'from the tone you take, that you did not care for my daughter.'

It was Medina-saroté who persuaded Nunez to face the blind surgeons.

'*You* do not want me,' he said, 'to lose my gift of sight?'

She shook her head.

'My world is sight.'

Her head drooped lower.

'There are the beautiful things, the beautiful little things – the flowers, the lichens among the rocks, the lightness and softness on a piece of fur, the far sky with its drifting down of clouds, the sunsets and the stars. And there is *you*. For you alone it is good to have sight, to see your sweet, serene face, your kindly lips, your dear, beautiful hands folded together. . . . It is these eyes of mine you won, these eyes that hold me to you, that these idiots seek. Instead, I must touch you, hear you, and never see you again. I must come under that roof of rock and stone and darkness, that horrible roof under which your imagination stoops. . . . No; you would not have me do that?'

A disagreeable doubt had arisen in him. He stopped, and left the thing a question.

'I wish,' she said, 'sometimes—' She paused.

'Yes?' said he, a little apprehensively.

'I wish sometimes – you would not talk like that.'

'Like what?'

'I know it's pretty – it's your imagination. I love it, but *now*—'

He felt cold. '*Now?*' he said faintly.

She sat quite still.

'You mean – you think – I should be better, better perhaps—'

He was realizing things very swiftly. He felt anger, indeed, anger at the dull course of fate, but also sympathy for her lack of understanding – a sympathy near akin to pity.

'*Dear*,' he said, and he could see by her whiteness how intensely her spirit pressed against the things she could not say. He put his arms about her, he kissed her ear, and they sat for a time in silence.

'If I were to consent to this?' he said at last, in a voice that was very gentle.

She flung her arms about him, weeping wildly. 'Oh, if you would,' she sobbed, 'if only you would!'

For a week before the operation that was to raise him from his servitude and inferiority to the level of a blind citizen, Nunez knew nothing of sleep, and all through the warm sunlit hours, while the others slumbered happily, he sat brooding or wandered aimlessly, trying to bring his mind to bear on his dilemma. He had given his answer, he had given his consent, and still he was not sure. And at last work-time was over, the sun rose in splendour over the golden crests, and his last day of vision began for him. He had a few minutes with Medina-saroté before she went apart to sleep.

'Tomorrow,' he said, 'I shall see no more.'

'Dear heart!' she answered, and pressed his hands with all her strength.

'They will hurt you but little,' she said; 'and you are going through this pain – you are going through it, dear lover, for *me*. . . . Dear, if a woman's heart and life can do it, I will repay you. My dearest one, my dearest with the tender voice, I will repay.'

He was drenched in pity for himself and her.

He held her in his arms, and pressed his lips to hers, and looked on her sweet face for the last time. 'Goodbye!' he whispered at that dear sight, 'goodbye!'

And then in silence he turned away from her.

She could hear his slow retreating footsteps, and something in the rhythm of them threw her into a passion of weeping.

He had fully meant to go to a lonely place where the meadows were beautiful with white narcissus, and there remain until the hour of his sacrifice should come, but as he went he lifted up his eyes and saw the morning, the morning like an angel in golden armour, marching down the steeps. . . .

It seemed to him that before this splendour he, and this blind world in the valley, and his love, and all, were no more than a pit of sin.

He did not turn aside as he had meant to do, but went on, and passed through the wall of the circumference and out upon the rocks, and his eyes were always upon the sunlit ice and snow.

He saw their infinite beauty, and his imagination soared over them to the things beyond he was now to resign for ever.

He thought of that great free world he was parted from, the world that was his own, and he had a vision of those further slopes, distance beyond distance, with Bogota, a place of multi-tudinous stirring beauty, a glory by day, a luminous mystery by night, a place of palaces and fountains and statues and white houses, lying beautifully in the middle distance. He thought how for a day or so one might come down through passes, drawing ever nearer and nearer to its busy streets and ways. He thought of the river journey, day by day, from great Bogota to the still vaster world beyond, through towns and villages, forest and desert places, the rushing river day by day, until its banks receded and the big steamers came splashing by, and one had reached the sea – the limitless sea, with its thousand islands, its thousands of islands, and its ships seen dimly far away in their incessant journeyings round and about that greater world. And there, unpent by mountains, one saw the sky – the sky, not such a disc as one saw it here, but an arch of immeasurable blue, a deep of deeps in which the circling stars were floating. . . .

His eyes scrutinized the great curtain of the mountains with a keener inquiry.

For example, if one went so, up that gully and to that chimney there, then one might come out high among those stunted pines that ran round in a sort of shelf and rose still higher and higher as it passed above the gorge. And then? That talus might be managed. Thence perhaps a climb might be found to take him up to the precipice that came below the snow; and if that chimney failed, then another farther to the east might serve his purpose better. And then? Then one would be out upon the amber-lit snow there, and halfway up to the crest of those beautiful desolations.

He glanced back at the village, then turned right round and regarded it steadfastly.

He thought of Medina-saroté, and she had become small and remote.

He turned again towards the mountain wall, down which the day had come to him.

Then very circumspectly he began to climb.

When sunset came he was no longer climbing, but he was far and high. He had been higher, but he was still very high. His clothes were torn, his limbs were bloodstained, he was bruised in many places, but he lay as if he were at his ease, and there was a smile on his face.

From where he rested the valley seemed as if it were in a pit and nearly a mile below. Already it was dim with haze and shadow, though the mountain summits around him were things of light and fire. The mountain summits around him were things of light and fire, and the little details of the rocks near at hand were drenched with subtle beauty – a vein of green mineral piercing the grey, the flash of crystal faces here and there, a minute, minutely beautiful orange lichen close beside his face. There were deep mysterious shadows in the gorge, blue deepening into purple, and purple into a luminous darkness, and overhead was the illimitable vastness of the sky. But he heeded these things no longer, but lay quite inactive there, smiling as if he were satisfied merely to have escaped from the valley of the Blind in which he had thought to be King.

The glow of the sunset passed, and the night came, and still he lay peacefully contented under the cold stars.

THE EMPIRE OF THE ANTS

§ 1

When Captain Gerilleau received instructions to take his new gunboat, the *Benjamin Constant*, to Badama[1] on the Batemo arm of the Guaramadema and there assist the inhabitants against a plague of ants, he suspected the authorities of mockery. His promotion had been romantic and irregular, the affections of a prominent Brazilian lady and the captain's liquid eyes had played a part in the process, and the *Diario* and *O Futuro* had been lamentably disrespectful in their comments. He felt he was to give further occasion for disrespect.

He was a Creole, his conceptions of etiquette and discipline were pure-blooded Portuguese, and it was only to Holroyd, the Lancashire engineer who had come over with the boat, and as an exercise in the use of English – his 'th' sounds were very uncertain – that he opened his heart.

'It is in effect,' he said, 'to make me absurd! What can a man do against ants? Dey come, dey go.'

'They say,' said Holroyd, 'that these don't go. That chap you said was a Sambo—'[2]

'Zambo – it is a sort of mixture of blood.'

'Sambo. He said the people are going!'

The captain smoked fretfully for a time. 'Dese tings 'ave to happen,' he said at last. 'What is it? Plagues of ants and suchlike as God wills. Dere was a plague in Trinidad – the little ants that carry leaves. Orl der orange-trees, all der mangoes! What does it matter? Sometimes ant armies come into your houses – fighting ants; a different sort. You go and they clean the house.

Then you come back again; – the house is clean, like new! No cockroaches, no fleas, no jiggers in the floor.'

'That Sambo chap,' said Holroyd, 'says these are a different sort of ant.'

The captain shrugged his shoulders, fumed, and gave his attention to a cigarette.

Afterwards he reopened the subject. 'My dear 'Olroyd, what am I to do about dese infernal ants?'

The captain reflected. 'It is ridiculous,' he said. But in the afternoon he put on his full uniform and went ashore, and jars and boxes came back to the ship and subsequently he did. And Holroyd sat on deck in the evening coolness and smoked profoundly and marvelled at Brazil. They were six days up the Amazon, some hundreds of miles from the ocean, and east and west of him there was a horizon like the sea, and to the south nothing but a sand-bank island with some tufts of scrub. The water was always running like a sluice, thick with dirt, animated with crocodiles and hovering birds, and fed by some inexhaustible source of tree trunks; and the waste of it, the headlong waste of it, filled his soul. The town of Alemquer, with its meagre church, its thatched sheds for houses, its discoloured ruins of ampler days, seemed a little thing lost in this wilderness of Nature, a sixpence dropped on Sahara. He was a young man, this was his first sight of the tropics, he came straight from England, where Nature is hedged, ditched, and drained into the perfection of submission, and he had suddenly discovered the insignificance of man. For six days they had been steaming up from the sea by unfrequented channels, and man had been as rare as a rare butterfly. One saw one day a canoe, another day a distant station, the next no men at all. He began to perceive that man is indeed a rare animal, having but a precarious hold upon this land.

He perceived it more clearly as the days passed, and he made his devious way to the Batemo, in the company of this remarkable commander, who ruled over one big gun, and was forbidden to waste his ammunition. Holroyd was learning Spanish industriously, but he was still in the present tense and substantive stage of speech, and the only other person who had any words of English was a Negro stoker, who had them all wrong. The second in command was a Portuguese, da Cunha, who spoke French, but it was a different sort of French[3] from the French Holroyd had learnt in Southport, and their intercourse was confined to politenesses and simple propositions about the weather. And the weather, like everything else in this amazing new world, the weather had no human aspect, and was hot by night and hot by day, and the air steam, even the wind was hot steam, smelling of vegetation in decay: and the alligators and the strange birds, the flies of many sorts and sizes, the beetles, the ants, the snakes and monkeys seemed to wonder what man was doing in an atmosphere that had no gladness in its sunshine and no coolness in its night. To wear clothing was intolerable, but to cast it aside was to scorch by day, and expose an ampler area to the mosquitoes by night; to go on deck by day was to be blinded by glare and to stay below was to suffocate. And in the daytime came certain flies, extremely clever and noxious about one's wrist and ankle. Captain Gerilleau, who was Holroyd's sole distraction from these physical distresses, developed into a formidable bore, telling the simple story of his heart's affections day by day, a string of anonymous women, as if he was telling beads. Sometimes he suggested sport, and they shot at alligators, and at rare intervals they came to human aggregations in the waste of trees, and stayed for a day or so, and drank and sat about; and, one night, danced with Creole girls, who found Holroyd's poor elements of Spanish, without either past tense or future, amply sufficient for their purposes. But these were mere luminous chinks in the long grey passage of the streaming river, up which the throbbing engines beat. A certain liberal heathen deity, in the shape of a demi-john, held seductive court aft, and, it is probable, forward.

But Gerilleau learnt things about the ants, more things and more, at this stopping-place and that, and became interested in his mission.

'Dey are a new sort of ant,' he said. 'We have got to be – what do you call it? – entomologie? Big. Five centimetres! Some bigger! It is ridiculous. We are like the monkeys – sent to pick insects. . . . But dey are eating up the country.'

He burst out indignantly. 'Suppose – suddenly, there are complications with Europe. Here am I – soon we shall be above the Rio Negro – and my gun, useless!'

He nursed his knee and mused.

'Dose people who were dere at de dancing place, dey 'ave come down. Dey 'ave lost all they got. De ants come to deir house one afternoon. Everyone run out. You know when de ants come one must – everyone runs out and they go over the house. If you stayed they'd eat you. See? Well, presently dey go back; dey say, "The ants 'ave gone." . . . De ants *aven't* gone. Dey try to go in – de son, 'e goes in. De ants fight.'

'Swarm over him?'

'Bite 'im. Presently he comes out again – screaming and running. He runs past them to the river. See? He get into de water and drowns de ants – yes.' Gerilleau paused, brought his liquid eyes close to Holroyd's face, tapped Holroyd's knee with his knuckle. 'That night he dies, just as if he was stung by a snake.'

'Poisoned – by the ants?'

'Who knows?' Gerilleau shrugged his shoulders. 'Perhaps they bit him badly. . . . When I joined dis service I joined to fight men. Dese things, dese ants, dey come and go. It is no business for men.'

After that he talked frequently of the ants to Holroyd, and whenever they chanced to drift against any speck of humanity in that waste of water and sunshine and distant trees, Holroyd's improving knowledge of the language enabled him to recognize the ascendant word *Saüba*,[4] more and more completely dominating the whole.

He perceived the ants were becoming interesting, and the nearer he drew to them the more interesting they became. Gerilleau abandoned his old themes almost suddenly, and the Portuguese lieutenant became a conversational figure; he knew something about the leaf-cutting ant, and expanded his knowledge. Gerilleau sometimes rendered what he had to tell to Holroyd. He told of the little workers that swarm and fight, and the big workers that command and rule, and how these latter always crawled to the neck and how their bites drew blood. He told how they cut leaves and made fungus beds, and how their nests in Caracas are sometimes a hundred yards across. Two days the three men spent disputing whether ants have eyes. The discussion grew dangerously heated on the second afternoon, and Holroyd saved the situation by going ashore in a boat to catch and see. He captured various specimens and returned, and some had eyes and some hadn't. Also, they argued, do ants bite or sting?

'Dese ants,' said Gerilleau, after collecting information at a rancho, 'have big eyes. They don't run about blind – not as most ants do. No! Dey get in corners and watch what you do.'

'And they sting?' asked Holroyd.

'Yes. Dey sting. Dere is poison in the sting.' He meditated. 'I do not see what men can do against ants. Dey come and go.'

'But these don't go.'

'They will,' said Gerilleau.

Past Tamandu there is a long low coast of eighty miles without any population, and then one comes to the confluence of the main river and the Batemo arm like a great lake, and then the forest came nearer, came at last intimately near. The character of the channel changes, snags abound, and the *Benjamin Constant* moored by a cable that night, under the very shadow of dark trees. For the first time for many days came a spell of coolness, and Holroyd and Gerilleau sat late, smoking cigars and enjoying this delicious sensation. Gerilleau's mind was full of ants and what they could do. He decided to sleep at last, and lay down on a mattress on deck, a man hopelessly perplexed; his last words, when he already seemed asleep, were to ask, with a flourish of despair. 'What can one do with ants? . . . De whole thing is absurd.'

Holroyd was left to scratch his bitten wrists, and meditate alone.

He sat on the bulwark and listened to the changes in Gerilleau's breathing until he was fast asleep, and then the ripple and lap of the stream took his mind, and brought back that sense of immensity that had been growing upon him since first he had left Para and come up the river. The monitor showed but one small light, and there was first a little talking forward and then stillness. His eyes went from the dim black outlines of the middle works of the gunboat towards the bank, to the black overwhelming mysteries of forest, lit now and then by a firefly, and never still from the murmur of alien and mysterious activities. . . .

It was the inhuman immensity of this land that astonished and oppressed him. He knew the skies were empty of men, the stars were specks in an incredible vastness of space; he knew the ocean was enormous and untamable, but in England he had come to think of the land as man's. In England it is indeed man's, the wild things live by sufferance, grow on lease, every-where the roads, the fences, and absolute security runs. In an atlas, too, the land is man's, and all coloured to show his claim to it – in vivid contrast to the universal independent blueness of the sea. He had taken it for granted that a day would come when everywhere about the earth, plough and culture, light tramways, and good roads, an ordered security, would prevail. But now, he doubted.

This forest was interminable, it had an air of being invincible, and Man seemed at best an infrequent precarious intruder. One travelled for miles amidst the still, silent struggle of giant trees, of strangulating creepers, of assertive flowers, everywhere the alligator, the turtle, and endless varieties of birds and insects seemed at home, dwelt irreplaceably – but man, man at most held a footing upon resentful clearings, fought weeds, fought beasts and insects for the barest foothold, fell a prey to snake and beast, insect and fever, and was presently carried away. In many places down the river he had been manifestly driven back, this deserted creek or that preserved the name of a *casa*, and here and there ruinous white walls and a shattered tower enforced the lesson. The puma, the jaguar, were more the masters here. . . .

Who were the real masters?

In a few miles of this forest there must be more ants than there are men in the whole world! This seemed to Holroyd a perfectly new idea. In a few thousand years men had emerged

from barbarism to a stage of civilization that made them feel
lords of the future and masters of the earth! But what was to
prevent the ants evolving also? Such ants as one knew lived
in little communities of a few thousand individuals, made no
concerted efforts against the greater world. But they had a
language, they had an intelligence! Why should things stop at
that any more than men had stopped at the barbaric stage?
Suppose presently the ants began to store knowledge, just as
men had done by means of books and records, use weapons,
form great empires, sustain a planned and organized war?

Things came back to him that Gerilleau had gathered about
these ants they were approaching. They used a poison like
the poison of snakes. They obeyed greater leaders even as the
leaf-cutting ants do. They were carnivorous, and where they
came they stayed. . . .

The forest was very still. The water lapped incessantly against
the side. About the lantern overhead there eddied a noiseless
whirl of phantom moths.

Gerilleau stirred in the darkness and sighed. 'What can one
do?' he murmured, and turned over and was still again.

Holroyd was roused from meditations that were becoming
sinister by the hum of a mosquito.

§ 2

The next morning Holroyd learnt they were within forty kilo-
metres of Badama, and his interest in the banks intensified.
He came up whenever an opportunity offered to examine his
surroundings. He could see no signs of human occupation whatever, save for a weedy ruin of a house and the green-stained
façade of the long-deserted monastery at Mojû, with a forest
tree growing out of a vacant window space, and great creepers
netted across its vacant portals. Several flights of strange yellow
butterflies with semi-transparent wings crossed the river that
morning, and many alighted on the monitor and were killed by
the men. It was towards afternoon that they came upon the
derelict cuberta.

She did not at first appear to be derelict; both her sails were set and hanging slack in the afternoon calm, and there was the figure of a man sitting on the fore planking beside the shipped sweeps. Another man appeared to be sleeping face downwards on the sort of longitudinal bridge these big canoes have in the waist. But it was presently apparent, from the sway of her rudder and the way she drifted into the course of the gunboat, that something was out of order with her. Gerilleau surveyed her through a field-glass, and became interested in the queer darkness of the face of the sitting man, a red-faced man he seemed, without a nose – crouching he was rather than sitting, and the longer the captain looked the less he liked to look at him, and the less able he was to take his glasses away.

But he did so at last, and went a little way to call up Holroyd. Then he went back to hail the cuberta. He hailed her again, and so she drove past him. *Santa Rosa* stood out clearly as her name.

As she came by and into the wake of the monitor, she pitched a little, and suddenly the figure of the crouching man collapsed as though all its joints had given way. His hat fell off, his head was not nice to look at, and his body flopped lax and rolled out of sight behind the bulwarks.

'Caramba!' cried Gerilleau, and resorted to Holroyd forthwith.

Holroyd was halfway up the companion. 'Did you see dat?' said the captain.

'Dead!' said Holroyd. 'Yes. You'd better send a boat aboard. There's something wrong.'

'Did you – by any chance – see his face?'

'What was it like?'

'It was – ugh! – I have no words.' And the captain suddenly turned his back on Holroyd and became an active and strident commander.

The gunboat came about, steamed parallel to the erratic course of the canoe, and dropped the boat with Lieutenant da Cunha and three sailors to board her. Then the curiosity of the captain made him draw up almost alongside as the lieutenant got aboard, so that the whole of the *Santa Rosa*, deck and hold, was visible to Holroyd.

He saw now clearly that the sole crew of the vessel was these two dead men, and though he could not see their faces, he saw by their outstretched hands, which were all of ragged flesh, that they had been subjected to some strange exceptional process of decay. For a moment his attention concentrated on those two enigmatical bundles of dirty clothes and laxly flung limbs, and then his eyes went forward to discover the open hold piled high with trunks and cases, and aft, to where the little cabin gaped inexplicably empty. Then he became aware that the planks of the middle decking were dotted with moving black specks.

His attention was riveted by these specks. They were all walking in directions radiating from the fallen man in a manner – the image came unsought to his mind – like the crowd dispersing from a bull-fight.

He became aware of Gerilleau beside him. 'Capo,' he said, 'have you your glasses? Can you focus as closely as those planks there?'

Gerilleau made an effort, grunted, and handed him the glasses.

There followed a moment of scrutiny. 'It's ants,' said the Englishman, and handed the focused field-glasses back to Gerilleau.

His impression of them was of a crowd of large black ants, very like ordinary ants except for their size, and for the fact that some of the larger of them bore a sort of clothing of grey. But at the time his inspection was too brief for particulars. The head of Lieutenant da Cunha appeared over the side of the cuberta, and a brief colloquy ensued.

'You must go aboard,' said Gerilleau.

The lieutenant objected that the boat was full of ants.

'You have your boots,' said Gerilleau.

The lieutenant changed the subject. 'How did these men die?' he asked.

Captain Gerilleau embarked upon speculations that Holroyd could not follow, and the two men disputed with a certain increasing vehemence. Holroyd took up the field-glass and resumed his scrutiny, first of the ants and then of the dead man amidships.

He has described these ants to me very particularly.

He says they were as large as any ants he has ever seen, black and moving with a steady deliberation very different from the mechanical fussiness of the common ant. About one in twenty was much larger than its fellows, and with an exceptionally large head. These reminded him at once of the master workers who are said to rule over the leaf-cutter ants; like them they seemed to be directing and co-ordinating the general movements. They tilted their bodies back in a manner altogether singular as if they made some use of the forefeet. And he had a curious fancy that he was too far off to verify, that most of these ants of both kinds were wearing accoutrements, had things strapped about their bodies by bright white bands like white metal threads. . .

He put down the glasses abruptly, realizing that the question of discipline between the captain and his subordinate had become acute.

'It is your duty,' said the captain, 'to go aboard. It is my instructions.'

The lieutenant seemed on the verge of refusing. The head of one of the mulatto sailors appeared beside him.

'I believe these men were killed by the ants,' said Holroyd abruptly in English.

The captain burst into a rage. He made no answer to Holroyd. 'I have commanded you to go aboard,' he screamed to his subordinate in Portuguese. 'If you do not go aboard forthwith it is mutiny – rank mutiny. Mutiny and cowardice! Where is the courage that should animate us? I will have you in irons, I will have you shot like a dog.' He began a torrent of abuse and curses, he danced to and fro. He shook his fists, he behaved as if beside himself with rage, and the lieutenant, white and still, stood looking at him. The crew appeared forward, with amazed faces.

Suddenly, in a pause of this outbreak, the lieutenant came to some heroic decision, saluted, drew himself together and clambered upon the deck of the cuberta.

'Ah!' said Gerilleau, and his mouth shut like a trap. Holroyd saw the ants retreating before da Cunha's boots. The Portuguese walked slowly to the fallen man, stooped down, hesitated, clutched his coat and turned him over. A black swarm of ants rushed out of the clothes, and da Cunha stepped back very quickly and trod two or three times on the deck.

Holroyd put up the glasses. He saw the scattered ants about the invader's feet, and doing what he had never seen ants doing before. They had nothing of the blind movements of the common ant; they were looking at him – as a rallying crowd of men might look at some gigantic monster that had dispersed it.

'How did he die?' the captain shouted.

Holroyd understood the Portuguese to say the body was too much eaten to tell.

'What is there forward?' asked Gerilleau.

The lieutenant walked a few paces, and began his answer in Portuguese. He stopped abruptly and beat off something from his leg. He made some peculiar steps as if he was trying to stamp on something invisible, and went quickly towards the side. Then he controlled himself, turned about, walked deliberately forward to the hold, clambered up to the fore decking, from which the sweeps are worked, stooped for a time over the second man, groaned audibly, and made his way back and aft to the cabin, moving very rigidly. He turned and began a conversation with his captain, cold and respectful in tone on either side, contrasting vividly with the wrath and insult of a few moments before. Holroyd gathered only fragments of its purport.

He reverted to the field-glass, and was surprised to find the ants had vanished from all the exposed surfaces of the deck. He turned towards the shadows beneath the decking, and it seemed to him they were full of watching eyes.

The cuberta, it was agreed, was derelict, but too full of ants to put men aboard to sit and sleep: it must be towed. The lieutenant went forward to take in and adjust the cable, and the men in the boat stood up to be ready to help him. Holroyd's glasses searched the canoe.

He became more and more impressed by the fact that a great if minute and furtive activity was going on. He perceived that a number of gigantic ants – they seemed nearly a couple of inches in length – carrying oddly-shaped burthens for which he could imagine no use – were moving in rushes from one point of obscurity to another. They did not move in columns across the exposed places, but in open, spaced-out lines, oddly suggestive of the rushes of modern infantry advancing under fire. A number were taking cover under the dead man's clothes, and a perfect swarm was gathering along the side over which da Cunha must presently go.

He did not see them actually rush for the lieutenant as he returned, but he has no doubt they did make a concerted rush. Suddenly the lieutenant was shouting and cursing and beating at his legs. 'I'm stung!' he shouted, with a face of hate and accusation towards Gerilleau.

Then he vanished over the side, dropped into his boat, and plunged at once into the water. Holroyd heard the splash.

The three men in the boat pulled him out and brought him aboard, and that night he died.

§ 3

Holroyd and the captain came out of the cabin in which the swollen and contorted body of the lieutenant lay and stood together at the stern of the monitor, staring at the sinister vessel they trailed behind them. It was a close, dark night that had only phantom flickerings of sheet lightning to illuminate it. The cuberta, a vague black triangle, rocked about in the steamer's wake, her sails bobbing and flapping, and the black smoke from the funnels, spark-lit ever and again, streamed over her swaying masts.

Gerilleau's mind was inclined to run on the unkind things the lieutenant had said in the heat of his last fever.

'He says I murdered 'im,' he protested. 'It is simply absurd. Someone 'ad to go aboard. Are we to run away from these confounded ants whenever they show up?'

Holroyd said nothing. He was thinking of a disciplined rush of little black shapes across bare sunlit planking.

'It was his place to go,' harped Gerilleau. 'He died in the execution of his duty. What has he to complain of? Murdered!

... But the poor fellow was – what is it? – demented. He was not in his right mind. The poison swelled him. ... U'm.'

They came to a long silence.

'We will sink that canoe – burn it.'

'And then?'

The enquiry irritated Gerilleau. His shoulders went up, his hands flew out at right angles from his body. 'What is one to *do*?' he said, his voice going up to an angry squeak.

'Anyhow,' he broke out vindictively, 'every ant in dat cuberta! – I will burn dem alive!'

Holroyd was not moved to conversation. A distant ululation of howling monkeys filled the sultry night with foreboding sounds, and as the gunboat drew near the black mysterious banks this was reinforced by a depressing clamour of frogs.

'What is one to *do*?' the captain repeated after a vast interval, and suddenly becoming active and savage and blasphemous, decided to burn the *Santa Rosa* without further delay. Everyone aboard was pleased by that idea, everyone helped with zest; they pulled in the cable, cut it, and dropped the boat and fired her with tow and kerosene, and soon the cuberta was crackling and flaring merrily amidst the immensities of the tropical night. Holroyd watched the mounting yellow flare against the blackness, and the livid flashes of sheet lightning that came and went above the forest summits, throwing them into momentary silhouette, and his stoker stood behind him watching also.

The stoker was stirred to the depths of his linguistics. '*Saüba* go pop, pop,' he said. 'Wahaw!' and laughed richly.

But Holroyd was thinking that these little creatures on the decked canoe had also eyes and brains.

The whole thing impressed him as incredibly foolish and wrong, but – what was one to *do*? This question came back enormously reinforced on the morrow, when at last the gunboat reached Badama.

This place, with its leaf-thatch-covered houses and sheds, its creeper-invaded sugar-mill, its little jetty of timber and canes, was very still in the morning heat, and showed never a sign of living men. Whatever ants there were at that distance were too small to see.

'All the people have gone,' said Gerilleau, 'but we will do one thing anyhow. We will 'oot and vissel.'

So Holroyd hooted and whistled.

Then the captain fell into a doubting fit of the worst kind. 'Dere is one thing we can do,' he said presently.

'What's that?' said Holroyd.

''Oot and vissel again.'

So they did.

The captain walked his deck and gesticulated to himself. He seemed to have many things on his mind. Fragments of speeches came from his lips. He appeared to be addressing some imaginary public tribunal either in Spanish or Portuguese. Holroyd's improving ear detected something about ammunition. He came out of these preoccupations suddenly into English. 'My dear 'Olroyd!' he cried, and broke off with 'But what *can* one do?'

They took the boat and the field-glasses, and went close in to examine the place. They made out a number of big ants, whose still postures had a certain effect of watching them, dotted about the edge of the rude embarkation jetty. Gerilleau tried ineffectual pistol shots at these. Holroyd thinks he distinguished curious earthworks running between the nearer houses, that may have been the work of the insect conquerors of those human habitations. The explorers pulled past the jetty, and became aware of a human skeleton wearing a loin cloth, and very bright and clean and shining, lying beyond. They came to a pause regarding this. . . .

'I 'ave all dose lives to consider,' said Gerilleau suddenly.

Holroyd turned and stared at the captain, realizing slowly that he referred to the unappetizing mixture of races that constituted his crew.

'To send a landing party – it is impossible – impossible. They will be poisoned, they will swell, they will swell up and abuse me and die. It is totally impossible. . . . If we land, I must land alone, alone, in thick boots and with my life in my hand. Perhaps I should live. Or again – I might not land. I do not know. I do not know.'

Holroyd thought he did, but he said nothing.

'De whole thing,' said Gerilleau suddenly, ''as been got up to make me ridiculous. De whole thing!'

They paddled about and regarded the clean white skeleton from various points of view, and then they returned to the gunboat. Then Gerilleau's indecisions became terrible. Steam was got up, and in the afternoon the monitor went on up the river with an air of going to ask somebody something, and by sunset came back again and anchored. A thunderstorm gathered and broke furiously, and then the night became beautifully cool and quiet and everyone slept on deck. Except Gerilleau, who tossed about and muttered. In the dawn he awakened Holroyd.

'Lord!' said Holroyd, 'what now?'

'I have decided,' said the captain.

'What – to land?' said Holroyd, sitting up brightly.

'No!' said the captain, and was for a time very reserved. 'I have decided,' he repeated, and Holroyd manifested symptoms of impatience.

'Well, – yes,' said the captain, '*I shall fire de big gun!*'

And he did! Heaven knows what the ants thought of it, but he did. He fired it twice with great sternness and ceremony. All the crew had wadding in their ears, and there was an effect of going into action about the whole affair, and first they hit and wrecked the old sugar-mill, and then they smashed the abandoned store behind the jetty. And then Gerilleau experienced the inevitable reaction.

'It is no good,' he said to Holroyd; 'no good at all. No sort of bally good. We must go back – for instructions. Dere will be de devil of a row about dis ammunition – oh! de *devil* of a row! You don't know, 'Olroyd. . . .'

He stood regarding the world in infinite perplexity for a space.

'But what else was there to *do*?' he cried.

In the afternoon the monitor started downstream again, and in the evening a landing party took the body of the lieutenant and buried it on the bank upon which the new ants have so far not appeared. . . .

§ 4

I heard this story in a fragmentary state from Holroyd not three weeks ago.

These new ants have got into his brain, and he has come back to England with the idea, as he says, of 'exciting people' about them 'before it is too late'. He says they threaten British Guiana, which cannot be much over a trifle of a thousand miles from their present sphere of activity, and that the Colonial Office ought to get to work upon them at once. He declaims with great passion: 'These are intelligent ants. Just think what that means!'

There can be no doubt they are a serious pest, and that the Brazilian Government is well advised in offering a prize of five hundred pounds for some effectual method of extirpation. It is certain too that since they first appeared in the hills beyond Badama, about three years ago, they have achieved extraordinary conquests. The whole of the south bank of the Batemo River, for nearly sixty miles, they have in their effectual occupation: they have driven men out completely, occupied plantations and settlements, and boarded and captured at least one ship. It is even said they have in some inexplicable way bridged the very considerable Capuarana arm and pushed many miles towards the Amazon itself. There can be little doubt that they are far more reasonable and with a far better social organization than any previously known ant species; instead of being in dispersed societies they are organized into what is in effect a single nation; but their peculiar and immediate formidableness lies not so much in this as in the intelligent use they make of poison against their larger enemies. It would seem this poison of theirs is closely akin to snake poison, and it is highly probable they actually manufacture it, and that the larger individuals among them carry the needle-like crystals of it in their attacks upon men.

Of course it is extremely difficult to get any detailed information about these new competitors for the sovereignty of the globe. No eye-witnesses of their activity, except for such glimpses as Holroyd's, have survived the encounter. The most extraordinary legends of their prowess and capacity are in circulation in the region of the Upper Amazon, and grow daily as the steady advance of the invader stimulates men's imaginations through their fears. These strange little creatures are credited not only with the use of implements and a knowledge of fire and metals and with organized feats of engineering that stagger our Northern minds – unused as we are to such feats as that of the *Saübas* of Rio de Janeiro, who in 1841 drove a tunnel under Parahyba where it is as wide as the Thames at London Bridge – but with an organized and detailed method of record and communication analogous to our books. So far their action has been a steady progressive settlement, involving the flight or slaughter of every human being in the new areas they invade. They are increasing rapidly in numbers, and Holroyd at least is firmly convinced that they will finally dispossess man over the whole of tropical South America.

And why should they stop at tropical South America?

Well, there they are, anyhow. By 1911 or thereabouts, if they go on as they are going, they ought to strike the Capuarana Extension Railway,[5] and force themselves upon the attention of the European capitalist.

By 1920 they will be halfway down the Amazon. I fix 1950 or '60 at the latest for the discovery of Europe.

THE DOOR IN THE WALL

One confidential evening, not three months ago, Lionel Wallace told me this story of the Door in the Wall. And at the time I thought that so far as he was concerned it was a true story.

He told it me with such a direct simplicity of conviction that I could not do otherwise than believe in him. But in the morning, in my own flat, I woke to a different atmosphere; and as I lay in bed and recalled the things he had told me, stripped of the glamour of his earnest slow voice, denuded of the focused, shaded table light, the shadowy atmosphere that wrapped about him and me, and the pleasant bright things, the dessert and glasses and napery of the dinner we had shared, making them for the time a bright little world quite cut off from every-day realities, I saw it all as frankly incredible. 'He was mystifying!' I said, and then: 'How well he did it! . . . It isn't quite the thing I should have expected him, of all people, to do well.'

Afterwards as I sat up in bed and sipped my morning tea, I found myself trying to account for the flavour of reality that perplexed me in his impossible reminiscences, by supposing they did in some way suggest, present, convey – I hardly know which word to use – experiences it was otherwise impossible to tell.

Well, I don't resort to that explanation now. I have got over my intervening doubts. I believe now, as I believed at the moment of telling, that Wallace did to the very best of his ability strip the truth of his secret for me. But whether he himself saw, or only thought he saw, whether he himself was the possessor of an inestimable privilege or the victim of a fantastic dream,

I cannot pretend to guess. Even the facts of his death, which ended my doubts for ever, throw no light on that.

That much the reader must judge for himself.

I forget now what chance comment or criticism of mine moved so reticent a man to confide in me. He was, I think, defending himself against an imputation of slackness and unreliability I had made in relation to a great public movement, in which he had disappointed me. But he plunged suddenly. 'I have,' he said, 'a preoccupation—

'I know,' he went on, after a pause, 'I have been negligent. The fact is – it isn't a case of ghosts or apparitions – but – it's an odd thing to tell of, Redmond – I am haunted. I am haunted by something – that rather takes the light out of things, that fills me with longings . . .'

He paused, checked by that English shyness that so often overcomes us when we would speak of moving or grave or beautiful things. 'You were at Saint Althelstan's all through,' he said, and for a moment that seemed to me quite irrelevant. 'Well' – and he paused. Then very haltingly at first, but afterwards more easily, he began to tell of the thing that was hidden in his life, the haunting memory of a beauty and a happiness that filled his heart with insatiable longings, that made all the interests and spectacle of worldly life seem dull and tedious and vain to him.

Now that I have the clue to it, the thing seems written visibly in his face. I have a photograph in which that look of detachment has been caught and intensified. It reminds me of what a woman once said of him – a woman who had loved him greatly. 'Suddenly,' she said, 'the interest goes out of him. He forgets you. He doesn't care a rap for you – under his very nose . . .'

Yet the interest was not always out of him, and when he was holding his attention to a thing Wallace could contrive to be an extremely successful man. His career, indeed, is set with successes. He left me behind him long ago; he soared up over my head, and cut a figure in the world that I couldn't cut – anyhow. He was still a year short of forty, and they say now that he would have been in office and very probably in the new Cabinet if he had lived. At school he always beat me without effort – as it were by nature. We were at school together at Saint Althelstan's College in West Kensington for almost all our school-time. He came into the school as my co-equal, but he left far above me, in a blaze of scholarships and brilliant performance. Yet I think I made a fair average running. And it was at school I heard first of the 'Door in the Wall' – that I was to hear of a second time only a month before his death.

To him at least the Door in the Wall was a real door, leading through a real wall to immortal realities. Of that I am now quite assured.

And it came into his life quite early, when he was a little fellow between five and six. I remember how, as he sat making his confession to me with a slow gravity, he reasoned and reckoned the date of it. 'There was,' he said, 'a crimson Virginia creeper in it – all one bright uniform crimson, in a clear amber sunshine against a white wall. That came into the impression somehow, though I don't clearly remember how, and there were horse-chestnut leaves upon the clean pavement outside the green door. They were blotched yellow and green, you know, not brown nor dirty, so that they must have been new fallen. I take it that means October. I look out for horse-chestnut leaves every year and I ought to know.

'If I'm right in that, I was about five years and four months old.'

He was, he said, rather a precocious little boy – he learnt to talk at an abnormally early age, and he was so sane and 'old-fashioned', as people say, that he was permitted an amount of initiative that most children scarcely attain by seven or eight. His mother died when he was two, and he was under the less vigilant and authoritative care of a nursery governess. His father was a stern, preoccupied lawyer, who gave him little attention and expected great things of him. For all his brightness he found life grey and dull, I think. And one day he wandered.

He could not recall the particular neglect that enabled him to get away, nor the course he took among the West Kensington roads. All that had faded among the incurable blurs of memory. But the white wall and the green door stood out quite distinctly.

As his memory of that childish experience ran, he did at the very first sight of that door experience a peculiar emotion, an attraction, a desire to get to the door and open it and walk in. And at the same time he had the clearest conviction that either it was unwise or it was wrong of him – he could not tell which – to yield to this attraction. He insisted upon it as a curious thing that he knew from the very beginning – unless memory has played him the queerest trick – that the door was unfastened, and that he could go in as he chose.

I seem to see the figure of that little boy, drawn and repelled. And it was very clear in his mind, too, though why it should be so was never explained, that his father would be very angry if he went in through that door.

Wallace described all these moments of hesitation to me with the utmost particularity. He went right past the door, and then, with his hands in his pockets and making an infantile attempt to whistle, strolled right along beyond the end of the wall. There he recalls a number of mean dirty shops, and particularly that of a plumber and decorator with a dusty disorder of earthenware pipes, sheet lead, ball taps, pattern books of wallpaper, and tins of enamel. He stood pretending to examine these things, and *coveting*, passionately desiring, the green door.

Then, he said, he had a gust of emotion. He made a run for it, lest hesitation should grip him again; he went plump with outstretched hand through the green door and let it slam behind him. And so, in a trice, he came into the garden that has haunted all his life.

It was very difficult for Wallace to give me his full sense of that garden into which he came.

There was something in the very air of it that exhilarated, that gave one a sense of lightness and good happening and well-being; there was something in the sight of it that made all its colour clean and perfect and subtly luminous. In the instant of coming into it one was exquisitely glad – as only in rare moments, and when one is young and joyful one can be glad in this world. And everything was beautiful there. . . .

Wallace mused before he went on telling me. 'You see,' he said, with the doubtful inflection of a man who pauses at incredible things, 'there were two great panthers there. . . . Yes,

spotted panthers. And I was not afraid. There was a long wide
path with marble-edged flower borders on either side, and these
two huge velvety beasts were playing there with a ball. One
looked up and came towards me, a little curious as it seemed.
It came right up to me, rubbed its soft round ear very gently
against the small hand I held out, and purred. It was, I tell you,
an enchanted garden. I know. And the size? Oh! it stretched far
and wide, this way and that. I believe there were hills far away.
Heaven knows where West Kensington had suddenly got to.
And somehow it was just like coming home.

'You know, in the very moment the door swung to behind
me, I forgot the road with its fallen chestnut leaves, its cabs and
tradesmen's carts, I forgot the sort of gravitational pull back to
the discipline and obedience of home, I forgot all hesitations
and fear, forgot discretion, forgot all the intimate realities of
this life. I became in a moment a very glad and wonder-happy
little boy – in another world. It was a world with a different
quality, a warmer, more penetrating and mellower light, with
a faint clear gladness in its air, and wisps of sun-touched cloud
in the blueness of its sky. And before me ran this long wide
path, invitingly, with weedless beds on either side, rich with
untended flowers, and these two great panthers. I put my little
hands fearlessly on their soft fur, and caressed their round ears
and the sensitive corners under their ears, and played with
them, and it was as though they welcomed me home. There was
a keen sense of homecoming in my mind, and when presently a
tall, fair girl appeared in the pathway and came to meet me,
smiling, and said "Well?" to me, and lifted me and kissed
me, and put me down and led me by the hand, there was no
amazement, but only an impression of delightful rightness, of
being reminded of happy things that had in some strange way
been overlooked. There were broad red steps, I remember, that
came into view between spikes of delphinium, and up these we
went to a great avenue between very old and shady dark trees.
All down this avenue, you know, between the red chapped
stems, were marble seats of honour and statuary, and very tame
and friendly white doves. . . .

'Along this cool avenue my girl-friend led me, looking down

– I recall the pleasant lines, the finely-modelled chin of her
sweet kind face – asking me questions in a soft, agreeable voice,
and telling me things, pleasant things I know, though what
they were I was never able to recall. . . . Presently a Capuchin
monkey, very clean, with a fur of ruddy brown and kindly hazel
eyes, came down a tree to us and ran beside me, looking up at
me and grinning, and presently leapt to my shoulder. So we
two went on our way in great happiness.'

He paused.

'Go on,' I said.

'I remember little things. We passed an old man musing
among laurels, I remember, and a place gay with paroquets,
and came through a broad shaded colonnade to a spacious cool
palace, full of pleasant fountains, full of beautiful things, full
of the quality and promise of heart's desire. And there were
many things and many people, some that still seem to stand out
clearly and some that are vaguer; but all these people were
beautiful and kind. In some way – I don't know how – it was
conveyed to me that they all were kind to me, glad to have me
there, and filling me with gladness by their gestures, by the
touch of their hands, by the welcome and love in their eyes
Yes—'

He mused for a while. 'Playmates I found there. That was
very much to me, because I was a lonely little boy. They played
delightful games in a grass-covered court where there was a
sundial set about with flowers. And as one played one loved. . . .

'But – it's odd – there's a gap in my memory. I don't remember
the games we played. I never remembered. Afterwards, as a
child, I spent long hours trying, even with tears, to recall the
form of that happiness. I wanted to play it all over again – in
my nursery – by myself. No! All I remember is the happiness
and two dear playfellows who were most with me. . . . Then
presently came a sombre dark woman, with a grave, pale face
and dreamy eyes, a sombre woman, wearing a soft long robe
of pale purple, who carried a book, and beckoned and took me
aside with her into a gallery above a hall – though my playmates
were loth to have me go, and ceased their game and stood
watching as I was carried away. "Come back to us!" they cried.

"Come back to us soon!" I looked up at her face, but she heeded them not at all. Her face was very gentle and grave. She took me to a seat in the gallery, and I stood beside her, ready to look at her book as she opened it upon her knee. The pages fell open. She pointed, and I looked, marvelling, for in the living pages of that book I saw myself; it was a story about myself, and in it were all the things that had happened to me since ever I was born. ...

'It was wonderful to me, because the pages of that book were not pictures, you understand, but realities.'

Wallace paused gravely – looked at me doubtfully.

'Go on,' I said. 'I understand.'

'They were realities – yes, they must have been; people moved and things came and went in them; my dear mother, whom I had near forgotten; then my father, stern and upright, the servants, the nursery, all the familiar things of home. Then the front door and the busy streets, with traffic to and fro. I looked and marvelled, and looked half doubtfully again into the woman's face and turned the pages over, skipping this and that, to see more of this book and more, and so at last I came to myself hovering and hesitating outside the green door in the long white wall, and felt again the conflict and the fear.

'"And next?" I cried, and would have turned on, but the cool hand of the grave woman delayed me.

'"Next?" I insisted, and struggled gently with her hand, pulling up her fingers with all my childish strength, and as she yielded and the page came over she bent down upon me like a shadow and kissed my brow.

'But the page did not show the enchanted garden, nor the panthers, nor the girl who had led me by the hand, nor the playfellows who had been so loth to let me go. It showed a long grey street in West Kensington, in that chill hour of afternoon before the lamps are lit; and I was there, a wretched little figure, weeping aloud, for all that I could do to restrain myself, and I was weeping because I could not return to my dear playfellows who had called after me, "Come back to us! Come back to us soon!" I was there. This was no page in a book, but harsh reality; that enchanted place and the restraining hand of the grave mother at whose knee I stood had gone – whither had they gone?'

He halted again, and remained for a time staring into the fire.

'Oh! the woefulness of that return!' he murmured.

'Well?' I said, after a minute or so.

'Poor little wretch I was! – brought back to this grey world again! As I realized the fulness of what had happened to me, I gave way to quite ungovernable grief. And the shame and humiliation of that public weeping and my disgraceful home-coming remain with me still. I see again the benevolent-looking old gentleman in gold spectacles who stopped and spoke to me – prodding me first with his umbrella. "Poor little chap," said he; "and are you lost then?" – and me a London boy of five and more! And he must needs bring in a kindly young police-man and make a crowd of me, and so march me home. Sobbing, conspicuous, and frightened, I came back from the enchanted garden to the steps of my father's house.

'That is as well as I can remember my vision of that garden – the garden that haunts me still. Of course, I can convey nothing of that indescribable quality of translucent unreality, that *difference* from the common things of experience that hung about it all; but that – that is what happened. If it was a dream, I am sure it was a daytime and altogether extraordinary dream. . . . H'm! – naturally there followed a terrible question-ing, by my aunt, my father, the nurse, the governess – everyone. . . .

'I tried to tell them, and my father gave me my first thrashing for telling lies. When afterwards I tried to tell my aunt, she punished me again for my wicked persistence. Then, as I said, everyone was forbidden to listen to me, to hear a word about it. Even my fairy-tale books were taken away from me for a time – because I was too "imaginative". Eh? Yes, they did that! My father belonged to the old school. . . . And my story was driven back upon myself. I whispered it to my pillow – my pillow that was often damp and salt to my whispering lips with childish tears. And I added always to my official and less fervent prayers this one heartfelt request: "Please God I may dream of

the garden. Oh! take me back to my garden!" Take me back to
my garden! I dreamt often of the garden. I may have added to
it, I may have changed it; I do not know. .... All this, you
understand, is an attempt to reconstruct from fragmentary
memories a very early experience. Between that and the other
consecutive memories of my boyhood there is a gulf. A time
came when it seemed impossible I should ever speak of that
wonder glimpse again.'

I asked an obvious question.

'No,' he said. 'I don't remember that I ever attempted to find
my way back to the garden in those early years. This seems odd
to me now, but I think that very probably a closer watch was
kept on my movements after this misadventure to prevent my
going astray. No, it wasn't till you knew me that I tried for the
garden again. And I believe there was a period – incredible as
it seems now – when I forgot the garden altogether – when I
was about eight or nine it may have been. Do you remember
me as a kid at Saint Althelstan's?'

'Rather!'

'I didn't show any signs, did I, in those days of having a
secret dream?'

§ 2

He looked up with a sudden smile.

'Did you ever play North-West Passage[1] with me? . . . No, of
course you didn't come my way!'

'It was the sort of game,' he went on, 'that every imaginative
child plays all day. The idea was the discovery of a North-West
Passage to school. The way to school was plain enough; the
game consisted in finding some way that wasn't plain, starting
off ten minutes early in some almost hopeless direction, and
working my way round through unaccustomed streets to my
goal. And one day I got entangled among some rather low-class
streets on the other side of Campden Hill, and I began to think
that for once the game would be against me and that I should
get to school late. I tried rather desperately a street that seemed
a *cul-de-sac*, and found a passage at the end. I hurried through

that with renewed hope. "I shall do it yet," I said, and passed
a row of frowsy little shops that were inexplicably familiar to
me, and behold! there was my long white wall and the green
door that led to the enchanted garden!

'The thing whacked upon me suddenly. Then, after all, that
garden, that wonderful garden, wasn't a dream!'

He paused.

'I suppose my second experience with the green door marks
the world of difference there is between the busy life of a
schoolboy and the infinite leisure of a child. Anyhow, this
second time I didn't for a moment think of going in straight
away. You see—. For one thing, my mind was full of the idea
of getting to school in time – set on not breaking my record for
punctuality. I must surely have felt *some* little desire at least to
try the door – yes. I must have felt that. ... But I seem to
remember the attraction of the door mainly as another obstacle
to my overmastering determination to get to school. I was
immensely interested by this discovery I had made, of course –
I went on with my mind full of it – but I went on. It didn't
check me. I ran past, tugging out my watch, found I had ten
minutes still to spare, and then I was going downhill into
familiar surroundings. I got to school, breathless, it is true, and
wet with perspiration, but in time. I can remember hanging up
my coat and hat. ... Went right by it and left it behind me.
Odd, eh?'

He looked at me thoughtfully. 'Of course I didn't know
then that it wouldn't always be there. Schoolboys have limited
imaginations. I suppose I thought it was an awfully jolly thing
to have it there, to know my way back to it; but there was the
school tugging at me. I expect I was a good deal distraught and
inattentive that morning, recalling what I could of the beautiful
strange people I should presently see again. Oddly enough I
had no doubt in my mind that they would be glad to see me. ...
Yes, I must have thought of the garden that morning just as a
jolly sort of place to which one might resort in the interludes
of a strenuous scholastic career.

'I didn't go that day at all. The next day was a half-holiday,
and that may have weighed with me. Perhaps, too, my state of

inattention brought down impositions upon me, and docked the margin of time necessary for the *détour*. I don't know. What I do know is that in the meantime the enchanted garden was so much upon my mind that I could not keep it to myself.

'I told – what was his name? – a ferrety-looking youngster we used to call Squiff.'

'Young Hopkins,' said I.

'Hopkins it was. I did not like telling him. I had a feeling that in some way it was against the rules to tell him, but I did. He was walking part of the way home with me; he was talkative, and if we had not talked about the enchanted garden we should have talked of something else, and it was intolerable to me to think about any other subject. So I blabbed.

'Well, he told my secret. The next day in the play interval I found myself surrounded by half a dozen bigger boys, half teasing, and wholly curious to hear more of the enchanted garden. There was that big Fawcett – you remember him? – and Carnaby and Morley Reynolds. You weren't there by any chance? No, I think I should have remembered if you were. . . .

'A boy is a creature of odd feelings. I was, I really believe, in spite of my secret self-disgust, a little flattered to have the attention of these big fellows. I remember particularly a moment of pleasure caused by the praise of Crawshaw – you remember Crawshaw major,[2] the son of Crawshaw the composer? – who said it was the best lie he had ever heard. But at the same time there was a really painful undertow of shame at telling what I felt was indeed a sacred secret. That beast Fawcett made a joke about the girl in green—'

Wallace's voice sank with the keen memory of that shame. 'I pretended not to hear,' he said. 'Well, then Carnaby suddenly called me a young liar, and disputed with me when I said the thing was true. I said I knew where to find the green door, could lead them all there in ten minutes. Carnaby became outrageously virtuous, and said I'd have to – and bear out my words or suffer. Did you ever have Carnaby twist your arm? Then perhaps you'll understand how it went with me. I swore my story was true. There was nobody in the school then to save a chap from Carnaby, though Crawshaw put in a word or so.

Carnaby had got his game. I grew excited and red-eared, and a little frightened. I behaved altogether like a silly little chap, and the outcome of it all was that instead of starting alone for my enchanted garden, I led the way presently – cheeks flushed, ears hot, eyes smarting, and my soul one burning misery and shame – for a party of six mocking, curious, and threatening school-fellows.

'We never found the white wall and the green door. . . .'

'You mean—?'

'I mean I couldn't find it. I would have found it if I could.

'And afterwards when I could go alone I couldn't find it. I never found it. I seem now to have been always looking for it through my schoolboy days, but I never came upon it – never.'

'Did the fellows – make it disagreeable?'

'Beastly. . . . Carnaby held a council over me for wanton lying. I remember how I sneaked home and upstairs to hide the marks of my blubbering. But when I cried myself to sleep at last it wasn't for Carnaby, but for the garden, for the beautiful afternoon I had hoped for, for the sweet friendly women and the waiting playfellows, and the game I had hoped to learn again, that beautiful forgotten game. . . .

'I believed firmly that if I had not told— . . . I had bad times after that – crying at night and wool-gathering by day. For two terms I slacked and had bad reports. Do you remember? Of course you would! It was *you* – your beating me in mathematics that brought me back to the grind again.'

§ 3

For a time my friend stared silently into the red heart of the fire. Then he said: 'I never saw it again until I was seventeen.

'It leapt upon me for the third time – as I was driving to Paddington on my way to Oxford and a scholarship. I had just one momentary glimpse. I was leaning over the apron of my hansom smoking a cigarette, and no doubt thinking myself no end of a man of the world, and suddenly there was the door, the wall, the dear sense of unforgettable and still attainable things.

'We clattered by – I too taken by surprise to stop my cab until we were well past and round a corner. Then I had a queer moment, a double and divergent movement of my will: I tapped the little door in the roof of the cab, and brought my arm down to pull out my watch. "Yes, sir!" said the cabman, smartly. "Er – well – it's nothing," I cried. "*My* mistake! We haven't much time! Go on!" And he went on. . . .

'I got my scholarship. And the night after I was told of that I sat over my fire in my little upper room, my study, in my father's house, with his praise – his rare praise – and his sound counsels ringing in my ears, and I smoked my favourite pipe – the formidable bulldog of adolescence – and thought of that door in the long white wall. "If I had stopped," I thought, "I should have missed my scholarship, I should have missed Oxford – muddled all the fine career before me! I begin to see things better!" I fell musing deeply, but I did not doubt then this career of mine was a thing that merited sacrifice.

'Those dear friends and that clear atmosphere seemed very sweet to me, very fine but remote. My grip was fixing now upon the world. I saw another door opening – the door of my career.'

He stared again into the fire. Its red light picked out a stubborn strength in his face for just one flickering moment, and then it vanished again.

'Well,' he said and sighed, 'I have served that career. I have done – much work, much hard work. But I have dreamt of the enchanted garden a thousand dreams, and seen its door, or at least glimpsed its door, four times since then. Yes – four times. For a while this world was so bright and interesting, seemed so full of meaning and opportunity, that the half-effaced charm of the garden was by comparison gentle and remote. Who wants to pat panthers on the way to dinner with pretty women and distinguished men? I came down to London from Oxford, a man of bold promise that I have done something to redeem. Something – and yet there have been disappointments. . . .

'Twice I have been in love – I will not dwell on that – but once, as I went to someone who, I knew, doubted whether I dared to come, I took a short cut at a venture through an unfrequented road near Earl's Court, and so happened on a white wall and a familiar green door. "Odd!" said I to myself, "but I thought this place was on Campden Hill. It's the place I never could find somehow – like counting Stonehenge[3] – the place of that queer daydream of mine." And I went by it intent upon my purpose. It had no appeal to me that afternoon.

'I had just a moment's impulse to try the door, three steps aside were needed at the most – though I was sure enough in my heart that it would open to me – and then I thought that doing so might delay me on the way to that appointment in which my honour was involved. Afterwards I was sorry for my punctuality – I might at least have peeped in and waved a hand to those panthers, but I knew enough by this time not to seek again belatedly that which is not found by seeking. Yes, that time made me very sorry. . . .

'Years of hard work after that, and never a sight of the door. It's only recently it has come back to me. With it there has come a sense as though some thin tarnish had spread itself over my world. I began to think of it as a sorrowful and bitter thing that I should never see that door again. Perhaps I was suffering a little from overwork – perhaps it was what I've heard spoken of as the feeling of forty. I don't know. But certainly the keen brightness that makes effort easy has gone out of things recently, and that just at a time – with all these new political developments – when I ought to be working. Odd, isn't it? But I do begin to find life toilsome, its rewards, as I come near them, cheap. I began a little while ago to want the garden quite badly. Yes – and I've seen it three times.'

'The garden?'

'No – the door! And I haven't gone in!'

He leant over the table to me, with an enormous sorrow in his voice as he spoke. 'Thrice I have had my chance – *thrice*! If ever that door offers itself to me again, I swore, I will go in, out of this dust and heat, out of this dry glitter of vanity, out of these toilsome futilities. I will go and never return. This time I will stay. . . . I swore it, and when the time came – *I didn't go*.

'Three times in one year have I passed that door and failed to enter. Three times in the last year.

'The first time was on the night of the snatch division on the

Tenants' Redemption Bill,[4] on which the Government was saved by a majority of three. You remember? No one on our side – perhaps very few on the opposite side – expected the end that night. Then the debate collapsed like eggshells. I and Hotchkiss were dining with his cousin at Brentford; we were both unpaired, and we were called up by telephone, and set off at once in his cousin's motor. We got in barely in time, and on the way we passed my wall and door – livid in the moonlight, blotched with hot yellow as the glare of our lamps lit it, but unmistakable. "My God!" cried I. "What?" said Hotchkiss. "Nothing!" I answered, and the moment passed.

'"I've made a great sacrifice," I told the whip as I got in. "They all have," he said, and hurried by.

'I do not see how I could have done otherwise then. And the next occasion was as I rushed to my father's bedside to bid that stern old man farewell. Then, too, the claims of life were imperative. But the third time was different; it happened a week ago. It fills me with hot remorse to recall it. I was with Gurker and Ralphs[5] – it's no secret now, you know, that I've had my talk with Gurker. We had been dining at Frobisher's, and the talk had become intimate between us. The question of my place in the reconstructed Ministry lay always just over the boundary of the discussion. Yes – yes. That's all settled. It needn't be talked about yet, but there's no reason to keep a secret from you. ... Yes – thanks! thanks! But let me tell you my story.

'Then, on that night things were very much in the air. My position was a very delicate one. I was keenly anxious to get some definite word from Gurker, but was hampered by Ralphs' presence. I was using the best power of my brain to keep that light and careless talk not too obviously directed to the point that concerned me. I had to. Ralphs' behaviour since has more than justified my caution. ... Ralphs, I knew, would leave us beyond the Kensington High Street, and then I could surprise Gurker by a sudden frankness. One has sometimes to resort to these little devices. ... And then it was that in the margin of my field of vision I became aware once more of the white wall, the green door before us down the road.

'We passed it talking. I passed it. I can still see the shadow of Gurker's marked profile, his opera hat tilted forward over his prominent nose, the many folds of his neck wrap going before my shadow and Ralphs' as we sauntered past.

'I passed within twenty inches of the door. "If I say good-night to them, and go in," I asked myself, "what will happen?" And I was all a-tingle for that word with Gurker.

'I could not answer that question in the tangle of my other problems. "They will think me mad," I thought. "And suppose I vanish now! – Amazing disappearance of a prominent politician!" That weighed with me. A thousand inconceivably petty worldlinesses weighed with me in that crisis.'

Then he turned on me with a sorrowful smile, and, speaking slowly, 'Here I am!' he said.

'Here I am!' he repeated, 'and my chance has gone from me. Three times in one year the door has been offered me – the door that goes into peace, into delight, into a beauty beyond dreaming, a kindness no man on earth can know. And I have rejected it, Redmond, and it has gone—'

'How do you know?'

'I know. I know. I am left now to work it out, to stick to the tasks that held me so strongly when my moments came. You say I have success – this vulgar, tawdry, irksome, envied thing. I have it.' He had a walnut in his big hand. 'If that was my success,' he said, and crushed it, and held it out for me to see.

'Let me tell you something, Redmond. This loss is destroying me. For two months, for ten weeks nearly now, I have done no work at all, except the most necessary and urgent duties. My soul is full of inappeasable regrets. At nights – when it is less likely I shall be recognized – I go out. I wander. Yes. I wonder what people would think of that if they knew. A Cabinet Minister, the responsible head of that most vital of all departments, wandering alone – grieving – sometimes near audibly lamenting – for a door, for a garden!'

§ 4

I can see now his rather pallid face, and the unfamiliar sombre fire that had come into his eyes. I see him very vividly tonight.

I sit recalling his words, his tones, and last evening's *Westminster Gazette*[6] still lies on my sofa, containing the notice of his death. At lunch today the club was busy with his death. We talked of nothing else.

They found his body very early yesterday morning in a deep excavation near East Kensington Station. It is one of two shafts that have been made in connection with an extension of the railway southward. It is protected from the intrusion of the public by a hoarding upon the high road, in which a small doorway has been cut for the convenience of some of the workmen who live in that direction. The doorway was left unfastened through a misunderstanding between two gangers, and through it he made his way.

My mind is darkened with questions and riddles.

It would seem he walked all the way from the House that night – he has frequently walked home during the past Session – and so it is I figure his dark form coming along the late and empty streets, wrapped up, intent. And then did the pale electric lights near the station cheat the rough planking into a semblance of white? Did that fatal unfastened door awaken some memory?

Was there, after all, ever any green door in the wall at all?

I do not know. I have told his story as he told it to me. There are times when I believe that Wallace was no more than the victim of the coincidence between a rare but not unprecedented type of hallucination and a careless trap, but that indeed is not my profoundest belief. You may think me superstitious, if you will, and foolish; but, indeed, I am more than half convinced that he had, in truth, an abnormal gift, and a sense, something – I know not what – that in the guise of wall and door offered him an outlet, a secret and peculiar passage of escape into another and altogether more beautiful world. At any rate, you will say, it betrayed him in the end. But did it betray him? There you touch the inmost mystery of these dreamers, these men of vision and the imagination. We see our world fair and common, the hoarding and the pit. By our daylight standard he walked out of security into darkness, danger, and death.

But did he see like that?

THE WILD ASSES OF
THE DEVIL

§ 1

There was once an Author who pursued fame and prosperity
in a pleasant villa on the south coast of England. He wrote
stories of an acceptable nature and rejoiced in a growing public
esteem, carefully offending no one and seeking only to please.
He had married under circumstances of qualified and tolerable
romance a lady who wrote occasional but otherwise regular
verse, he was the father of a little daughter, whose reported
sayings added much to his popularity, and some of the very
best people in the land asked him to dinner. He was a deputy-
lieutenant and a friend of the Prime Minister, a literary knight-
hood was no remote possibility for him, and even the Nobel
prize, given a sufficient longevity, was not altogether beyond
his hopes. And this amount of prosperity had not betrayed him
into any un-English pride. He remembered that manliness and
simplicity which are expected from authors. He smoked pipes
and not the excellent cigars he could have afforded. He kept
his hair cut and never posed. He did not hold himself aloof from
people of the inferior and less successful classes. He habitually
travelled third class in order to study the characters he put into
his delightful novels; he went for long walks and sat in inns,
accosting people; he drew out his gardener. And though he
worked steadily, he did not give up the care of his body, which
threatened a certain plumpness and what is more to the point,
a localized plumpness, not generally spread over the system but
exaggerating the anterior equator.[1] This expansion was his only
care. He thought about fitness and played tennis, and every
day, wet or fine, he went for at least an hour's walk. . . .

Yet this man, so representative of Edwardian literature – for it is in the reign of good King Edward[2] the story begins – in spite of his enviable achievements and prospects, was doomed to the most exhausting and dubious adventures before his life came to its unhonoured end. . . .

Because I have not told you everything about him. Sometimes – in the morning sometimes – he would be irritable and have quarrels with his shaving things, and there were extraordinary moods when it would seem to him that living quite beautifully in a pleasant villa and being well-off and famous, and writing books that were always good-humoured and grammatical and a little distinguished in an inoffensive way, was about as boring and intolerable a life as any creature with a soul to be damned could possibly pursue. Which shows only that God in putting him together had not forgotten that viscus the liver which is usual on such occasions. . . .

The winter at the seaside is less agreeable and more bracing than the summer, and there were days when this Author had almost to force himself through the wholesome, necessary routines of his life, when the south-west wind savaged his villa and roared in the chimneys and slapped its windows with gustful of rain and promised to wet that Author thoroughly and exasperatingly down his neck and round his wrists and ankles directly he put his nose outside his door. And the grey waves he saw from his window came rolling inshore under the hurrying grey rain-bursts, line after line, to smash along the undercliff into vast, feathering fountains of foam and sud and send a salt-tasting spin-drift into his eyes. But manfully he would put on his puttees and his waterproof cape and his biggest brierwood pipe, and out he would go into the whurry-balloo of it all, knowing that so he would be all the brighter for his nice story-writing after tea.

On such a day he went out. He went out very resolutely along the seaside gardens of gravel and tamarisk and privet, resolved to oblige himself to go right past the harbour and up to the top of the east cliff before ever he turned his face back to the comforts of fire and wife and tea and buttered toast. . . .

And somewhere, perhaps half a mile away from home, he became aware of a queer character trying to keep abreast of him.

His impression was of a very miserable black man in the greasy, blue-black garments of a stoker, a lascar probably from a steamship in the harbour, and going with a sort of lame hobble.

As he passed this individual the Author had a transitory thought of how much Authors don't know in the world, how much, for instance, this shivering, cringing body might be hiding within itself, of inestimable value as 'local colour' if only one could get hold of it for 'putting into' one's large acceptable novels. Why doesn't one sometimes tap these sources? Kipling,[3] for example, used to do so, with most successful results. . . . And then the Author became aware that this enigma was hurrying to overtake him. He slackened his pace. . . .

The creature wasn't asking for a light; it was begging for a box of matches. And, what was odd, in quite good English.

The Author surveyed the beggar and slapped his pockets. Never had he seen so miserable a face. It was by no means a prepossessing face, with its aquiline nose, its sloping brows, its dark, deep, bloodshot eyes much too close together, its V-shaped, dishonest mouth and drenched chin-tuft. And yet it was attractively animal and pitiful. The idea flashed suddenly into the Author's head: 'Why not, instead of going on, thinking emptily, through this beastly weather – why not take this man back home now, to the warm, dry study, and give him a hot drink and something to smoke, and *draw him out*?'

Get something technical and first-hand that would rather score off Kipling.

'Its damnably cold!' he shouted, in a sort of hearty, forecastle voice.

'It's worse than that,' said the strange stoker.

'It's a hell of a day!' said the Author, more forcible than ever.

'Don't remind me of hell,' said the stoker, in a voice of inappeasable regret.

The Author slapped his pockets again. 'You've got an infernal cold. Look here, my man – confound it! would you like a hot grog? ...'

§ 2

The scene shifts to the Author's study – a blazing coal fire, the stoker sitting dripping and steaming before it, with his feet inside the fender, while the Author fusses about the room, directing the preparation of hot drinks. The Author is acutely aware not only of the stoker but of himself. The stoker has probably never been in the home of an Author before; he is probably awe-stricken at the array of books, at the comfort, convenience, and efficiency of the home, at the pleasant personality entertaining him. ... Meanwhile the Author does not forget that the stoker is material, is 'copy', is being watched, *observed*. So he poses and watches, until presently he forgets to pose in his astonishment at the thing he is observing. Because this stoker is rummier than a stoker ought to be—

He does not simply accept a hot drink; he informs his host just how hot the drink must be to satisfy him.

'Isn't there something you could put in it – something called red pepper? I've tasted that once or twice. It's good. If you could put in a bit of red pepper.'

'If you can stand that sort of thing?'

'And if there isn't much water, can't you set light to the stuff? Or let me drink it boiling, out of a pannikin or something? Pepper and all.'

Wonderful fellows, these stokers! The Author went to the bell[4] and asked for red pepper.

And then as he came back to the fire he saw something that he instantly dismissed as an optical illusion, as a mirage effect of the clouds of steam his guest was disengaging. The stoker was sitting, all crouched up, as close over the fire as he could contrive; and he was holding his black hands, not to the fire but *in* the fire, holding them pressed flat against two red, glowing masses of coal. ... He glanced over his shoulder at the Author with a guilty start, and then instantly the Author perceived that the hands were five or six inches away from the coal.

Then came smoking. The Author produced one of his big cigars – for although a conscientious pipe-smoker himself he gave people cigars; and then, again struck by something odd, he went off into a corner of the room where a little oval mirror gave him a means of watching the stoker undetected. And this is what he saw.

He saw the stoker, after a furtive glance at him, deliberately turn the cigar round, place the lighted end in his mouth, inhale strongly, and blow a torrent of sparks and smoke out of his nose. His firelit face as he did this expressed a diabolical relief. Then very hastily he reversed the cigar again, and turned round to look at the Author. The Author turned slowly towards him.

'You like that cigar?' he asked, after one of those mutual pauses that break down a pretence.

'It's admirable.'

'Why do you smoke it the other way round?'

The stoker perceived he was caught. 'It's a stokehole trick,'[5] he said. 'Do you mind if I do it? I didn't think you saw.'

'Pray smoke just as you like,' said the Author, and advanced to watch the operation.

It was exactly like the fire-eater at a village fair. The man stuck the burning cigar into his mouth and blew sparks out of his nostrils. 'Ah!' he said, with a note of genuine satisfaction. And then, with the cigar still burning in the corner of his mouth, he turned to the fire and *began to rearrange the burning coals with his hands* so as to pile up a great glowing mass. He picked up flaming and white-hot lumps as one might pick up lumps of sugar. The Author watched him, dumbfounded.

'I say!' he cried. 'You stokers get a bit tough.'

The stoker dropped the glowing piece of coal in his hand. 'I forgot,' he said, and sat back a little.

'Isn't that a bit – *extra*?' asked the Author, regarding him. 'Isn't that some sort of trick?'

'We get so tough down there,' said the stoker, and paused discreetly as the servant came in with the red pepper.

'Now you can drink,' said the Author, and set himself to mix a drink of a pungency that he would have considered murderous ten minutes before. When he had done the stoker reached over and added more red pepper.

'I don't quite see how it is your hand doesn't burn,' said the Author as the stoker drank. The stoker shook his head over the uptilted glass.

'Incombustible,' he said, putting it down. 'Could I have just a tiny drop more? Just brandy and pepper, if you *don't* mind. Set alight. I don't care for water except when it's super-heated steam.'

And as the Author poured out another stiff glass of this incandescent brew, the stoker put up his hand and scratched the matted black hair over his temple. Then instantly he desisted and sat looking wickedly at the Author, while the Author stared at him aghast. For at the corner of his square, high, narrow forehead, revealed for an instant by the thrusting back of the hair, a curious stumpy excrescence had been visible; and the top of his ear – he had a pointed top to his ear![6]

'A-a-a-a-h!' said the Author, with dilated eyes.

'A-a-a-a-h!' said the stoker, in hopeless distress.

'But you aren't—!'

'I know – I know I'm not. I know. . . . I'm a devil. A poor, lost, homeless devil.'

And suddenly, with a gesture of indescribable despair, the apparent stoker buried his face in his hands and burst into tears.

'Only man who's ever been decently kind to me,' he sobbed. 'And now – you'll chuck me out again into the beastly wet and cold. . . . Beautiful fire. . . . Nice drink. . . . Almost home-like. . . . Just to torment me. . . . Boo-ooh!'

And let it be recorded to the credit of our little Author, that he did overcome his momentary horror, that he did go quickly round the table, and that he patted that dirty stoker's shoulder.

'There!' he said. 'There! Don't mind my rudeness. Have another nice drink. Have a hell of a drink. I won't turn you out if you're unhappy – on a day like this. Have just a mouthful of pepper, man, and pull yourself together.'

And suddenly the poor devil caught hold of his arm. 'Nobody good to me,' he sobbed. 'Nobody good to me.' And his tears ran down over the Author's plump little hand – scalding tears.

§ 3

All really wonderful things happen rather suddenly and without any great emphasis upon their wonderfulness, and this was no exception to the general rule. This Author went on comforting his devil as though this was nothing more than a chance encounter with an unhappy child, and the devil let his grief and discomfort have vent in a manner that seemed at the time as natural as anything could be. He was clearly a devil of feeble character and uncertain purpose, much broken down by harshness and cruelty, and it throws a curious light upon the general state of misconception with regard to matters diabolical that it came as a quite pitiful discovery to our Author that a devil could be unhappy and heartbroken. For a long time his most earnest and persistent questioning could gather nothing except that his guest was an exile from a land of great warmth and considerable entertainment, and it was only after considerable further applications of brandy and pepper that the sobbing confidences of the poor creature grew into the form of a coherent and understandable narrative.

And then it became apparent that this person was one of the very lowest types of infernal denizen, and that his role in the dark realms of Dis had been that of watcher and minder of a herd of sinister beings hitherto unknown to our Author, the Devil's Wild Asses, which pastured in a stretch of meadows near the Styx. They were, he gathered, unruly, dangerous, and enterprising beasts, amenable only to a certain formula of expletives, which instantly reduced them to obedience. These expletives the stoker devil would not repeat; to do so except when actually addressing one of the Wild Asses would, he explained, involve torments of the most terrible description. The bare thought of them gave him a shivering fit. But he gave the Author to understand that to crack these curses as one drove the Wild Asses to and from their grazing on the Elysian fields was a by no means disagreeable amusement. The ass-herds would try who could crack the loudest until the welkin rang.

And speaking of these things, the poor creature gave a picture of diabolical life that impressed the Author as by no means unpleasant for anyone with a suitable constitution. It was like the Idylls of Theocritus[7] done in fire; the devils drove their charges along burning lanes and sat gossiping in hedges of flames, rejoicing in the warm, dry breezes (which it seems are rendered peculiarly bracing by the faint flavour of brimstone in the air), and watching the harpies and furies and witches circling in the perpetual afterglow of that inferior sky. And ever and again there would be holidays, and one would take one's lunch and wander over the sulphur craters picking flowers of sulphur[8] or fishing for the souls of usurers and publishers and house-agents and land-agents in the lakes of boiling pitch. It was good sport, for the usurers and publishers and house-agents and land-agents were always eager to be caught; they crowded round the hooks and fought violently for the bait, and protested vehemently and entertainingly against the Rules and Regulations that compelled their instant return to the lake of fire.

And sometimes when he was on holiday this particular devil would go through the saltpetre dunes, where the witches-brooms grow and the blasted heath is in flower, to the landing-place of the ferry whence the Great Road runs through the shops and banks of the Via Dolorosa[9] to the New Judgement Hall, and watch the crowds of damned arriving by the steam ferry-boats of the Consolidated Charon Company. This steam-boat-gazing seems about as popular down there as it is at Folkestone. Almost every day notable people arrive, and, as the devils are very well informed about terrestrial affairs – for of course all the earthly newspapers go straight to hell – whatever else could one expect? – they get ovations of an almost under-graduate intensity. At times you can hear their cheering or booing, as the case may be, right away on the pastures where the Wild Asses feed. And that had been this particular devil's undoing.

He had always been interested in the career of the Rt Hon. W. E. Gladstone. . . .[10]

He was minding the Wild Asses. He knew the risks. He knew the penalties. But when he heard the vast uproar, when he heard the eager voices in the lane of fire saying, 'It's Gladstone at last!' when he saw how quietly and unsuspiciously the Wild Asses cropped their pasture, the temptation was too much. He slipped away. He saw the great Englishman landed after a slight struggle. He joined in the outcry of 'Speech! Speech!' He heard the first delicious promise of a Home Rule movement which should break the last feeble links of Celestial Control. . . .

And meanwhile the Wild Asses escaped – according to the rules and the prophecies. . . .

§ 4

The little Author sat and listened to this tale of a wonder that never for a moment struck him as incredible. And outside his rain-lashed window the strung-out fishing smacks pitched and rolled on their way home to Folkestone harbour. . . .

The Wild Asses escaped.

They got away to the world. And his superior officers took

the poor herdsman and tried him and bullied him and passed this judgement upon him: that he must go to the earth and find the Wild Asses, and say to them that certain string of oaths that otherwise must never be repeated, and so control them and bring them back to hell. That – or else one pinch of salt on their tails. It did not matter which. One by one he must bring them back, driving them by spell and curse to the cattle-boat of the ferry. And until he had caught and brought them all back he might never return again to the warmth and comfort of his accustomed life. That was his sentence and punishment. And they put him into a shrapnel shell and fired him out among the stars, and when he had a little recovered he pulled himself together and made his way to the world.

But he never found his Wild Asses and after a little time he gave up trying.

He gave up trying because the Wild Asses, once they had got out of control, developed the most amazing gifts. They could, for instance, disguise themselves with any sort of human shape, and the only way in which they differed then from a normal human being was – according to the printed paper of instructions that had been given to their custodian when he was fired out – that 'their general conduct remains that of a Wild Ass of the Devil'.

'And what interpretation can we put upon *that*?' he asked the listening Author.

And there was one night in the year – Walpurgis Night, when the Wild Asses became visibly great black wild asses and kicked up their hind legs and brayed. They had to. 'But then, of course,' said the devil, 'they would take care to shut themselves up somewhere when they felt that coming on.'

Like most weak characters, the stoker devil was intensely egotistical. He was anxious to dwell upon his own miseries and discomforts and difficulties and the general injustice of his treatment, and he was careless and casually indicative about the peculiarities of the Wild Asses, the matter which most excited and interested the Author. He bored on with his doleful story, and the Author had to interrupt with questions again and again in order to get any clear idea of the situation.

The devil's main excuse for his nervelessness was his pro-found ignorance of human nature. 'So far as I can see,' he said, 'they might all be Wild Asses. I tried it once—'

'Tried what?'

'The formula. You know.'

'Yes?'

'On a man named Sir Edward Carson.'[11]

'Well?'

'*Ugh!*' said the devil.

'Punishment?'

'Don't speak of it. He was just a professional lawyer-politician who had lost his sense of values. . . . How was *I* to know? . . . But our people certainly know how to hurt. . . .'

After that it would seem this poor devil desisted absolutely from any attempt to recover his lost charges. He just tried to live for the moment and make his earthly existence as tolerable as possible. It was clear he hated the world. He found it cold, wet, draughty. . . . 'I can't understand why everybody insists upon living outside of it,' he said. 'If you went inside—'[12]

He sought warmth and dryness. For a time he found a kind of contentment in charge of the upcast furnace of a mine, and then he was superseded by an electric fan. While in this position he read a vivid account of the intense heat in the Red Sea, and he was struck by the idea that if he could get a job as stoker upon an Indian liner he might snatch some days of real happi-ness during that portion of the voyage. For some time his natural ineptitude prevented his realizing this project, but at last, after some bitter experiences of homelessness during a London December, he had been able to ship on an Indiaward boat – only to get stranded in Folkestone in consequence of a propeller breakdown. And so here he was!

He paused.

'But about these Wild Asses?' said the Author.

The mournful, dark eyes looked at him hopelessly.

'Mightn't they do a lot of mischief?' asked the Author.

'They'll do no end of mischief,' said the despondent devil.

'Ultimately you'll catch it for that?'

'*Ugh!*' said the stoker, trying not to think of it.

§ 5

Now the spirit of romantic adventure slumbers in the most unexpected places, and I have already told you of our plump Author's discontents. He had been like a smouldering bomb for some years. Now, he burst out. He suddenly became excited, energetic, stimulating, uplifting.

The Author uplifts the devil.

He stood over the drooping devil.

'But my dear chap!' he said. 'You must pull yourself together. You must do better than this. These confounded brutes may be doing all sorts of mischief. While you – shirk. . . .'

And so on. Real ginger.

'If I had someone to go with me. Someone who knew his way about.'

The Author took whisky in the excitement of the moment. He began to move very rapidly about his room and make short, sharp gestures. You know how this sort of emotion wells up at times. 'We must work from some central place,' said the Author. 'To begin with, London perhaps.'

It was not two hours later that they started, this Author and this devil he had taken to himself, upon a mission. They went out in overcoats and warm underclothing – the Author gave the devil a thorough outfit, a double lot of Jaeger's[13] extra thick – and they were resolved to find the Wild Asses of the Devil and send them back to hell, or at least the Author was, in the

shortest possible time. In the picture you will see him with a
field-glass slung under his arm, the better to watch suspected
cases; in his pocket, wrapped in oiled paper, is a lot of salt to
use if by chance he finds a Wild Ass when the devil and his
string of oaths is not at hand. So he started. And when he had
caught and done for the Wild Asses, then the Author supposed
that he would come back to his nice little villa and his nice little
wife, and to his little daughter who said the amusing things,
and to his popularity, his large gilt-edged popularity, and –
except for an added prestige – be just exactly the man he had
always been. Little knowing that whosoever takes unto himself
a devil and goes out upon a quest, goes out upon a quest from
which there is no returning—

Nevermore.

Precipitate start of the Wild Ass hunters.

Appendix

H. G. WELLS'S INTRODUCTION TO
THE COUNTRY OF THE BLIND AND
OTHER STORIES (1911)

The enterprise of Messrs T. Nelson & Sons and the friendly accommo-
dation of Messrs Macmillan render possible this collection in one
cover of all the short stories by me that I care for anyone to read again.
Except for the two series of linked incidents[1] that make up the bulk
of the book called *Tales of Space and Time*, no short story of mine
of the slightest merit is excluded from this volume. Many of very
questionable merit find a place; it is an inclusive and not an exclusive
gathering. And the task of selection and revision brings home to me
with something of the effect of discovery that I was once an industrious
writer of short stories, and that I am no longer anything of the kind.
I have not written one now for quite a long time, and in the past five
or six years I have made scarcely one a year. The bulk of the fifty or
sixty tales from which this present three-and-thirty have been chosen
dates from the last century. This edition is more definitive than I
supposed when first I arranged for it. In the presence of so conclusive
an ebb and cessation an almost obituary manner seems justifiable.

I find it a little difficult to disentangle the causes that have restricted
the flow of these inventions. It has happened, I remark, to others as
well as to myself, and in spite of the kindliest encouragement to
continue from editors and readers. There was a time when life bubbled
with short stories; they were always coming to the surface of my mind,
and it is no deliberate change of will that has thus restricted my
production. It is rather, I think, a diversion of attention to more
sustained and more exacting forms. It was my friend Mr C. L. Hind[2]
who set that spring going. He urged me to write short stories for the
Pall Mall Budget, and persuaded me by his simple and buoyant

conviction that I could do what he desired. There existed at the time
only the little sketch, 'The Jilting of Jane',[3] included in this volume –
at least, that is the only tolerable fragment of fiction I find surviving
from my pre-Lewis-Hind period. But I set myself, so encouraged, to
the experiment of inventing moving and interesting things that could
be given vividly in the little space of eight or ten such pages as this,
and for a time I found it a very entertaining pursuit indeed. Mr Hind's
indicating finger had shown me an amusing possibility of the mind. I
found that, taking almost anything as a starting-point and letting my
thoughts play about it, there would presently come out of the darkness,
in a manner quite inexplicable, some absurd or vivid little incident
more or less relevant to that initial nucleus. Little men in canoes upon
sunlit oceans would come floating out of nothingness, incubating the
eggs of prehistoric monsters unawares; violent conflicts would break
out amidst the flower-beds of suburban gardens; I would discover I
was peering into remote and mysterious worlds ruled by an order
logical indeed but other than our common sanity.

The 'nineties was a good and stimulating period for a short-story
writer. Mr Kipling[4] had made his astonishing advent with a series of
little blue-grey books, whose covers opened like window-shutters to
reveal the dusty sun-glare and blazing colours of the East; Mr Barrie
had demonstrated what could be done in a little space through the
panes of his *Window in Thrums*.[5] The *National Observer* was at the
climax of its career of heroic insistence upon lyrical brevity and a vivid
finish, and Mr Frank Harris[6] was not only printing good short stories
by other people, but writing still better ones himself in the dignified
pages of the *Fortnightly Review*. *Longman's Magazine*, too, represented a *clientèle* of appreciative short-story readers that is now scattered. Then came the generous opportunities of the *Yellow Book*, and
the *National Observer* died only to give birth to the *New Review*.[7]
No short story of the slightest distinction went for long unrecognized.
The sixpenny popular magazines had still to deaden down the conception of what a short story might be to the imaginative limitation of
the common reader – and a maximum length of six thousand words.
Short stories broke out everywhere. Kipling was writing short stories;
Barrie, Stevenson, Frank Harris; Max Beerbohm wrote at least one
perfect one, 'The Happy Hypocrite'; Henry James[8] pursued his wonderful and inimitable bent; and among other names that occur to me,
like a mixed handful of jewels drawn from a bag, are [here Wells lists
a further nineteen names]. I dare say I could recall as many more
names with a little effort. I may be succumbing to the infirmities of
middle age, but I do not think the present decade can produce any

parallel to this list, or what is more remarkable, that the later achievements in this field of any of the survivors from that time, with the sole exception of Joseph Conrad,[9] can compare with the work they did before 1900. It seems to me this outburst of short stories came not only as a phase in literary development, but also as a phase in the development of the individual writers concerned.

It is now quite unusual to see any adequate criticism of short stories in English. I do not know how far the decline in short-story writing may not be due to that. Every sort of artist demands human responses, and few men can contrive to write merely for a publisher's cheque and silence, however reassuring that cheque may be. A mad millionaire who commissioned masterpieces to burn would find it impossible to buy them. Scarcely any artist will hesitate in the choice between money and attention; and it was primarily for that last and better sort of pay that the short stories of the 'nineties were written. People talked about them tremendously, compared them, and ranked them. That was the thing that mattered.

It was not, of course, all good talk, and we suffered then, as now, from the *a priori* critic. Just as nowadays he goes about declaring that the work of such-and-such a dramatist is all very amusing and delightful, but 'it isn't a Play', so we had a great deal of talk about *the* short story, and found ourselves measured by all kinds of arbitrary standards. There was a tendency to treat the short story as though it was as definable a form as the sonnet, instead of being just exactly what anyone of courage and imagination can get told in twenty minutes' reading or so. It was either Mr Edward Garnett or Mr George Moore[10] in a violently anti-Kipling mood who invented the distinction between the short story and the anecdote. The short story was Maupassant;[11] the anecdote was damnable. It was a quite infernal comment in its way, because it permitted no defence. Fools caught it up and used it freely. Nothing is so destructive in a field of artistic effort as a stock term of abuse. Anyone could say of any short story, 'A mere anecdote', just as anyone can say 'Incoherent!' of any novel or of any sonata that isn't studiously monotonous. The recession of enthusiasm for this compact, amusing form is closely associated in my mind with that discouraging imputation. One felt hopelessly open to a paralysing and unanswerable charge, and one's ease and happiness in the garden of one's fancies was more and more marred by the dread of it. It crept into one's mind, a distress as vague and inexpugnable as a sea fog on a spring morning, and presently one shivered and wanted to go indoors. ... It is the absurd fate of the imaginative writer that he should be thus sensitive to atmospheric conditions.

But after one has died as a maker one may still live as a critic, and I will confess I am all for laxness and variety in this as in every field of art. Insistence upon rigid forms and austere unities seems to me the instinctive reaction of the sterile against the fecund. It is the tired man with a headache who values a work of art for what it does not contain. I suppose it is the lot of every critic nowadays to suffer from indigestion and a fatigued appreciation, and to develop a self-protective tendency towards rules that will reject, as it were, automatically the more abundant and irregular forms. But this world is not for the weary, and in the long-run it is the new and variant that matter. I refuse altogether to recognize any hard and fast type for the Short Story, any more than I admit any limitation upon the liberties of the Small Picture. The short story is a fiction that may be read in something under an hour, and so that it is moving and delightful, it does not matter whether it is as 'trivial' as a Japanese print of insects seen closely between grass stems, or as spacious as the prospect of the plain of Italy from Monte Mottarone.[12] It does not matter whether it is human or inhuman, or whether it leaves you thinking deeply or radiantly but superficially pleased. Some things are more easily done as short stories than others and more abundantly done, but one of the many pleasures of short-story writing is to achieve the impossible.

At any rate, that is the present writer's conception of the art of the short story, as the jolly art of making something very bright and moving; it may be horrible or pathetic or funny or beautiful or profoundly illuminating, having only this essential, that it should take from fifteen to fifty minutes to read aloud. All the rest is just whatever invention and imagination and the mood can give – a vision of buttered slides on a busy day or of unprecedented worlds. In that spirit of miscellaneous expectation these stories should be received. Each is intended to be a thing by itself; and if it is not too ungrateful to kindly and enterprising publishers, I would confess I would much prefer to see each printed expensively alone, and left in a little brown-paper cover to lie about a room against the needs of a quite casual curiosity. And I would rather this volume were found in the bedrooms of convalescents and in dentists' parlours and railway trains than in gentlemen's studies. I would rather have it dipped in and dipped in again than read severely through. Essentially it is a miscellany of inventions, many of which were very pleasant to write; and its end is more than attained if some of them are refreshing and agreeable to read. I have now re-read them all, and I am glad to think I wrote them. I like them, but I cannot tell how much the associations of old happinesses gives them a flavour for me. I make no claims for them and no apology; they will be read as long as people read them. Things written either live or die; unless it be for a place of judgement upon Academic impostors, there is no apologetic intermediate state.

I may add that I have tried to set a date to most of these stories, but that they are not arranged in strictly chronological order.[13]

NOTES

1. 'A Story of the Stone Age' and 'A Story of the Days to Come' (not included in this volume).

2. Journalist and author C. Lewis Hind (1862–1927), editor of the *Pall Mall Budget* (1893–5) and the *Academy* (1896–1903). For the *Pall Mall Budget*, see also note 8 to 'The Remarkable Case of Davidson's Eyes'.

3. Published in the *Pall Mall Budget* on 12 July 1894 (not included in this volume).

4. See note 9 to 'The Moth', and note 3 to 'The Wild Asses of the Devil'.

5. *A Window in Thrums* (1889), an early 'kailyard' novel by Sir James Matthew Barrie (1860–1937).

6. Frank Harris (1856–1931) edited the *Fortnightly Review* (1886–94) and the *Saturday Review* (1894–8), for which Wells became chief fiction reviewer.

7. The *Yellow Book* (published 1894–7) quickly became notorious as the chief organ of the 'Decadent' school of writers and artists. 'A Slip under the Microscope' was Wells's sole contribution to the journal. Both the *National Observer* and the *New Review* were edited by William Ernest Henley (1849–1903). Wells published an early version of *The Time Machine* as a serial in the *National Observer*. When the paper folded in 1894, Henley encouraged him to rewrite it at greater length, and serialized it in the *New Review*.

8. For Robert Louis Stevenson, see, note 8 to 'The Moth'. Sir Max Beerbohm (1872–1956), essayist, caricaturist and author of the novel *Zuleika Dobson* (1911). Henry James, American novelist (1843–1916) who frequently met and corresponded with Wells between 1898 and their quarrel in 1915. He wrote nearly 100 short stories.

9. Joseph Conrad (1857–1924) began his career as a novelist with *Almayer's Folly* (1895), a book which Wells reviewed favourably

in the *Saturday Review*. Conrad's short stories include *Tales of Unrest* (1898) and the novella 'Heart of Darkness' (1899).

10. For Garnett and Moore, see note 3 to Introduction. Wells caricatured Moore, together with Henry James, in *Boon* (1915).

11. French novelist Guy de Maupassant (1850–93), one of the pioneers of the modern short story.

12. A mountain close to Lake Maggiore in northern Italy.

13. Here Wells named five stories which were reprinted for the first time in *The Country of the Blind and Other Stories*.

Wells's London and Surrounding Region

Wells set many of his stories in the London he studied and worked in after he entered the Normal School of Science at South Kensington in 1884, and in the surrounding counties he lived in before and after his time in London.

These regions include the area around the Normal School (later the Royal College) of Science, and the fashionable residential, commercial and entertainment area of London's West End, roughly between The Strand, Oxford Street, and Regent Street and Mayfair, Westminster, and Hyde Park. Bordering this was Regent's Park and the residential areas of Camden Town, Holloway and Highgate to the north, Chelsea to the west, and Lambeth and Waterloo to the south.

Bordering Wells's London are the suburbs which shade into what was then a fast-growing network of small towns in the surrounding 'Home Counties' of Kent, Surrey and Sussex, which the railway had made desirable homes for London office-workers. In some stories ('The Argonauts of the Air') we can see this network almost as it grows, extending into the future. Other stories ('The Plattner Story') show the countryside of this area, especially the North and South Downs, sometimes under assumed names. 'A Story of the Stone Age' shows this region before any names were applied to it.

The following gazetteer gives locations mentioned in the stories. Where they have a particular significance to the story, they are included in the Notes or Glossary.

Bloomsbury: Area in central London centred on Bloomsbury Square, surrounding the British Museum.

Camden Town: District of London two or three miles north of the river, just beyond King's Cross station and bordering Regent's Park.

Campden Hill: Between Kensington High Street and Notting Hill Gate, an exclusive residential area during the mid nineteenth century.

Chelsea: Now part of the Borough of Kensington and Chelsea but then a borough in its own right, Chelsea is on the north bank of the Thames to the west of Westminster. During Victorian times it became something of a Bohemian area of artists and students.

Chiltern Hills: Range of hills running north-west of London from Reading to Hitchin in Hertfordshire.

Chislehurst: Near Bromley in Kent, where Wells was born. The nearby caves have a reputation for hauntings.

Ealing: West London suburb.

Gower Street: Parallel with Tottenham Court Road; University College Hospital was established there in 1834 as the North London Hospital.

Great Portland Street: Parallel to Portland Place, running north from Oxford Street to Marylebone Road.

Hampstead village: Now a fashionable area of North London, overlooked by Hampstead Heath.

Highgate: Highgate Cemetery in North London, in the southern part of the residential district of Highgate itself.

Highgate Archway: Bridge, originally constructed 1812, in North London carrying Hornsey Lane over what is now Archway Road, which shortly afterwards becomes Holloway Road.

Holloway: District of North London, south of Highgate.

Kensington: West and south of Hyde Park, noted for Kensington Gardens (immediately west of Hyde Park) and many of London's most important museums.

Kew: District of London south of the River Thames, the location of the Royal Botanic Gardens.

Landport: Part of Portsea island, itself part of the city of Portsmouth in Hampshire.

Langham Place: Short continuation north of Regent Street leading to Portland Place.

North Downs: Chalk ridge which runs south of London through Surrey and Kent to meet the sea at the 'White Cliffs' of Dover.

Piccadilly: Fashionable street running between Knightsbridge and Shaftesbury Avenue through the district of Mayfair. Piccadilly Circus, linking Regent Street, Piccadilly and Shaftesbury Avenue is renowned as the heart of London's West End.

Pool of London: Dockland area of the River Thames reaching upstream to London Bridge: the heart of London's maritime trading.

Primrose Hill: North of Regent's Park.

Regent's Park: Between Marylebone in the south and Camden Town in the north, it was opened to the public during the nineteenth century after attempts to make it an exclusive parkland for the wealthy, with terraces designed by John Nash (1752–1835). It is the site of the Zoological Gardens, opened in 1828 and made open to the public in 1848. It is linked southwards to Piccadilly Circus by Portland Place and Regent Street.

Rugby: Town in Warwickshire on the main railway line to London from the Midlands and the North-west.

St Catherine's Hospital: North of Hyde Park and Kensington Gardens in West London.

St Martin's Church: St Martin-in-the-Fields, at the north-east corner of Trafalgar Square.

Sark: One of the Channel Islands, off the coast of northern France.

Seven Dials: Junction of seven streets, and its surrounding area, in London, between Shaftesbury Avenue and Covent Garden.

Shadwell: On the north bank of the Thames, between Wapping and Stepney, a dockland region with a bad reputation and a transient population of foreign sailors.

Sidmouth: Small port in the county of Devon on the south coast of England.

South Downs: Line of chalk ridges running from Hampshire through Sussex.

Southport: Coastal town north of Liverpool; then in Lancashire, now part of the metropolitan county of Merseyside.

Tottenham Court Road: Runs roughly north–south from Euston Road to Oxford Street, with Bloomsbury to the east.

Wealden mountains: Line of ridges and hills running through Surrey and Kent.

West Kensington: Residential area of London, bordering the Borough of Kensington and Chelsea and now part of the borough of Hammersmith and Fulham.

Andy Sawyer

Glossary

Where cited *OED* is the *Oxford English Dictionary* (second edition).

A. B.: Able Seaman.

affection: In the sense of something influencing or affecting the eyes in 'The Remarkable Case of Davidson's Eyes'.

albumens: Albumen is egg-white or similar tissue.

Aldebaran: Bright reddish star in the constellation Taurus (The Bull).

alisphenoid: Bone at the base of the skull.

ambuscade: Ambush.

Antares: Bright red star in the constellation Scorpio (The Scorpion).

Antipodes Island: Island south of New Zealand, the closest land to the 'antipodes' or opposite point to Britain on the globe.

a priori: 'From the former' (Latin): a term used in reasoning to argue from cause to effect.

Argonauts: The crew of the ship *Argo*, captained by Jason in the Greek legend.

Aurora: Dawn, but the capital (in 'A Dream of Armageddon') suggests the personified figure of the Greek goddess of the same name.

axis fibre: Cell through which impulses are transmitted.

Baffin's Bay: Or Baffin Bay, a stretch of sea to the west of Greenland between the Atlantic and Arctic Oceans.

ball governors: Device which regulates the speed of a steam engine by adjusting the flow of steam.

bath-chair: Chair on wheels for invalids.

black art: Magic.

blackleg: Someone who works while his colleagues are on strike.

blastopore: Opening in an embryo which will develop into the mouth or anus.

Bogota: Capital of Colombia.

bosh: Nonsense (slang).

buckram: Coarse, stiffened linen cloth.

bulldog: Short brierwood pipe.

burthen: Alternative spelling for 'burden' or load.

cab-runner: Someone who calls cabs for gentlemen in hopes of a tip.

cachalot: Sperm whale.

Capella: Bright yellow star in the constellation Auriga (The Charioteer).

capelline: Hood-like garment, especially for evening wear.

capo: Short for 'Captain' or 'Capitan' (Spanish), but could simply mean 'boss'.

Capricorn: Tropic of Capricorn, latitude at 23° 26' 22" south of the Equator (which runs through southern Africa).

caramba: Spanish exclamation of delight or surprise. It may be a euphemism for *carajo*, 'penis'.

casa: House (Spanish).

cephalopods: Molluscs such as octopus or cuttle-fish, with tentacles attached to the head.

chapped: Cracked.

charabancs: Omnibuses, especially for tourists (from the French *char-à-bancs*, meaning 'benched carriages').

Charon: In ancient Greek legend, the ferryman who took the souls of the dead across the River Styx.

chloroform: Began to be used as an anaesthetic in 1847.

cockney: Londoner, strictly one 'born within the sound of Bow Bells'.

Cordilleras: Mountain ranges.

coruscating: Flashing.

Cotopaxi: Volcano in Ecuador, about 150 miles from the sea.

coup d'état: Sudden attempt at overthrowing a government or authority by force (French).

cramming: Learning for an examination.

Creole: Descendant of European settlers of mixed blood in Brazil and the Americas generally.

cretonnes: Printed cloth, originally from Creton in France.

'crib-hunting': Looking for a job: 'crib' being a contemporary slang expression for 'position' or 'job'.

cribs: Previously-prepared answers.

crinoid: Plant-like sea animals (such as the sea lily).

crosiers: Staffs held by bishops to signify their pastoral roles, suggested by the rolled tops of the ferns which resemble such staffs.

cryohydrates: 'A solid hydrate formed by the combination of a salt or other crystalloid with water (ice) at a temperature below freezing-point' (*OED*).

cuberta: Small sailing-boat used on the Amazon river (Spanish).

cutaneous: Affecting the skin.

davits: Small cranes on the side or stern of a ship by which boats may be raised or lowered.

demi-john: Large slender-necked glass bottle enclosed in wicker-work, frequently used to hold spirits such as rum.

deputy-lieutenant: Deputy to the Lord-Lieutenant of an English county, an honorary post whose responsibilities include acting as representative of the Monarch and chairing legal and taxation committees.

devil's tattoo: The act of drumming, tapping or thumping, often used to describe rapping on a table with one's fingers to express irritation or impatience.

diatoms: Single-celled vegetable organisms.

Dis: Roman name for the Greek god Hades or Pluto, god of the underworld.

éclat: Energetic display (French).

electrometers: Instruments for ascertaining the quality and quantity of electricity in an electrified body.

Elysian Fields: Abode of the dead in Greek mythology.

en rapport: In communication (French).

epicycles: Circles whose centres move round in the circumference of a greater circle, as rotating planets revolve around the sun.

Faraglioni: Craggy islets, one of Capri's most famous tourist attractions.

forecastle: Also fo'c'sle; upper deck of a ship forward of the foremast, where the crew's living-quarters were situated.

frangible: Breakable.

furies: Monsters from Greek mythology and the embodiments of revenge.

Futurus: (To) the future (Latin).

galvanometer: Apparatus for detecting the existence, direction and intensity of a galvanic (electric) current.

ganglion cell: A ganglion is a collection of nerve cells.

genus: Next highest classification of animal or vegetable life above the single species.

Great Bear: Ursa Major, the constellation also known as The Plough or Big Dipper.

grog: Rum and water, traditionally drunk by sailors.

Grotta del Bove Marino: On the north coast of Capri, known as the cave of the 'Sea-cow' because of the noise generated by waves during storms.

harpies: Monsters from Greek mythology with the heads and bodies of women and with the wings and claws of vultures.

Hedon: Name signifying 'pleasure' (Greek).

Hercules: Constellation named after the Ancient Greek hero.

Himmel: Heaven (German).

Hindustan: Modern India.

holland aprons: Made from brown linen cloth originally manufactured in Holland.

hypophosphites: Compounds containing phosphorous and hydrogen. In combination with other chemicals, they can be explosive.

impressed: Press-ganged, or forced into service.

incubus: Vampiric demon which preys upon sleeping people.

intercalary: 'Inserted' as a leap-year inserts an extra day (29 February) into the calendar.

ironclads: Warships plated with metal for defence in war.

Ischia: Largest island in the Bay of Naples, on the far side of the bay from Capri.

Isle of the Sirens: The Grotte delle Sirene on the Sorrento peninsula is supposed to be the cave from which the Sirens, in Homer's *Odyssey*, lured sailors with the sweetness of their songs.

jack-o'-lantern: Or 'will-o'-the-wisp'; light caused by the natural combustion of methane drifting around swamps, associated with stories about spirits leading travellers astray.

jigger: In nautical terms, apparatus used to secure cables for hoisting equipment on or off the ship; also a tropical flea.

jobbing . . . appointments: Using influence to secure positions for his favourites.

Juggernaut: Title given to the Hindu god Krishna, and by extension a vast overwhelming object or force, after the huge wagon on which a statue of Krishna was drawn through the streets of the Indian town of Puri on the Bay of Bengal. Frequent accidental deaths of devotees gave rise to a myth that they threw themselves under the wheels of the wagon to gain the god's favour.

knacker's yard: Slaughterhouse for worn-out horses.

Kümmel: German liqueur flavoured with cumin and caraway seeds.

laminaria: Type of seaweed.

lascar: Asian seaman.

leading-strings: Reins to guide and keep safe children learning to walk.

lenticel: Lens-shaped spots on tree bark, around the pores.

Lisle hose: Stockings made from smooth cotton fabric named after Lille in France.

loggia: Open, elevated gallery (Italian).

Manitoba: Canadian province west of the Great Lakes.

'mesoblast': Middle layer of the bodily structure.

mesoblastic somites: Middle layers of the body segments of embryos from which develop the skeleton and the muscular and connective tissues.

microlepidoptera: Informal rather than scientific term for small moths.

middy: Short for midshipman; junior non-commissioned officer or young cadet.

Monte Solaro: Highest point on the island of Capri, in the Bay of Naples.

monitor: Ironclad gunboat.

mumchancer: From 'mumchance'; to be sullenly silent (originally referring to mime or masquerade).

muslin: Thin cotton cloth of open weave.

nefas: Monster (Latin).

niente: Nothing (Italian).

Nobel prize: The Swedish industrialist Alfred Nobel (1833–96) established a Foundation to award prizes for achievement in various categories, including Literature. Prizes have been awarded since 1901.

odium theologicum: 'Hatred of the kind which proverbially characterizes theological disputes' (*OED*).

opera hat: Collapsible tall hat.

opium: Frequently used as an anaesthetic or for pain relief.

Orion: Constellation named after the Greek hero Orion, the Hunter.

ostended: Revealed.

ovum: Egg.

pachydermatous: Thick-skinned (like an elephant).

Palaeolithic: Early Stone Age, roughly two million to ten thousand years ago.

Panama hat: Wide-brimmed hat made from fine straw or similar material.

pannikin: Small pan or drinking vessel.

pantoum: A Malayan verse form. The beginning and ending rhyme are identical, here pointing out the circular form of 'The Man who could work Miracles'.

pariah dog: Indian ownerless dog; 'pariah' also means outcaste.

paroquets: Variant spelling of 'parakeets' (small parrots).

peccant: Offending, from the Latin *peccare*, to transgress, mistake or sin.

perfect transport: Rapture or fit of strong emotion.

personalities: Personal remarks.

pharmacopoeia: 'Stock' of medical drugs and compounds.

placoid: Plate-like scales, as of fishes.

Pleiades: Cluster of stars (also known as The Seven Sisters) in the constellation Orion.

pneumatics: Study of the mechanical properties of gases.

Pole Star: Polaris, or the North Star; the last star in the tail of the constellation Ursa Minor (The Little Bear) which marks the North Celestial Pole.

Pollux: One of the two main stars (the other is Castor) in the constellation Gemini (The Twins), named after mythological heroes.

post-prandial: After-dinner.

pot-banks: Local term for the potteries of the Stoke-on-Trent area.

Preventive Service: Old term for the Coast Guard, originally established to prevent smuggling.

privet: Shrub often used for hedges in suburban gardens.

prognathous: Having projecting jaws, a suggestion of the 'primitive'.

pteropods: Marine molluscs with a modified foot that acts as a kind of fin.

puddlers' furnaces: Furnaces in which 'pig-iron' is purified into 'wrought-iron'.

puttees: Strips of cloth wound in a spiral from ankle to knee, worn as leggings by soldiers.

rancho: Hut or hovel (Spanish). The North American term 'ranch', meaning extensive farm, is derived from this.

Rangoon: Capital city of Burma, now Yangon.

ranunculus: Family of flowering plants including the crowfoot, lesser celandine, and buttercup.

Regulus: Brightest star of the constellation Leo (The Lion).

Rhodian arch: In Greek legend, the island of Rhodes was guarded by a colossal animated statue of bronze, one of the Seven Wonders of the World.

rocker microtome: Instrument for cutting material in very thin slices for examination under a microscope.

rouleau: The cylinder (French) of money given Eden earlier, in 'The Story of the late Mr Elvesham'.

St Lawrence valley: The St Lawrence river flows through Canada eastwards from the Great Lakes to the Gulf of St Lawrence.

salaamed: Bowed in greeting; from the Arabic *Salaam Aleikum* (Peace be upon you).

sconces: Ornamental brackets for carrying a light.

sea lilies: Animals related to starfish but attached to rocks by thin
stalks.

seidlitz-powder: Mild laxative or remedy for over-indulgence, named
after a German spa-town.

senior wranglers: Cambridge graduates who had come top of the list
of Part 2 of the Mathematical Tripos.

shake-up: *OED* gives shake-*down* for a makeshift bed.

Sirius: Blue-white 'Dog Star', in the constellation Canis Major (The
Great Dog), is the brightest star in the sky.

skerry: Stretch of rocks or reef, covered at high tide.

slop suit: Overalls.

snatch division: Unexpected vote, with the result that the Government
in 'The Door in the Wall' has not made sure that enough of its
supporters are present to enable it to win comfortably.

solar corona: Light around the disc of the sun, visible during an eclipse.

somnambulistic: Sleep-walking.

Southern Cross: Constellation only visible in the southern hemisphere.

spectroscope: Instrument (especially used in astronomy) to analyse the
chemical makeup of an object by means of the light it emits. Invented
in 1859 by Gustav Robert Kirchhoff (1824–87) and Robert Wilhelm
Bunsen (1811–99).

spin-drift: Continuous driving spray whipped up from the sea.

spiring: Shooting or sprouting like plants.

spirit-lamps: Fed by methylated or other spirits.

stoker: Person whose job it is to shovel fuel into the furnace of steamships, railway engines, etc.

Styx: River which the souls of the dead had to cross to reach the
Underworld (see note 2 to 'Under the Knife').

talus: Slope of loose material fallen from a cliff-face.

tamarisk: Shrub often used for hedges in suburban gardens.

tapestry: Imitative of decorated woven or embroidered textiles.

taxidermic material: Material for preparing, stuffing and mounting
dead animals for display.

temerarious: Heedless, rash or haphazard.

tender: Carriage behind a locomotive engine which carries fuel and
water for it.

Terceira: Third largest island of the Azores group in the North
Atlantic.

thaumaturgist: Worker of magic.

Theriomorpha: Victorian (largely superseded) classification of
mammal-like reptiles which flourished in the Early Mesozoic age,
about 245 million years ago.

Titans: Giants in Greek mythology, children of Uranus and Gaea.

Trappistine: Liqueur made by the Trappist order of monks originally founded at the Abbey of La Trappe in France.

Tropic of Capricorn: *See* Capricorn.

truckle-bed: Low bed running on castors, which can be stored away when not in use.

tuyères: Also known as 'twyers', pipes through which air enters a blast furnace (French).

unpaired: When Members of Parliament are not going to be present at a vote, they arrange to be 'paired' with members of the opposite party who would have voted the opposite way. In this way their votes cancel out.

vans: Blades or leading-edges for the aircraft's screw-propellers in 'The Argonauts of the Air'.

Vega: In the constellation Vega or Lyra (The Lyre), the fifth brightest star in the sky.

velveteen: Fabric consisting of poor-quality velvet, consisting largely of cotton instead of silk.

vertebrata: Backboned animals.

vertebrated: With a backbone.

vestry-meeting: Meeting of Church parishioners (from 'vestry', the room where the clergy and choir stored their robes) or the more secular Parish Council, part of the British system of local government.

villas: Small (suburban) houses.

viperine: Like the viper (or adder), the only poisonous British snake, identified by a 'V'-shaped marking on the head.

viscus: One of the soft internal organs.

vittles: Food (pronounced thus, but spelled 'victuals').

Walpurgis Night: 30 April, or May Day Eve. In German folklore, it is traditionally a festival for witches.

welkin: Sky.

Welsh rarebit: Traditional Welsh dish of melted cheese on toast.

the whip: Official of a political party responsible for seeing that its members turn out for Parliamentary votes.

Whitsun week: The week beginning with Whit Sunday or Pentecost, the seventh Sunday after Easter.

whurryballoo: Clamour or uproar (a variant of 'hullabaloo').

Widdy, Widdy Way: Children's street game in which the person who is 'on' chases the others.

zodiacal light: Glow (caused by reflected light from interplanetary dust) seen in the sky after dusk.

Notes

Quotations from the Bible are from the Authorized Version.

THE LORD OF THE DYNAMOS

1. *Camberwell*: District of London south of the Thames, now part of the London Borough of Southwark. The City & South London Railway, London's first deep underground electric railway, was opened in 1890 although the generators that powered it were not actually in Camberwell, but nearby Stockwell.

2. *Carnot's cycle*: Principle formulated by the French physicist Nicholas Léonard Sadi Carnot (1796–1832), describing the cycles of expansion and contraction in an ideal 'heat-engine' (engine powered by heat).

3. *Azuma-zi*: Azuma is a Japanese name (meaning 'east'), but there is no particular significance here other than to evoke the 'mysterious East'.

4. *Pooh-bah*: The pompous 'Lord High Everything Else' in the popular comic opera *The Mikado* (1885) by William Schwenck Gilbert (1836–1911) and Arthur Sullivan (1842–1900). This, as with 'nigger help' later, is Holroyd's casual racism, but the story also points towards a more sophisticated unease towards other races which Wells and his readers were not free from.

5. *Lord Clive . . . Straits Settlements*: Ship named after Robert Clive (1725–74), general whose military victories in India helped establish British rule in the following century. The Straits Settlements were former East India Company-controlled colonial territories along the Strait of Malacca: Penang, and Malacca, in what is now Malaysia, and Singapore.

6. *Twelve per cent*: The dividend which the railway shareholders were expected to receive.

7. *British Solomon*: The biblical King Solomon (c. 1000 BC–928

BC), famous for his wisdom, was also associated, especially in Arabic folklore, with stories of supernatural beings. There might also be an echo of the British Solomon Islands in the South Pacific, established as a British protectorate in 1893, as the region of 'beyond' from where Azuma-zi might have originated.

8. *a meteoric stone*: The pre-Islamic Arabs venerated a black stone, said to be of meteoric origin, around which the Kaaba at Mecca was built.

9. *anointing of the coils with oil*: Applying oil to a body as a mark of respect is a custom in many religions.

THE REMARKABLE CASE OF
DAVIDSON'S EYES

1. *Wade's*: Investigator (fictional) into the 'case' of Davidson.

2. *Harlow Technical College ... Highgate Archway*: Harlow in Essex is over 15 miles north-east from the Highgate Archway. Wells may have been thinking of Holloway although the Northern Polytechnic Institute in Holloway was not opened until 1896.

3. *Scott ... everyone swore by that personage*: Various 'personages' have been suggested, from the American Civil War General Winfield Scott (1786–1866) to the author Sir Walter Scott (1771–1832). The *OED* (2nd edn.) gives 1885 as the first instance of 'Great Scott' as an exclamation, citing *Tinted Venus* by F. Anstey (Thomas Anstey Guthrie (1856–1934)): 'Great Scott! I must be bad!', but the expression seems to have been used in 1864 in *Eye of the Storm: A Civil War Odyssey*, a diary by Private Robert Knox Sneden.

4. *hull down*: So far away that the hull is below the horizon and cannot be seen.

5. *Bishop Berkeley*: George Berkeley (1685–1753), Bishop of Cloyne in Ireland, 'idealist' philosopher who argued against the distinction of 'matter' and 'spirit', suggesting that what we believe exists is a product of our sensory perception or the mind of God.

6. *penguins*: Only found in the southern hemisphere, giving a clue to the whereabouts of Davidson's perception.

7. *Dogs' Home ... King's Cross*: The Dogs' Home was founded in Holloway in 1860 and moved to its present location in Battersea, south of the river Thames, in 1871. King's Cross railway station is to the south of Camden Town.

8. *the special Pall Mall*: The *Pall Mall Budget* (where, of course,

this story first appeared) was a weekly supplement to the *Pall Mall Gazette*, London evening paper.

9. *group of stars like a cross*: The Southern Cross constellation, only visible from the Southern hemisphere.

10. *changing views of a lantern*: Projected images from 'magic lantern' slides dissolving into one another; a popular entertainment during the mid nineteenth century. (See also 'The Story of the late Mr Elvesham'.)

11. *Fulmar*: A possibly fictional naval vessel, named after a sea-bird.

12. *Fourth Dimension*: Wells's *The Time Machine* (1895) begins with a discussion of Time as the Fourth Dimension after Length, Breadth and Thickness, but here and in 'The Plattner Story' it is seen more as an extra spatial dimension.

13. *Saint Pancras installation*: The station (between Euston and King's Cross stations on Euston Road) designed by William Henry Barlow (1812–1902) was opened in 1868. It and the associated Midland Grand Hotel (opened 1877), designed by George Gilbert Scott (1811–78), were among the glories of Victorian railway architecture.

THE MOTH

1. *Periplaneta Hapliia*: Latin name for the (fictional) 'Hapley's cockroach'.

2. *Geological Society*: Scholarly and professional society, formed in 1807.

3. *burn Sir Ray Lankester at Smithfield*: Edwin Ray Lankester (1847–1929) was Professor of Zoology at University College London and Professor of Comparative Anatomy at Oxford. A friend of Wells, he wrote the entry on 'Mollusca' for the 9th edition of the *Encyclopedia Britannica* (1875–89). Criminals, traitors and, during the sixteenth century, heretics were executed at Smithfield Market in the City of London.

4. *Royal Entomological Society*: Scholarly society dedicated to the study of insects, founded 1833.

5. *Chamber of Deputies*: The Lower House of the French Parliament, since 1946 known as the National Assembly. French politics in the late nineteenth century was often turbulent, with many short-lived governments.

6. *Quart. Journ. Entomological Soc.*: The Royal Entomological Society issued various 'Proceedings' and journals, but nothing with this precise title.

7. *along Piccadilly . . . societies abide*: Burlington House in Picca-
    dilly is the home of a number of learned scientific societies,
    including (until 1968) the Royal Society, as well as the Royal
    Academy of Fine Arts. Wells is joking about the artistic com-
    munity's ignorance of the scientific world.
8. *'Island Nights' Entertainments'*: Collection of stories (1893) by
    Robert Louis Stevenson (1850–94), which includes 'The Bottle
    Imp'.
9. *Kipling*: Rudyard Kipling (1865–1936), the popular author of
    poems, short stories and novels. See also note 3 to 'The Wild
    Asses of the Devil'.
10. *Besant's 'Inner House'*: Dystopian novel (1888) by Sir Walter
    Besant (1836–1901).
11. *monograph*: The original meaning of 'monograph' (now 'a work
    in one volume' – *OED*) was a treatise on a single specialized
    subject such as a zoological or botanical species.

A CATASTROPHE

1. *4¾d.*: Fourpence and three-farthings. In British currency of the
    time, there were four farthings to a penny, twelve pennies to a
    shilling and twenty shillings to a pound. 'Half a crown' is two
    shillings and sixpence. A guinea was worth 21 shillings.
2. *Bandersnatch*: From the poem 'Jabberwocky' in *Through the
    Looking Glass* (1871) by Lewis Carroll (1832–98). Here,
    'snatch' evokes the greed of Winslow's competitors, just as one
    of his wholesale dealers is named 'Grab'.
3. *Black Care*: Term used to signify depression or turn of fortune,
    from Horace (Quintus Horatius Flaccus (65–8 BC)), 'post equi-
    tem sedet atra Cura' ('Behind the rider sits black care'), *Odes*
    3.1.40.
4. *Y.M.C.A.*: The Young Men's Christian Association was founded
    in 1844 to encourage the spiritual and educational development
    (and later, the physical fitness) of young men. Its roots in the
    drapery trade make it an obvious alternative to the public-house
    for Winslow.
5. *Christian World*: Weekly journal which began publishing in
    1857.
6. *tempering the wind to the shorn retailer*: The proverbial
    expression 'tempering the wind to the shorn lamb' refers to a
    providential act of mercy.

THE CONE

1. *Gehenna*: The (Greek) name of a valley outside Jerusalem where fires continually burned to consume rubbish and where pagans allegedly sacrificed children (Jeremiah 19:3–6). It became a synonym for Hell in Christian writing.

2. *penthouse brows*: Overhanging eyebrows, possibly from the libretto to the opera *King Arthur* (1691) by John Dryden (1631–1700) and Henry Purcell (1659–95), III.1.30: 'My Pent-House Eye-Brows, and my Shaggy Beard'.

3. *Hanley and Etruria*: Hanley is one of the six 'Potteries' towns in Staffordshire which make up the present Stoke-on-Trent. Etruria, west of Hanley, was where Josiah Wedgwood (1730–95) settled upon for his pottery factory, and Wells lived there for a few months in 1888. Burslem (mentioned later) is another of the 'Potteries' towns.

4. *season of 'play'*: Term used in industrial relations in the north and midlands to signify lack of work through illness or strike action.

5. *Jeddah*: Port city in Saudi Arabia, near the holy city of Mecca. The company is probably reminiscent of the Shelton Iron Steel and Coal Company in Etruria.

6. *pillars of cloud by day*: When Moses led the Israelites out of Egypt, God guided them 'by day in a pillar of a cloud ... and by night in a pillar of fire' (Exodus 13:21).

7. *Newcastle*: Newcastle-under-Lyme, in Staffordshire, just west of the 'Potteries' towns.

THE ARGONAUTS OF THE AIR

1. *South-Western main line*: Constructed in the 1830s, the London and South-Western Railway network ran from Vauxhall in London through Wimbledon, Surbiton and Woking in Surrey to Southampton on the south coast. A number of suburban railways branched off and connected to this line. From Wimbledon, a line ran via Worcester Park to Leatherhead and Guildford.

2. *Maxim*: Sir Hiram S. Maxim (1840–1916), inventor of an early machine gun and a pioneer of heavier-than-air flight, on whom Monson, his 'successor', is obviously based. In 1894, before a crowd of invited guests which included Wells, Maxim flew two hundred feet before crashing. See also note 10.

3. *over Trafalgar Square*: Trafalgar Square in central London com-

memorates the naval victory of the Battle of Trafalgar (1805) where Horatio, Lord Nelson (1758–1805) met his death. As an iconic location it would be expected that the first aircraft would be seen over the square in the same way as French pioneers of aviation in the early 1900s made sure that they were seen near the Eiffel Tower.

4. *Isle of Wight trippers*: The island on the south coast of England off Southampton, was a popular holiday destination reached by the railway network (line) alluded to earlier. The working- and lower-middle-class 'trippers' would be entertained and amused by Monson's failures.

5. *Romeike*: Henry Romeike (dates unknown) was the founder of a press cuttings agency in the 1880s.

6. *ceased from troubling*: Echo of Job 3:17: 'There the wicked cease from troubling; and there the weary be at rest.'

7. *Folly*: Often used for a costly and striking but essentially useless enterprise, such as an ornamental building.

8. *Esher*: Five miles west of Worcester Park.

9. *aluminium rod*: Although the very light metal aluminium was first extracted in 1825, it was expensive to produce until 1886 when the process of electrolysis was perfected.

10. *Lilienthal's methods*: Otto Lilienthal (1848–96), German experimenter with gliders, who died following a crash. His experiments with flying were based upon the close observation of the flight of birds, while Maxim attempted to generate power by other means, such as the propeller. Monson is trying to combine the two methods and keep his aircraft gliding like a gull through mechanical adjustments of the wings and the force generated by the engines and propeller.

11. *petroleum*: Petroleum (or gasoline), extracted from oil, became increasingly important as a fuel in the second half of the nineteenth century and the development of the internal combustion engine in automobiles boosted the idea of applications in powered flight. The first successful powered flight using a gasoline engine was Orville Wright's on 17 December 1903.

12. *eminent literary people from Haslemere*: Haslemere in Surrey is close to Hindhead, where the writers Grant Allen (1848–99) and Richard Le Gallienne (1866–1947), friends of Wells, lived.

13. *Albert Hall*: Concert hall in Kensington, opened 1871 in memory of Prince Albert (1819–61).

14. *Imperial Institute*: South Kensington, London. Founded 1881 as a museum/research institute. Part of it was incorporated

into Imperial College of Science, Technology and Medicine in
1899.

15. *Royal College of Science*: See note 4 to 'A Slip under the Microscope'. 'Formerly' implies that it was damaged or destroyed in
the crash.

UNDER THE KNIFE

1. *Regent's Park Canal*: Running through the northern end of
Regent's Park, the canal was constructed in 1816 to connect the
Grand Union Canal to the London Docks. The Broad Walk is
part of the park's formal gardens. The 'crescent' is Park Crescent
between Marylebone Road and Portland Place.

2. *a black barge . . . white horse*: The images here may be taken
from Greek mythology (souls of the dead were ferried across the
River Styx) and the Bible (in Revelation 6:8 Death is described
as riding on a 'pale horse').

3. *winged globes*: The symbol of the winged sun disc probably
originated in Assyria but was used frequently in ancient Egypt.

4. *a thousand years was but a moment*: An echo of 'For a thousand
years in thy sight are but as yesterday' (Psalm 90:4), adapted by
Isaac Watts (1674–1748) in the popular hymn 'Oh God, Our
Help In Ages Past': 'A thousand ages in thy sight / Are like an
evening gone'.

5. *the hour had come . . . a noise of many waters . . . 'There will be
no more pain'*: References to Revelation 3:3: 'thou shalt not
know what hour I will come upon thee'; 19:6: 'as the voice of
many waters'; 21:4: 'neither shall there be any more pain'.

A SLIP UNDER THE MICROSCOPE

1. *News from Nowhere*: Utopian novel (1890) by William Morris
(1834–96). See also note 15.

2. *Oratory clock*: At Brompton Oratory, in Brompton Road near
the Royal College of Science.

3. *mixed classes*: Men *and* women; women were beginning to
receive a scientific education in some institutions. The University
of London accepted women for graduation in all faculties in
1878. Oxford and Cambridge took until 1920 and 1948 respectively to do the same.

4. *College of Science*: The Royal College of Science in South
Kensington, London, formed in 1881 as the Normal School of

Science by amalgamating courses of the Royal School of Mines with the teaching of other science subjects. One of its aims was to train school science teachers. Students from unprivileged backgrounds like Hill (and Wells himself, 1884–7) were recruited by means of state scholarships. The Normal School was renamed the Royal College of Science in 1890 and is now part of Imperial College, London.

5. *blue paper*: The offer of a scholarship to candidates who had done well in school examinations.

6. *a guinea a week*: Something under the average income of a skilled worker.

7. *seventh standard of the Board school*: The highest class of the Board Schools, established in 1870 to educate working-class children.

8. *Carlyle*: Thomas Carlyle (1795–1881), historian and writer on social issues. His books included *Sartor Resartus* (1833–4; see also note 11 to 'The New Accelerator'), *History of the French Revolution* (1837) and *On Heroes* (1841).

9. *a paying student*: Paying her own fees, in contrast to Hill who is receiving a State grant.

10. *Browning*: Robert Browning (1812–89), poet.

11. *Harvey Commemoration Medal*: An apparently fictional award in memory of William Harvey (1578–1657), who pioneered research into the circulation of the blood.

12. *Longfellow ... Mrs Hemans*: The American poet Henry Wadsworth Longfellow (1807–82), Alfred, Lord Tennyson (1809–92), Alexander Pope (1688–1744) and Percy Bysshe Shelley (1792–1822) were all 'canonical' poets. They are contrasted with more popular versifiers Eliza Cook (1818–89) and Mrs (Felicia) Hemans (1793–1835).

13. *'mugger'*: 'Crammer' or 'swot' who memorizes facts for examinations rather than learning with full understanding or enjoyment. (But Hill is also being looked down upon by the Oxford man because of his humbler origins.)

14. *counted to him for righteousness*: Cf. Psalm 106:31: 'And that was counted unto him for righteousness.'

15. *Bernard Shaw's ... Walter Crane's*: George Bernard Shaw (1856–1950), playwright and socialist activist, was a friend and rival of Wells. As well as being a novelist, poet, and socialist activist, William Morris's printing and household designs were issued through his Kelmscott Press and the Morris & Co. design firm. Walter Crane (1845–1915) was celebrated for his children's

book illustrations and his cartoons and art supporting the Social-ist cause.

16. *'dined late'*: A characteristic of a 'gentleman'.

17. *finger-bowl shibboleths*: Only the wealthy and cultivated used finger-bowls to wash during meals. Judges 12:5–6 relates how the pronunciation of 'shibboleth' (Hebrew, 'ear of grain') was used to distinguish between the Gileadites and their enemies the Ephramites, who were slaughtered when they could not pass the test. It now refers to specialist jargon or customs used to distinguish members of a privileged group (like Wedderburn) from outsiders (like Hill).

18. *Ruskin*: John Ruskin (1819–1900), art critic and influential writer on social issues. In *Sesame and Lilies* (1865) he argued that men's roles were public, while women's influence was more to be felt in the private sphere, an attitude common in Victorian times.

19. *aerated bread shop*: The Aërated Bread Company began by introducing carbon dioxide into dough, to make the bread rise faster. In 1864 it started to serve food and drink in its shops. The ABC 'tea shops' introduced into Victorian society a cheap and (for women) unthreatening alternative to eating and socializing in the home or public-houses and lasted well into the second half of the twentieth century.

20. *Bradlaugh and John Burns*: Charles Bradlaugh (1833–91) advocated birth control and was prevented from taking his seat in Parliament for five years because as an atheist he refused to take a religious oath. John Burns (1858–1943) was a socialist and trade union leader who was elected to Parliament in 1892.

21. *Hindu god*: Like the statue of a Hindu god positioned for all to see.

22. *Q. Jour. Mi. Sci.*: *Quarterly Journal of Mining Science*.

23. *threepenny or ninepenny classics*: Cheap editions of classic books.

24. *The Meistersingers*: *Die Meistersinger von Nürnberg*, an opera by Richard Wagner (1813–83), first performed 1868.

THE PLATTNER STORY

1. *Eusapia's*: The medium Eusapia Palladino (1854–1918) was the subject of a number of investigations during the 1880s and 1890s. Numerous reputable scientists (such as the physicist Oliver Lodge (1851–1940)) attended her seances and were convinced of her

genuine ability. Others considered her an ingenious but blatant fraudster, and Wells is mocking the alleged gullibility of the scientific investigators who took her side.

2. *Alsatian*: From the (now) French province of Alsace, on the border of Germany, a large proportion of whose population was of German ancestry. From 1648, the region was ruled by France, but between 1871 and 1918 it was German.

3. *a cyclist*: Cycling became a craze (in which Wells participated) in the 1890s.

4. *cheap 'Gem' photographs*: Small 'tintype' photographs mounted on decorated card, known as 'Gem' or 'American Gem' pictures, and popular from the late 1870s onwards.

5. *Nordau*: Max Nordau (1849–1923), whose *Degeneration* (translated into English 1895) argued that the 'decadent' art of the *fin de siècle* was symbolic of a tendency to hysteria and morbidity.

6. *Fourth Dimension*: See note 12 to 'The Remarkable Case of Davidson's Eyes'.

7. *Board ... schools*: See note 7 to 'A Slip under the Microscope'.

8. *the Three Gases*: Hydrogen, oxygen and nitrogen, which Antoine Lavoisier (1777–94) identified as chemical elements.

9. *left not a wrack behind*: Allusion to *The Tempest* (1611) by William Shakespeare (1564–1616), IV. 1. 156: 'Leave not a rack behind'.

10. *Society for the Investigation of Abnormal Phenomena*: A fictional version, perhaps, of the Society for Psychical Research, founded in 1882 to investigate spiritualism and psychic phenomena scientifically.

11. *Journal of Anatomy*: The journal of the Anatomical Society, founded 1887 and still a major scholarly body.

12. *Euclid riders*: An exercise in geometry to deduce propositions from previous propositions (from 'rider': 'corollary or addition supplementing, or naturally arising from, something said or written' (*OED*)).

13. *human heads beneath which a tadpole-like body swung*: The heads and underdeveloped bodies are reminiscent of the Martians of *The War of the Worlds* (1898), and the evolved humans of 'The Man of the Year Million' (1893), but the physical description also seems to suggest sperm cells.

14. *devil's dyke*: There is a valley in the South Downs called the Devil's Dyke, and other 'Devil's Dykes' in Cambridgeshire and Hertfordshire.

THE STORY OF THE LATE
MR ELVESHAM

1. *Trentham*: Wells's father Joseph worked as a gardener at Trentham Hall, near Stoke-on-Trent, for a brief period following his marriage to Wells's mother Sarah in 1853.

2. *University College, London*: Founded 1826, opening up education for a wider social mix than could attend Oxford or Cambridge.

3. *Shoolbread's premises*: James Shoolbread & Co. was a furniture supplier in Tottenham Court Road, but the restaurant (Blavitski's) appears to be fictional.

4. *dissolving views*: See note 10 to 'The Remarkable Case of Davidson's Eyes'.

5. *Psychical Research Society*: The Society for Psychical Research: see note 10 to 'The Plattner Story'.

6. *powers of three*: Multiplying three by itself and continually multiplying the product by three.

IN THE ABYSS

1. *Myers apparatus*: Device to absorb carbon dioxide and release stored oxygen, invented by Henry Fleuss in 1879. By 1900 a similar system was developed in Britain for escape from sunken submarines. 'Myers' may be fictional.

2. *Daubrée*: French geologist Gabriel Auguste Daubrée (1814–96) worked on metamorphic rocks and the influence of pressure and vulcanism in creating them.

3. *eight bells*: In naval custom, the 24-hour day, beginning at noon, is divided into five 'watches' of four hours with two two-hour afternoon 'dog watches'. In each watch, after half an hour, a bell is rung, followed by two bells the next half-hour, three the next and so on. 'Eight bells' therefore signifies here the end of the Forenoon watch at noon.

4. *since the waters were gathered together*: The separation of land and sea in the biblical creation account: Genesis 1:9: 'Let the waters under the heaven be gathered together in one place.'

THE SEA RAIDERS

1. *Haploteuthis ferox*: A mock scientific name for the invented creature; translated from the Greek and Latin, it means something like 'Fierce squid'. There are several species of giant squid, including *Architeuthus dux*, which live at great depths and of which little is known although occasional sightings led to numerous legends and tall tales. Observations during the nineteenth century became more common due to wider exploration of the oceans and a series of unexplained strandings of giant squid on the shores of Newfoundland and of New Zealand. There are few credible instances of people being attacked, although in 1873 a boy is reported to have hacked off a tentacle of a squid which attacked a small boat off the coast of Bell Island, Newfoundland.

2. *Prince of Monaco's discovery*: Prince Albert I of Monaco (1848–1922) was an enthusiastic researcher into giant squid and in 1895 described several species including 'Lepidoteuthis grimaldii' which bears his family name. He founded the country's Oceanographic Institute.

3. *The downward bend . . . grotesque suggestion of a face*: Reminiscent of the description of the Martians in *The War of the Worlds*.

4. *straw hat and whites*: Summer-holiday clothing.

THE CRYSTAL EGG

1. *thirty shillings*: One pound ten shillings, less than a third of the asking price of five pounds. Cave's claim to his wife that the crystal is worth 'ten guineas' is just over twice his asking price.

2. *sugar and lemon and so forth*: The 'so forth' would presumably be gin or brandy or some such alcoholic addition.

3. *Pasteur Institute*: Medical research institute founded in Paris in 1887 by the French chemist and pioneer of germ theory Louis Pasteur (1822–95).

4. *a wide and shining canal*: The first clue, along with the reddish cliffs, that this may be Mars. During the 1877 opposition (when the earth is between the sun and Mars, and the two planets are at their closest), the Italian astronomer Giovanni Virginio Schiaparelli (1835–1910) had observed 'canali' (channels). Percival Lowell (1855–1916) continued Schiaparelli's mapping, and argued in his book *Mars* (1895) that they were probably actual canals, built by Martians. Further evidence of identity is

the 'two small moons': the two Martian moons, Phobos and
Deimos, were discovered in 1877.

5. *methyl*: Methanol (methyl alcohol) or a number of chemicals
   derived from it, probably used in the preserved animals on sale
   in Cave's shop.

6. *certain clumsy bipeds*: Something like those fed on by the Martians
   of *The War of the Worlds*.

7. *The Daily Chronicle and Nature*: The *Daily Chronicle* was a
   Liberal newspaper established in 1872 and merged with the *Daily
   News* in 1930. *Nature* was one of the most important scientific
   journals of the time, founded in 1869 and still published today.

A STORY OF THE STONE AGE

1. *Leith Hill, and Pitch Hill, and Hindhead*: Leith Hill (south of
   Dorking in Surrey) is the highest place in south-east England,
   and with Pitch Hill and Hindhead, is part of a line of ridges and
   hills running through Surrey. See also note 12 to 'The Argonauts
   of the Air'.

2. *Wey*: The River Wey is a tributary of the Thames about forty
   miles long which flows through Godalming and Guildford to the
   Thames at Weybridge, nine miles west of Epsom.

3. *Fifty thousand years ago*: In *The Outline of History* (1920)
   Wells places the extinct sub-species 'Neanderthal Man' as having
   flourished in Europe fifty thousand years ago, at the height of
   the Fourth Ice Age. The descriptions of the bodies and customs
   of the tribe in this story resemble his account of *Homo Neander-
   thalis* there.

4. *little pointed tips*: A mark often used to signify 'elvish' or 'faery'
   folk, and suggesting a common belief that tales of such supernatural beings were folk-memories of more 'primitive' races of
   humanity.

5. *Epsom Stand*: Epsom racecourse, on the North Downs in Surrey,
   is the home of the Derby, the most important horse race in the
   British sporting calendar. Wells is pushing the area's association
   with horse racing back thousands of years.

THE STAR

1. *Neptune*: The eighth planet of the solar system, discovered in
   1846 after investigations of discrepancies in the apparent orbit
   of Uranus. It is the furthermost planet (after the redefining of

planets in 2006). Its satellite is Triton, and it is now known to have at least seven other moons.

2.   *Ogilvy*: An astronomer of that name is a friend of the narrator of *The War of the Worlds*.

3.   *Boers . . . Hottentots*: The Boers were the people of Dutch descent who settled in South Africa in the seventeenth and eighteenth centuries. The Gold Coast was the name given to what is now Ghana. 'Hottentots' was the name (now seen as pejorative) given to the Khoikhoi people, the native inhabitants of Namibia and Cape Province in South Africa.

4.   *telegraph . . . telephone wires*: A number of different inventions and improvements developed the electric telegraph in the early nineteenth century. The first successful transatlantic telegraph cable came into operation in 1886. The invention of the telephone is likewise complex, but Alexander Graham Bell (1847–1922) patented an electro-magnetic telephone in March 1876.

5.   *throbbing tape*: The 'ticker tape' used to record telegraph messages.

6.   *Centrifugal, centripetal*: Centrifugal force is the outward force acting on a body that revolves around a central point. Centripetal force is the gravitational force that draws the body towards the centre. In a stable orbit they are equal and opposite forces.

7.   *the pointers of the Bear*: The 'pointers' are the stars Dubhe and Merak in Ursa Major (The Great Bear), which point to Polaris, the North Star.

8.   *the year 1000*: When many people believed that the Second Coming of Christ would take place.

9.   *Greenwich time*: 'Greenwich Mean Time' is the standard time calculated from the sun's crossing of the line of longitude running through the observatory at Greenwich, London.

10.   *mouth of the Indus to the mouths of the Ganges*: The Indus flows westwards to the Arabian Sea in what is now Pakistan. The Ganges flows eastwards to the Bay of Bengal.

11.   *The Martian astronomers*: As in 'The Crystal Egg', Wells speculates that Mars is an inhabited world. (Martians appear in a more sinister guise in *The War of the Worlds*.)

THE MAN WHO COULD
WORK MIRACLES

1. *Torres Vedras*: Portuguese town after which were named the Duke of Wellington's successful lines of defensive forts in the Peninsular War (1808–14).

2. *safety-match*: Earlier matches could be struck by rubbing against any rough surface. The safety-match needed a specially prepared surface to ignite it, and came into use in Britain after the manufacturers Bryant and May established a factory in 1862.

3. *Moses' rod ... Tannhäuser*: It was actually Aaron's rod that turned into a serpent in the story told in Exodus 7:9–10, but he cast it down on Moses's orders. *Tannhäuser* (first performed 1845, revised extensively in 1861) is an opera by Richard Wagner, set in medieval Germany. In Act III the staff of the minstrel-knight Tannhäuser sprouts leaves.

4. *Poona-Penang lawyer*: Made from the stem of the Malaysian dwarf palm *Licuala acutifolia* native to Penang off the west coast of Malaysia. 'Lawyer' is a dialect word signifying 'bramble' but the *OED* suggests that the term may also be a jocular reference to the use of these canes in settling disputes.

5. *Immering*: Fictional Sussex village, also used in *Love and Mr Lewisham* (1900).

6. *Mahomet ... Yogi's ... Blavatsky*: Mohammed (570–632), was the founder of Islam. Yogi is a general term for a Hindu mystic; the capitalization suggests that Wells had a particular adept in mind. Helena Blavatsky (1831–91) was the founder of Theosophy, a religious sect based upon Eastern mysticism and stressing 'yogic' powers of mind over matter – hence the later reference to the 'miracles of Theosophists' who sometimes claimed psychic abilities.

7. *Duke of Argyll*: George Douglas Campbell, the 8th Duke of Argyll (1823–1900) was a prominent politician and an opponent of the theory of evolution by natural selection proposed by Charles Darwin (1809–82). He disputed these ideas with Thomas Henry Huxley (1825–95), under whom Wells studied and whose work he admired.

8. *Sunday, Nov. 10, 1896*: That date was actually a Tuesday.

9. *Joshua*: The biblical prophet Joshua is reputed to have stopped the motion of the sun and moon for a day (Joshua 10:12–13).

10. *a thousand miles an hour*: In 'A Theory of Errors: The Altered

Worlds of Fiction' (*Foundation* 36 (Summer 1986), pp. 45–57), David Lake points out that there is a contradiction here between this figure and the continued forward movement (as the globe stops) of nine miles per second. He suggests 'about eleven miles per minute' as the speed from the latitude of Sussex.

A DREAM OF ARMAGEDDON

1. *Armageddon*: The final battle between good and evil or, more loosely, a cataclysmic conflict that brings down a civilization. The Bible refers to Armageddon as a place: 'And he gathered them together into a place called in the Hebrew tongue Armageddon' (Revelation 16:16), which is usually identified with Mount Megiddo in Israel, the site of several battles.

2. *Dream States*: While Fortnum-Roscoe seems to be a fictional author, there was much interest in dreams and their meaning at this time. Sigmund Freud (1856–1939) published *The Interpretation of Dreams* in 1900, although it was not translated into English until 1913.

3. *pleasure city*: In the future described in *When the Sleeper Wakes* (1899, revised as *The Sleeper Awakes* (1910)), there are 'pleasure cities' or resorts devoted to luxury, one of which seems to be Capri, celebrated as such since the days of the Emperor Tiberius (42 BC–AD 37) and which was still a resort of the rich and famous in the late nineteenth century.

4. *Evesham*: Changed to 'Gresham' in the Atlantic Edition, presumably because Wells had used the name Evesham in *The New Machiavelli* (1911) for a contemporary political figure.

5. *Vesuvius*: The volcano which erupted in AD 79, destroying Pompeii. Torre Annunziata and Castellamare are nearby towns on the bay, to the north and south of Pompeii.

6. *aeroplanes*: Although airships were becoming increasingly successful, powered flight in a heavier-than-air machine was not to be achieved until 1903. (See note 11 to 'The Argonauts of the Air'.) Powered flight, for Wells, was *the* symbol of technological progress which, however, brought anxieties about its use in war: see, for instance, *The War in the Air* (1908).

7. *Rhinemouth*: At the time of writing of this story, anxieties about a future war with Germany were common although Wells is careful not to specify if his warlike power *is* Germany. The major port of the Rhine delta is, in fact, Rotterdam in Holland.

8. *South-west*: Salerno, where the narrator and his companion head for as mentioned later, is actually east and somewhat north of Capri, but they could have changed course.
9. *Marina Piccola*: The 'small harbour', one of the two harbours on the south side of Capri.
10. *Cava . . . Paestum*: Trying to find a refuge in Italy, they tried to cross from Salerno to Taranto in south-east Italy, but were turned back crossing the central mountains, ending up at Paestum in the Gulf of Salerno south of the Bay of Naples, the site of a Greek city.

THE NEW ACCELERATOR

1. *guinea*: See note 1 to 'A Catastrophe'.
2. *The Strand Magazine*: Published 1891–1950, it was one of the most celebrated of the 'gaslight' fiction magazines, and where, of course, this story was first published.
3. *Mephistophelian*: Devilishly sinister; from Mephistopheles, a devil associated with Dr Faustus in *The Tragical History of Doctor Faustus* (published 1604) by Christopher Marlowe (1564–93).
4. *Upper Sandgate Road*: In Folkestone, Kent, where Wells was living at the time.
5. *Gibberne's B Syrup*: In *Tono-Bungay* (1909) Wells was to satirize similar patent medicines.
6. *Jews and Orientals*: Part of the racial thinking of the time was to assume differences between groups of humanity such as an alleged (and unproven) propensity of some groups to greater intelligence, quickness of thought and shorter life-spans.
7. *Harley Street specialist*: Harley Street was – and still is – a centre for medical specialists.
8. *'gas'*: Nitrous oxide, or 'laughing gas', was used as an anaesthetic from the late eighteenth century.
9. *Analysed sounds*: The *OED* has for 'analysed', 'Resolved or reduced to its elements or essential constituents'; the sense is that the sense of hearing is also affected by the change in the perception of time and that they are hearing a kind of generalized mixture of slowed-down sounds which are mostly below the perception level of the human ear.
10. *Leas*: Promenade offering a panoramic view over Folkestone and the English Channel. The Metropole was one of the country's most luxurious hotels.

11. *that Time Garment of which Carlyle speaks*: In *Sartor Resartus*,
     Carlyle writes of how we are 'clothed' from the real, transcendent
     reality by the 'garments' of the senses, custom, philosophy, and
     Space and Time. See also note 8 to 'A Slip under the Microscope'.

THE TRUTH ABOUT PYECRAFT

1. *Jamrach's*: Charles Jamrach (1815–91), a dealer in wild animals
    for zoos and menageries.
2. *Santos-Dumont*: Alberto Santos-Dumont (1873–1932), Brazilian
    aviation pioneer.
3. *euphuism*: Elaborate, affected language as in the prose fiction
    Euphues (1578) by John Lyly (1553–1606). Wells surely means,
    though, *euphemism*, the substitution of a less disagreeable word
    for a more accurate if offensive one. He makes the same mistake
    in Chapter Nine of *Ann Veronica* (1909), but the OED cites
    instances of other nineteenth-century writers confusing the two
    words.
4. *British Encyclopaedia*: The tenth edition of the *Encyclopedia
    Britannica* (1902–3) had just been issued in thirty-six volumes.

THE COUNTRY OF THE BLIND

1. *Chimborazo*: Volcano in Equador. This sentence foreshadows
    'Chimborazo, Cotopaxi, / Took me by the hand', lines from the
    poem 'Romance' in *The Hunter* (1916) by W. J. Turner (1889–
    1946).
2. *Mindobamba*: And 'Parascotopetl' and 'Arauca' later, are fic-
    tional mountains. Quito, however is the capital of Ecuador, and
    Yaguachi is a town in southern Ecuador on the river Guayas,
    north of Guayaquil, the country's main port. Wells is mixing
    fictional and real places to create the scene for his imaginary
    country.
3. *old Peru*: The Incas, who ruled most of Peru and Ecuador at the
    time of the conquest by Francisco Pizarro (1478–1541). They
    were known for their architecture and command of agriculture,
    and the highly developed political and religious organization
    made somewhat mysterious by their failure to develop writing.
4. *Matterhorn*: Mountain in the Alps on the borders of Switzerland
    and Italy. During the nineteenth century it became a favourite of
    climbing expeditions, and because of its difficulty was not
    ascended until 1865.

5.   *'In the Country . . . is King'*: A proverb dating back to at least the sixteenth century.
6.   *Medina-saroté*: There may be a meaning in this name. 'Medina' (Arabic) means 'city' and is a Spanish place-name and surname. Sarote or Sarotte is a rare variant of Sarah ('Princess' in Hebrew). Medina-saroté could therefore mean 'Princess of the City'.

THE EMPIRE OF THE ANTS

1.   *Benjamin Constant, to Badama*: Ship either named after the French politician and novelist (1767–1830), or after the Brazilian city named after him. Badama is fictional as are most of the other place names (although there is a Badema in the African country of Guinea). There is a Parahyba or Paraíba river in Brazil which runs through the state of Rio de Janeiro.
2.   *Sambo*: The (now) offensive term 'Sambo' may have come from the Spanish 'zambo' (bandy-legged) applied to a person of mixed race.
3.   *a different sort of French*: Partly a joke about the state of language teaching in Britain: in Southport, Holroyd may have experienced rigid and narrow lessons. But both he and da Cunha have French as a second language and communication would not automatically have been easy.
4.   *Saüba*: The South American sauba or umbrella ant, referred to earlier as the 'leaf-cutting ant', which devastates areas of the forest, is the source for the ants in this story.
5.   *Capuarana Extension Railway*: A railway line opened in Brazil in 1854, but in 1898 a British company took over and extended the Brazilian railway system.

THE DOOR IN THE WALL

1.   *North-West Passage*: The discovery of a passage around Canada through to the Pacific Ocean and Asia was the dream of many nineteenth-century explorers.
2.   *Crawshaw major*: It was customary when two brothers attended the same public school for the elder to be 'Major' (Latin, 'greater') and the younger 'Minor' (lesser).
3.   *counting Stonehenge*: Many stone circles are associated with legends to the effect that one can never count the stones and get the same answer twice.
4.   *Tenants' Redemption Bill*: A fictional bill, but reminiscent of the

turbulent politics of the time, particularly around the question of employment. 1906, the year of the story's publication, was notable for a massive Conservative Party defeat by the Liberals, aided by the electoral rise of the Labour Party.

5. *Gurker and Ralphs*: Representing political leaders of the day: presumably 'Gurker' is the Prime Minister.

6. *Westminster Gazette*: Liberal Newspaper published from 1893 until 1928, when it was merged with the *Daily News*.

THE WILD ASSES OF THE DEVIL

1. *anterior equator*: I.e. his stomach.

2. *King Edward*: Edward VII (1841–1910), who reigned from 1901.

3. *Kipling*: Rudyard Kipling (see note 9 to 'The Moth') with whom Wells at times had something of a rivalry for the popular market.

4. *went to the bell*: Middle-class houses were equipped with a system of bells to summon servants.

5. *a stokehole trick*: Picked up among his fellow stokers in the furnace-rooms of the steamships (but Hell, of course, is also a location famous for furnaces).

6. *a pointed top to his ear*: See note 4 to 'A Story of the Stone Age'.

7. *Idylls of Theocritus*: The pastoral poems of the Greek poet (*c.* 310–250 BC).

8. *flowers of sulphur*: The fine powder obtained by heating sulphur and allowing the vapours to condense.

9. *Via Dolorosa*: (Latin, 'The Way of Grief'). The name of a street in Jerusalem, traditionally the route taken by Jesus on his way to his crucifixion.

10. *W. E. Gladstone*: William Ewart Gladstone (1809–98), Liberal Prime Minister in four governments. He finally resigned as leader in 1894 over the rejection of his bill for Home Rule for Ireland.

11. *Sir Edward Carson*: (1854–1935), Irish Unionist leader who campaigned against Home Rule for Ireland in the years before the First World War, threatening Protestant resistance in Ulster and establishing the paramilitary Ulster Volunteer Force. He also took a leading part in Oscar Wilde's disastrous libel action against the Marquis of Queensberry in 1895.

12. *If you went inside*—: Wells presented a utopian underground city of the future, free from germs carried in the open air, in *Things to Come*, the film based upon *The Shape of Things to Come* (1933).

13. *Jaeger's*: Clothing store in London's West End, established in 1884 to specialize in 'healthy' clothing from wool and other animal fibres, rather than cotton or linen.

A.S.